GW00597950

A Seventeenth-Century Chinese Classic

Ling Mengchu

Amazing Tales
Second Series

Translated by Perry W. Ma

Panda Books

A Seventeenth-Century Chinese Classic

Ling Mengchu

Amazing Tales

Second Series

Translated by Perry W. Ma

Panda Books

Panda Books
First Edition 1998
Copyright ©1998 by CHINESE LITERATURE PRESS
ISBN 7-5071-0401-X
ISBN 0-8351-3225-0

Published by CHINESE LITERATURE PRESS
Beijing 100037, China
Distributed by China International Book Trading Corporation
35 Chegongzhuang Xilu, Beijing 100044, China
P.O. Box 399, Beijing, China
Printed in the People's Republic of China

CONTENTS

Introduction

*A*mazing Tales — *Second Series* is another short-story collection that Ling Mengchu wrote at the request of his publisher after *Amazing Tales* — *First Series* became a hit upon its publication. According to the author, this second collection contained forty stories but only thirty-eight are in existence today. From those highly popular and wonderful stories we have chosen nineteen for this selection. (The tales have been renumbered.)

Quite a good part of the current selection are stories about women and love affairs, in addition to a wide range of other subject matters. These stories display the dialectal contradictions in women's lives at the time: their affliction under the yoke of marriage in a polygamous society and their continual struggle for love and happiness, their humiliation as targets of the lechery of the senior officials and noble lords and their courage in breaking shackles in search of new lives, and their personalities distorted by women's low social status and their innate character of goodness and honesty. These unique characteristics of women are vividly depicted in these stories.

The plots of these nineteen short stories are complicated but deftly developed through to their climaxes. These highly entertaining and brilliant tales have been adapted on stage, screen and in many books. Each story is full of clever twists in plot which eventually arrive at a satisfying ending, an edifying moral.

Furthermore this literary work gives a broad-range projection of life encompassing the imperial court, government office, farmer's quarters, bandits' lairs and brothels with a range of characters including senior officials, nobles, scholars, young ladies, servant-girls, prostitutes, gigolos and a remarkable thief. A distinctive writing feature that stands out in the book is a realistic portrayal of women characters in terms of the author's comprehensive and profound insight into their inner world, which unfolds in the development of moving love stories. The tales become at times explicit in descriptions of the love affairs that develop, but the writing is always artistically tasteful and full of fine sentiment. The stories are all highly readable and engaging.

The historically famed author, Ling Mengchu, was born in Wucheng, Zhejiang Province, in 1580. He went to school at the age of twelve. In his late forties, while living in Nanjing, he started writing his *Amazing Tales*. When he was in his fifties, he was appointed magistrate of the county of Shanghai and in the same year, as the county director of the coast guard. In 1642, he was made an assistant-governor of Xuzhou. Two years later he died at the age of sixty-four. Apart from *Amazing Tales* he authored many other works.

This translation of the work has used the Wang Gulu (王古鲁)-annotated edition and the edition published in 1992 by the Shanghai Classics Press (上海古籍出版社) as the original text. Nineteen stories are translated and some omissions are made, particularly at the beginnings of the stories, which usually serves as a lead-in. Some poems, which usually come scattered through the stories, were also omitted in agreement with the editor's intention of facilitating the Western reader's understanding. We hope that completely translated versions of all the "Amazing Tales" in full will soon be made available to readers.

The Translator

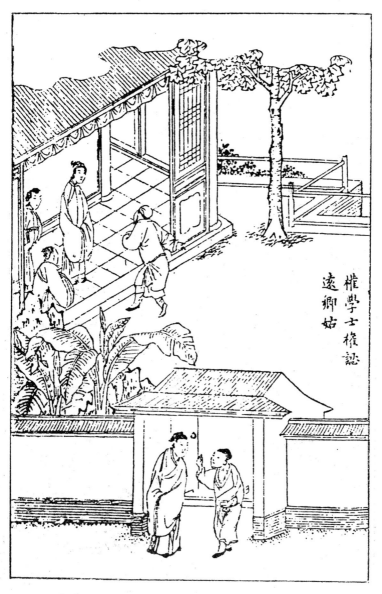

權學士權認
遠鄉姑

Scholar Quan Plots to Relate Himself to a Distant Aunt

白嬌人白嫁親生女

Mother Bai Is Deceived in Marrying off Her Daughter

青樓市探人蹤

Inquiring About a Lost Man in Courtesans' Quarters

Hearing Howls of Ghosts in the Saffron Garden

Wang Xiangmin Loses His Son at the Lantern Festival

The Thirteenth Boy at Age Five Pays Respects to His Majesty

李將軍錯
認劉君妹

General Li Claims a Brother-in-law by Mistake

劉氏女詭從夫

Lady Liu Contacts Her Husband by Stealth

Shen Binges with Thousands in Silver

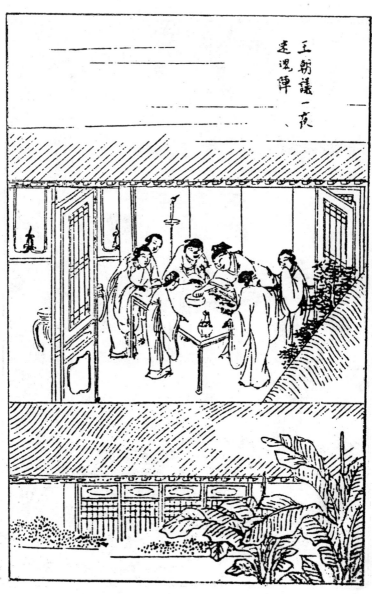

王朝議一夜
迷魂陣、

Lord Wang Lays a One-night Trap

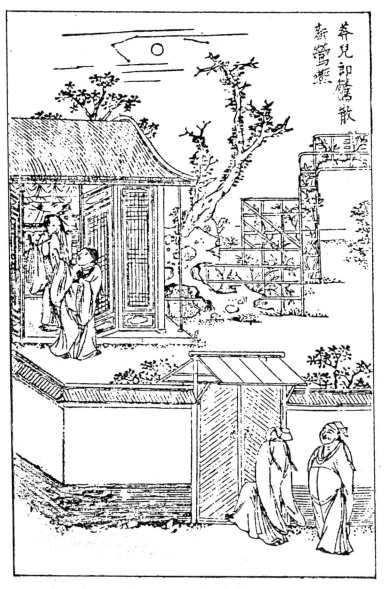

莽見卽驚散
燕鶯薪

Rash Young Men Startle Lovers

偷梅香暗合
玉蟾蜍

Clever Young Women Recognize Jade Toads

趙
五
虎
合
計

挑
家
篡

Five Tigers Cunningly Plot a Family Dispute

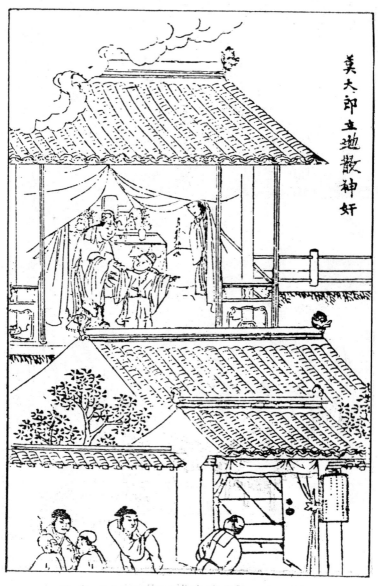

美大郎立地散神奸

Big Brother Mo Wisely Shatters a Sinister Scheme

滿少卿飢附
飽颺

Lord Man Deserts His Benefactor Spouse

冤報　焦文姬生雞

Jiao Wenji Wreaks Vengeance After Death

A Senseless Young Master Squanders His Fortune in Liberal Donations

賢丈人巧騰囮頭婿

The Virtuous Father-in-law Plots to Bring Him Back to a Sensible Life

徐茶酒秉
鬧動新人

Tea-and-wine Master Xu Kidnaps the Bride Amid Wedding Festivities

Zheng Ruizhu Utters Her Grievances Ending an Unsettled Case

憒教官雲
女不受報

A Muddle-headed Instructor is Mistreated by His Pampered Daughters

A Once Poor Scholar Finances His Teacher for a Happy Old Age

程朝奉單遇
無頭婦

A Rich Man Encounters a Headless Female Body

王通判雙雪不明冤

An Assistant Prefect Clears up Two Unsettled Cases

誓褔娘一心

貞守

Zhang Funiang Resolves to Stay Unmarried for Integrity

朱天錫萬里荷名

Zhu Tianxi Takes a Long Journey to Identify a Name

Yang Chouma Asks to Be Thrashed

富家卹涙受驚

A Rich Man Is Frightened

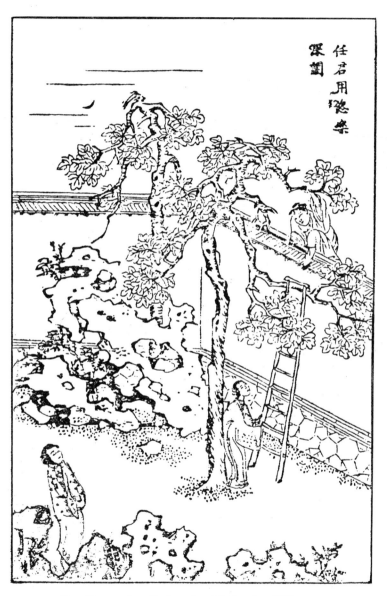

任君用恣樂
深閨

You Use-me Lustily Revels with Confined Women

Minister Yang Sinisterly Castrates His Literary Hack

Mother Reproaches Daughter for a Suspected Affair

Youth Takes Wife from a Mistaken Lawsuit

王漁翁捨鏡
宗三寶

Fisherman Wang Donates a Mirror in Worship of Buddha

白水僧盗物
喪雙生

Two Monks Lose Their Lives for Stealing the Treasure

両錯認莫大
且私奔

Sister Mo Elopes with the Wrong Lover

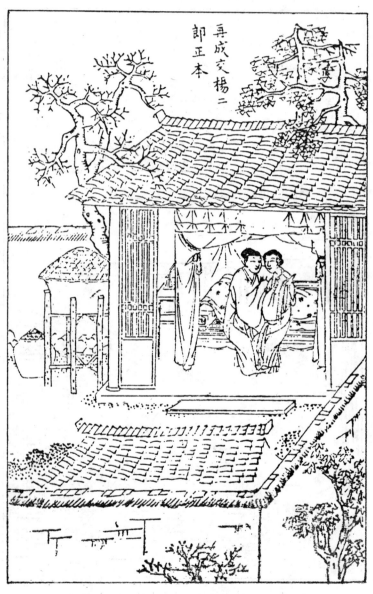

再成交楊二
卽正本

Second Brother Yang Marries His Former Mistress

神偷寄與
一枝梅

An ingenious Thief Conveys His Sentiment with a Plum

A Gallant Burglar Plays His Game with Adroitness

Tale 1

Scholar Quan Plots to Relate Himself to a Distant Aunt;
Mother Bai Is Deceived in Marrying off Her Daughter

In our [Ming] Dynasty there was an official whose family name was Quan, given name, Ciqing and formal name, Wenchang. He was from the Ningguo Prefecture of Southern Zhili Province. In his early years he passed the imperial examinations and was appointed to be a clerk of the chronicle at the Imperial Academy. As a member of the academy, he was handsome, gallant and well versed in all the things he did. He was compared to a divine bard who was banished from Heaven to lead a worldly life, and regarded as a very talented man. After he won the title of *jinshi*, he lived in the capital city [Beijing] for more than one year. At that time in the capital city it was popular to hold a fair on the 1st, 15th and 25th days of each month. During such events, thousands of goods were lined up on display from the town god's temple all the way up to the street on which the Board of Punishments was located. Such fairs drew large crowds for browsing and business. The officials who were less occupied and curious would go out in casual dress with one or two servants from their household and make a few purchases of their favorite things and antiques. At the imperial court the Imperial Academy had the least work to do, so the men working there usually spent their time doing nothing but reading, playing chess, drinking and calling on their friends. Quan Ciqing was young and inclined to have fun. So he would stroll out on the street whenever such an occasion was available.

One day he saw an elderly man at a sales-stand on which there were many odd articles, most being household wares such as candlesticks, copper ladles, teapots, bowls, plates, teacups, etc. There was nothing in particular that might draw the attention of a learned man. Yet Quan did catch a glimpse of an item with a peculiar color. He picked it up and realized it was a lid that had come off of an antique bronze box. He knew it was precious but felt sorry that it was incomplete.

He asked the elderly man, "It's incomplete. Where's the body of the box?"

The man answered, "I only have this lid. I've never seen the body."

Quan said, "How could that happen? Tell me where you acquired the lid so we can find the body."

The elderly man said, "I have a few extra rooms near the Dongzhi Gate. I rented them to a family of five. Later they contracted an epidemic disease and two young members of the family died. The rest of the family became frightened and moved out before they had recovered. Because they owed me some rent, they gave me a few articles instead. I accepted them and am trying to make some money by selling them. This lid is one of the articles they left behind. It also has a bamboo container for it, which is wrapped in a few pieces of paper. I don't know what is the use for the lid, so I have put it out on the table for sale, hoping someone might like to buy it."

Quan replied, "It is a shame it is not a complete set. But I will buy it. Can you show me that bamboo container?"

The elderly man reached under the table and brought out the paper-wrapped, worn bamboo container. Quan said, "These things are not valuable. Can you sell them to me at a low price?"

The man said, "They are worth little. It's up to you, sir, to pay whatever you want." Quan told his household-keeper, Quan Zhong, to pay him one hundred coins. The elderly man took out the old paper from the bamboo container, wrapped the lid in it and placed it inside the bamboo container again. Then he presented it with both hands to Quan, who asked his servant to carry it, while they went on to purchase a few more antique writing materials.

After he returned home, Quan set his purchases on a small marble table and studied them one by one, very satisfied. Finally he came to the bamboo container. He removed its cover and took out the paper package. Then he removed the wrapping and looked steadily at the item, which was shining brightly. It was indeed a treasure. As he turned it over, he pondered, "Where is the body? I'll put it away. I may have a chance to get the other part later. Who knows?" While wrapping it again with the original paper, he noticed something red sticking out. He spread out the wrapping and discovered a red slip of paper inside. He picked it up and looked. Then he said with surprise, "Here's the answer!" What was it, reader? The paper said,

> I am putting down this note on paper. I am a woman from the family of Bai and live on Dashiyong Street. I have a two-year-old daughter called Xu Dangui. I have a brother called Bai Da, who has a son of the same age as my daughter. The boy is called Liuge. My husband, Xu Fang, is from Suzhou. In order for my daughter and nephew to identify each other in the future after years of separation, this bronze money box is divided between the two families as a token of evidence.

At the end of the note were the month, year, and signature. Quan thought to himself, "This has turned out to be the proof for a marriage. It is vital, but why was it abandoned? The old man sold it to me! She was careless indeed." He then thought, "Since the woman had a husband, why didn't she let her husband write the note?" Counting the years on his fingers, he said with a smile, "Since the time the note was written, it has been seventeen years. The girl should be nineteen now, in the bloom of her youth. I wonder whether she has married or not." Then he laughed and said, "Why should I care about that? I will keep the box top for the time being." So he put the things away.

On the next fair date Quan saw the elderly man again. He said to the elderly man, "The other day you sold the top of a money box to me and told me it was left behind by a family. Can you tell me where the family has gone?"

The elderly man replied, "I have no idea. The family had a succession of deaths starting from the youngest. They were frightened and fled one night. Maybe they have all died by now."

Quan said, "Did they have any relatives who got in touch with them when they stayed in your rooms?" The man replied, "The man had a younger sister who had married a man from the lower reaches of Yangtze River and that sister's family lived at the Qianmen Gate. For many years I have never seen them come to visit, so I don't know where they are now."

Quan thought to himself, "If I can find out their whereabouts, I will be able to return the top to them. It will be something worthy of praise to do. Since there's no trace of the family, I will have to let the matter run its own course."

He returned to his residence. A letter arrived from his home notifying him that his wife had died. He cried. Depressed, he packed things for a trip back home. He presented a memorial to the emperor requesting sick leave. The imperial decree stated, "Quan is granted sick leave to go home and should report back immediately upon recovery. The Emperor has thus decreed." Quan then left the capital city for home.

Let's now leave him for awhile and turn to the unidentified money box. In Suzhou there was a man called Xu Fang and styled West Spring, who was from a family of ancient nobility. He was a student in the Imperial College. He had stayed in the capital city in order to get a promotion. As he felt lonely, he arranged through a matchmaker to obtain a daughter of a local family called Bai as his concubine. Later a baby girl was born. The birth was in the eighth month of the lunar calendar, so the daughter was called Dangui.* During the same year, the concubine's brother, Bai Da, had a son, whose given name was Liuge. The concubine was narrow-minded and thought only of her own clan. Besides, officials and their family members living in the capital city seldom had many connections outside the home and did not trust marriage beyond kinship. Therefore she set her mind on a marriage between her daughter and her nephew. Scholar Xu was not planning to live in the capital city for very long, knowing that he would leave for his hometown sooner or later. He wanted to marry the daughter to a man from his home region. So he was rather dissatisfied with his concubine's marriage arrangement.

One day Supervisor Xu was appointed to be an assistant prefect in central Fujian Province. He prepared to go there with his concubine and take the position. Disappointed at leaving her relatives, the woman wrote a note behind his back. In that note, although she did not state clearly her intention for her daughter to marry her nephew, she said that a money box was divided between the girl and boy so that if they met each other in future, this would be proof of identity. The two parts of the box would be sufficient identification either when her daughter had the opportunity to go to the capital city or if they encountered one another in a different part of the country.

The concubine went to Suzhou with Xu. Because Xu Fang had been

---

*In Chinese, "gui" (literally meaning, bay tree) is another name for the moon. Popular legend has it that there are bay trees and toads on the moon. During the Mid-autumn Festival, which falls on the fifteenth day of the eighth lunar month each year, people traditionally enjoy the full moon.

a single for a long time, Xu was made his formal wife. Later they had a son, who was born in the ninth month and called Gaoer. After two terms of tenure in office, Xu returned home. He then betrothed his daughter to a local family called Chen, and the wife had to drop her hopes for a marriage between her daughter and nephew. However, she kept thinking about it. Periodically she prayed in front of a figure of Bodhisattva to be able to go back to the capital city and recover the other part of the money box. Later Xu died, leaving his wife behind as a widow living with her daughter and son. Now she gave up any thoughts of going back to the capital city. She realized that it had been more than fifteen years since they had left there. Dangui grew up to be an extremely beautiful young girl. The son of the Chen's family had also grown up, but before the young man had a chance to send formal gifts and marry her, he contracted a consuming disease and died. Dangui's horoscope was harsh and bound to bring ill fate to her kin. She became a widow-to-be* instead of wife-to-be because she had not been betrothed to a healthy man. Dangui in plain dress led a meager life with her mother and brother. She was like:

> *A single star in the sky*
> *Looking for a partner in vain.*

Leaving Xu Dangui to her solitary life, we return to scholar Quan, who was on sick leave at home after the death of his wife. He remained unmarried for one year. One day he was bored and wandered to Suzhou with the idea of looking for a beautiful concubine. He feared that if local prefecture and county government officials learned of his arrival, they would offer him horses or chariots to greet him and

---

*In feudal times in China, especially during the Ming and Qing dynasties when the rationalist Confucian school was prevalent, a woman, once betrothed to a man, should belong to him all her life. Even if the man died before wedding, the woman could not marry another man if she wanted to maintain her reputation of chastity. So a woman whose husband-to-be died was called a "widow-to-be."

involve him in welcome and farewell parties, and that would make him uneasy. So he decided that, since he was young and had a boyish face and short stature, no one would consider him to be an official — he posed as a traveling scholar and rented a room next door to the Moonbeam Temple outside town. The temple housed monks and nuns. One old nun was called Abbess Miaotong. She was over sixty, experienced in Buddhist rites, conventions and worldly affairs, and she exclusively associated with influential families. Impressed by Quan's appearance and good conduct, Miaotong knew he was no ordinary person, though she was ignorant of his real identity. She did not want to slight him in her treatment of him, so she kept sending a lay brother to bring tea to his room and called him over for chats. One day Quan took the chance to reveal his intention of obtaining a concubine to Miaotong, who replied, "I'm a nun and should keep away from mundane affairs." Quan thus had to quit the subject for the time being.

It was the seventh day of the seventh month, but Quan was away from home and felt lonely. The solitude caused him to think of the love story of the Herdsman and the Weaving Maid.* In the moonlight he suddenly saw a woman in white step into the temple. He rushed in following her, stealing glimpses of her in the darkness. Abbess Miaotong emerged to meet the woman. The woman didn't say anything but lit a stick of incense in front of the figure of Buddha. What did the woman look like?

She is praised for her phoenix-like braids
And admired for her flimsy gauze dress.
Oh, for whom does she burn incense at night
And gaze at mist-veiled still waves?

---

*This comes from a love story of Chinese mythology, in which a Herdsman and a Weaving Maid, identified with the stars Altair and Vega, are ordained to be separated by the River of Heaven, or Milky Way, and are only able to meet once a year on the seventh day of the seventh lunar month.

Her hair over her forehead flutters in a breeze,
Roses shine through her fair cheeks.
Why should the lovely night be passed idle —
The night illuminated by the beauty and the moon?

With a stick of incense in her hands the woman knelt in front of the figure of Buddha. She looked up and murmured a great deal in a soft voice, but nothing reached Quan's ears. Then Miaotong came up and put a conclusion to her prayer, "Young lady, you can never pour out all your worries. Let me put your wishes in one word."

The woman rose and asked, "Abbess, what is it?"

Miaotong replied, "Buddha bless you! Marry a good man. How about that?"

The girl said, "Don't be fooling me. I was born with bad luck. My father is dead and my mother is old. I'm single and have no one to turn to for a living. So I've come to pray to Buddha for blessing."

Laughing, Miaotong said, "Generally you have the same idea as I just told you." The woman laughed too. Miaotong brought out tea and food, and the woman had two cups of tea and then took leave.

The scholar, as he was watching, was getting excited. He could scarcely hold himself back from leaping out to hug her. After she left, he could not keep his passion in check. As he was wildly pondering, Miaotong turned back from seeing the woman off and saw him. Miaotong then said to him, "You're not sleeping? At what time did you come here?"

Quan answered, "I saw a bodhisattva dressed in white arrive, so I came to show my reverence."

Miaotong said, "She's the daughter of the Xus, one of my neighbors. Her name is Dangui. She is extremely beautiful, the rarest beauty I've ever seen." Quan then asked, "Is she married?"

Miaotong said, "Hard to say. She was betrothed by her father, when he was alive, to a young master of the family of Chen. But, about the time of their wedding, the young master had bad luck and died, leaving his young lady a widow-to-be. No one has proposed to her yet."

Quan said, "No wonder she was dressed in plain clothing. But why did she come at so late an hour?"

Miaotong said, "Tonight it's the time for the meeting of the Herdsman and the Weaving Maid. She suffered much affliction in her engagement and is rather sad about her future. So she received permission from her mother to come to burn a nightly stick of incense."

Quan asked, "Who is her mother?" Miaotong said, "Her mother is from the family of Bai, originally from the capital city. Dangui's father waited for an appointment to a position in the capital city long ago, married her mother and then brought her here. Dangui's mother is outspoken and easy to get along with. She told me that she has a brother in the capital city, who had a two-year-old son of the same age as her daughter at the time her husband family left the capital city. But they've lost track of her brother's family during the past twenty years. She is worried about how things have gone with the brother's family, so she often asks me to pray for them in front of Buddha."

Having heard this, Quan thought to himself, "I bought the lid of a money box more than a year ago. It said on the paper, 'I am a woman from the Bai family... I have a daughter called Xu Dangui. I have a brother called Bai Da, who has a son... called Liuge.' That woman must be Xu Dangui and her mother is Bai. They're surely this family. I was told by the old man that the family lost two juniors, and then the master of the family took a hasty leave with the rest of his family, leaving the note and lid behind in the rush. I think one of the juniors who died was probably her nephew, Bai Liuge. The woman turns out to be quite good-looking. She had a betrothal and then lost her intended. Now I am in possession of the lid and the note. And by chance I have seen her. What a coincidence! Probably it will make for my happy marriage." He checked his motives with his conscience and made up his mind, saying, "It is a matter of an interval of almost twenty years and a distance of over three thousand *li*. How can the matter be examined closely? I should do as I desire."

With this idea in mind, he said to Miaotong, "Could you tell me how old is the mother you talked about just now?"

Miaotong replied, "More than forty."

Quan asked, "Is her brother in the capital city Bai Da, with a son called Liuge?"

Miaotong said, "Exactly! How did you know that, sir?"

Quan replied, "The lady is none other than my aunt. I'm Bai Liuge, her nephew."

Miaotong said, "You're kidding. Your family name is Quan. How can you say it is Bai?"

Quan said, "I left the capital city in my early years. I wandered around in the south for the purpose of learning, with the idea of enjoying the southern landscape and seeking my relatives. That's why I later changed my name completely and came here. Today I'm glad that you mentioned this story. This is a heavenly arrangement. Otherwise how could I know the names of her brother and nephew?"

Miaotong said, "It's absolutely a coincidence! Please go to them tomorrow, sir, and claim your kinship. I will be with them for congratulations."

Quan took his leave and went back to his room. He was lost in fantasy that night. The next morning he called Quan Zhong and talked to him about the matter. Then the scholar dressed himself up and walked with Quan Zhong to the home of Xu.

They saw an old man sitting by the side of the gate. The scholar bid Quan Zhong to tell the old man, "Please take a report to your master of the arrival of Master Bai from the capital city."

The old man responded, "Our master is dead. The little master's still young. Which one do you want to see?"

Quan said, "Is your mistress a person with the family name of Bai from the capital city?"

The old man said, "Yes, she is."

Quan Zhong said, "Here's my lord, Master Bai, her nephew."

The old man said, "Really? Come with me, please. I'm going to report." The old man led Quan Zhong to Bai. Quan Zhong knew what he was supposed to do. He kowtowed to her and said, "Master Bai, my lord, is waiting outside. He has come from the capital city."

The mother asked, "Is it really my brother's son Liuge?"

Quan Zhong said, "Yes, it was his pet name."

Overjoyed the mother said, "It's wonderful!" At once she called her son and said, "Your cousin is here, Gaoer. Go and see him." The boy was happy and ran out to meet the scholar.

With a little nervousness, Quan walked inside. When he saw Bai rise, he called out, "Aunt," making a deep bow. He was about to kowtow to her before she stopped him, saying, "You've had a long exhausting journey. You can save the formal etiquette." Tears welled up in her eyes as she looked at the scholar, impressed by his very outstanding bearing. She said joyfully, "When I left the capital city, you were only two. Now you've grown up with such handsome looks. How is your father?"

Pretending to weep sadly, with his hand shielding his face, Quan said, "He died long ago. I have no family members and relatives to depend on. My father told me, when alive, that my aunt had married a southerner. So I toured the south for learning as well as in an effort to find you. Yesterday I talked with Abbess Miaotong of the Moonbeam Temple, who mentioned you by accident. So I discovered that your are here. I have come to visit you."

Bai said, "Why don't you speak with a northern accent?"

Quan said, "I've been in the south for a long time and like to speak southern dialects. So you find me with a change of accent."

Quan then had Quan Zhong present the gifts. The mother accepted them gladly, saying, "We're close relatives. I'm so happy that you've come to see me. Why do you bother to give me gifts?"

Quan said, "It was hard to find satisfactory gifts along the journey. I'm sorry they are only humble gifts. I'm glad you're in good health, aunt. Miaotong told me yesterday that my uncle died. A moment ago I saw my boy cousin. I think I should have a girl cousin who is of the same age as me. Is she around?"

The mother said, "When your uncle was alive, she was betrothed to another. But it was predetermined to be a bad match. The young man died before the wedding. My daughter has not been engaged yet."

Quan said, "May I meet her?"

The mother answered, "Yesterday she went to the temple to burn incense and caught a cold. She's not up yet. You should stay here for awhile, so you will have plenty of chances to see her. Please put your luggage in the west room first." She ordered that a dinner be prepared and led Quan by his hand to the western chamber.

They went past a small-yard gate and the mother said, pointing at it, "There's your girl cousin's bedroom." Quan smelled the fragrant musk and felt confused.

Bai had dinner together with Quan, and then saw to the moving of his luggage into the study and his settlement before returning to her room. Left alone in the study, Quan thought, "I posed as her nephew and wanted to see the girl. Unfortunately I didn't get the chance. I'm glad the mother was deceived. I'll stay here from now on, and eventually I'll have the opportunity to be with the girl. I don't need to worry. I expect to see her tomorrow."

Meanwhile Xu Dangui was rather frustrated ever the failure of marriage. That night when she went to the temple to burn the incense, she was quite downcast. And then she caught a cold. So she didn't feel well enough to rise in the morning. She heard that her cousin had arrived from the capital city. Her mother had told her before that she was meant, in childhood, to marry him. She was also told that her cousin was tall and handsome. The thought of getting a chance to see him tickled her fancy. Though unwell, she compelled herself to rise and dress. Looking into the mirror, she sighed, "I wonder to whom such good looks will go?"

After dressing, she was about to go to see her cousin when her brother, Gaoer, rushed in to tell her, "Mother suddenly had a chest pain and fainted. I'm going out to buy some medicine. Please go and see to Mother right now, Sister." Dangui rushed out to take care of her mother, leaving her cosmetic box behind and the door open.

That morning the scholar had gotten dressed and was ready to request a meeting with Dangui. Then he heard someone calling, "The mistress had a chest pain and has fainted." He pondered, "To cure this sickness, a 'composing pill' is the most effective. That medicine is only sold by a drugstore on Chessboard Street at Qianmen in the capital city. I happened to bring the medicine with me in the small gift case. I'll go, as her nephew, and make an inquiry about her health and give her the medicine. By restoring her health, I'll have the chance to gain favor with her." He took the medicine out of the case and tucked it in into his sleeve. He then made his way toward the mother's room.

As he went through the small courtyard, he noticed the room in which Dangui lived, as he had been told the day before. Seeing the door open, he decided, "She must be inside. I'll just enter her room, pretending to know nothing about it, and see what will happen." Nervously, Quan stepped into the bedroom and saw,

The sweet dressing case was open, and the precious mirror was left untended; the face powder and eyebrow pigment remained strewn in a basin, and the flower-like ornaments and colorful jewels were left littered about on the small table. When she did her make-up with her slender fingers, she needed a man around to paint her eyebrows.

Quan became intoxicated. He picked up the things one after another, sniffing at them. But he felt unsatisfied. Then a strong, sweet smell drifted over from another direction. He turned around. It was her exquisitely decorated bed with embroidered bed-drapes, and a silk quilt and a pillow adorned with animal horns, all clean and neat. Quan thought to himself, "Let me take a nap on her bed, smelling some of the fragrance as though I were close to her skin." So he lay down on his back, his head on the pillow and became lost in a daydream. After awhile, as nothing turned up, he got up and hesitated for a moment before he walked out. When he came near to Bai's room, he reached into his sleeve but couldn't find the pill. He paused and tried to recall where he might have dropped it. He made his way back to his study.

Dangui was with her mother. As her mother's pain abated, Dangui remembered that she had left her door open and her cosmetics untended. She ran back to her room and put things away. A little tired, she lifted the bed drape and was about to take a nap when she saw a package on the bed. She picked it up and opened it. It was a medical pill with the paper wrapping that carried the words, "Composing pill, effective on chest pains and the best medicine." Dangui wondered, "Where did this pill come from? If my brother brought it, why didn't he bring it to my mother's room instead of putting it here on my bed? But if it was not my brother, who could have put it here? It is the medicine needed for a chest pain! It's strange. Anyway I'm going to take it to my mother's room and ask her about it."

She took it with her, shut the door, went to her mother's room and asked her, "Has my brother come back with the medicine yet, mother?"

Mrs. Bai answered, "I'm running out of patience waiting. I wonder where the boy has gone and who he is playing with."

Dangui said, "Listen, Mother. Just now when I went back to my bedroom, I saw a medicinal pill on my bed. The paper wrapping says, 'Composing pill, effective on chest pains and the best medicine.' I wonder whether it was my brother who put it there. But why didn't he bring it here to you instead? Since my brother has not come back yet, it is dubious where the medicine came from."

Bai said, "The composing pill is only available, daughter, in a drugstore on a street at Qianmen in the capital city. How could it get here? It's clear that the gods are touched by your filial attitude toward me and have bestowed it on me. Come on and give it to me. I'm going to take it." Dangui brought water and handed the pill to her mother, who gulped it down. Soon her pain was gone. The mother and daughter were delighted.

With the pain gone and being tired, Bai fell asleep. Dangui sat by her bed in watchful attendance. The scholar, unable to recover the lost pill, came to see Bai for her health. He encountered Dangui, who guessed he was her cousin whom she would eventually meet. Thus she didn't move. Quan intended to strike up an intimate relationship with her, so smiling, he walked up with a huge bow and clasped hands and said, " Sister, please accept my greetings."

Dangui returned a curtsy saying, "Good luck to you, Brother."

Quan asked, "How's my aunt?"

Dangui said, "She feels better. She fell asleep a moment ago."

Quan said, "I arrived yesterday and expected to see you and enjoy your beauty. I was told that you were not well, so I did not intrude upon you." Dangui said, "I heard of your arrival and desired a meeting. To avoid being untidy, I had to dress carefully. But this morning when I was about to come out for a meeting with you, my mother developed a sudden illness and I had to be with her. I'm surprised to meet you here at this moment. But I'm glad to see you looking so well."

Quan said, "I traveled a few thousand *li* to be here. It is well worth my trip, Sister, to take a look at your beauty."

Dangui said, "My mother and you are related in a close aunt-and-nephew kinship. I'm a fated unfortunate. How can I, worthless as I am, be somebody that calls for your attention?"

Quan asked, "Why are you saying that? You're young and beautiful.

You'll have abundant happiness later in life."

The conversation went on unreservedly. Dangui was a mature young lady and was immediately attracted to the scholar's good looks and refined conduct. Besides, the cousin relationship gave her the courage to be on easy terms with him so she chatted sweetly. She said, "You're new here. If you're not comfortable in your room for any reason, just feel free to talk to me."

Quan replied, "Why should I feel uncomfortable?"

Dangui said, "Don't you think you may need something?"

Quan said, "Well, I do have a need. But I feel uneasy about expressing it in front of you."

Dangui said, "Tell me, please."

Quan said, "What I need, I think, is something you may not be willing to offer. But you're the only person who can do so."

Dangui asked, "What is it?"

Smiling, Quan said, "I need a bed partner at night." Blushing and saying nothing, Dangui turned around and was about to leave. Quan rushed over and grabbed her, saying, "Would you please lead me to your bedroom so that I can show my respect for you?"

Dangui realized he was getting presumptuous with her. As they were in an awkward situation, they heard the mother say, "Who is talking in the room?"

Quan had to release his grip of Dangui and say to Bai, "I'm here to greet you, Aunt." Dangui seized the chance to run back to her room. The mother flipped up the bed-drape and saw the scholar.

She said, "It's you. My son is not back with the medicine yet. Why is your cousin not here? Who were you talking to?"

Guilty-conscienced, Quan lied, "I am here alone. There is nobody else."

Bai said, "Well, I'm old. Maybe I didn't hear clearly." The scholar seemed absentminded, and, after a brief perfunctory talk, he stood up and left.

The mother was puzzled at his brusqueness and distraction, thinking to herself, "The composing pill is from the capital city. I'm sure that my nephew brought it here. But how did it happen to get into my daughter's room? I was disturbed in my sleep just now and heard my daughter's voice. However, he said he was alone! I'm worried that they may get to know of the early marriage arrangement and start to fool around with each other. That may develop into an affair later. They are grown up. I originally had planned to bring them together. The reason that I've not broached the subject is that he is new here and I don't know whether he's married or not. I'll wait for a time and then find an opportunity to get them married."

At this point Gaoer entered the room with the medical plaster he had purchased and said, "The goddamn doctor was not in, so I had to wait a long time to purchase this medicine."

Mrs. Bai was not happy with the boy's being late and said, "If I had depended upon the medicine you bought, I would have died long ago. Now I'm fine and you can put the medicine aside. Go and see your cousin."

Gaoer said, "I don't think my cousin is honest. I saw him awhile ago hanging around my sister's room. When he spotted me, he left."

The mother said, "Stop talking like that."

Gaoer replied, "To my mind, my cousin is handsome, and my sister has lost her betrothed. Why don't you get my sister to marry my cousin so as to complete a life business? That will keep him from becoming impatient and doing something ridiculous."

The mother replied, "You're young and talking nonsense! I know what to do." Though she reproved her son, she understood that her son's words made sense, so she stored the thought in her mind before she had a chance to say anything more about it.

After their first chat, the scholar and Dangui often traded amorous glances. He was infatuated with her, day and night kept writing on a piece of paper with a brush, reluctant to take his meals, while she was not up to doing anything either. She was tired and sleepy and neglected her needle work. The mother noticed this change in their behavior. They, though attracted to each other, could only restrain themselves from acting rashly because there was always someone around.

One day the scholar was on his way to the mother's room when he ran into Dangui, who had just finished dressing and was leaving her own room. He blocked her way and said in greeting her, "I have long heard of your beautifully adorned room, but have never had a chance to take a look at it. Now I've got the chance and you must let me in."

Without waiting for a reply, he slid inside. Dangui had to follow him in. Seeing no one around, he seized her in his arms, saying, "I'm pleading, Sister. Please do me the great favor of granting a request."

Dangui, for fear of making a disturbance, said in a low voice, "Please behave, Brother. I appreciate your high valuation of me. Why not go to my mother and make a proposal? She will approve it. Why should you act in secret and frivolously?"

Quan said, "I appreciate your advice, Sister, and the treatment you are giving me with warmth and sincerity. I understand the value of decent conduct. But it does not satisfy my current need. I just can't wait that long."

With a stern face, Dangui said, "I absolutely cannot comply with your precipitant request. If I did, you would despise me after marriage." She wrenched herself free from his embrace and stalked toward the door, her hairpins slanted and her hair disheveled. She then ran to her mother's room, panting.

The mother was surprised at the sight of her daughter and said, "What happened to you?"

Dangui replied, "I was leaving my room when my cousin came up. So I started to run, a little too fast."

The mother said, "You're cousins. Why do you have to avoid seeing him?" Bai thought her nephew might be in shortly, but he was not. Quan, in fact, was a little disappointed with Dangui's reaction and so he turned around and went back.

Bai now became even more apprehensive. She should like to get the two of them to marry at an early date, but a matchmaker was wanting. Suddenly she thought, "My nephew told me that he had come to our home after he heard of us from Abbess Miaotong. It might be a good idea to let Miaotong be the matchmaker for them." At once she sent Gaoer to ask Miaotong to come. Let's now leave her for the moment.

After going back to his room, Quan was rather discouraged, thinking about what happened a short time before. Then he decided that Dangui was inclined to accept his love and what she had said made sense, though she turned him down on his advances. "She doesn't know I'm an impostor. But who can I talk to about this?" he wondered. Then he mused, "She and her mother have no doubt as to my identity as the son from the family of Bai. Their confidence in this marriage hinges on the money box. If I show them the box, what reason will I have for worrying about my chances of marrying her?" But on second thought, he said to himself, "It's not a good idea. If someone else has an identical name and the money box is not from Dangui's family, that will confuse the whole thing, given the trust of the mother and daughter in me up to now. I'd better keep the box top hidden and try to be intimate with Dangui. I'll have her eventually."

As he strolled out into the yard, locked in thought, Abbess Miaotong entered. She greeted him and said, "You've been with your relatives quite a while, sir, and have not recently stopped at our temple!"

Smiling, Quan said in returning her greeting, "To be frank, my aunt would not let me go. Besides, I hate being alone and want to stay with my kinfolk. So I haven't gone out."

Miaotong said, "Well, if you're bored with being alone, I can do the matchmaking for you."

Quan said, "I wanted to buy a concubine when I first talked with you, but you said you didn't care about worldly affairs. So I didn't discuss the matter with you. It would be good to have you as my matchmaker now."

Miaotong said, "I've got someone in mind for your marriage, but Lady Bai just now sent for me. I'll come back to discuss it with you after I meet with her."

Quan said, "I am interested in a girl, so I need to talk to a matchmaker and you're the right person to talk to. Please be sure to come to my room after you see my aunt. We can talk."

"I see," Miaotong agreed.

Then Miaotong went in. Bai said to her, "It's been long time since your last visit here."

Miaotong replied, "I learned that you're not in good health. I was about to come to see you when your son came and called me. So I've arrived."

Bai said, "A few days after my nephew arrived, I was both happy and sad. I was also a little tired. So I fell sick. Now I've recovered. Please don't worry about me. I do, however, have one thing to talk over with you, Abbess."

Miaotong asked, "What is it?" Bai said, "I'm worried day and night about the fact that my daughter is not married."

Miaotong said, "It's not easy to be satisfied on such a matter."

Bai said, "But I have someone in mind. I want to talk to you about him."

Miaotong asked, "Why do you want to talk to me, a nun, about the matter?" Bai said, "Let me ask you something first. I have a nephew who has come from the capital city. He said he got to know you first. Do you know him?"

Miaotong replied, "Why not? He stayed in our temple for a time. After I told him something about you, he went to see you, claiming kinship. How could I not know him? He's handsome."

Bai said, "My nephew is the same age as my daughter. This I have told you before. Years ago when I was in the capital city, I wanted to betroth her to him. But my husband disagreed. Before I left the capital city, I secretly split a money box in half as proof of identity. One half I left with my nephew's family and the other half I kept with me. I also wrote a note. At that time my nephew was a baby. So many years have passed and we're worlds apart. I wonder whether they still have the other half of the money box and the note, but I believe he is my nephew. I'm worried about my daughter since there has not been a satisfactory choice for her marriage. Maybe it is the heavenly arrangement for him to come here. In any case, I desire to fulfill my promise made years ago. But it is not suitable for me to bring up the matter with my nephew. Furthermore, I don't know whether he is married or not. I would appreciate it if you could go to the western chamber and talk to him. If he's not married, I will arrange for their marriage. Would you please do this favor for me?"

Miaotong replied, "My pleasure. I think it's going to be very successful match. I'll take that half of the box with me. It will help to start a conversation."

Bai said, "Exactly." She went into her room, brought out the bottom part of the box and gave it to Miaotong.

With the body of the box tucked in her sleeve, Miaotong made straight for the west room. Upon meeting, Quan said to her, "Did you see my aunt, Abbess?"

Miaotong rejoined, "Yes I did."

Quan asked, "Can I know what you talked about?"

Miaotong replied, "Nothing particular. We had not seen each other for a long time."

Quan said, "Did you see my cousin?"

Miaotong said, "No, I did not. But I'll see her later in her room."

Quan then said, "She has a pretty nice room. Unfortunately she has to stay alone."

Miaotong said, "She should also be taken care of in terms of matchmaking."

Quan continued, "A short time ago you said something about a marriage for me. What's that?"

Miaotong said, "The woman is one of my patrons, very good-looking and a perfect match for you, sir. But you only want to obtain a concubine, so you must have a wife at home. The woman I have in mind doesn't want to be a concubine."

Quan replied, "I had a wife but she died a year ago. I was thinking that I might not find another satisfactory match from a family well matched in social status, so I said to you I wanted a concubine. If you propose a girl from a good origin and satisfactory, I'll naturally take her as my formal wife."

Miaotong said, "What requirement will satisfy you?"

Pointing to Dangui's room, he said, "To tell you the truth, someone like her would be the best."

Miaotong smiled and said, "Well, her features will certainly meet your requirement."

Quan asked, "How many gifts does her family require for the betrothal?"

Miaotong slipped the bottom of the money box out of her sleeve and said, "They don't want any gifts. But their requirement is rather harsh. They have this part of a money box. Anyone who owns the other part of it can marry her."

Quan took the object and saw that it was the bottom part of the money box. Secretly delighted, he asked, concealing his true feelings, "Since they want to have this box matched, there must be a story behind it. I wonder whether you know anything about it."

Miaotong replied, "This family originally lived in the capital city. A conjugal relationship was agreed upon for the girl and her brother's son. The two families split the money box between them, each to keep one part as proof of identity for the future. Anyone who has the other part of the box is the predestined match."

Quan said, "Speaking of this money box, I've got a part of it. But I'm not sure whether it is the right part to match." He quickly took the lid of the box out of his gift case. It matched Miaotong's part perfectly.

Miaotong said, "They indeed go together. It is surprising that you've kept it."

Quan replied, "Please let me know who owns the other part?"

Miaotong, said, "Who else? Why do you pretend to be ignorant? It's your cousin Dangui. Didn't you know that?"

Quan said, "I watched you beat about bush before, Abbess, so I didn't talk directly either, just teasing you. Another thing is that my aunt planned on this marriage in our childhood, but why does she need you as the matchmaker?"

Miaotong replied, "Your aunt told me that it's been long time since then and she suspects you might have married a wife. Therefore it was not appropriate for her to bring up the matter. She asked me to make an inquiry. Since you lost your wife and have not remarried ever since, and your part of box matches hers, I should report to her about this. The marriage can be fulfilled immediately."

Quan said, "I appreciate your kindness in doing me this great favor. I wonder when we will marry — I hope it will be early?"

Miaotong said, "What an impatient bridegroom you are! It should be during the Mid-autumn Festival tomorrow. I'm going to talk Bai into holding your wedding ceremony tomorrow. You should not wait any more."

"Thank you," Quan said, "I am much obliged to you."

Tucking the two parts of the money box into her sleeve, Miaotong left in high spirits for the mother's room. Believing that the other part of the box had been found and the long-planned marriage could now come true Bai was overjoyed. She got ready to hold the wedding party the next day. At this moment of excitement, how could she have conceived of the fact that her nephew was a fraud? Indeed,

The box was genuine;
The man not,
A blessing is concealed
In a plot.

The scholar Quan was in extreme bliss, staying awake the whole night. He got up unusually early the next day and bade Quan Zhong to hire a scholar's hat and dress for him. He prepared for the performing of the wedding rites. The mother was up early, too, seeing to the wedding party arrangements and urging her daughter to dress quickly and properly. The bride and bridegroom were supposed to worship heaven and earth with bows during the wedding ceremony. Dressed in the scholar's garment, Quan was at his best, trying to conceal his quiet happiness, and Quan Zhong, too, kept smiling. Others believed Quan was in marital bliss. Who might be suspicious? The house was immersed in the splendor of candlelight as if in a fairyland. After the wedding party, the bride and bridegroom were led into their room, which was Dangui's bedroom on the east side, where Quan had dreamed so much of being with her and had intruded into to take liberties with her. Now he was sleeping with her for the night. Can you imagine how happy he was? He felt as though he were asea on an immortals' wonderland. He and she got into the bed and made love with immeasurable joy.

Their love complete, Quan, caressed and hugged Dangui, and said, "Our conjugal bond across great distance has now finally come true. I am blessed for my past, present and next lives."

Dangui said, "Our marriage was arranged in our early years and we get married today. It is not something strange. I'm happy that, despite the elapse of all these years and the great distance that separated us, we've managed to marry each other. It is just like a heavenly design. But I've got one thing to talk about with you. You're not a native here and have married into my family without any idea about where you will settle in future. Besides, I don't know whether you want to pursue learning or business in terms of your career. Now that I'm your wife, I will follow you whatever you do. But we have to plan on our future. We should not indulge ourselves in moments of merriment."

Quan responded, "Don't worry. But you would have to, otherwise. Since you're married to me, I can guarantee that you will be better-off."

Dangui said, "What good can you promise me? I'm sure that I won't have the honor and wealth of the wife of a senior official."

Quan laughed and said, "Something else may be hard to come by. But if you want the position of the wife of a senior official, I can give that to you as easily as I can take something from my wardrobe."

With a "pooh", Dangui said, "Shame on you!" Dangui did not take what she said to heart, while Quan smiled in silence. He spent the whole night with her in intimacy and gentleness.

The next morning, they washed and dressed in gowns. Then they went together to greet Lady Bai and to thank Miaotong for her efforts in doing the matchmaking. As they were making obeisance, sounds of gongs were heard from the yard, then about ten clamoring people entered, sending Gaoer into a frantic sprint.

Quan emerged and asked, "Who are making such a noise?"

He had barely uttered that question when Quan Xiao, one of his old housekeepers, came forward with a herd of messengers from the capital city. He kowtowed to scholar Quan and said, "The messengers have come from the capital city to notify you of your promotion. I have looked for you everywhere. A moment ago I saw Quan Zhong and learned you were here. But why are you in such clothes? Please be quick to change them."

Quan gestured to silence them, attempting to maintain the concealment of his identity. However, he was bombarded with one shout after another of "Master Quan." The messengers took out a sheet of announcement, saying he had been conferred upon the fellowship in the Imperial Academy. They all shouted for a tip from him, who kept telling them not to call him by his family name "Quan." The men did not listen to him but posted high on the wall the good news written on red paper, which said,

An immediate announcement:
    Lord Quan from your honorable household has been granted promotion to fellow in the Imperial Academy.

Quan Zhong brought out an official hat and girdle for the scholar and said to him, "I don't think you will be able to conceal your identity any more. You'd better let them know." The scholar took off his scholar's hat and garment, smiling, and changed into the official dress. The incense table fixed in front, he kowtowed before it, in expressing his gratitude to the emperor. He told the messengers to wait outside for the reward and then went in to greet his mother-in-law once more.

The news came as a great surprise to the lady and sent her into a fluster. The scholar kowtowed to her, as she said, "What should I do? I did not know your family name was Quan and that you were a senior official at the imperial court. It is a shame that I have eyes but failed to see a huge mountain. Please forgive me for the slighting treatment I gave you."

The scholar responded, "Now that we're one family, don't mention it."

The mother-in-law said, "Could you do me a favor and let me know why you posed as my nephew and came to our humble home, since you're not from the family of Bai? There must be a reason."

The scholar replied, "I stayed in the Buddhist temple. One night I took a stroll and caught a glimpse of your daughter. I admired her beauty. Then I talked to Abbess Miaotong, who told me about your family. So I faked it and came over as your nephew. Fortunately you believed in what I said and took me as your son-in-law. It's my great fortune."

Miaotong said, "When the scholar first arrived at my place, he said his family name was Quan. Later when we talked about Lady Bai, he said he was from the family of Bai. I asked him why he called himself Quan and he then told me that he had changed his name for the sake of searching for his relatives. It is the game of a noble. We were all deceived. This is a stupid mistake we've made."

Lady Bai said, "I have another curiosity. Where did you obtain that part of the money box? Is it possible that you, son-in-law, are supernatural?"

The scholar said smiling, "I'm not your genuine nephew. But that part of the money box is not something I faked. The whole thing seems predestined, something beyond human endeavor."

Surprised, the mother and Miaotong said, "Could you please let us know how?"

The scholar said, "One day long ago I strolled on a street in the capital city. There I purchased the lid of a money box in the market. It was wrapped in a piece of paper that bore the characters you wrote to your nephew, Liuge, and included your daughter's name. With the note you wrote, I became confident that I might pose as your nephew. Please forgive me, mother-in-law, for my offense of deception."

Lady Bai said, "Alright, you can drop this matter. But I don't understand why my nephew's family sold the part of the money box and who sold it to you. You should know everything about it, son-in-law."

The scholar said, "The seller was an elderly man. He told me that he was the owner of the house in which your brother's family lived. He said the family contracted an epidemic disease. The young members died and the old folks fled, leaving some things behind. So the old man sold them in the market."

Lady Bai said, "My nephew died. My brother may have died, too.

They only left this thing behind." She started to weep.

Miaotong tried to calm her by saying, "Old Lady, marriage is predestined. Don't worry about whether he is or is not your nephew, and whether he is from the family of Quan or that of Bai. Now with a fellow in the Imperial Academy as your son-in-law, your daughter will be graced."

The mother replied, "What you say is correct." Thus everyone was happy.

Dangui had listened carefully in silence. She recalled that the scholar had promised to make her the wife of a senior official the previous night. She now understood that he had something in mind at that time but did not want to brag. The money box worked out magically to bring them together. Her joy knew no bounds.

Scholar Quan loved Dangui's beauty and marveled at the adventure of the money box. He and she were deeply in love. He thanked Abbess Miaotong with generous gifts and left with the whole family, his wife, mother-in-law and brother-in-law, on his way to the assumption of his office. Later, when his tenure of office expired, the title of Yiren was conferred on Dangui. The husband and wife lived together into their old age.

Everything in the world is predestined;
Even a chance meeting is at the mercy of Fate.
Without the help of a box lid,
How could the scholar come from afar to his mate?

Tale 2

Inquiring About a Lost Man in Courtesans' Quarters; Hearing Howls of Ghosts in the Saffron Garden

It is said that during the Ming Dynasty there once lived a retired official surnamed Yang in the county of Xindu, in Sichuan Province. He won the title of *jinshi*, but later met a violent end. So we'll omit his given name. Of wealthy stock, his disposition was one of avarice, fierceness and brutality, which made him a despot of his native place. While holding a post of subsidiary governor of Yunnan Province, he had a bullying subordinate named Zhang Yin, a grant-aided student. After his mother had died young, his father had entrusted the management of the household to Zhang Yin. His father was a man of immense wealth, whose wife gave birth to Zhang Yin and whose concubine gave him a much younger son named Zhang Bin. Zhang Yin was quite good at school work and never failed to top the list in examinations. Soon he became a local celebrity, easily associating with the prefecture and county officials. But his father was worried about him because he was treacherous and vile by nature, and he seized every opportunity to profit at another's expense. The father often advised him, saying, "Our family has enough wealth to meet all your needs and those of coming generations. Besides, you are making rapid progress in learning and will have a successful career sooner or later. Why do you bother to haggle over trifles and gaining advantage over others?"

Zhang Yin was not only disgusted with these sincere admonishments but he became suspicious. My father must have had some private savings, he thought. Therefore he takes things lightly and dislikes my style of frugality. Besides, my mother has died, and he has his concubine and her son. The larger portion of his wealth will belong to them. Part of property that I am looking after will go to my brother. How much shall I have then?

He started to calculate day and night and began to acquaint himself with local government officials so that he might call upon their power after his father's death to place the concubine and her young son at his mercy. In this way he hoped to seize all his father's legacy in days to come.

Some time later, the father died. Zhang Yin, fearing that the younger brother might insist on dividing the family fortune between them, immediately asked the concubine for the private savings that the old man had left behind. The concubine's response was "no."

Zhang Yin rummaged through the chests and cupboards but could find nothing. He did not let the matter drop and began to suspect that the money was buried somewhere underground or had been shifted to someone else's home. Finally, the concubine demanded a split of the family property between the two brothers. Zhang Yin refused. "Since you have kept my father's private savings for yourself," he said, "I am entitled to the rest of the property." Relatives of the family took sides, some standing by the elder brother and others with the younger one. The heated dispute eventually led to a lawsuit. By this time, Zhang Yin's two sons had become students of official schools. They were well established both financially and socially and had friends in government. The widow and her young son, however, had no one to turn to, so they instituted a lawsuit against Zhang Yin. It came before the subsidiary governor Yang.

Hearing that Yang had accepted the indictment, Zhang Yin felt panic. Do you know why this was so? It's because Yang was greedy, ruthless and never spared anyone's feelings. If he was annoyed, he would show nobody mercy. He would find any excuse he could to settle a matter in favor of one party and disfavor of another. His only virtue was love of silver. There was no cure for him except silver. He was well-known as Madman Yang, meaning he could not be offended. Zhang Yin reasoned that the lawsuit over the family property would eventually be settled by the prefecture or county authorities, and so he would by no means lose it since he had connections in the county's and prefect's government. But what counted was the fact that this Madman Yang held a written complaint against him. If he did not buy him off, the man would create trouble and divide the father's legacy between himself and his half-brother. That would be a grave matter.

Experienced and crafty, Zhang Yin selected a trusted follower of Yang, and made a deal through him with Yang in which Zhang promised to pay a reasonable five hundred *liang* of silver so that Yang would decide the lawsuit in Zhang's favor. Yang agreed to the terms and said, "Please bring the silver over and I'll take care of it. If the verdict does not satisfy you, I'll return the silver to you in perfect condition."

Zhang Yin scraped up the three hundred *liang* along with a golden tea pot and a glimmering and ingeniously constructed set of gold jewelry, which was estimated to be worth two hundred *liang* of silver. Then he asked the go-between to write a statement and have a redeeming permit issued to him in exchange for his silver. An agreement was reached that when the report about the dispute was delivered by county or prefect authorities, Yang would write a comment in favor of Zhang so that he would get rid of any trouble posed by his half-brother for good. To assure Zhang, a counter complaint was accepted first. Zhang was allowed to claim back all his deposit if his terms were not completely met.

The go-between led Zhang in plain clothes to a side entrance to Yang's office. The two parties conducted the exchange with a tacit understanding. Zhang ruminated that he was perfectly safe. With this small payment, the wealth of the great household would roll into his pocket. He thought to himself, what a deal I am going to have! He was overjoyed.

If Zhang Yin had been a little kind, he would have made a present of the five hundred *liang* of silver to his half-brother, instead of arguing over the family property, thus keeping the money within the household and leaving the widow and her young son with immense gratitude toward him. What a heartless man he was to cudgel his brains over how to skin his half-brother and to give his own money to somebody else! If Zhang Yin had achieved his end, the natural laws would have been in great disorder.

However, there are always unpredictable vicissitudes in life. After Yang had taken the money and valuables, and passed Zhang's counter-complaint down to the concerned officials to be processed, the Day of Longevity to the Emperor arrived. According to national practice, the provincial departments of administration and justice were expected to send a representative with a memorial to the capital, to present congratulations to the emperor. The task fell this year to Yang. Unable to shirk this duty, he packed to make ready to go. The news tossed Zhang Yin into a pool of anxiety. He went to the go-between to inquire about his case, and the reply came back from Yang, who said, "This trip won't take me more than a year. In addition, the proceeding of your lawsuit is still at its early stage since the county's department of justice has not required the complaint to be turned in yet. I'll have plenty of time to handle the matter after I come back."

With no way out, Zhang Yin had to bribe county and prefect court to have them set aside the issue until Yang's return.

But things seemed to work against Zhang's wishes. After Yang arrived in Beijing to attend the imperial ceremonies he was assessed by the Board of Civil Personnel. Because of his notoriety of avarice, he was rated as an "indiscreet" official. So he was forced to stay idle although he was nominally demoted.

Yang left the capital city in disappointment while sending for his wife and children to join him in his native place. When Yang's family was about to set out on the journey, Zhang voiced his concern about his money through the go-between, only to receive the response from the family members that, "This is the business of the master, not ours, and you'd better go and talk to the master himself if you have a right to claim the money. We know nothing about it."

Zhang could push the matter no further and so shelved it, helplessly looking on as his sum of silver dropped into the east seas never to be recovered. It was only natural that Zhang Yin's stupid tricks had incurred this consequence, and he would have been better off if he had been content with his incompetence and swallowed the humiliation at the beginning. But Zhang Yin was not one for generosity, and he begrudged letting five hundred *liang* of silver be snatched away so easily from him. He mused, with the redeeming permit on me, Yang can have no reason to refuse to return my money. I will go to his native town in the county of Xindu and talk to other members of his family, who may be able to redeem part of my deposit, at least those pieces of gold jewelry, if not the silver. This year, I will be recommended to enter the school for State's Scions and will sit for examinations in Beijing. On my way to Beijing, I'll have to go to Chengdu, and, from Chengdu, I will make a detour, a short distance of about fifty *li*, to Xindu county. If I can get back some of my money from Yang's family, that will cover part of my traveling expenses. He kept his plan to himself, not even telling his own wife for fear he would be secretly sneered at for his greed.

Then Zhang Yin had passed the selective tests for students to be recommended. He rushed back home excitedly to receive congratulations. He laid aside the matter of lawsuit and drank to his fill for days before packing for the long journey.

As usual, he picked Zhang Long, Zhang Hu, Zhang Xing and Zhang Fu as his traveling companions. They traveled day and night, and sometime had to pass a night by the waterside and take their dinner in the wind. Before long, they reached Chengdu. After they had put up for the first night in an inn, Zhang Yin thought to himself, "I have to make a trip to Xindu to retrieve my money, and it's inappropriate to leave our heavy baggage here at the inn. Since I am feeling quite bored after these days of traveling, why not divert myself a little by visiting one of the local brothels and staying there for a couple of nights? I may as well leave my baggage there when I go on my way to Xindu, and pick it up upon my return."

He summoned his four traveling companions and told them his idea. These servants were used to staying outside. Hearing their master would go whoring, they realized they would also benefit. Who, after all, would pass up such a chance? They escorted Zhang Yin towards downtown brothels.

As Zhang Yin cruised the streets of parlor houses, he saw girls richly attired and heavily made-up leaning on their own door-frames in flirtatious postures. He was dazzled, but none of them particularly intrigued him. As he was hesitating over which harlot should be his target, a man meandered over. He had been watching Zhang Yin and his followers looking around in all directions with an air of whoring but in need of a pimp. The man came up and inquired, "I'm sure you are born to the purple, but why are you fooling around in this vulgar place?"

With a cupped-hand salute, Zhang Yin replied, "As a student visitor, I have just settled at an inn, and I have ventured out into this part of your town to dispel my boredom."

The man smiled, remarking, "I wonder whether you can complete the true task of whoring with your eyes only."

"How do you know I won't get into bed with one of these girls?" Zhang Yin rejoined with a grin.

The man laughed heartily. "If you are really in a mood to enjoy yourself, I would like to show you the way," he said.

The man's suggestion fitted in with Zhang's wishes. He seized the opportunity and inquired, "May I ask your name?"

"My name is Loaf, with the sobriquet of Do-nothing," replied the man, "and I'm quite familiar with this place and its people. May I know where you are from?"

Zhang Yin answered, "I'm from Dianzhong."

"Then you're from central Yunnan Province," remarked the man.

"Our master," butted in Zhang Xing, "will enter the school for State's Scions and is currently on his way to the capital city for the examinations at the imperial court."

"Sorry I didn't recognize you," responded Loaf Do-nothing promptly, "I'm very honored to meet you, and it will be my pleasure to accompany you on your tour around here as your host. What do you think?"

"Marvelous," replied Zhang Yin, "I wonder who is the best whore here?"

Counting on his fingers, Loaf Do-nothing mentioned a few names, "Liu Jin, Zhang Sai, Guo Shishi and Wang Diu'er are all of the rising generation."

"Who is an expert at the trade then?" questioned Zhang Yin.

"As to who is good at this business," commented Loaf Do-nothing, "these young girls are inexperienced, a far cry from Tang Xingge, who is soft, warm and full of tender affection. She was a popular girl, too. But it is a shame that she is close to thirty, a few years over her prime. I'm sure you will find a great deal of fun in her."

"I'm no youngster anymore myself," said Zhang Yin, "and I have already had enough of childish stuff. I think older girls are more enjoyable."

"Okay then," said Loaf Do-nothing, "let's go to Xingge's place right now," and he guided his customer toward the house of Tang.

Xingge emerged to meet them. She looked really balanced, filled with charm and the manners of an expert. Zhang Yin was delighted.

While having some tea, the host and guest told each other their names. From time to time, Loaf Do-nothing would supply other information required by either part. Noticing that Zhang Yin was satisfied, Loaf Do-nothing assumed the appearance of a host and sent Zhang's followers to get things ready for dinner.

That night, Loaf Do-nothing stayed drinking in their company. Zhang had always been a good drinker, and now set on having all the fun of a traveler, drank to his heart's content. The Loaf was also an enormous vessel for liquor. Xingge was no less mature at drinking, and many drinks down her throat left her still steady and sober. The three vied with one another in consuming food and wine until well into the night.

After Loaf Do-nothing left for home, Zhang Yin shared a bed with Xingge, who, using all her resources, entertained her visitor throughout the night. The following day, Zhang Yin brought all the baggage to Xingge's house.

A few days' stay in Xingge's home cost Zhang Yin quite a sum of silver. But he hated to part from this woman, as he was bewitched by her charms. I don't have much money left on me, he thought, so why not go now to Xindu and have that business of mine completed so I will have more money to spend on Xingge? Thus thinking, he emerged to talk to his followers, then had them put saddles on the horses to get ready for the trip.

Thinking he would get the business settled and return in a few days, he told Xingge, "I have a sum of silver in Xindu. It's a half-day's journey. I'll go and collect the debt and then play with you for some time more."

"Why don't you send your men to fetch the money while you stay here with me?" asked Xingge.

"This is something special," replied Zhang Yin. "I have to go and do it personally. They won't give the money to anyone except me."

"How much is it?" asked Xingge.

"Five hundred *liang*," answered Zhang Yin.

"Then I'd better not stop you," said Xingge, "as this matter is rather important. But if you don't come back to me, I'll be waiting in vain."

"Here's our baggage," said Zhang Yin, "I'll leave it with you. We won't need to take it with us, except for the bedding and a couple of presents. No matter what happens, I'll be back in a couple of days. If I have good luck, I may bring back more money than I expect and then I'll definitely give you a larger share."

"I don't care about that," laughed Xingge, "but you should make haste and return as soon as possible." Then they bade farewell to each other.

Suppose a wise man had shown up at this moment and admonished him, "You originally harbored evil designs, and that's why you've dropped this amount of silver into the black pit never to be retrieved. You can blame nobody but yourself. For those government officials, their role is to take hold and not to give up. You'd better forget about recovering your silver. It would be as difficult to get it as it would be to snatch a chunk of tender meat from a tiger's jaws or to pull a tusk from an elephant's cheek. Even if you get the money, you will want to squander it at the cathouse which, like a deep well, can never be filled up. Why do you scheme to no avail? I think it is time for you to accept your lousy luck and give up."

If this advice would have helped Zhang Yin change his mind, he would have had good fortune. However, there was no one around at that time to present him with this assistance. And even if there were, the warning would undoubtedly have fallen on deaf ears.

The result of this trip was: an elderly scholar went to his early grave in the park of saffrons, while a vicious local official became a prisoner. Thus:

The hogs and sheep are straying into the butcher's house,
And heading step by step toward the moment of slaughter.

Let's leave Zhang Yin and his men for awhile and take a look at Yang, who had by now returned home. Aware that his official career had come to its end, he fleeced the local people more intensively than before, for his family's wealth never abated his insatiability for more money. He engrossed himself in designing one scheme after another and in committing crimes.

He, too, had a younger brother. But this second child of the family was rich, law-abiding and never snooped into others' business. Occasionally, his younger brother would remonstrate his elder brother. But Yang would rebuke him, saying, "You've abused my power in bullying others and made a fortune for your own family. Now are you trying to teach me a lesson?" Their disagreeable conversation never went any further.

The younger brother knew Yang harbored sinister intentions, and would sooner or later direct his pernicious plots against his own family. Therefore, the younger brother hired a few able servants to prepare for this eventuality. But before long he fell seriously ill and took to his bed, never to rise again. He called his wife, only son aged eight, and family servants to his death bed and told them, "I'll leave this boy, my only flesh and blood, behind. Look, on the other side of the house my elder brother, with his power and high-ranking position, has been coveting our property like a tiger eyeing its prey. You should take precautions and not fall into his snares. This heavy load on my mind won't let me rest in peace even after my death." Tears streamed down his cheeks as he heaved a last sigh and died. After that his wife and the family servants kept a close watch over their household, seldom ventured out, and gave up all thoughts of making use of Yang's power.

Seeing there was no loophole he could take advantage of, Yang thought to himself, what an inheritance my second brother must have left behind! Unfortunately it will fall to that brat of a son. If I have the boy murdered, who will that wealth belong to except me? However, he couldn't carry out this plan, because the widow and her son shut themselves within the surrounding walls of their home and scarcely ever paid a visit to Yang's house.

If I have them killed with poison, the evil official thought to himself, the public will definitely point an accusing finger at me as the perpetrator of the crime. In addition, there is little chance of success in implementing such a plot. But I can throw dust in the eyes of the public by having a bunch of bandits kill them as they rob their home. Then I'll pretend to be sympathetic and fair. The blame will fall on the bandits. Who would suspect the ins and outs of such a matter! Even if the two of them survive the calamity, I can still achieve my goal by seizing all their property, and they will have to admit that they just had bad luck.

He usually maintained a retinue of over thirty hardened bandits at his house, who shared their booty with him after every robbery. Sometimes a part of their crime would be exposed, and he would emerge to cover it up and protect his men. Local governments knew about his cunning, and the public feared his power. Hence there was no brave soul to stare him down on the street, and he would send his men out to seize the property of anyone he disliked and bring it back to share with him. His deeds became routine, as he hardly gave any thought as to the consequences. Now he was waiting for his opportunity to topple his nephew's family. But the servants of the widow's family patrolled day and night with a host of dogs, as fierce as wolves, guarding the entrance. It might have been God's will that, although Yang had always been successful in the past, a number of attempts on the house of the second brother's widow came to naught.

One day as Yang was racking his brain for a solution, a note was suddenly handed in to him notifying him that Zhang Yin was calling on him. Yang remembered that this used to be one of his subordinates when he held tenure of office in Yunnan Province. He was startled, thinking to himself, "I took his bribe of five hundred *liang* of silver but did not do any work for him before I was dismissed from office and went home. I knew this sum would be a root of future trouble. Now as I apprehend, he has come for it. Since I was not able to help him in the lawsuit, he has every reason to get his bribe returned to him. Yet how can I willingly spit out the food I have already gulped down? Nevertheless, this petty scholar won't drop this matter. If this matter is brought to the authorities, not only will my reputation suffer, but I will have to waste a lot of breath in argument. Maybe I should show him courtesy and meet with him. He might turn out to be sensible enough not to mention the matter. If that happens, I'll give him some money for his journey and send him away. But if he does bring the matter up, I'll play it by ear."

Yang went over his idea in his mind several times so as to make sure there was no risk, then walked into the reception room and summoned his visitor. Zhang Yin adjusted his hat and clothes and came in. He made a formal salute in the way a subordinate greeted their superior, and presented some local products as a gift. Yang accepted them and had tea brought in, saying, "I used to work in your hometown, and committed many blunders. After I lost my post, I have been staying at home. It is a shame that I didn't get the chance to revisit your native land again. Even today I feel ashamed whenever I see a friend from your native place."

Zhang Yin answered, "Your Excellency was upright and outspoken and therefore offended a few people. But the majority of our officials and common people have always thought highly of your noble character."

"I'm flattered," replied Yang, adding with one hand cupped in the other, "Congratulations on your being selected as a student of the School of State's Scions."

"Oh, that luck of mine is worthless," said Zhang Yin.

"Then where are you heading by way of my humble place?" asked Yang.

"I just stopped by here," replied Zhang Yin, "to pay you a visit on my way to Beijing for the examinations at the imperial court."

"It's a distance of fifty *li* from here to Chengdu," said Yang, "and I feel uneasy and yet grateful that you've made such special detour to see me."

Zhang Yin was now sure that his host was purposely avoiding the subject of the bribe and so he addressed the topic directly. "I gave you a payment in advance for your assistance in solving our family's dispute over the property," he said. "But before its completion, you left on your business tour and returned to your hometown afterwards. Originally I didn't mean to bother you, but I'm indeed falling short of funds for the journey. So I'm here to beg you to return this money so as to aid my travel."

Yang flared up. "When staying in your hometown, I only consumed some water for survival. How could I have performed such a foul deed? This is absolutely a false charge! I wonder if you have perhaps been swindled by some racketeer?"

If he had been a wise man, Zhang Yin would have stopped pushing at this point, since he knew his host was denying his debt. However, not being one who could swallow an insult like this, Zhang Yin got excited and fiercely replied, "I personally handed the silver to you in front of the side entrance to your office, and I have kept the statement and the redeeming permit. How can you make off with it against your conscience?"

On hearing that his caller had the statement and redeeming permit, Yang corrected himself, assuming an air of pleasure. "I'm sorry," he said. "I'm getting too old to remember things. Now I recall one of my wife's brothers once asked me for some gifts and funds when he was about to leave for home. I had an empty pocket at that time, and so I sent him away with your silver. But later things were not smooth for me, so I haven't been able to do your bidding. I should give the money back to you, but to tell you the truth, I have nothing to give you right now. Will you allow me a few days to scrape the money together and pay you back?"

Zhang Yin felt a little easier now that his host had agreed to return the money, but he regretted that he might lose the two valuable pieces of gold he had also given to the man. "But I'm worried about the gold wares," said Zhang Yin. "They are family heirlooms, and I hope you can return them to me in perfect condition."

Yang answered with a grim smile, "If that is true, then who would have been willing to give them out as a deposit? Please rest assured that I'll take care of this after I give you a simple welcoming dinner." So saying, he rose to have his guest led away to his study and to have a feast prepared.

During the time before the meal, Yang turned the matter over and over again in his mind. His original plan was to repudiate the debt and expect Zhang Yin to meet him halfway by dropping the issue. Then he would certainly have given him ample presents in return to cover his traveling expenses, thus satisfying both sides. However, this narrow-minded Zhang Yin showed no due respect for his concerns and brought everything out into the open. Yang thought about returning half of the money as a token to satisfy Zhang's desire. But the gold pot and jewelry that Zhang Yin had given to him really touched his fancy. He fondled them whenever he had a chance and occasionally showed them to his relatives. How could he part with them? And now Zhang Yin was making a particular request to get them back. After a moment of hard thinking, a wicked idea came into his mind. I have to brazen through regardless of the consequences, he thought to himself. The man is a Yunnan native and currently away from home. Who will be able to discover the plot if I have him killed and his body disposed of!

Then he let a few competent servants gather those bandits he kept in his household, telling them to get ready for his order after dinner. This done, he invited Zhang to the table for a feast, and entertained him by addressing some idle topics and state concerns and having a few handsome boys repeatedly pour wine into his cup during the meal.

Zhang Yin found it hard to ignore his host's kindness, thinking to himself, with such hospitality, he will undoubtedly keep his word and return my things. Thus making himself at ease, he drank one cup after another until he got drunk. Then Yang asked his servants, "Are Zhang's followers being attended to?" He was told that they were also engaged in drinking. Those mean fellows of Zhang Yin's saw such good wine and delicious food that they rejoiced over the fact that they were in a place of such rapture. They ate and drank extravagantly, regardless of the consequences, until they were dead drunk and could no longer recognize anybody. After learning of the condition of his visitors, Yang ordered, "Carry them all to the Garden of Saffrons and finish them off!"

Yang owned this Garden of Saffrons, with an area of more than a thousand *mu*, where saffron plants were grown and reaped, bringing him a yearly income of eight hundred to nine hundred *liang* of silver. Around the garden were many houses accommodating visitors as well as providing lodging for the bandits. When Zhang Yin and his men were being carried away to their dwelling place in the Garden, they were completely drunk and asleep, snoring thunderously with no concern in their minds.

A gong echoed in the garden mustering a number of the bandits. With one stroke of their swords after another, they chopped off the heads of all the drunkards. Even if these pitiful men had each had three heads and six arms, it would not have taken the murderers but a few minutes to finish their mission. Not to speak of a student and a few stupid servants. In almost no time, they were all dead. The murderers then dug a pit in one part of the garden where the plants grew sparsely, tossed the bodies into a pile in the pit, and buried them there. Poor Zhang Yin! His wishful dream of regaining his possessions and, with them, going to Chengdu where he could have a good time with his sweetheart was over. But he would never know that he had met such a miserable end.

One year later, the two sons of Zhang Yin who had remained at home became worried because their father had sent no letter back after he left for the capital city. Occasionally they would meet someone returning from Beijing, and the general reply to their inquiries would be, "I didn't meet your father and have no idea as to his whereabouts." Suspicious, the sons said to each other, "Our Yunnan Province is one of the country's border areas, far away from the capital city. How can we get information here? We'd better travel to Sichuan to make inquiries. That's where people usually stop over on their way to and from Beijing."

The two young men gathered some money and then journeyed to Chengdu. After settling for their lodging, they strolled around the streets but encountered no one who could enlighten them regarding their father. Ten days soon passed and boredom began to take over their minds. "There are many well-known hookers around here," the two brothers reasoned in talking with one another, "and we can each pick one up and thus entertain ourselves." With mutual assistance, they each found a young harlot, Tong Xiaowu and Gu Adu. Led to their lodging, the two brothers made merry for days on end and utterly forgot their task of locating their father's whereabouts.

One day, the elder brother said that he wanted to find another girl. The two young prostitutes, knowing he was from Yunnan Province, teased him by saying, "We have learned that men from Yunnan Province are only interested in middle-aged strumpets. Are we so dull that although you've stayed here only for a few days, you already want to leave for another woman?"

"Where did you get the idea that men from Yunnan are only interested in middle-aged strumpets?" the two brothers asked.

Tong Xiaowu replied, "Uncle Loaf Do-nothing told us that one of his friends from Yunnan Province stayed here last year and asked him to find a whore for him. That man had a particular interest in mature ones. Later he was introduced to Xingge at the House of Tang. This Xingge belongs to my mother's generation. But this gentleman had a good time with her and spent a great deal of money on her. When he left, he promised to come back and spend more money on her. However, there is no telling where he has been ever since. Isn't this a typical instance that shows Yunnan natives are fond of mature women?"

"What was the name of that Yunnan native?" asked the two brothers. "And what did he look like?"

"Who cares!" answered Tong Xiaowu and Gu Adu, clapping their hands and laughing. "And is that any of our business? We don't care whether his family name was Zhang or Li, nor did we ever see him. We just think Uncle Loaf Do-nothing's story about this man is rather amusing."

Then the two brothers began to question them closely. "Who is this Loaf Do-nothing, and where does he live? You can certainly answer those questions!"

Again clapping their hands, the two girls said, "How can you go whoring if you don't know Uncle Loaf Do-nothing?" And Tong Xiaowu explained, "Uncle Loaf Do-nothing is a busy man. He usually appears unexpectedly and is quite difficult to get a hold of. If you insist on finding out about your fellow provincial, go and talk to Tang Xingge."

"That's a good idea," said the two brothers. So the younger brother stayed in the company of the two girls, and the elder brother made his way to the House of Tang.

It had been more than a year since Zhang Yin had left Tang Xingge behind on his trip of fifty *li*, which should have taken only one or two days. Xingge had heard nothing from him since and nobody had come to pick up the baggage he had left with her. As a prostitute, she was so accustomed to visitors coming and going that she had not worried much. On this day she had no business, and so Xingge shut the door and went to sleep. She sank into a dream in which she saw Zhang Yin arrive bringing back his silver. As she was about to greet him, she was awakened by rapid knocking on her door. Still half asleep, she thought to herself, I haven't missed him, but why did his image come into my dream? I wonder whether someone is sending word and picking up his clothing for him. Then there came up another knock on the door. She adjusted her attire and sent a serving girl out to answer the knock.

"Here's a visitor," reported the serving girl, ushering in Zhang, the elder brother. Looking up, Xingge was surprised to see that this gentleman looked exactly like Zhang Yin. But how, she wondered, has he become so much younger?

She led the visitor into the living room and both seated themselves. After learning that this young man was also from Yunnan and had the family name of Zhang, Xingge was puzzled about the matter, but said nothing about it to him.

The elder brother broke the silence. "Madam," he said, "I have an inquiry. I have just learned that a man from Yunnan came and stayed here in your house last year. May I know who he was?"

"Yes, a rather mature traveler stopped here last year," responded Xingge. "He said his family name was Zhang, and he was on his way to the capital city for the national examinations at the imperial court. He lingered here a couple of days before leaving for Xindu to retrieve the payment of a debt. He was supposed to come back soon, since it is only a half-day trip there, but nobody knows why he has not shown up since."

"How many were traveling with him?" questioned Zhang, the elder brother.

"He had four servants with him," answered the hostess.

Now Zhang was assured of his father's identification and went on with the questions. "If he has disappeared, maybe he started off for his long-planned journey without letting you know."

"I don't think so," said Xingge, "He entrusted me with the care of his baggage, because he intended to come back and pick up his belongings before his departure for Beijing."

"Why didn't he return then?" asked the elder brother. "Did he want to stay there for a long time and abandon his plan for his journey?"

"I think he might have had some problem obtaining the payment," replied Xingge. "But if he was held up there, he should have sent word or a servant back to let me know about it. It's strange that I've heard nothing from him so far."

"What kind of debt was he dealing with?" asked Zhang.

"He said," Xingge answered, "it involved five hundred *liang* of silver, but I have no idea of any details."

Stamping the floor, the elder brother shouted, "So that's it! I will have to go to Xindu to locate him."

"Does he have something to do with you that you need to make that trip?" inquired Xingge.

"To be frank," replied Zhang, "he is my father."

"Excuse me for my impropriety," said Xingge. "Now I understand why you and he look exactly alike. You're father and sons." Then, smiling, she sent the cook to make dinner and asked her visitor to wait for awhile.

Zhang told her, "It's very kind of you, but I have a younger brother awaiting me in the other part of town. I just want to double-check to see if you're serious about what you've just said."

"Of course I'm serious," responded Xingge quickly. "I've got his baggage here with me, and you may take a look at it and see whether it is his or not." She then led the elder brother into an inner room and showed him his father's belongings.

After he made sure everything was correct, he bade her good-bye, saying, "This is urgent business. I must hurry and set out tonight with my younger brother for Xindu. We'll be back with my father soon." Xingge pretentiously asked him to stay a little longer before seeing him off at her entrance.

The elder brother scurried back to his dwelling place and told his younger brother, "I've learned our father's whereabouts. He was here whoring last year at the House of Tang. However, the prostitute said our father didn't go to Beijing at all."

"Where did he go then?" asked the younger brother.

"He should be staying in Xindu right now," replied the elder brother. "We must go there and find him."

"Why did he tarry there so long?" asked the younger brother.

"This woman told me," answered the elder brother, "he wanted to get back his five hundred *liang* of silver. I'm sure he went to find Yang the Madman!"

"He shouldn't have delayed his trip to Beijing whether he was successful or not in claiming his money. How can he be still lingering in Xindu?"

"I saw his baggage in Xingge's home a moment ago. I don't think he would have departed without picking that up. I believe he has been held up in Xindu. Since it is not a long way from here, let's pack our things and go there so we can get to the bottom of the matter." Having made up their minds, the two young men paid the two prostitutes some silver and started off for Xindu.

They stayed at a hotel in Xindu. Knowing they were not natives, the hotel manager asked, " I guess you two gentlemen are travelers away from home?"

The two brothers told him they came from Yunnan and they were there to look for someone. "Yunnan," said the manager, "are you here really to look for someone or to retrieve some former bribe?"

This question surprised the brothers. "What are you talking about?" they asked.

"I was joking," replied the manager.

After taking their seats, the brothers inquired, "Do you have any idea about a certain Yang who lives somewhere around here?"

The manager paused, sticking out his tongue, "I don't think you want to mess around with that man," he said. "You're not from these parts. Why are you inquiring about him?"

The brothers answered, "We're just inquiring about him. But why are you afraid of mentioning his name?"

The manager said, "If he is a little displeased, he will make you suffer through a lawsuit. But if he is annoyed by you, he may send bandits to rob you. If a stranger offends him he may have him killed in one way or another!"

"How can he remain at large in today's society of law and order," asked the brothers, "after committing such homicide?"

"For what does he need to pay with his own life?" asked the manager, and then he recalled, "Last year, a gentleman, also from Yunnan Province, came here, with four servants, to make a claim for some bribery that Yang had once accepted when holding a post. But they were simply killed one night, and the wrong has not been redressed so far. Has he been punished any way? Because I heard you two are from Yunnan, too, so I joked with you awhile ago."

The manager's story made the brothers' hair stand on end. Staring at each other, they remained silent for some time before asking another question. "I wonder whether you, by any chance, know that gentleman's name?" they asked, trembling.

"I have no idea," said the manager. "But Yang has a household manager called Third Brother who still maintains some standards. He frequents my tavern and, while having a drink with me, revealed everything about the atrocities his boss had perpetrated, believing that justice would someday be done. After the murder of the five Yunnan natives last year, a rumor about it circulated and many people learned of it. I was suspicious at first and did not immediately believe this story, until Third Brother, feeling indignant about the injustice, convinced me. These five men died a miserable death unknown to their family members. Now you two have again brought forth the topic of the Yang family, so I picked up the thread and chatted idly. Gentlemen, only sweep away the snow in front of your own home, and don't try to remove the frost on the roof of your neighbor's house."

The two brothers now recognized that the victim must have been their father, but they dared not say so. They were profoundly grieved. After a sleepless night they wandered about the streets probing high and low. But the scraps they garnered all converged on the story of their father's murder. In a secluded place the two brothers wailed broken-hearted. They realized any leak as to their identity might draw the same destruction onto themselves. The family of Yang was so powerful in this area that the local government could do nothing about it. Grief-stricken and frightened, they went back to Chengdu.

After they recounted the story to Tang Xingge, the woman also shed some tears. "Why not sue the man and bring him to justice?" asked Xingge.

"Exactly!" replied the two brothers. At that time an imperial commissioner, Shi by name, was in Chengdu. The two young men retrieved their father's baggage from Xingge, and sorted out the official dispatch regarding the title of their father and kept it in a safe place. Then they filed a bill of indictment and appealed to the court. The bill of indictment read as follows:

An Indictment by Zhang Zhen and Zhang Qiong
Concerning the Murder of Five Innocent Men

Your Lordship:
  Zhang Yin, our father, went to the home of Yang, a local

tyrant in Xindu last year in an effort to obtain payment of a debt.
But he disappeared. We hunted around Xindu for clues and
discovered this Mr Yang had him, along with his four followers,
murdered for the purpose of appropriating our father's property.
The story of this iniquity has been widely circulated and
universally accepted in the local area.

Their bodies have vanished, the crime is towering, and this
injustice is extraordinary. We are presenting this indictment and
plead for your permission to capture the criminal.

Sincerely
Zhang Zhen
(a Yunnan native)

After reading this bill of indictment, Shi recalled that Yang of
Xindu had long had a bad reputation for cruelty and despotism, and he
had personally gathered many complaints against this man. Because
this bully was a *jinshi* and no bold man had ever before brought a suit
against him, Shi hadn't found a way to punish him by law. Now, with
this indictment in front of him, he knew the suit was no false charge.
But he was, indeed, in need of testimonies about the crime before he
could undertake this case. A rash action would only result in grave
consequences. Shi told his subordinates to leave him and the two
accusers alone.

"I've learned a great deal about the atrocities this criminal has
committed," he said to the brothers, "and now your suit adds a further
charge against him. I think you should hurry back home without delay,
in case this treacherous man might learn of your intention and lay
murderous hands on you. I'll look into this matter and gather criminal
evidence. When ready, I'll have a summons sent to you so that you
will be here for his trial. Please tell nobody anything about this." This
said, he tucked the bill of indictment under his sleeve. The two young

men kowtowed, thanked him for his advice and took their leave. Having packed their possessions, the brothers left for home.

One day after a routine conference with officials of the two administrative departments of the provincial government, Shi asked Master Xie, the department head of justice for the province, to stay a little longer and have a chat. He slipped the bill of indictment out of his sleeve and showed it to Master Xie, remarking, "I've heard a great deal about this man's crimes, and it is outrageous that such an outlaw has remained at large for so long. Now someone has brought a lawsuit against him. Would you please take charge and make an investigation of the case?"

"He is cruel and crafty, and a government of law and order cannot tolerate his evil," replied Master Xie.

Shi exhorted, "I hear that he has thousands of servants and dozens of hatchet men. If we act rashly without solid evidence against him, we may be outwitted. Please act with caution."

"Be content with me in charge, Your Lordship," answered Master Xie, sticking the bill of indictment into his sleeve and bowing farewell. Then he left.

Master Xie was a competent official, and, with Shi's advice, he prepared a careful scheme. He had two runners, one called Shi Ying and the other called Wei Neng, who always understood their master's intentions thoroughly and were particularly dependable. Master Xie immediately called them in and dictated, "I've a confidential errand for both of you."

Kowtowing, the two men answered, "We're at your disposal and will defy all difficulties and dangers to accomplish the mission."

Master Xie took the bill of indictment out from his sleeve and showed it to them. He said, pointing to Yang's name, "The imperial commissioner wants to condemn him for this murder he committed, but is short of evidence because the bodies of the five victims have never been discovered. Your mission is to take a careful look into this matter and to find the exact place where those bodies are buried. Then we will be able to bring the man to justice. This bully is noted for his fierce and treacherous character, so this will be no easy task. On the contrary, any sort of security disclosure might shatter the whole mission and give rise to disastrous results. That's where your difficulty lies."

The two runners responded, "This villain has committed crimes in every nook and corner of his native place. If he manages to find out about his superiors' current intention of bringing about his downfall, he will take the initiative and gain the upper hand. Even our presence in his hometown will easily give away our identity as yamen runners and arouse his suspicions that might lead to some unpredictable consequences. The only way to complete the task you entrust us is to disguise ourselves as casual visitors and try to seize any possible opportunity to find out the details of the matter."

"What you've said is right," said Master Xie, "and you'd better hurry to start the work."

The two subordinates compared notes and then reported to Master Xie. "Here's a ruse we have designed, but we have no idea whether it is feasible or not."

"Please tell me about it," said Master Xie.

One of the men replied, "Xindu abounds in saffron, and we've heard that the Yang family possesses a garden of them, which reaps a big profit. We can go in disguise as buyers of such plants and thus eventually get in touch with managers for his family. As we gradually get to know the place and the local people better, they will not be suspicious of us and we can have a chance to inquire into this matter. If we work in this way, you cannot set a deadline for us."

"That's a very good idea," commended Master Xie. "Take care. If your work is successful, I will not only treat you with increased respect, but I will put in a good word for you to the governor and you may get a promotion."

"We appreciate your kindness," the two men said. They kowtowed and left.

Shi Ying and Wei Neng were married men. They worked in the government office for a better future. Conscious of the significance of their task, they set about their assignment in earnest. Each carried one hundred *liang* of silver and headed for Xindu in the disguise of customers. Claiming to be buying saffron, they roamed the streets of the town and learned there was a third manager who had the family name of Ji, who ran the saffron business for the Yang family. It was said that he was honest by nature and fair in business, thus doing rather brisk saffron sales and earning a yearly average of 1,000 *liang* of silver for the master. Without him, few customers would have gone to the manor of such a brutish master.

The two disguised officials went to the home of Third Brother Ji. After exchanging greetings, they presented a gift of local products and let their host know their intention to buy saffron. Delighted, Third Brother Ji showed them courtesy by treating them with wine. The two officials were experienced in their profession, and at once realized that their host was a good person who could be depended on.

They heaped praise on their host, which the latter accepted readily. Then Wei Neng said to his colleague, "Brother Shi, we're strangers here doing business. An old saying goes like this, 'A man seeks his master while a bird flies into the woods.' Seldom does one encounter such a good host. We three should become sworn brothers today based on the sequence of our dates of birth. What do you think?"

"I agree," replied Shi Ying. "But this is our first meeting. Besides we've not completed our business transactions. I think we should finish our purchases before performing such a ceremony for brotherhood."

Third Brother Ji said, "It is kind of you to show such hospitality and pay me such high respect. Let's conclude the deal of saffron tomorrow. Then I will throw a small party and we'll go through the rite of becoming sworn brothers as you propose. Do you agree?"

"Wonderful," said the two runners. That night, Third Brother Ji gave his visitors a northern room in the Garden of Saffron.

The following day, the two buyers looked at the saffron. They were willing to pay a higher price, but the host insisted on coming down for them. The business was done to the satisfaction of both sides. Later that day, Third Brother acted as host. He slaughtered hens and bought pork, while the two officials went into the town and bought paper and candles for the ceremony. They set up an altar, and first paid tribute to the gods and then put down their dates of birth in sequence on paper. It turned out Shi Ying was the eldest, Third Brother Ji was six years younger, and Wei Neng one year younger still. Standing in order of age, they prostrated themselves before the gods and revealed their willingness to become sworn brothers, swearing in chorus, "From now on, we will be faithful to each other, help each other and rush to the rescue to anyone of us in time of plight. We will bear this in mind. If anyone violates this code of conduct, he will be punished by the gods." From then on, the two officials began to call Ji the Second Brother. Ji, in turn, called them the Eldest and Third Brother. Overjoyed, they ate and drank a great deal that night.

This practice of becoming sworn brothers had been handed down from the period of Three Kingdoms (AD 220-280) when three heroes from the state of Shu — Liu Bei, Guan Yu and Zhang Fei — became sworn brothers. Now Shi Ying and Wei Neng were carrying on this convention in order to make Ji their confident. But at that time they carefully avoided the subject of the murder. They simply took their purchases back to Chengdu and resold it via a local warehouse, reaping a little profit. Thus, with the silver earned, they journeyed to and fro between Chengdu and Xindu five or six times over the next few months. Whenever they got together with Ji, they had a meal hosted by one side or the other, and all three became as close as real brothers.

One day after some drinks, Shi Ying stretched himself and said, "It's wonderful that we've met such a good brother here. Every time we come we have such a good time."

Picking up the thread of his colleague's remark, Wei Neng added, "Brother Ji has treated us very well. However, I still feel short of assistance in terms of one concern that is on my mind."

"Did I offend you, Brother?" asked Ji. "Please air whatever it is that is on your mind. Since we are brothers, you needn't avoid anything."

"We need a sound sleep at night," said Wei Neng, "and you should have settled us in a quiet place. Instead, I have been disturbed every night at our dwelling place by the howling of ghosts. I'm scared of ghosts, and to be frank, I have to bring this up as your fault, Brother."

"Is it true that you heard ghosts' howls?" asked Ji.

"It is true," Shi Ying cut in. "It's strange. But I heard those howls, too, just as Brother Wei did."

"Would I tell you a lie if it wasn't true?" asked Wei Neng.

"It's possible," answered Ji, nodding toward a servant pouring wine into his cup. Then he said, "You know who is yelling? I'm sure it must be that man from Yunnan Province."

Hearing Ji say this, the two officials pretended it was no news to them, and calmly seized the chance by saying, "We heard a long time ago that one from Yunnan was killed here. But we think you, Brother, should have been merciful to him and begged your master to find a plot of land in which to bury his body. It is a shame that his body was merely flung out there so that his soul has been howling each night ever since."

"It's true he died a tragic death," Ji said. "But you can be assured that his body was buried. Don't believe all the rumors and gossip you hear."

"But speculation has it," remarked the two officials, "that his remains were strewn all over the place after his death. If you're sure they were buried, why is he now howling?"

"If you two brothers don't believe me," Ji said, "I'll show you the place. Believe it or not, no saffron grows on that spot where his body was buried."

Then Shi Ying said, "I think we should take advantage of the rapture aroused by the wine and have a stroll over there now. Let's pour a cup of warm wine over his tomb so as to calm him down at night. In addition, it gives more pleasure to down a couple of cups of wine outdoors."

Getting up, the two officials sauntered into the Garden of Saffron. Believing the two men were just out for some fresh air after the wine, Ji went with them, ordering a servant to accompany him with a container of wine. He thus led the way to the place. Pointing toward it, Ji said, "Beneath that barren surface of earth are the bodies of those five men. Why did you think their bodies were scattered?"

Pouring wine into a large cup, Shi Ying made a bow with his hands clasped toward the skies, and prayed, "Please take a cup of wine, brothers from Yunnan. We would appreciate it if you did not disturb us any more at night."

"Here's my share of the contribution," said Wei Neng, "so that he can have two cups of wine."

"Every bite of food and every drop of drink in one's life are determined by fate," Ji commented. "If you brothers had not honored them with your presence here, they would have never had a taste of this wine."

"It is their luck," said Shi Ying. The three of them laughed. Then setting the container of wine and cups on the ground, they sat down and each had a couple of drinks while playing finger-guessing games. They didn't stop until darkness overcame them. The two officials then took careful note of the place and went back to their rooms for the night.

The following day, the two said to Ji, "We had a good sleep last night. Probably our libation worked in satisfying the souls."

They all laughed. That same day they bade farewell to Ji, saying, "Second Brother, would you like to come down to Chengdu some day in the future to visit us? We will play the role of host so as to extend our appreciation in return for your hospitality. Otherwise, we will always feel indebted, since we have bothered you a lot."

"What are you saying, brothers?" answered Ji. "I only make trips down there on business. But I'll surely pay a special visit to you on New Year's Eve when I have to do shopping for the New Year." Then they parted.

Shi Ying and Wei Neng went back to give a thorough account of what they had discovered to Master Xie, who commended them, "You're indeed competent. Don't breathe a word about this at this time. As soon as that Ji arrives here in the capital city of the province, let me know at once, and I'll take care of the matter."

The two men departed to await the arrival of Ji.

As the year drew to its end, Ji traveled to Chengdu, as he had promised, for the seasonal purchases. He made special visits to the homes of Shi and Wei, which were not far apart. The two officials were delighted and said to their visitor, "You're a distinguished guest coming here by good luck!"

Shi Ying then said to Wei Neng, "Would you please stay here with Brother Ji while I go downtown to purchase some groceries for dinner."

"Okay, but please hurry." answered Wei Neng.

Shi Ying dashed out with a young servant holding a shopping basket and hundreds of *liang* of silver. He purchased some meat and fruit, and sent the young fellow back home first to fix the dinner, as he scurried to the office to tell Master Xie about the arrival of Ji.

"Go home and stay with him," ordered Master Xie. "Don't let him go." Then he wrote a summons in cinnabar and commanded two of his runners, "Take this with you and bring Ji of the Yang family in Xindu here for interrogation!" The two runners took the summons and rushed directly to Shi Ying's home.

Shi Ying had already returned and was preparing the wine and food. During the course of the dinner, the two officials and Ji heard a knock at the door. When Shi Ying let a young boy open the door, the two runners dashed inside. They greeted Shi Ying and Wei Neng, then turned to Ji, asking, "Is this man Mr. Ji, a manager for the Yang family?"

"Yes," replied Shi Ying and Wei Neng realizing the situation. "He is Uncle Ji from the Yang family."

The two runners, cupping one hand in the other as a salute, said, "The boss of our government office is asking you to come over for a meeting."

Taken by surprise, Ji asked, "Why does he want to see me? Is this some mistake?"

"No mistake at all," replied the runners. "Here's the summons." They showed him the summons. Shi Ying and Wei Neng feigned ignorance and asked, "What's happened?"

The runners answered, "Our boss has been working on an investigation regarding matters related to the Yang family and has told us to report to him immediately if a manager of the Yang family came to the provincial capital city. Moments ago, Lord Shi was spotted on the street buying groceries and talking about a dinner to be prepared for Ji the manager. Somebody, we have no idea who, reported this to His Lordship and so we've been sent here to extend the invitation."

Ji was nonplused for a moment, then murmured, "Why is he calling me since I have nothing to do with him? And I didn't commit any felony."

The two runners answered, "Nobody knows whether you've committed a felony or not. You'll understand after your meeting with our boss."

"You've a clean record, Second Brother," advised Shi Ying and Wei Neng, "so it won't hurt you to go and see him."

"I'm sure that's true," said Ji. "It is obviously because of the old man of our household, and nobody else."

Shi Ying and Wei Neng then said, "If you're questioned about your family's business, just tell the truth. I'm sure you won't be injured. By the way, you two officers, why not sit down and have some drinks with us since you happen to be here?"

"It's kind of you," replied the two runners, "but our boss is waiting for us so we can't delay."

Allowing for no excuses, Shi Ying grabbed a big bronze vessel, and made each of them take a few drinks from it. When the runners said they had to leave, Shi Ying said, "I'll go with Brother Ji to the government office. Brother Wei, please stay at home to keep the wine warm and to get things ready. We'll be back shortly for another round of merry-making."

"I know nobody in the government office," Ji said. "It's kind of Brother Shi to go with me."

Ji could do nothing but follow the two runners to the provincial office. After learning of Ji's arrival, Master Xie met him in his private office. He asked him, "Are you a manager for the Yang family?"

"Yes, sir, I am," Ji answered.

"Do you know anything about the atrocities your master has committed?" asked Master Xie.

"Yes," Ji answered. "I think my master has performed one or two evil deeds. But I'm a subordinate and dare not make them public."

"If you make a clean breast of his crimes," Master Xie said, "I'll spare you flogging. Otherwise, I'll put you on the rack."

"Which one of his crimes do you want to find out about?" answered Ji. "I'll tell the truth. My master is guilty of more than one kind of evil. Where do you want me to start?"

"Indeed, he's committed too many crimes." Master Xie said with a sneer. He picked up the bill of indictment and went through it quickly, then asked, "Tell me about the death of Zhang Yin and his followers from Yunnan Province. Where are their bodies?"

"This is what I should tell you, sir." said Ji. "My master really defied divine justice in doing this."

"Please tell me about it at leisure," commanded Xie.

Ji recounted how Zhang Yin went to Yang's place for his silver, how he and his men were asked to stay for dinner, and how they were killed and buried in the plot of saffron fields.

Master Xie required him to put his words down in a written statement, saying, "You're honest, I think, so I won't give you a harsh treatment. But I will have to keep you behind bars until the criminal is arrested." Immediately Ji was put in jail. Considering their recent relations with Ji, Shi Ying and Wei Neng made their due efforts in bidding the jail guards not to give him a rough time.

Having acquired all the details concerning the murder, Master Xie issued a plate as a token of authority ordering Shi Ying and Wei Neng to go to Xindu and have the county magistrate there arrest Yang on a charge of murdering the five men. If the criminal was not arrested the county magistrate should be arrested in his stead. After that, he gave out another token of authority ordering that the remains of the five men be unearthed from the saffron field.

The two officials took the order with them and raced to Xindu on New Year's Eve. The county magistrate accepted the order, and, pressed by the two officials, was overwhelmed by the urgency of the matter. He thought to himself, today is the last day of the year, and I think the old man should be at home. I'll send troops right away to surround his manor and launch a surprise attack so everything will work out right. At once he sent out a token of authority to the garrison troops and had three hundred soldiers mustered. Led by himself, the troops besieged the Yang's family so tightly that it seemed as if the household was enclosed in an iron barrel.

At the moment Yang was having a New Year's Eve wine party. The night had fallen and the gates of the yard were tightly closed. Yang was enjoying the dinner with his concubines, having songs and dances performed for him. One of the concubines sang a song entitled "A Black-naped Oriole," which went like this:

Chill in spring now seeps in rain drops;
Blossoms fall off all tree tops.
Languidly I ascend and see the paths soaked,
Winding streams
And hills in clouds cloaked.
Oh, all that in the wide world looms
Casts over me a gloom!
The wild goose, messenger bird,
Can't reach Yunnan in distance
And deliver to my love my word.

Hearing the words "Yunnan" uttered in her singing, Yang caught his heart missing a beat. He threw a tantrum, roaring, "'Yunnan' is no word you're to use!" He felt uneasy.

Outside his house at this point the county magistrate had already stationed his troops to completely encircle the house. Since the entrance gate was shut, Shi Ying and Wei Neng climbed over a flank wall into the yard and opened it to let in the troops. Seating himself in the main hall, the county magistrate sent for the host of the family. Yang was still angered by the mention of "Yunnan." He suddenly heard the county magistrate had come to his main hall. He wondered what the man was doing there at that time of night. This was something unusual. Had someone reported on him about the former crime? Panic-stricken, he dashed into the kitchen and squatted in front of the range thinking to himself, better to avoid encountering him now, and I'll manage to work out some way later.

Seeing that his summons brought no sign of Yang, the county magistrate became anxious about the fulfilling of his task. He personally walked into the inner part of the house. His search led him to Yang's wife and concubines, who had not yet hidden away. The county magistrate ordered, "Bring one of them in front of me." So one of the ladies had to emerge to answer his call.

"Where's your master?" asked the county magistrate.

"He's out, not at home," replied the lady.

"Nonsense!" said the county magistrate. "It's the last day of the year today. Is he staying away from his family?" He told his followers to get the finger-squeezer ready to torture her.

Scared, the lady shouted, "All right, he's at home." She pointed in the direction of the kitchen range. The county magistrate led his men to that part of the kitchen to make a search. Unable to stay there any longer, Yang had to come out. "What is the important business that has brought you here on New Year's Eve?" he asked.

"Well, it is none of my business," said the county magistrate. "It is His Excellency the governor and His Excellency the head of the provincial department of justice that want you to attend a meeting regarding something about a murder of five men. You're to set out right away this night and report to them immediately. Otherwise I'll have to emerge in court in your stead. So I have no alternative but to intrude on you."

"Whatever the business, you should allow me to spend the holiday at home first," refuted Yang.

The county magistrate replied, "But I'm getting a lot of pressure from the superiors and the two runners sent here are waiting for me to carry out the mission. I simply can't delay in spite of the holiday. If you make the trip, I will be happy to be in your company." So he and the two runners left no room for further discussion. Utterly without hope, Yang followed the county magistrate out of his house. The latter signed a statement to go to his superiors about his accomplishment in arresting Yang. The criminal was sent under escort directly to the provincial capital. Shi Ying and Wei Neng took care to lead some of the troops to the spot in the Garden where they excavated the five corpses. Then they caught up with the county magistrate. Seeing their master arrested, Yang's bandits realized the situation had turned foul for them. So they abruptly dispersed.

Master Xie convened court to handle this case on New Year's Day. The county magistrate brought in Yang, who, in informal dress, knelt down articulating plausibly, "I've no idea of what sort of felony I have committed to be brought here in this way as an outlaw."

Master Xie then read to him the bill of indictment, approved by the provincial department of justice. Yang asked, "Do you have any evidence for this charge?"

"Here's the evidence!" replied Master Xie. He sent for Ji, and then turned to Yang, "Can you deny the fact that this man has worked for you? And his confession is clear and detailed. What do you say about that?"

"I think this servant of mine simply gave vent to his personal grievance and made a false charge against me," carped Yang. "Why do you believe him?"

Master Xie said, "Whether it is a false charge or not will be clear shortly."

Hardly had he uttered these words than the police officers and magistrate's assistants from Xindu set on the ground outside the court the five bodies unearthed from the Garden of Saffrons. "How do you now account," asked Master Xie, "for the fact that the five bodies were excavated on you estate?"

Turning to the police officers, Master Xie asked, "Did you examine the bodies?"

The police officers answered, "The magistrate had the bodies examined and discovered that these men were all beheaded, their heads and trunks separated."

"Then this result and the account of Ji both tally," said Master Xie to the accused. "What else can you say in making a denial?"

Yang was tongue-tied and lowered his head. Then he said, "I admit I flew into a rage under intoxication after drinking that day and then performed this deed. I beg you to take into consideration the service I've done as a government official and show me some leniency."

"Do we have anybody else like you among the government officials?" remarked Master Xie. "You're a beast in human society, and a wolf in the kingdom of animals! Master Shi, governor of the province, has long known about his case and he made secret investigations. We won't let you off easily." Yang was immediately carried away to jail and kept there for further interrogation when the accusers would be summoned. After that, Master Xie rewarded Shi Ying and Wei Neng lavishly and sent Ji back home.

When the summons had reached Yunnan Province, the two brothers knew Yang was in prison. They set off on their journey to Chengdu without delay, and made their way directly to the provincial department of justice which was handling this business. Master Xie let them go to the mortuary to identify their father's body, and had Yang brought up to confront his accusers. The two young men immediately began to attack him. Master Xie shouted to stop them, "Stop acting like that," he said. "He has already been brought to justice and will soon receive whatever punishment he deserves."

According to penal code, a criminal deserved a lingering execution as the harshest punishment if he committed three homicides. Since Yang was the murderer of five men, Master Xie without hesitation meted out the death penalty by a slow process to the convict. He also issued an order to round up for trial Yang's followers who were involved in the crime. As Yang had been a government official, the sentence was reviewed at a higher level for the final decision.

However, while staying in jail waiting for the final decision to arrive Yang could no longer bear the mental torment. He also saw the ghosts of Zhang and his four followers come to torture him everyday. Before long, he died in jail. Yang left behind no son, and since there was nobody in charge of the family affairs, his former concubines dispersed. Yang Qing, Yang's eight-year-old nephew, the only son of the second brother in Yang's family, became the heir to the large estate. When Yang had nursed the sinister motive of seizing his nephew's property, he could not have foreseen that his own property would go to his nephew. This evinces that the heavenly law is indeed very fair.

Zhang Yin had also died a violent death in an alien land because of his wrongdoing in bullying his younger brother. Thanks to the upright authorities, his wrongdoing was redressed. Nevertheless, after the settling of the case and official summons being sent to the government of his local place, the story of his bribing the superior in an effort to seize family property began to be talked about everywhere.

Zhang Bin, the younger brother of Zhang Yin, reported with his mother to the county magistrate that, "If it had not been right to divide my father's legacy equally between us two brothers, why would my elder brother have gone out of his way to suborn somebody? Due to his ruse, he lost his life. Since his murder has been officially cleared up, our family dispute over the splitting-up of the property has become easier to handle. The case has been processed in Chengdu and concerning documents make everything clear. The documents can't be fabrications."

Unable to counter them the county magistrate let the property of the Zhang's family be divided in two halves: one to Zhang Bin, and the other to his two nephews. The two nephews could argue no more, but accepted the decision.

If Zhang Yin had known the conclusion of his life, would he have striven for such adversity? He lost five hundred *liang* of silver and paid a death toll of five. His tragedy gives proof to the old saying: Go for wool and come back shorn. All in all, it pays to be honest and law-abiding.

Tale 3

Wang Xiangmin Loses His Son at the Lantern Festival; The Thirteenth Boy at Age Five Pays Respects to His Majesty

During the reign [1068-1086] of the emperor Shenzong of the Song Dynasty, there was a minister posthumously styled as Xiangmin, whose family name was Wang and given name Shao. He lived with his family in luxury, enjoying high honors in a beautiful, imposing mansion in the capital city Kaifeng. It was a time when peace reigned and prosperity held sway across the land. As the Lantern Festival, [15th day of the first lunar month] was drawing near, candles were lit in each house, festival lanterns were displayed from door to door, and thousands of people thronged the streets at night to celebrate the holiday season, which began on the 13th day of the lunar month.

At midnight on the 15th day, the emperor emerged, as was the custom each year, to tour the city center and watch the splendid spectacle. Women and men throughout the city awaited that moment to catch a glimpse of the strikingly elegant bearing of His Majesty. The occasion was graced by a lovely night sky hung with a bright full moon. The moonlight wrapped the city in a cloak of brilliance, mingled with multi-colored candlelight beams radiating from the exquisite lanterns in an extraordinary display.

To enjoy themselves, all the family members of Wang Xiangmin's household, old and young, except for the master himself, turned out onto the street in neat and joyous attire with their servants carrying the heavy curtains. You may ask why they carried such big heavy curtains. It was widely accepted at that time that it was scandalous and outrageous for ladies of the family of a high-ranking official to be walking among ordinary people. Therefore a covering made of silk or cloth was used to shield the lady walking within it. Thus she was separated from strangers, while able to clearly see outside. Handed down as a convention from the Jin Dynasty [AD 265-420], such curtains were called "walking blinds" or "brocade blinds".

The master, Wang Xiangmin, had a son named Nangai who was the youngest among his children. This boy was thirteenth among his brothers. At five, he was good-looking, bright, obedient and well-liked both inside and outside of the family. The master and his wife also treated him with great affection. This boy was now out with his fellow fun-seekers. Boys of rich stock undoubtedly appeared in fine clothing, but his outfit was particularly notable because of his cap. The cap was decorated with a string of western-made beads of soybean size in the shape of twin phoenixes perched on a peony plant as well as a gleaming gem named "cat's eye" fixed in front, circled with colorful precious stones, mostly sapphires and emeralds. This cap must have cost at least one thousand strings of coins.* The master had a servant, named Wang Ji, carry the boy on his back during the walk with other family members for the viewing of lanterns.

As an obedient male servant, Wang Ji knew he was to walk along

---

*In ancient China coins were strung together, and one string of cash was equal to 1,000 coins.

beside one of the walking blinds. The moment the family entourage proceeded to the front of the Xuande Gate, the emperor, arrived and ascended the tower of the Gate. He issued a decree that the visitors were permitted to look up at him and the imperial guards were ordered not to stop the people.

On the tower was set up a small mount of glittering lanterns of all colors, with clouds of incense smoke curling up, and palace music playing to the accompaniment of drums and reed pipes. At the foot of the tower, plays and acrobatics performed for the emperor were tightly encircled with a large crowd of spectators.

Among the throngs of people, Wang Ji couldn't catch a satisfactory view of the excitement because of the little master sitting on his shoulders. Then in an instant, he found himself released of the load on his back, but he was too fascinated by the spectacle to notice what had happened. Stretching himself and raising his head, he felt comfortable and continued his play-watching.

It suddenly struck him, "Where's my little master?" He noticed the boy was no longer on his shoulders. He turned around only to be met with strange faces and no sign of the boy. He wanted to pull away from the crowd, but everyone was too tightly crammed together. Quite flurried, he edged through the crush and finally found his way to a less crowded spot, exhausted.

Then some of his fellow servants came over, and he asked them, "Did you see the little master?"

One of them answered, "You're supposed to be taking care of him. Why are you asking us?"

Wang Ji said, "I was engrossed in the performance when someone grabbed him from my back. I though perhaps one of you might have worried about my burden with the five year old and helped me by taking him away. I took delight in being unburdened, so I didn't check carefully among the crowd. When I looked for the boy, he had disappeared. Are you sure you have no idea who might have done this?"

His words plunged the other servants into agitation. They scolded him: "What a poor job you have done! This is no joking matter. How come you were so negligent! You lost the little master out there in the crowd of people, but you are here to inquire about him. How could you be so amiss as to delay the search? Let's go back to the crowd and hunt for him in different directions."

The group of about ten, along with Wang Ji, started to push their way in and out of the multitude of fun-seekers, shouting at the top of their voices. But the crowd was so large their efforts were useless. They searched, shouting, until their eyes were dim and their voices were hoarse. But no sign was found. At last they gathered together, checking with each other. As the answers were all a "no", they were fluttering with anxiety.

One of them said, "Probably one of the other servants carried the boy back home."

Another answered, "How could that happen, since all of us are here?"

An elderly man said, "I'm sure the little master is not at home. Those eye-catching gems on his cap were rather inviting. I guess some villain must have swept away him with those valuable things. We'd better go home and let the master know about it, but we should certainly not frighten the madam with the news. The master will send troops to hunt for the villain."

The mention of informing the master about this turn of events panicked Wang Ji. He said to the rest, "Is it a good idea to report to the master at this moment? I think we should take more time to search, and not make haste."

Overwhelmed by anxiety, the other servants simply turned a deaf ear to what Wang Ji was saying and raced back home. After making a covert inquiry about the little master, they assembled in front of Wang Xiangmin, and kept whispering to one another, but no one dared to bring up the matter.

The master, puzzled by the strange behavior of his servants, said, "You weren't out very long. Why did you all return so soon? Besides, you are in such a flurry that you must be hiding something behind my back."

Then the servants had to tell him about the loss of the little master. Wang Ji knelt down and kowtowed, asking for the penalty of death. But Wang Xiangmin didn't seem to be too worried and said with a smile, "He'll be back. Don't worry about that."

The servants asked, "If the little master was abducted by some rascal, how will we be able to bring him back? We suggest that Your Highness report the matter to the court of justice in Kaifeng and see about sending troops to capture the criminal."

Shaking his head, the master responded, "Unnecessary." His inferiors were perplexed that their superior so lightly treated such a burning issue.

They then went to the madam, who was within the walking-blind. The master's wife became quite perturbed at the news and returned home instantly. With tears welling up in her eyes, she consulted the master. The master said, "If one of my other sons had been lost, I would have positively mounted a search. But it's the lovely thirteenth son of mine that got lost. I'm sure he'll come back home shortly. Don't worry about it."

The madam said, "I know he's smart. But he's at most a boy of four or five. If he gets lost among crowds of people, how can he find his way back home?"

The nurses also stepped in saying, "It's said rogues often kidnap little children. They make those children blind by stabbing their eyes, or chop off their feet or mutilate their bodies in other ways, and then send them onto the streets as beggars. We're pleading with you to take emergency steps. Otherwise the boy would be subject to torture." The ladies all wept.

The servants said to the master, "If you, my lord, do not want to bother to report the matter to the court of justice, we think you should put up some posters or a big notice offering a reward for some clue as to his whereabouts. I'm sure someone greedy for money will come up with a tip."

So opinions varied and the household was in an uproar of concern. Nevertheless, Wang Xiangmin remained unflustered, remarking, "Regardless of what you say, it's not necessary to do anything now. He'll be back home in a couple of days."

The madam said, "How can we be deprived of a our lovely doll-like boy! You should not take it lightly and say something like that!"

The master said, "I'll take the full responsibility for everything. I assure you I will bring him back in perfect condition. Take it easy, please." The madam would not listen, nor did other family members and nurses. So the madam sent out servants to search for him.

It turned out that when Nangai was sitting astride his guardian's back watching the festivities that night, one man had pushed his way through the crowd and suddenly reached out to snatch the boy away. Soon the little master was sitting on the shoulders of the stranger, not Wang Ji. The boy was utterly fascinated by the ongoing performances and hadn't, at first, realized what had taken place. Then, noticing he was being carried forcefully through the throngs of people, Nangai had shouted to his bearer, "Where are you going, Wang Ji?" But a closer look assured him that the man carrying him was not his trustee any more. The unfamiliar apparel of the man told the smart little child that he was at the hands of a rascal. Nangai wanted to scream for help. But, seeing he was surrounded by strangers, he decided, this evil man is aiming to get the gems on my cap — if he is able to make away with those precious stones, it will be hard to recover them. I'll take off my cap and hide it somewhere. I don't think he will do anything to me." Thus thinking, he slipped his cap into his sleeve, remaining calm and quiet as he was carried forward, as if nothing had happened.

As they approached the Donghua Gate, four or five sedan chairs came toward them in a single file. Nangai thought to himself, I'm sure that some high-ranking officials or dignitaries are riding in those sedan chairs. Here's a good chance to shout for help. So as one sedan chair passed them, the boy stuck out his hand to lift its curtain and yell, "Stop thief! Stop thief! Help! Help!" The villain carrying Nangai was quite nervous, conscious of the sinful deed he was performing and the danger of being captured at any time. The boy's scream so frightened him that he put the boy down and took to his heels amid the sea of people. Hearing the call of a boy, the man sitting inside the sedan chair raised the blind and looked at the little boy with black hair and white complexion, a doll-like lovely child. He was delighted and called to his carriers to set down the sedan chair. He then picked up the boy and asked him, "Where are you from?"

Nangai answered, "I was kidnapped by a villain."

The sedan-chair rider asked, "Where's the villain?"

Nangai said, "As I shouted for help just now, he ran away into the crowd."

Impressed by the boy's fluency and eloquence, the gentleman said, stroking his head, "Oh, little boy, don't worry. Come with me." He placed Nangai on his lap and resumed his tour through the Donghua Gate and toward the imperial palace. You might wonder who the gentleman was who was riding the sedan chair. He was the head eunuch, a favorite of the emperor. He and four or five of his fellows were on their way, after the emperor's viewing of the lanterns, to make arrangements for an imperial banquet in the palace. He took Nangai into his room in the palace, gave him some fruit to eat and set him under bedding to keep him warm, in case he might be frightened. Eunuchs had an inborn fancy for little children and unquestionably took good care of them.

The following morning, the head eunuch, along with his colleagues, appeared in the imperial court and reported to the emperor. "Last night on our way back to the palace after the lantern viewing, we picked up a lost boy and brought him into the palace. We were delighted, thinking it's a good omen leading to Your Majesty's fortune in obtaining a son. We have no idea where the boy comes from and can't take further steps without Your Majesty's permission. Now we're presenting the issue for Your Majesty's discretion."

The emperor did not yet have a son and was in great need of an heir. Overjoyed at the news of coming across a lost child, particularly a boy, he responded, "Bring him here."

The head eunuch went back to his room. He took Nangai into his arms, saying, "At the imperial request, you're now going to see His Majesty. Don't panic."

Knowing he was going to see the emperor, the boy, not at all nervous, calmly took his cap with gems out of his sleeve and adjusted it on his head as he had worn it the day before. He followed the head eunuch to the Emperor Shenzong. As a child, he didn't, of course, know the imperial etiquette of kowtowing and chants of "longevity." But his movement of cupping his hands and bending his legs, as if he were performing the required code of conduct at court, overwhelmed the emperor with pleasure.

"Little boy," asked the emperor, "where are you from? What's your family name?"

Nangai answered, "My family name is Wang. I'm the youngest son of Wang Shao, one of Your Majesty's ministers."

The emperor was surprised to see that the boy had a clear voice and logical flow of speech. The emperor then asked further, "How did you come here?"

The boy said, "I was out with one family servant last night for the lantern viewing and observing of the imperial countenance of Your Majesty. Later I was kidnapped by a villain and carried away on his back. When I saw some sedan chairs coming toward me, I shouted for help. The villain put me down and fled. So I came here with your honorable attendants. It's a great honor for me to see Your Majesty."

The emperor asked, "How old are you?"

Nangai said, "I'm five years old."

The emperor then said, "At such a young age you have such appropriate manners. What a promising son Wang Shao has! I think your family must be very worried about you because you were lost last night. I'm going to send you back home at once. But I have no idea how to catch that villain."

Nangai replied, "That's easy, if Your Majesty wants to do so."

The emperor asked, "What do you mean?"

Nangai said, "After I was kidnapped, I knew I was not on my servant's back any more. So I took off my gem cap and hid it in my sleeve. My mother once pinned an embroidery needle with a silk thread on the top of my gem cap in order to fend off bad luck. I realized it would be hard to capture this villain later, if he bore no mark of identification. So I sewed a line of thread along his collar and pinned the embroidery needle in his coat as a sign. Now if Your Majesty is going to launch a hunt for the villain, all that needs to be done is to find the one who carries this embroidery needle and silk thread on his collar. That should be the kidnapper. It's that simple."

The emperor was stunned and said, "What a precocious child you are! You're still an infant, but you're well developed mentally. If I fail to capture the villain, I'll be no match for a child like you. Now I'm going to keep you inside the palace until I have that villain arrested."

Turning around, the emperor praised the boy to all the officials and servants surrounding him, "Such a brilliant child, I should definitely show him to my wife." Then the empress was instantly summoned.

As Her Excellency arrived at the court and the routine greeting was performed, the emperor said to her, "I've a boy here with me, the son of one of my ministers. I'd like you to take care of him for me in the palace for a couple of days in order to make his stay here a good omen toward the birth of our own first son."

The empress accepted the assignment but felt bewildered by it. Then the emperor said, "The boy will tell you the details of his story, if you're interested." So the empress led Nangai into the palace.

The emperor issued a secret imperial edict for the immediate capture of the outlaw, which was delivered by a major eunuch to the prefect of Kaifeng. The prefect understood the significance of this mission, a far cry from his usual responsibilities of catching pilferers. He did not waste a minute, but immediately called in He, the head arrest-runner, saying, "I allow you three days to seize those rascals who conducted unlawful deeds on the night of the Lantern Festival."

The head arrest-runner said, "Without spoils and evidence, how can I do so?" The prefect bent over and whispered in his ear the story of the boy's making a mark with an embroidery needle and the silk thread on the villain's coat. Then the head arrest-runner said, "I'll have no problem fulfilling this mission in three days. It will not be necessary to disturb the local people."

The prefect said, "Do a good job, please. This is a task assigned by His Majesty, absolutely different from your regular duty of rounding up thieves. Take care."

The head runner returned to his patrol station, gathered a few intelligent and capable arrest-runners and said, "I don't think this rascal was the only one who took advantage of the Lantern Festival to commit evil deeds, and the boy's family was not the only one that suffered that night. In addition, though this villain failed to kidnap the child this time, he would not have given up and might have succeeded somewhere else. With time, he may have eased off and now be celebrating in a house of prostitution or in a tavern. Though we don't know his name and address, there shouldn't be any problem getting hold of him because of the mark he carries. Even criminals with no clues for us have been found and caught by us. There are about ten of us professional runners. Let's go in different directions and make individual searches. We should be able to get some results soon."

Then they went about the job independently, probing tea-houses, taverns, and other places where people gathered, carefully looking for anyone who appeared suspicious.

It turned out that the kidnapper was nicknamed "Vulture's Talon." He was one of a gang of ten who, each occasion a crowd of people gathered, seized opportunities to conduct offenses. That night of the Lantern Festival this "Vulture's Talon" had been in hiding outside the mansion of Wang Xiangmin and spotted the little master, neatly dressed, as he was carried out on the back of a servant — the gang member had made up his mind to follow them closely. When they were among the jam of fun-seekers at the foot of the tower of the Xuande Gate, he had snapped up his chance to grab the boy and carry him away on his back, assuming the little master was no more than an infant who could do nothing but cry out in fright. The villain's negligence had soon turned into panic when the boy started to shout "stop thief" as the sedan chairs passed by. "What a tough child!" had thought the villain. He quickly had set the boy down on the ground and taken to his heels. But he never knew he had been marked by the boy. No man or spirit could have expected the boy to do this.

Later that night, the escaped gang member had joined his colleagues, who displayed the various booty that they had plundered, such as emerald hairpins, gold jewels, jade beads, marten-fur ear flaps, fox-tail neck-pads. This man was the only one who had come back empty-handed. After learning about the incident, his fellow rascals had asked, "Why didn't you just take the boy's cap of gems away?" The man had replied, "The boy was well-dressed. His clothing was full of gems and valuable beads, with a bracelet on each of his wrists and ankles. As a four-or-five-year old, he himself would sell for two strings of coins. Why should I let him go so easily?" The gang members had asked, "Where's the boy, then? Clearly you bit off more than you can chew!" The abductor had said, "The boy shouted for help as the palace sedan chairs went by. There was a large group of capable court guards around at that moment. I should celebrate the stroke of good fortune that I didn't get caught. What else should I extravagantly hope for outside of obtaining those precious things?" His fellow men had said, "It was truly a thrilling experience of yours. Now you're back safe and sound. Let's share the booty first, and then go and drink to get over the upset." With each of them playing the role of host for one day by turns, they found an out-of-the-way tavern and drank excessively.

That same day, one arrest-runner called Li Yun happened to pass by a tavern close to Yuyin Garden and heard an uproar over drinking and finger-guessing games coming from inside. An observant and conscientious person, he entered and from the peculiar bearings and manners he got an inkling what this group of customers were. Then he took a seat at a table for one and called, "Bring me food and wine, please."

The waiter came over and set a cup and a pair of chopsticks on his table. The runner stood up and paced up and down the room, casting sidelong glances at the drinking men one by one. He soon spotted one of them who carried a one-inch-long, colored thread on his collar. Li Yun realized he had found his target. Then he called to the waiter, "Please don't warm the wine right now. I'm going to bring my friends in to join me here."

He hurried out, and a whistle immediately mustered seven or eight runners around him. "What's up, Brother Li?" they asked.

Pointing to the tavern, Li Yun said, "They're inside. I double-checked, and there is no mistake. Let's have someone watch the door and send someone else to bring ten more of our fellow men here. Then we can attack."

One of them, a fleet-footed runner sprinted away and brought back the reinforcements. They mounted the assault on the tavern, shouting, "We're carrying out the imperial edict for capturing the criminals who conducted evil deeds on the night of the Lantern Festival. Boss of the tavern, we need your help. Don't let any one of them get away!"

Hearing it was an imperial edict, the tavern-keeper understood that this could be no trifle. He at once called waiters, cooks and cooks-helpers to come with kitchen tools for assistance. All the outlaws had been forced down onto the floor and tied up. Indeed, as the saying goes, if one performs no misdemeanor by day, he should not panic at hearing knocks on his door at night.

In general, thieves get terrified whenever confronting government arrest-runners, as if they are rats facing a cat. At the same time, government arrest-runners can identify at first sight whatever suspects they run into, just like a red-crowned crane, by its keen sense of smell, never fails to locate the hollow lair of a snake, its prey. The two parties — thieves and runners — usually get along on tacit terms: an arrest-runner would demand some money, called "the absolution charge," from the captured thief and then let him go. It was a common practice, particularly in matters of minor note. It gave the government arrest-runners an extra income. But their current assignment was ordained by the emperor and the villain carried the clearly defined sign of the needle and thread on his collar. So the patrol runners would not allow themselves any negligence. They first stripped off the marked coat of the villain. The rest of the gang, though grumbling complaints, shuddered with pale looks on their faces. A body search yielded some booty on each of them. Then they were sent to the prefect of Kaifeng.

The prefect convened court and had the needle and thread examined to verify the identity of the villain. Then he ordered loudly, "Torture him until he tells all!" This hardened criminal bore the pain and yielded nothing. The prefect then showed him the needle and string and asked, "Where did you come by these things?"

The man was baffled and faltered. Laughing, the prefect said, "It's a shame that a professional thief like you was outwitted this time by a little boy. Isn't it because Heaven's laws have prevailed? Do you remember the boy who shouted for help when some palace sedan chairs passed on the night of the Lantern Festival? By that time the boy had already made a mark on you. Do you want to deny this fact?"

Now the villain realized his little victim had gotten the better of him. He could think of nothing to say in denial, but made a clean breast of all the crimes he had committed. It turned out that this man and his fellow outlaws had gone on their spree of burglary and theft on each occasion of a festival, and had conducted the traffic and torture of children all year around. Their felonies were monstrous and numerous but had never before been brought to light. This villain would not have believed he could be outwitted by a boy he had kidnapped at this year's Lantern Festival and that his offense would be brought to the attention of the emperor so as to cause his downfall. To him, it seemed he was doomed to be captured and executed. The prefect had his confession recorded and filed. At the same time this case reminded the prefect of another unsettled one from the year before. What was the case? — gentle readers may ask. Now let me tell you the story.

It took place also during the Lantern Festival when women of imperial and noble families sat behind curtains that had been set up on either side of the main entrance to their mansion so that they could nightly view the lanterns. A prince lived in the east end of the city. He had a daughter called Zhenzhu, who, at age seventeen and unmarried, was beautiful and always appeared in a dazzling costume. Since she belonged to the same clan with the emperor, she was also called Royal Lady Zhenzhu. The prince's younger sister, her aunt, was out admiring lanterns in the west end of the capital. That aunt knowing that her niece was there, sent a servant girl to invite Zhenzhu, saying, " If you're interested in joining me, I will send sedan chairs to bring you over here."

Zhenzhu was pleased with the idea and said to her mother, "I originally thought about going over to see my aunt. Now my aunt has sent me an invitation. I should go there at once." Her mother gladly permitted her request and sent a servant girl over to answer the request.

After awhile, a sedan chair came from the west. Zhenzhu was childish and eager to play. Hearing from her nurses that it was the sedan chair that had arrived to pick her up she impatiently ordered her attendants to come after while she herself slipped into it and was carried away.

Not long after Zhenzhu went, the maid servant who had come to deliver invitation came again with a sedan chair, saying, "I'm waiting for Zhenzhu to come over. Please get in the sedan chair."

The people of the prince's house said, "Zhenzhu went in a sedan chair a moment ago. Why have you come to take her again?"

"Only I and this sedan chair have been sent here," replied the maid. "What a sedan chair came before us?"

Realizing that something unexpected had taken place, the family became agitated. They reported this to the prince. He sent some servants to inquire about Zhenzhu and found she was not there. He hurriedly dispatched his guards and attendants everywhere in search of the girl, but no clue was found. So he prepared a report at once and submitted it to the prefect of Kaifeng. The prefect dared not delay in sending out search parties because he knew this was a matter concerning a prince. The prince also offered a prize of two thousand strings of coins for anybody who could provide a clue. With all these efforts, no news was heard of the lost girl.

As for Zhenzhu, as soon as she got inside the sedan chair, the carriers started to run. Zhenzhu was puzzled. She thought to herself, it's probably these carriers were normally used to sprinting. A short time later, the sedan chair made a turn and went into a strange narrow alley. The carriers began to grope their way with uncertain steps in the darkness. As the young lady was pondering the situation, the sedan chair came to a standstill and the carriers scattered. As no one came to meet her, she lifted the curtain and stepped out. What she saw terrified her. In front of her was an ancient shrine. Inside the shrine, she saw the figure of a god sitting there in the middle, with about ten demon guards standing on either side of him holding different weapons in their hands. The figure of the god had a large face that was about a foot wide, with a thick beard on its chin and two torch-like flashing eyes. Occasional movements of its arms and shoulders made the figure look like a grotesque human being. Quite frightened, Zhenzhu knelt down before the figure in greeting.

The figure said loudly, "Don't panic, please. You and I were predestined to meet in this life. So I've brought you here with divine power."

Seeing that the figure could talk, Zhenzhu was even more terrified and broke into wailing. Two of the demon guards stepped over to hold her up. The figure said, "Bring a cup of wine here so as to remove her fear!"

A demon held a cup of warm wine toward her lips. Zhenzhu would normally have turned it down, but overwhelmed with fright, she reluctantly let the cup touch her mouth and the wine soon poured down her throat in one gulp. Immediately the young lady felt dizzy and drunk. She dropped into a coma and fell to the floor.

"We've done it!" said the figure of the god, grinning. The demon guards came closer. Then they stripped off their disguises and masks. It turned out that they were humans, a gang who committed offenses undercover. The wine they had just given Zhenzhu to drink contained knockout drops. They carried her into an inner room of the shrine and an old woman emerged to put her into a bed. Then the men started to rape her in turn. It was outrageous that a young lady of noble lineage could be victimized by a herd of villains. Later they dispersed to conduct a new round of felonies, leaving the old woman to attend to the young lady.

The next morning Zhenzhu woke up and didn't know where she was, but she saw an old woman sitting beside her. A pain came over her from her private parts, and she touched them to find they were swollen. Thus she realized she had been ravished. She asked the old woman, "Where am I? Why did they put me here?"

The old woman said, "Those gallants brought you here last night. Don't worry. I'll send you to a satisfactory place."

Zhenzhu said, "I'm a girl from a prince's house. How could you have the audacity to defy the law by committing atrocities like this?"

The old woman said, "There is no use talking about a prince's house. I can tell that you are from aristocracy. I will treat you differently."

Zhenzhu couldn't understood the old woman's words. She sobbed sadly with her hands covering up her eyes. It so happened that this old woman was a trafficker in girls and children, and her customers were rich families. The gang of villains often left persons they had seized with the old woman, and she watched such victims for a few days before some customer came and took his purchase away. That day the old woman made an effort to console Zhenzhu. In two days, a sedan chair turned up and shipped her away — she was sold to a rich family outside of town as a concubine.

After the wedding, the bridegroom who bought her started to make love to Zhenzhu. Though he was aware of the fact that his new partner was no longer a virgin, her beauty enraptured him. So he was quite content. He never even broached the subject of her background. Zhenzhu herself didn't mention it either, because of her sense of shame. However the old man had a sizable body of concubines who were consumed by envy at the favor the master was bestowing on the newcomer. Their gossip began to fall on the ears of the old master. According to them, his newly obtained girl had a hazy background, and possibly was a maid servant driven out of her family due to some offenses she had perpetrated. The endless speculation eventually pushed the master to the limits of his patience. He asked Zhenzhu directly about her past. His question struck the right note. The young lady started to wail and told him about her noble birth and suffering. The master was shocked to learn of her story. His memory of notices posted in many places as to information about the gang convinced him this issue was no trifle. He sent for the old woman who had sold him the girl, but she had disappeared long before.

The master meditated about the matter. "The crimes of these felons will be brought to light sooner or later," he said to himself. At that time will I any longer be able to keep from the public the facts about this victimized girl and escape the accusation of my participation in their evil deed? Apart from this, she is a lady of a family of imperial kinship and will be eventually located. Can I be so stupid as to be a scapegoat for the wrongdoing conducted by somebody else?" After further deliberation, he called for two servants and told them to get a worn-out bamboo sedan chair. Then he sent for Zhenzhu.

The master kowtowed before her, saying, "I apologize to you for my failure to recognize you as a member of a noble family and my insolence toward you. I didn't know those villains imposed such affliction upon you. Today I am willing to suffer losses financially and send you back home. I entreat you to do your best to keep my name out of the responsibility for this evil deed when you are relating the details in front of your family."

Knowing she was going home, Zhenzhu was overjoyed, as if an amnesty had been granted. She felt indebted to the master for treating her kindly and expressing his regrets. She said to him, "I won't mention your name to my parents when I return home."

After she got into the sedan chair, the two carriers set off at a sprint before she even had a chance to say "good-bye" to the master. A run over a distance of six or seven *li* took her into some wild country. The sedan chair was then set down, and the carriers disappeared in the blink of an eye.

Zhenzhu stuck her head out from behind the curtains and spotted no one around. She climbed out of the sedan chair and was astonished to realize that she was alone. Dread overcame her. "What a lousy fate I have!" she said aloud. "Why should I be left here alone? What can I do if a villain shows up?" She climbed back into the chair and broke into mournful sobbing, her body trembling and hair disheveled. It was the third month, the regular season for outings in the wilderness. She was noticed by someone, who was shocked at the scene. Then a crowd gradually gathered around her, bombarding her with one question after another. Zhenzhu was so disturbed that she could not give tongue to her distress. A senior stepped up at this point.

He gestured with his hand for silence and then asked her earnestly, "Young lady, where are you from, and why are you sitting in a sedan chair alone in the wild?"

With tears in her eyes, Zhenzhu stopped her crying and replied, "I'm the daughter of a prince, and was abducted and dumped here by some rascals. If one of you can do me the favor of reporting this to my family, I will make sure that he gets an ample reward." No sooner had her voice dropped to silence than one of the onlookers darted away to report the matter to her family.

After awhile, some assistants and guards of the family came. They at once identified the lost young lady. A family sedan chair was brought and it carried Zhenzhu back home. The wretched sight of her with disordered hair and tear-stained cheeks gave rise to much sadness and crying on the part of her parents and other family members. Zhenzhu wailed even more with desperate bitterness. After they had all given vent to their feelings, the family settled down to learn Zhenzhu's full account of her sufferings.

Her father asked her, "Do you know the name of the person who purchased you, so I can have this situation checked through him?"

Conscious of her promise not to involve the master who bought her in the crime, Zhenzhu replied, "I can recognize him. But I certainly have no idea of his name and cannot remember where he lives because it's so remote. Besides, I'm sure that gentleman was absolutely an outsider in this crime. Those villains should take the spear."

The prince though to himself, "I should not let this family disgrace become public knowledge. Otherwise I will have difficulty marrying my daughter off. So he said nothing outside the home about the issue. Meanwhile he sent a report to the court of justice in Kaifeng so they would hunt for the criminals.

Now the prefect had in front of him the group of criminals who had committed the crime in relation to the family of Wang Xiangmin on the night of this year's Lantern Festival. He wondered whether it was possible that this might be the same gang who had committed this separate crime the year before. His follow-up interrogation confirmed his suspicion. Grinding his teeth, he struck the table and severely reprimanded them.

"You're just a bunch of detestable male and female hoodlums," he said, "and even capital punishment is too lenient for you!" He sternly commanded that they be tortured, sixty cudgel blows to each, and then cast into jail until a final decision could be made.

To the emperor he sent a memorial, which was briefly as follows:

This band of criminals went on a spree of theft and abduction on the eve of the Lantern Festival this year. They are professional brigands who have so far committed many murders. Is it not outrageous to allow such heartless gangsters to roam at large in the capital? I am submitting this request to Your Majesty for sentencing them to a severe penalty so as to maintain our country under law and order.

The emperor read the memorial and learned that all the criminals had been arrested. He smiled and said, "The little boy really did a good job in helping to capture these criminals!"

Delighted, he granted the request and commanded that the official in charge carry out the executions at an appropriate time. He also demanded the prefect of Kaifeng submit a copy of the confessions made by the criminals. Later the court of justice in Kaifeng carried out the emperor's order, executed the criminals and sent the report to the emperor along with a copy of the record of the jail confessions made by the individual criminals. The emperor slid the record of the jail confessions into his sleeve and, smiling, returned to his palace.

The empress had taken the imperial command to take care of the boy with gratitude and had returned to the palace with Nangai, believing that her careful watch of the boy would be a good omen for getting pregnant with a baby son. She asked the boy about his background. Nangai was comfortable and at home, as he had been in front of the emperor. His clear and fluent reply filled the empress with joy. She held him on her lap and kept saying, "My dear boy!" Then she called a girl servant to fetch a cosmetic kit and started to comb his hair and apply make-up to his face so that he would appear at his best. The news of a boy with whom the empress was entrusted drew the imperial concubines and female servants of the whole palace to the empress' room to present their congratulations, as well as to have a glimpse of this boy. No little boy had been around the palace for a long time. Now present was Nangai, a boy with wonderfully strong features, red lips and snowy teeth, a lovely, doll-like lad who was capable of expressing himself clearly and answered each question addressed to him. How could one not be thrilled? Eager to please the empress and being fond of little boys, these ladies vied with one another to slip into Nangai's sleeves many toys, such as gold beads and jade bracelets, as tokens of kindness at their first meeting. Quickly, his sleeves became too full to hold those toys. So the empress told an old woman servant to keep the toys for him. Shortly thereafter the boy was being led around and was playing in the chambers of the palace. A flurry of excitement prevailed among the concubines and female servants, who took the occasion as a time of celebration, competing for the boy's attention and giving him presents. What a commotion inside the palace!

Such hustle and bustle did not die down until about ten days passed. The emperor suddenly arrived at the palace of the empress one day and summoned the boy to appear before him. The empress led him to greet the emperor, who asked, "Did the boy feel restless?"

The empress answered, "Many thanks for the kindness of Your Majesty in granting me the mission of taking care of the boy. This boy is very intelligent. Though he stayed in the forbidden quarters, he behaved as naturally as usual. He has the bearing that might be expected from an adult. And it is indeed a revelation of Your Majesty's towering blessing. I'm very pleased that the emergence of such a precocious child has been bestowed on our country."

The emperor replied, "Here's the news. Those criminals were captured by the court of justice in Kaifeng because of the clue of the embroidery needle and the silk thread on the villain's collar. None of them escaped. The boy's precocious ability is astonishing. Now all the criminals have been executed. The boy's family has undoubtedly been worried and are looking for clues in their search for him. He should be sent back home today."

The empress and Nangai expressed their gratitude. At the imperial command, the boy was to be taken back home by the head eunuch who had brought him into the palace a few days before, and he was provided with a small basket of gold trinkets to amuse him.

The head eunuch stepped forward in the front of the emperor, picked up the boy and left with him in his arms. To part with the boy was admittedly the last thing the empress wanted. She presented more gifts to the boy, and had someone collect all the gifts in a small chest and hand it to the head eunuch. Outside the imperial palace, the head eunuch arranged for a young-ox-drawn carriage. With the imperial edict in his sleeve and Nangai on his lap, he rode toward the house of Wang.

The loss of the little master had turned the home of Wang Xiangmin into an abode of sorrow. Everyone had tears of distress in his or her eyes, old and young, family members and servants alike. Only the master himself seemed not mindful of the situation and sent no one to search. Instead, search teams had been dispatched by the madam and household manager, but all came back empty-handed. One day as the frustration dragged on, a message suddenly arrived reporting that the head eunuch had come with an imperial edict. Wang Xiangmin did not know what this might be about, but he instructed the servants to set up an incense burner table and he dressed himself with a formal hat on his head, a girdle around his waist and a tablet held before his breast. He knelt down and readied himself to listen to the announcement of the imperial edict. From the carriage alighted the head eunuch with a boy in his arms. The family members made their way to the front, and were stunned to see it was none other than the lost little master. They were overwhelmed with joy.

The head eunuch said solemnly, "Get ready to listen to my presentation of the edict from His Majesty." Then he began to read:

You lost one of your sons at the Lantern Festival this year. I found him and brought him back to the palace. Now I am returning him to you. In addition, I am granting him a small basket of gold trinkets as a token of commendation for his extraordinary talents. Accept my imperial edict.

Wang Xiangmin kowtowed and expressed his indebtedness as he received the imperial edict. Then he and the head eunuch took seats as host and guest. The head eunuch smiled and remarked, "My old chap, you have a very smart boy!" As Wang Xiangmin was about to ask him how the boy had come under the emperor's care, the head eunuch took out a rolled up file and said, "This file will tell you everything you want to know."

Wang Xiangmin took it and read it. The text was an account of criminal's prison-confession recorded by the court of justice in Kaifeng, acting under the auspices of the emperor. Then Wang Xiangmin said, "My son is quite young but His Majesty was disturbed by his loss and made a personal effort to have the criminals brought to justice. Such a tremendous debt of gratitude I owe to His Majesty, I will not be able to repay even a tiny bit of it should I live and die a thousand times!"

Grinning, the head eunuch said, "But, in fact, it was your son who made the major contribution to the capture of these criminals. His Majesty did not have to do anything." Then Nangai started to chatter away about how he had been kidnapped that night, brought to meet His Majesty and stayed with Her Excellency. It was a detailed and clear narration.

The family members and servants who waited inside the main entrance of the mansion for the reception of the imperial edict had been overwhelmed with excitement and bewilderment as Nangai had gotten off the carriage. Now the little master's account of his adventure cleared up their puzzlement, and a shower of praise flowed over him for his mental abilities. Everyone was convinced Wang Xiangmin demonstrated foresight when he refused to take action to search for the lost boy and believed he would be back home soon.

At the order of Wang Xiangmin, a dinner was held in honor of the head eunuch. At the same time the head eunuch displayed the gold trinkets granted by His Majesty and the presents given by the empress, concubines and servants. Those gold trinkets and jewels of immeasurable value glittered brilliantly in the room. The head eunuch said to Nangai, stroking his head, "Little boy, you will be tempted to buy fruits with those things!"

Wang Xiangmin kowtowed in the direction of the imperial palace and had the children's tutor compose a gratitude-memorial which would be carried by the head eunuch back to the emperor. It read, "I will lead my son in being present at court tomorrow morning and express our gratitude personally."

The head eunuch said to Wang Xiangmin, "I happened to run into your boy and brought him to the presence of His Majesty. Here's my humble gift to your son as a souvenir." He presented the boy with two shoe-shaped gold ingots and colorful satin which was enough for eight suits of clothes. Unable to turn down the gifts, Wang Xiangmin accepted them and presented an ample gift of his own in return. The head eunuch then took off to report to the emperor.

Wang Xiangmin came back from his send-off of the guest to a family union of celebration, saying, "You see, what I originally did turns out to be absolutely correct, when I said you should not be worried and my thirteenth son would come back by himself. Now he has not only returned home but brought back many rewards due to the capture of the villains on the basis of his wisdom." The whole family was convinced.

In the years that followed Nangai took the name of Wang Cai. He was very successful in both his literary and official careers during the reign of Zhenghe [1111-1118]. The remarkable intelligence he displayed as a little boy revealed his potential and set the stage for his future professional triumphs.

Tale 4

General Li Claims a Brother-in-law by Mistake; Lady Liu Contacts Her Husband by Stealth

This story is about the Liu family, who lived in the area south of the Huaihe River during the period of Zhiyuan [1335-1341] under Emperor Shundi. They had a daughter called Cuicui, who was particularly bright, quick to learn, and could read poetry and prose by the age of five. Convention banned women from undertaking official careers. Seeing this, her parents decided to send her to school with the thought that she might acquire more knowledge and become a woman of letters. There was a local, free private school taught by an old, knowledgeable instructor, and hence it had many school-age children. Cuicui was sent there.

Among her schoolmates was a boy the called Jin Ding, who was cute and intelligent. He and Cuicui stood out from the rest of the class in learning. They were of the same age and others often teased them by saying, "You two are both smart and of the same age. You'll eventually form a couple." Though Jin Ding and Cuicui said nothing about this, they acquiesced to it. An attachment was formed between them. Jin Ding once presented his poem to Cuicui as an expression of affection. It went like this:

The gemmed balusters on terraces
Enjoy the sun and spring wind with zest.
Oh, why not transplant them together —
The peach in east garden and willow in west?

In reply, Cuicui wrote a poem to him. It read:

I always feel sorry for the timid girl
Why should she keep her love unexpressed?
Oh, floral goddess, pray thee, be kind
To let the peach and willow stand abreast!

After more than one year in the school, Cuicui had a retentive memory and read many books. When she was older, she quit school. At age sixteen, her parents decided to betroth her. But whenever a visitor came to discuss the issue of marriage, she would shut herself in her room and sob, and even refuse to eat. At first her parents didn't mind but later they noticed that obstinacy had become her way of life. Perplexed by her distress, they talked to her. But they could obtain no explanation for her behavior. After repeated coaxing, they had to make a promise that her request would be granted once it had been uttered. Then Cuicui told them, "Jin Ding of our west neighbor is the same age as I am. When I studied in the same school with him, I promised to marry him in the future. Now if you don't grant my request, I would rather die! I'm determined not to marry anybody else."

The old couple pondered. "That son of the Jins' is handsome and smart. But his family is rather poor, far from being a match for our daughter!" But seeing that their daughter stood firm in her determination and would take to tears and refuse to take food, they feared she might act rashly if her hopes were dashed. They had to promise her, "Since you've made up your mind, we'll find a matchmaker to pass the word. It's going to be alright."

Her father went to a woman matchmaker and told her that his daughter wished to be betrothed to Jin Ding. The matchmaker said, "The young man's family is poor. How can his family match yours in social status?"

The mother said, "My girl, Cuicui, and their boy, Jin Ding, are of the same age. They used to be classmates. Our Cuicui will marry no one but him. So we have to make the betrothal accordingly."

The matchmaker replied, "I thought you would be concerned about his unprivileged family background. Since you have no objection to the marriage, there won't be any problem. I will go and talk to his parents about a betrothal."

The matchmaker made straight to the Jin's and talked about the issue. The parents of Jin Ding felt they were too humble to accept such a proposal. "Look at our disadvantaged background," they said. "How can we expect to have them as our relatives?"

The matchmaker replied, "You have no idea about the issue. The young lady of the Liu's has resolved to marry your little master. She often weeps and eats nothing. The family has turned down quite a few marriage proposals. It's very kind of her parents to approve her request because of her firm position. Now if you decline her on the excuse of your poor financial condition, you will lose a good chance for a marriage. Besides, you'll be unworthy of the young lady's kindness."

The old couple said, "In terms of appearance and talent, our son can be a match for their daughter. But given our scanty income, how can we afford a betrothal gift? That's why we can't say a yes."

The matchmaker said, "You should say a yes. But you have to use a mild wording to smooth away your embarrassment."

The old couple asked, "What kind of wording do you suggest?"

The matchmaker replied, "Leave me pass them message on behalf of you, I will say, "Our son is well read but socially inferior. We appreciate your kindness and warmth in deigning to choose him for marriage. But our family stems from a humble line of descent and has survived on meager livelihoods. The marriage expenses, including gifts and ceremonies, are far beyond our means. We're just financially inadequate. We're pleading with you to show understanding and concern so that we'll be able to work out a way of handling the issue.' If you give such a full account of your dilemma, they will understand that you are too poor to prepare the betrothal gifts. But they can't act against their daughter's wish. So they will surely give in to you."

The old couple was overjoyed and said, "Many thanks for your advice. We would appreciate it if you would take care of this matter."

So the old woman took her version of the Jins' state of mind to the Liu's. The parents doted on their daughter and anticipated nothing but success in this marriage. Upon the matchmaker's recounting of the boy's family's lack of funds to pay for betrothal gifts, the old couple of the Liu's family said, "An old saying goes, 'It is the barbarian way of living to demand a huge sum of money in marital terms.' We highly value our son-in-law's character rather than his gifts. But we do have some terms they will have to comply with: since they're poor, our daughter will find it hard to adjust herself to a meager living in their home, so their son should come to live with our daughter in our home."

When this word reached Jins through the matchmaker, the family was quite satisfied and readily accepted the terms. Happiness filled the house. A date for the marriage was to be chosen by the girl's family, a date on which Jin Ding would go to Cuicui's home for the marriage. All the expenses, such as silks, brocade, meat and wine, would be provided by the girl's family. There is an old saying, "A son-in-law who marries into the girl's family brings only his genitals along with him." Thus the Jins fulfilled a marriage without spending a single coin.

All this was because Cuicui's parents had to comply with their daughter's choice in marriage.

On the chosen date, the bride and groom met at the wedding ceremony, quite content. In bed that night, Cuicui chanted an improvised poem as a present to Jin Ding:

We once companions in classroom
Have become bride and groom.
We frolic in our wedding chamber
Permeating with musk perfume.

I frown for I'm not used
To your forceful shove.
But your billing and cooing
Will kindle my ardent love.

Her husband also improvised a poem in reply:

I remember our days in classroom.
No stranger is your bridegroom.
We're blessed to wander in fairyland
Enjoying exotic flowers in bloom.

Our hearts are bound in vows
That your eyes say is enough.
Yet I'll repeat my oath
To you my only love.

They enjoyed each other's companionship as if they were a pair of falcons freely soaring into clouds or a couple of mandarin ducks joyously swimming around a green pond.

However, sorrow came in the wake of joy. Their marital joy lasted for less than a year before the country sank into turmoil and chaos due to lack of order in the Yuan government. A salt-seller, Zhang Shicheng, and his brother led in a military rebellion in Gaoyou. The coastal prefectures and counties all fell into his hands. A general called Li, a subordinate of Zhang Shicheng, fought in the vanguard and his troops abducted beautiful women wherever they went. When he arrived in Huai'an, the reputation of Liu Cuicui's beauty attracted his attention. He led a platoon of his guards to break into Cuicui's home. Seeing she was to his liking he took her away. The seizure frightened the whole family, and everyone ran for their lives. Who might have dared to step forward to reason? So the newlywed girl was taken away with the family watching helplessly. Jin Ding cried and swooned. He initially wanted to track the rebelling troops in order to find his wife. But then the government troops arriving from the north quickly engaged the rebels in prolonged confrontation and destruction. All roads were blocked and travel suspended. If he ventured around in those areas, he might be captured by the troops of either side, with the possible loss of his life. Therefore, Jin Ding stayed at home and spent his days in distress.

By the end of the period of Zhizheng [1341-1368], Zhang Shicheng had brought large areas of land under his control, areas on both sides of the Yangtze River, including Jiangsu and Zhejiang Provinces. His territory reached into Guangdong and Guangxi Provinces and Yizhou [in present-day Sichuan Province]. Unable to suppress his rebellion, the central government offered amnesty and government positions. Zhang Shicheng was not ambitious for one unified country and was satisfied with his achievements. So a cease-fire was declared and the terms of amnesty by the central government were accepted. He was granted the title of prince and some territories to govern. Order was restored and travel renewed. Jin Ding missed his wife and could not set his mind at ease. He planned to make a trip to find his wife. After scraping together a few *liang* of silver and packing his things into a roll, he bade his parents farewell and then took leave of his parents-in-law, saying, "I've resolved to go and find my wife. I will never come back if I don't see her." Then he cried and departed.

He went by Yangzhou, crossed the Yangtze River and arrived at Runzhou [present-day Zhenjiang]. With only brief stopovers at night, he reached the city of Suzhou. On the way he heard that General Li now guarded the city of Shaoxing. He hurried to Lin'an, crossed the Qiantang River, and boated from Xiling through the night to reach Anfeng, only to be told by the people there, "If you had come here two days earlier, you would have found General Li. He just left with his troops to return to Huzhou."

Jin Ding said, "I wonder if I can find him by the time I get there. He may have left by then."

An Anfeng man said, "No. Huzhou is the station for his troops. He won't move to other places."

Jin Ding replied, "If that is so, I'll get there no matter how far away it is."

Then he made his way toward Huzhou. Since the day he left home, he had traveled thousands of *li* and more than two years had passed. Still there was no trace of his wife. But without meeting his wife, he would never relax his efforts. The money he had brought with him was all gone so he had to beg for food and had to sleep outdoors. But his desire was unflinching and his will was firm.

Finally he reached Huzhou and heard that there was indeed a General who had his office established there. General Li was a henchman of Zhang Shicheng, who entrusted him with important missions and granted him a great deal of power. As Jin Ding approached General Li's residence, an imposing mansion came into sight:

The gate and walls were freshly painted and guarded with axes and halberds. The beast faces on the gate were hung with

*copper hoops. Two dignified iron figures of soldiers stood facing
each other. On each of the gate frames was posted a blank
peach charm. A stone lion was sitting on a stone block on either
side of the gate. Though not a heavenly abode, this was surely
the residence of a rich and noble family.*

Jin Ding stood in front of the gate for awhile. He did not venture to
intrude, nor did he dare to speak. He poked his head inside for a peep
and backed up two steps. As he hesitated, an old house retainer came
out and asked, "What are you up to here, scholar? Why are you
snooping around at the entrance? I wonder whether you're a spy. If our
general knows you are here, you'll land yourself in trouble."

Jin Ding made a greeting and said, "My regards, old gentleman."
The old house retainer made a half bow in reply and asked, "What can
I do for you?"

Jin Ding answered, "I'm a native of Huai'an. My younger sister got
lost in the chaos of the war some time ago. I have heard she is staying
in your house, so I've traveled thousands of *li* to get here in order to
see her. Just now I was not sure whether I had reached the right place,
so I was about to make an inquiry. I'm lucky to have met you."

The house retainer asked, "What's your name? And what's your
younger sister's name? How old is she? Tell me in detail. I'll go and
check and then let you know."

Jin Ding didn't reveal his family name but only told his wife's
family name and said, "My family name is Liu and my name is Jin
Ding. My younger sister is called Cuicui. She can read and write. At
the time we lost her, she was only seventeen. She should be twenty-
four this year."

The old retainer nodded and said, "Oh, yeah. We do have a young
lady surnamed Liu. She is from Huai'an, twenty-four this year. She
can read and write poems. She is clever and thoughtful. She
monopolizes the favor of our general more than others. What you said

just now is quite correct. Since she is your younger sister, you should be a brother-in-law of our general. Please come in and wait in the janitor's room for a minute. I'm going to report to the general." The old retainer rushed in. Jin Ding waited patiently in the janitor's room. Let's leave him for now.

As for Cuicui, after she was taken by General Li, she had wept day and night — she was ready to take her own life but had refused to obey the general. The general intimidated her by saying, "If you keep this up, I'm going to wipe out your whole family, old and young. If you're obedient, I won't touch them." Concern for the safety of her family and that of her parents-in-law had compelled her to reluctantly submit. Seeing that she was quick-witted, well-read and knowledgeable, the general lavished affection on her, putting a high valuation of her and complying with her whims. Cuicui started to give him forced smiles, though not out of any willingness. But her husband was constantly in her thoughts and her days were still plagued with sadness. A faint gleam of hope lingered that she might have a chance to see him. But as she followed General Li on successive military maneuvers east and west, seven years had passed before she realized this.

Now, as the general received the old retainer's message, he turned to Cuicui and asked, "Do you have a brother?"

Cuicui thought to herself, "I've never had a brother. I guess it must be my husband. He doesn't want to reveal his identity and so he is posing as my brother." She promptly replied, "Yes, I do. But I've not heard from him for years. Tell me what his name is and I'll see if he is my brother."

The general said, "The door-keeper said he is called something like Liu Jin Ding."

The mention of "Jin Ding" struck her like a heavy blow. She realized her husband was there to see her under the false family name of Liu. "That's correct," said Cuicui. "My brother is indeed here. I'm going to see him now."

The general said, "Well, let me go out and see him first. Then I'll call you."

He turned to the old retainer and said, "Have Liu Jin Ding come in."

Jin Ding was led into the room. As a professional soldier, General Li was very arrogant. He swaggered into the reception hall and took the seat in the middle.

Jin Ding had to bow in greeting him, which the general accepted. Then the general asked, "Why have you come, scholar?" Jin Ding replied, "My family name is Liu. I'm from Huai'an. I have a younger sister who became lost during the war years ago. I have learned she is living with your family, so I've come and beg you to grant us a meeting."

The general saw he was refined in his manner and speech, so he said, with pleasure, "Please rise, brother-in-law. Your younger sister is doing well here. She'll be out to see you shortly."

He turned to a boy servant called Xiaoshu, who was standing nearby, and said, "Mr. Liu has made a long, special trip here from his hometown. Tell Lady Cui to come here to see him at once."

In the meantime, Cuicui was nervously waiting, after learning about her husband's arrival. Now, as she was called to a meeting, she rushed into the hall. As she looked up at the man, she saw it was truly her husband. But, with the general present, she had to restrain herself. So she assumed her supposed blood relationship. She stepped forward as a sister and called her husband, "Brother." They thus met on the terms of brother and sister. My gentle readers, if this story teller was there, he might have dragged the general away, and thus let the young couple pour out their innermost thoughts and tell each other about their respective experiences of the past a few years. That would be an exchange they might have expected. Unfortunately, the general was not sensible enough to offer the help. He sat there staring at them like an imperial examiner. The husband and wife could not exchange words of intimacy, but merely talked about their parents. They held a tacit affection for one another and repressed their sadness.

Fortunately, General Li, as a rough military man, was not suspicious at all since this husband-wife reunion appeared to be nothing special to him. He took Jin Ding to be brother of Cuicui and thus to be his brother-in-law. He said to Jin Ding, "Brother-in-law, you have traveled all the way here. You must be very tired now. Stay with us for a time and take a good rest. I'll make arrangements for you."

Then he commanded, "Bring a new set of clothes for my brother-in-law so he can take off his old, dusty ones." Another order followed that a small study in the west chamber be tidied up and provided with a bed, curtain, set of bedding, and so on, to be prepared to accommodate Jin Ding. This order exactly fitted Jin Ding's wishes. He gladly moved into the study for the night. But the thought of his separation from his wife, who was well within reach, depressed him.

The next morning when Jin Ding got up, Xiaoshu came and said to him, "Our general wants to talk to you, scholar. Please come to the hall."

After an exchange of greetings, the general asked, "Your sister can read and write. I wonder whether you're educated, too?"

Jin Ding replied, "Yes. I grew up as a Confucianist and have made a career of learning. I've even dabbled in historical and ancient literary works of various schools. Do you think I qualify as a scholar?"

The general was delighted and replied, "To be frank, I missed school when I was a little boy. Later I had a rough time during the war. Then I became a soldier and have earned this position through my military career. Fortunately, my lord had a lot of trust in me and so many local lords have come to submit to my rule. Every day I'm swamped with appointments to meet visitors and guests, so I greatly need an assistant to share my duties. Letters and reports coming in to me pile up each day. I need a secretary to take care of them for me.

I've been bothered for a long time with these problems. Now I'm glad you, brother-in-law, are here. Since you're learned and good at social intercourse, why not work for me as a secretary. That will help me a lot. Besides, we're relatives and I don't think you will despise me. What do you think?"

Jin Ding really wanted to stay longer and so he replied, "I doubt whether I qualify for the position with my smattering of knowledge and my incompetence. But I can't turn you down."

The general was very satisfied and took out about ten letters and reports from his inner-office. He handed them to Jin Ding and said, "Would you please go through them and prepare a reply. I have been worried about them. Now I can have them done."

Jin Ding took them to his study, read them one by one and wrote a letter of reply to each. Then he came back and read his drafts to the general, explaining various aspects when necessary. The general was pleased and said, "Wonderful! You've taken the words out of my mouth. A very capable brother-in-law! Heaven has helped me by sending you here!" From then on Jin Ding received even better treatment.

An intelligent person, Jin Ding knew the ways of the world and treated others with warmth and courtesy. He was popular among both his superiors and subordinates. In addition, he took care to use gentle words in public interaction. When talking to the general, he only heaped praise on him, making the general rather proud of himself. Jin Ding figured he would seize a chance, once he settled down, to meet his wife and vent his sorrow. In addition to this thought, he had no idea about his wife's future plans since she had been separated from him for so many years. He had to talk to her about this in detail. However, after their first meeting there was no sign in sight of their next meeting. Occasionally he was tempted to make his desire clear to the general, but withdrew for fear of giving rise to suspicion and any grave consequences that might ensue. He wanted to work out a way to send a word to his wife, but his wife's boudoir was cut off from the outside, and there was no opportunity for him to take advantage of. He watched for a chance day after day, but months flew by before he realized it.

It was late autumn. The west wind picked up at night and a bitter cold frosted the land in white. Jin Ding felt lonely and miserable in his isolated room and usually lay awake through out the night. He mused, "At this time, Cuicui must feel quite comfortable with someone in a brocade-draped bed. Is she still missing me? Does she know I'm lonely and sad?" He wrote this poem to express his state of mind:

Since a fair flower is moved in a yard enclosed
To the spring color it has never been exposed.
How can one in blitheness know the wanderer's pain?
It's easy to sever, but not to meet again!

When shall the horse straying in alien earth return home?
Now a phoenix prances all alone.
Her beauteous chamber veiled in mist is beyond my sight.
For whom does the moon shine in the lovely night!

The poem was written on a sheet of paper. He wanted to send it in to Cuicui and let her know his thoughts but feared it might draw attention to them. Then he hit upon an idea. He ripped out the stitches along the seam of the collar of his cloth robe and tucked the paper inside it, then sewed it up again. He called for the serving boy, Xiaoshu, and said to him, "It's getting cold. I need more clothing. This cloth robe is dirty with dust and grease. Please take to my sister. Let her wash it for me, after removing the lining and sewing it up again, and then bring it back to me." So saying, he took out a hundred or so coins and gave them to the boy, saying, " This is an errand I am asking you to run for me. Take this money to buy yourself some fruit."

The boy was glad at the sight of money. He took the robe and dashed inside Cuicui's room, where he said, "Master Liu out there needs your ladyship to fix this." Cuicui understood that the robe sent in by her husband was meant for some special reason. She told the boy to leave it with her and pick it up the next day. Xiaoshu then went out.

Cuicui carefully examined the robe, thinking to herself, "This is my husband's clothes. It's been long time since the last time I sewed for him!" Tears ran down her cheeks. It suddenly dawned on her, "My husband has stayed here for some time. Now he's sending this robe to me. I don't think he simply means for me to wash it. He must have some other motive." She shut the door and carefully took out the stitches along the seams. As soon as she parted the seam of the collar, a sheet of paper jumped into view. She took it and read the poem written on it. She sobbed as she read it, and tears kept trickling down her cheeks. After finishing, she broke into a crying, saying, "My dear husband, you just can't understand me!" With tears welling up in her eyes, she neatly washed and sewed up the robe. Then she wrote a poem of her own and tucked it inside the collar. The boy Xiaoshu was called in to take the newly washed robe back to Jin Ding.

When Jin Ding got it back, he took out the note from inside the collar. He read the poem with great sadness. It went like this:

Since war plagued our hometown years ago,
I have been overwhelmed by lingering woe.
My heart is broken, but not my faith.
If I can't keep you company, I will after death.
I hope the shattered mirror will be pieced together
And you will sing a rhapsody for our get-together.
Many a girl martyr died with her mate.
Alas! This seems to be also my fate!

After reading this, Jin Ding knew Cuicui had submitted to fate against her will, as her faithfulness was clearly expressed. His spirits sank at Cuicui's promise to meet him in another life, because he realized a reunion was impossible for the rest of their present life. He wept day after day and took little food and water. Eventually his sadness developed into sickness and a lump developed in his abdomen. The general was worried about him and sent for several doctors. But as the old saying goes, "An illness mentally procured is mentally cured." How could doctors bring him back to health? As the days went by, he was getting from bad to worse and soon death was at hand.

At the news of his sickness Cuicui felt her heart pierced. She plucked up her courage to ask the general for a leave to see her brother in the study. The general knew his brother-in-law was in critical condition and so approved her request. Cuicui hurried into Jin Ding's study. This was their second meeting in the general's house. Jin Ding was on his bed, breathing feebly. He couldn't get up. Cuicui was deeply depressed. With tears welling up in her eyes, she propped up his head and said at a low voice, "Brother, hang on. Here's your sister Cuicui to see you." Then she burst into tears. Her words awakened him.

He opened his eyes with difficulty and saw his wife at his side supporting him. He heaved a long sigh and said, "Sister, I will not be able to recover! It's a rare chance for you to come out and see me. I will die at your side and be content." So he let Cuicui sit at the side of his bed as he struggled to raise his head. Then he put his head into Cuicui's lap and breathed his last.

Cuicui's cried until she fell into a swoon. The general heard about it and felt sorry for her. Fearing that Cuicui would become sick due to her grief, he ordered that a grand funeral and burial be held for Jin Ding. He also promised to bury him on a smooth plot of land at the foot of a hill in a place where Taoist rites were performed. Cuicui told the general she would attend the funeral. She went there and watched the burial being completed. She cried and fainted a couple of times.

After she returned, a sickness seized her and she fell into a deep trance and began to live in restlessness. General Li did his best to find doctors for her, but Cuicui intended to die and took no medicine. So her sickness lingered on for two months.

One day, she sent for the general and tearfully said to him, "Since I left my home and followed you at age seventeen, it's been eight years. I've lived estranged from my kin. My brother was the only family member of mine who came to see me. Unfortunately he died here. Now I'm sick. If I can't make it, remember to bury me at the side of my brother's grave. My soul would be content to be in his company after death. I would appreciate your kindness very much." Then she burst into tears. The general felt quite sorry for her and offered her a great deal of consolation, telling her to take it easy and have a good rest. But moments later she fell into a coma and stopped breathing.

The general wailed. Feeling obliged to comply with her dying request, he had her body buried at the side of Jin Ding's grave. It was deplorable that Jin Ding and Cuicui failed to become united once again in life, but their misery was compensated for as they posed as brother and sister and were buried together after death.

By the early years of the Hongwu period [1368-1399] of the Ming Dynasty, the rebellion led by Zhang Shicheng was suppressed, unity was restored to the country and travel became possible again.

One day a former servant of Cuicui's parents in Huai'an came to Huzhou to traffic in silk wadding. He happened to pass the place of Taoist rites performances at the foot of the hill. He saw a large residential dwelling there, which, with green walls surrounding it and a big vermilion gate, was shaded by scholar trees and willows. A man and a woman were sitting in front of the gate, side by side. The servant figured they were members of a noble household and he was about to make a detour so as to keep a respectful distance. Suddenly he heard the couple call to him. As he approached them, he was shocked to recognize they were none other than Jin Ding and Cuicui. Cuicui inquired of him about her folks and changes in her hometown. The servant made a detailed reply.

Then the servant asked them, "Your lady and lord, why did you leave home and stay here for so long?"

Cuicui answered, "When the war broke out that year, I was captured by General Li and brought here. Later my husband came all the way to see me. The general was very kind in returning me to my husband. So we decided to settle down here."

The servant said, "I'm leaving for Huai'an today. Would you please write a letter to your parents and let me take it to them? Or they will worry about you.

Cuicui replied, "That's a good idea."

Then they led the servant into their home and provided him with a dinner and a room for the night. The following day, Cuicui handed him a letter to her parents and asked him to take her best regards to them.

The servant thanked them and made his way back to Huai'an. He handed the letter to the old father Liu. The parents of Jin Ding and Cuicui had long before lost track of their son and daughter and thought they must have been killed in the chaos of war. When the letter reached the family from Huzhou, Cuicui's parents were overjoyed to learn that their daughter and son-in-law were living in Huzhou. They summoned the whole family and read the letter together. The letter was written in Cuicui's name. It was parallel prose. After reading it the whole family was quite happy.

Father Liu asked the servant, "Do you remember the place where they live?"

The servant answered, "Sure. It's a big house. I stayed there for a night and have brought the letter to you. How can I forget it?"

The father said, "If you're sure, I'm going to make a trip with you to see them."

So the father gathered together some traveling money, said a good-bye to his family and set off with the servant on the journey to Huzhou.

When they arrived in the place where the servant spent the night, they exclaimed: "Strange!" There was no sign of a shack, not to speak of any imposing residence. The only thing they saw was a wilderness of weeds and bushes, with foxes roaming and hares running about. In the woods were two tombs standing side by side.

The father asked, "Have we come to the wrong place?"

The servant answered, "I'm sure I was here just a few days ago. They treated me to a dinner of good Huzhou rice, fresh crucian carp from Tiaoxi River and wine from Wucheng. I spent one night here. How could I be wrong?"

As they were puzzling over the matter, an old monk shuffled by leaning on his walking stick. The father and his servant said to the monk, "Old master, there was a big house here days ago, with a Lord Jin and a Lady Liu living in it. But where are they?"

The old monk answered, "No. This is the grave where General Li buried Master Liu and his younger sister Cuicui. There has never been such a thing as a big house! I wonder if you saw phantoms?"

The father replied, "How could that happen? I received the letter they sent to me and so I came here to see them. I have the letter with me. How can there be phantoms?"

He took the letter from his bag. It was blank. Then he realized what had shown up were phantoms and here were their graves. He then asked the old monk, "Do you have any idea where that General Li is now? I might inquire of him about my child."

The old monk replied, "General Li was a follower of Zhang Shicheng. Their forces were stamped out by the central government. Nobody knows where they got killed. He was not lucky to be buried like Liu and Cuicui. How can you locate him?"

The father was grief-stricken at the loss of his daughter and son-in-law. He spoke in the direction of the graves, saying, "My daughter, you sent me a letter and I traveled a thousand *li* to be here. I thought you wanted to see me. Now I'm here but you're out of sight. I have no idea where you are. I feel very sad. We are father and daughter, and we can contact each other although we belong to the different realms of the living and dead. If you can hear me, be sure to show up and talk to me. Then I will feel at ease."

The old monk consoled him, "Please don't grieve, patron. I often see the souls of this gentleman and lady in my meditations. I live not far from here in a Buddhist temple. Now it's a late hour. It isn't fit for you to stay in the wilds. Why not come with me to my temple and put yourselves up for the night? I'll contact their souls in my meditations and see what they say. What do you think?"

The father replied, "I appreciate your kindness very much."

He and his servant followed the old monk to the temple after walking half a *li*. The old monk served them a vegetarian meal and made arrangements to accommodate them for the night. He then left to engage in his meditation. Later that evening, the father entered his bedroom. As he was about to get into bed, he heard the door creaking open. A young couple walked in. He took a close look at them and recognized them as Cuicui and Jin Ding. The two got down on their knees and wept, all choked up. Tears gushed from the father's eyes, as well. He stroked Cuicui's head saying, "My daughter, please tell me what is on your mind."

Cuicui replied, "It was bad luck that the ravages of war fell on us that year and I was carried away. I lived in estrangement and disgrace far away from home. I had no one to turn to for help. The days dragged on like years. I was happy my husband kept me in his mind. He came to see me one day posing as my brother. But our meeting was short. After that we lived separately. The sorrow was so deep that my husband died first and then my death followed. I was glad my request was granted that I be buried beside my husband's grave so our souls can keep one another company. I wanted to let you know what had happened to us so I sent a letter by way of the servant. Though my husband and I were separated in life, we are together after death. Now my wishes are fulfilled. Father and Mother, please don't worry about us."

The father sobbed and said, "I didn't think that you were dead. I came over a long distance and expected to go home with you. But you're both dead! Tomorrow I'll only be able to take your remains back home. I'll bury you by the side of our ancestors' graves. Therefore I won't have made this trip in vain."

Cuicui replied, "I was worried about you, my parents, so I sent that letter. I appreciate that out of fatherly love you journeyed all the way here. That's why I have made a special trip with my husband out of the infernal regions in order to meet you. Now we're having a family reunion. Our longing is satisfied. However, I would be very grateful if you would leave us here instead of moving our remains home."

"Why do you say that?" asked the father.

Cuicui answered, "I understand that I failed to assume my filial duty to attend to you, my parents, during my life. After death I should undoubtedly stay with our ancestors. But the infernal regions are quiet and should be left undisturbed. Besides, it's a beautiful landscape here with babbling brooks, rolling hills and lush bushes and trees. I'm happy to be with my husband here day and night. The Buddhist temple is also within reach. We're often instructed in Buddhist scriptures. We'll soon be reborn and become husband and wife again. Since we're pretty much settled down, please don't mention this matter any more." Then she threw herself on her father's shoulder and started to cry. At that moment the bells rang in the temple and Cuicui and Jin Ding instantly vanished.

Father Liu woke up crying and found it was a dream. The old monk came in and asked, "Did you see anything last night?"

The father narrated the occurrences in his dream. The old monk remarked, "Your daughter's spirit is alive. Her words are true. Now you know everything. Set yourself at ease, please." The father expressed his gratitude and then went into town with his servant. They purchased some animal sacrifices, sweet wine and food. Then they came back to the graves, made a libation and presented sacrificial offerings. The father cried again. Then the two of them left for Huai'an.

Today, the graves of Jin Ding and Cuicui are still located at the place at the foot of the hill. The story of the couple has become a favorite topic among passersby. It is a legend of a husband and wife who were separated in life but brought together after death. Since they are satisfied with their state, they often produce extraordinary phenomena. Indeed, love works wonders.

Tale 5

Shen Binges with Thousands in Silver;
Lord Wang Lays a One-night Trap

This tale is about an official surnamed Shen, who lived in Pingjiang Prefecture during the reign of Xuanhe [1119-1126] under the emperor Huizong in the Song Dynasty. Because of his ancestors' influence, he inherited the qualification for a minor official. To receive the nomination he went to the capital city. Because his family was rich, this young man often carried many treasures of gold and silver with him when he frequented song and dance halls to flirt with young ladies, or traveled extensively across beautiful lands for merriment in tea-houses and taverns. He was such a prodigal that he squandered his money wherever he found he could have fun. It is universally true, in human society, that a prodigal always finds himself in the company of someone who is interested in encouraging a style of wasteful living. Not far away from his lodging lived two good-for-nothing men, one surnamed Zheng and the other Li. They were shiftless and lazy. They had never obtained full names, so they were simply remembered as Tenth Brother Zheng and Third Brother Li, or simply Tenth Zheng and Third Li. They usually spent the whole day at Shen's place, talking and eating with him. Shen would not part from them either, even for a moment. Occasionally they spent some money and ordered a feast in one of the brothel on Pingkangli*. When they drank their full and felt happy, they would sleep with the girls there. Very often, while offering services, Zheng and Li worked in collusion with a prostitute to cheat some money out of Shen. They usually shared the profits and in the end they had to spend none of their own money. Because Shen was fickle and was never interested in one lady for long, they could not coax him into giving a huge sum. So Zheng and Li had to be satisfied with whatever fringe benefits they could receive in the company of their patron — good food and wine in most cases.

Half a year went by quickly and they had been to all the places of interest in town. One day Shen said to his two companions, "We've gone through all the entertainment of this town. Besides, it's too noisy and crowded in the city, not much fun. I want to go out of town to the country for a change. How about you?"

Zheng and Li said, "Wonderful! You are indeed somebody who knows where to go. But we're sorry we can't go today, because we have a little business to attend to. We would appreciate it if you could put off going until tomorrow."

Shen said, "Tomorrow is fine with me. But don't be late."

The two men said, "No, we won't, sir. We appreciate your trust in us. We would be a couple of useless fellows if we went back on our word. We'll surely be here with you tomorrow."

The two left and came back the next day, asking Shen, "Are you ready for the trip out of town?"

Shen said, "Yes, I'm ready."

Zheng asked, "I wonder whether you, Master, want to go there by

---

*A well-known street for prostitution during the Song Dynasty.

riding a horse or taking a sedan chair?"

Li said, "Since we want to take a leisurely stroll, what is the point of using a horse or sedan chair?"

Shen said, "Exactly, Brother Li. If we have servants coming with us, tending to the horses and sedan chairs, we won't feel free to move around. We're just going to take a stroll for relaxation. It will be up to us where we go and where we stay. What fun it's going to be! So we'll just bring one or two servants along with us." Then he had one of his favorite serving boys carry a small leather suitcase with his valuable things inside and follow them. The three of them sauntered out of the Changan Gate. What they saw out of town was quite a different sight:

The city walls began to blur and fade, and also retreating into the distance were their mundane affairs; in the wilds, old towering trees stood with branches and twigs in entanglement, and streams meandered along with threads of gossamer covering their banks; a humble wine store was there, patronized by only farmers and elderly locals; fishing-boats sailed back home with their catch and met buffalo boys and woodsmen awaiting them to make purchases; wisps of smoke spiraled skyward from the chimneys of houses shrouded in dense fog; roads branched out and forks were submerged in thick bushes.

The three men were fascinated by the charms of country life, free from worldly worries. They walked slowly, enjoying the wild landscape and chatting with one another. A short stroll of two or three *li* brought them to a pond. They saw several burly men with stout legs and big feet, who, stripped to the waist and holding straps in their hands, were washing a few good horses in the pond. Spotting some people approaching, these men sprang out of the pond, slipped into their clothing and bowed in greeting.

Surprised, Shen asked his companions, "They're strangers, so why are they showing such respect toward us?"

The two companions said, "They're servants of Lord Wang. Wang is on good terms with both of us. That's why they have to be courteous."

Shen said, "Yes, I understand."

Then they strolled along the side of the pond chatting for another a couple of hundred of steps. Suddenly Li stopped Shen and said, "Master, I've an idea."

Shen asked, "What is it?"

Li said, "We are having a lot of fun enjoying the rustic charm out here today. But we're walking without a specific purpose, and there is no place for a break. It's going to be pretty boring soon if we keep walking like this. Why not check out the horses of Lord Wang we saw just now, and take a ride to visit him at his home today? Isn't that a good idea?"

Shen said, "Who's Lord Wang? I don't know him. Is it appropriate to intrude upon him?"

Li replied, "Well, he's a marvelous old person. He used to be chief of a prefecture. He owns some extremely valuable property and keeps an army of concubines. He likes to entertain people and is never tired of offering them hospitality. Now he is becoming old and suffers from asthma, so his concubines all want to leave him. But he keeps his gate under close watch. Nobody except the two of us is allowed entry, because we are close to him. By the way, those concubines of his have nothing to attend to, so they gather to play and have fun all day long. If we go to see him, I'm sure he'll be quite happy. Though you haven't met him before, you can simply come with us and say you admire his noble character and would like to make his acquaintance. He'll definitely show courtesy since you're our friend. We may let him know you're to go to the capital city and assume a position. He'll think he and you are in the same profession and treat you with particular attention, and probably provide a special feast. If that happens, we can drink like fish tonight. That'll give us a lot of fun. Isn't it much better than going back home after a lonesome walk?"

Shen hesitated, but Zheng pushed him by saying, "He is a very cheerful old guy. He enjoys living with many beautiful concubines, and his generosity toward his friends is also remarkable. He always has such fun entertaining visitors that he sees to it that the food served is carefully chosen and cleaned. He does his best to avoid causing any offense and ruining an otherwise good appetite. I wonder whether you will ever meet another person as generous as he is. Today we've stopped by here. I suggest you take this opportunity and get to know him. Don't miss the chance."

Shen said, "Alright, I'd like to go and see him."

Li said, "Let's go back to the side of the pond and check out some of the horses."

Then they made their way back. Zheng and Li shouted toward those horsemen, "Bring us four horses, please."

The horsemen didn't dare delay and said, "These horses are our lord's property. Feel free to use them."

Zheng, Li and Shen each took a horse. Even the servant-boy who carried the suitcase for his master was provided with one. One leading horseman grabbed the rein of one horse and asked, "Can you let me know where you're going?"

Zheng, pointing his whip in the direction, said, "To your lord's home."

The horseman said, "Thank you, sir. I understand." And he led the way for them.

They rode three abreast and, after turning past two hamlets, came to a large residence with a huge gate. Li said, "Here we are. Zheng, please wait here with Shen, the master, for a moment. Let me go inside and tell the host. He'll be out to meet you." Shen opened his case, took out a name card and handed it to Li. Li took the card and went in.

Shortly afterward, he came out and said, "He's very glad to hear there is a new visitor here. Unfortunately, he's been sick for a long time and feels uncomfortable putting on his official hat and girdle. He wonders whether he could meet you in casual dress."

Shen said, "Well, the dress code requires formal attire for a new visitor — but since he's not up to dressing, I should not bother him to do so. He will feel more comfortable and at ease in casual dress."

Li then went inside again. A moment later, Lord Wang emerged supported by two serving boys and in the company of Li. Shen looked up and saw that Wang, though quite old, still carried the bearing of a high-ranking official. Shen was struck with awe. Seeing his visitor was young and handsome, Wang smiled and courteously led the way into a reception hall. There the three visitors met their host formally.

Shen first offered some words of admiration and then said, "Fortunately, it's through the introduction of my friends, Zheng and Li that I have the chance to make your acquaintance, probably an essential step toward future success in my career. Today's meeting has fulfilled my wishes, but I apologize for the intrusion."

Wang made this reply. "I take any friend of these two gentlemen as one of my own. Besides, the two gentlemen are well-accomplished in learning. A person in their company, like you, should be unquestionably one of a high caliber of intelligence. I'm old and incompetent so I will feel honored to make friends with you."

After tea, Wang showed his guests into an east room and told the house manager to fix a dinner. Soon afterwards, the food and fruit arrived with the dinnerware. Shen noticed, though it was not a feast, the serving of the food was refined, delicate and professional, absolutely beyond the achievement of an ordinary family.

Wang said politely, "I'm sorry I was in a rush and could only present a humble dinner of a few dishes. I hope you don't mind."

Zheng and Li said, "Shen is rather casual. Since he's our friend, please don't treat him as a new guest. Just feel free to do what you please as our host. Drink and have fun! No formality is needed." Then the three visitors started to drink in large quantity, attended by two servant-boys who kept pouring wine into their cups, while the host, though in a sick condition, struggled to keep up with the occasion.

Darkness started to gather and candles were lit. Wang managed to sit for another few moments, but he suddenly fell short of breath and had a coughing fit. His continuous loud spitting denied his efforts to bring himself under control and disturbed the others. He had the two servant-boys prop him up and said to his guests, "Sorry I'm not feeling well. You're honorable guests, but I don't feel up to doing my duty as the host. What an embarrassment this is!"

Then he turned to Zheng and said, "Sorry, Brother Zheng. I just can't do anything but let you take charge as host to see to that everyone enjoys himself. I'm going to take a recess and have some brewed medicine. I'll be back with you shortly. I am terribly sorry." Then he departed in the attendance of the two servant-boys, leaving the three men at the table. The boys who had poured wine for them were also gone.

Li said, "Let me go and bring us some company," and he went inside.

With the host gone and dinner suspended, Shen was a little disappointed. He would have left but thought he should say good-bye to the host. In addition, he had just had a few cups of wine and had gotten into the spirit of things. So he strolled down into the yard. Suddenly he heard the sound of dice-throwing and the roar of excitement. Following the sound, he reached a small room and saw some candlelight radiating from a crack in the window. He pulled the crack larger and peeped through it. If he had not done this, everything would have been fine. But as he stole a glance through it, his limbs became weak and numb and his body disintegrated.

Reader, what do you think was going on inside? In the middle of the room was a large square table, surrounded by seven or eight standing beauties. On the table was a high candle. There was a wine vessel and a dice pot in the center of the table. Each pretty girl had a pile of things in front of her, things used as stakes. With their sleeves rolled up, these young ladies seemed eager to try their chance. Shen gazed at them. Each was as beautiful as the moon goddess. Staring lustfully at them, Shen lost his head.

As his eyes remained riveted on the women, Li sprang from nowhere into the game-playing party. He grabbed the dice and was about to throw them when these women, in the heat of the moment, saw his intrusion and shouted, "Scholar Li, you've come here to make trouble again. You're interrupting our game!"

Li said shamelessly, "I think you need me to add more fun to your game of dice."

One woman said, "He's an old friend. Let him play. But you should play a fair game. Take out your money and bet it!"

The other women chimed in, "Look at him, a wretch! Do you expect him to bet a big sum?"

Such hoots of derision bombarded him one after another. Li made a few more throws of the dice, with a wry smile. He became a target of ridicule, but he bore it shamelessly, not caring what they said. The women eventually yielded to his brazenness and let him join in the game.

The sight of Li having fun with the women fascinated Shen. He stamped feet, saying to himself, "Here is paradise! If I got the chance to enjoy myself there as Li does, I would be absolutely satisfied even if I were to die soon after!" Shen became flurried and fidgeted about like a jumping bean. He went to find Zheng, hoping to talk to him about what he had seen. Zheng was having a little nap on the seat.

Shen woke him with a shove and said, "It's weird you should be content to be sleeping out here. Brother Li is alone sucking honey inside!"

Zheng asked, "What's up?"

Shen pulled him by the hand to the window and, pointing inside, said, "Look!"

Zheng looked in and saw Li was gambling with those women. Zheng said to Shen, "Li is shameless."

Shen replied, "What a party of fun! How can I let him know that I want to join them in the game? That'll make my trip here worthwhile."

Zhen said, "Those women are Wang maids. The old gentleman has gone to sleep so they have the chance to enjoy themselves. Li and I are frequent visitors here so he has no problem messing around with them. But the women don't know you and the host is not around. I think it would be hard for you to play with them. It's quite a different case."

Shen said, "My good brother, do me a favor and get me in."

Zheng said, "If you're really interested, you will need something to bet."

Shen said, "Sure, I've some valuable things in my case worth about a thousand *liang* of silver. I also have a couple of thousand of tea-coupons. I can use them for bets. If you manage to get me in the game to satisfy me tonight, I'll be willing to give them all up."

Zheng said, "Alright, lower your voice and come with me quietly. I'm going to find a chance to sneak you in at the right time. It's best not to disturb them."

Shen kept quiet and Zheng led him forward by grasping his hand and making a few turns like he was quite familiar with the compound. A moment later, they stole to the side of the gambling table. The women were in high spirits, bent over the table, and didn't notice them. Zheng pinched Shen and pulled him to an empty space. They waited for some time until that round was over.

As the roar died down, Zheng said loudly, "Would you mind if I have a shot?" The women all raised their heads and realized Zheng was there. But they saw a strange face nearby.

They shouted, "Who's that man, and how did he get in here?"

Zheng replied, "He's my friend Master Shen. He learned you were having a party here, and he wanted to have a look. Don't be surprised."

The women said, "Our master and you have been on good terms for some time and you've never hidden anything from one another. But why are you bringing a young man here tonight without letting our master know? You're intruding upon us."

One middle-aged lady said, "I think it's fine — since this gentleman is a friend of yours, he is no stranger to us. As he's here already, why not have a late drink of wine?" She picked up a big vessel, poured a cup of warm wine and presented it to Shen.

A thrill seized Shen's whole body. Seeing the lady offer the wine with both hands, he dared not decline it. He took the cup in both hands and downed the wine completely. The lady commented, "He's really interesting! You should each offer him a drink, too."

Zheng said, "No, don't ruin your spirits in playing by doing that. Master Shen would like to participate in a round of the game with you. Let's throw the dice while having drinks. This will give us more fun."

The middle-aged lady said, "You bet! But we'd better not let our master know what's going on here." She called a young girl servant, "Go to Lord's room and take a look. If the master is sleeping, hurry back and let us know. Don't make any mistakes, alright?" The young girl servant left. The girls renewed the dice game with Shen.

Shen was overjoyed that he had the good luck to be in an abode of female angels. As his wishes were now fulfilled and his enthusiasm was running high, luck seemed to be on his side. He won one game after another. To find something to bet, the women had to strip jewels off their heads, items such as hairpins and jade earrings worth of about one thousand *liang* of silver. But they were all won by Shen. The women were stunned, with nothing left in front of them. With a pull at Shen, Zheng said to him, "You've had enough. Won't you stop now?"

Shen was feeling a tremendous surge at energy. He was anxious to stay longer, and was not mindful of his wins and losses. How could he be willing to quit the game at that moment? He went on with his spree of throwing dice and drinking. The women added spice to his play by making teasing remarks to him. Shen continued to play with even more gusto. Soon his good luck had left the women empty-handed. One of them was the youngest and most beautiful. She lost more games than anyone and became irritated at Shen's incessant winning and drinking. She, scowling, rose and went back to her room.

A few moments later she returned with a white jade wine vessel with patterns. She set it on the table and said, "Here's a vessel worth of one thousand strings of cash. I'm going to have a last shot with it."

The other women were shocked and said, "It's not yours. How can you use it as a stake?"

The young woman said, "I know it's our master's. But it'll give me a last chance. If I win, that's fine. But if I lose again, I won't get back the vessel. Tomorrow the master will inquire about it and I'll be ready for his lashes. But I am in such a desperate situation, I have no choice."

The rest said, "No, you can't let yourself be driven by emotions. If you lose the vessel, you'll never be able to get it back."

Infuriated, the young girl said, "I'll take care of that. Don't say anything any more." She wouldn't change her mind.

Seeing her becoming angry, the rest said, "We meant to have fun. Why are you taking it so seriously?"

The young woman's obstinacy attracted Shen. He took a liking of her and at the same time felt sorry for her. He figured, "Originally I was not interested in the results of the game. But luck has been on my side. Now I think I should do her a favor by losing the next game so as to calm her down. Otherwise I'm going to be blamed for dashing all the fun."

Reader, dice, though not human, do have inspiration and run according to one's wishes and mood. At first, Shen was very enthusiastic so the dice brought him a number of wins in succession. After awhile, things started to turn. In addition, he was worried about the young woman and intended to give up the game, and hence his high mood. Shen was indeed carried away by the young woman's behavior, her anger and persistence. As a result, he cast the dice in a flurry and lost the round.

The young woman shouted, "Alright. Good luck has not left me after all!" So saying, she turned the wine vessel upside down and dumped the contents onto the table. Originally Shen had thought the wine vessel cost up to the value of one thousand strings of coins. He never thought it would be full of jewels and pearls. The dazzling jewels were quite precious. Since the wine vessel and jewels were stakes for the game, Shen, as the loser, had nothing to do but pay that sum of money.

This sum was about three thousand strings of cash, estimated by Zheng, Li and the women. Shen couldn't deny it. He turned in what he had won previously, worth less than one thousand *liang* of silver. Then he went out and asked his servant-boy to get him the more than two thousand tea-coupons from his case, which were counted in value and all paid as the stake.

Reader, you may wonder what the tea-coupons were and how they could be used in the place of gold and silver. Well, during the Song Dynasty, the government imposed a levy on tea and issued tea-coupons to tea vendors who had paid their taxes. This tax payment receipt was accepted everywhere and could be traded at the value of more than one *liang* of silver. Some rich families made profits from tea-coupon deals. That is why the tea-coupons could be used as silver. There was a well-known story about a girl called Su Xiaoqing, who was sold by a brothel owner for three thousand tea-coupons.

The two thousand or so tea-coupons Shen lost were approximately worth of two thousand *liang* of silver. Though the loss of this game cost him a great sum, he still had hundreds of tea-coupons left and all the treasures were intact. He figured he would play another round of the game and thus turn the tide. Suddenly the sound of coughing coming from the inner house caught his attention. It was Lord Wang, who needed a spittoon. Agitated, the women pushed the three men out of the room, put out the candle and raced inside to attend to their master.

The three men returned to the room in which they had been drinking earlier that evening. As they seated themselves, two servant-boys came over to offer them more drinks of wine, saying, "Our master appreciates your coming as honorable guests. However, it is late and he's tired. He doesn't feel up to being with you now, but he asks that you have one more drink."

The three men said, "We've had enough. Thank you. We're taking off."

The servant-boys took in the report of their visitors' leaving and returned the next moment, saying, "Our master said, 'I was caught in a rush and apologize for not attending to you very well. Now it's some time after midnight. I'm sorry I can't see you off. Please come again in three days and I'm sure we'll have more fun. Please don't turn me down.' He also made arrangements for having the horsemen take you back home and report to him after that."

The three men and Shen's servant-boy left the house of Lord Wang, riding the four horses they had ridden on their way there earlier that day. As they came to the city gate, dawn was breaking and the gate was opened. The horsemen took Shen back home. Shen tipped the horsemen for himself as well as for Zheng and Li. Then the horsemen left. Taking their leave, Zheng and Li said to Shen, "We've played the whole night. Now we can go home and have some sleep. Let's make sure we'll keep the appointment and go to the party in a couple of days." Then they left.

Shen recalled with pleasure that, although he lost a couple of thousands *liangs* of silver that night, he had received the tender feelings of a middle-aged lady and observed the young woman's fury at him with amusement. It was also a pleasant memory for him that, as the girls offered drinks to him in turn and competed with him in the game, he was thrilled with bewitchment and felt proud of himself. He soliloquized, "All this was done behind the back of the host. However, I hate to realize that Zheng and Li snatched such a good chance of enjoyment ahead of me. But since I am now started on the right track, things will ease up for me in learning the ropes. Eventually I'm going to have an equal share in the gains of those two. Probably I may get the better of them someday. Who knows?" He was happy.

Sleepiness overcame him and he stayed inside the next two days. As the third day arrived, he woke up at dawn and got ready for the appointment with Wang. However, Zheng and Li didn't show up. He was anxious and sent two servants to their homes to fetch them. The servants came back with the report, "They're out." He had to wait hopelessly until noon. However, there was still no sign of them. He waited nervously. Then the thought hit him, "They might have set out for Wang's place without letting me know. Since I've been there, I know the way and don't need their company. But I do need their help for getting inside Wang's house. I'd better bring some gifts with me as a token of my gratitude for all the service I received the other night. If they're there ahead of me, that's good. If they're not there yet, they must be on their way. I can simply wait for them." So he called a servant-boy to saddle his horse and prepare some gifts. Then he went out of town and traveled toward Wang's home, as he had the previous day.

When he arrived, the gate was shut. His servant-boy saw a side door and entered. There was nobody inside. The servant-boy was puzzled and came out to tell Shen about it. Shen was shocked. Uncertain about whether or not he had come to the right place, he went in with the servant-boy for a double-check. It was indeed an empty residence, although there was the familiar sight of the reception hall, east porch, and small room that reminded him of the gambling party the other night. Quite confused, Shen said, "It should be here. This is weird."

He dashed outside and found a man running a fur store to the left side of the gate. He said to the store owner, "Excuse me, sir. Lord Wang lives in this residence. But where has his family gone?"

The fur dealer answered, "This is the property of Lord Hou, minister of domestic affairs. He has left the residence empty and unused. There has never been a person living here by the name of Wang."

Shen replied, "A Lord Wang with his family was here three days ago. I came to visit him and he hosted and treated me to dinner with wine the whole night. I'm sure this is the right place. How can you say no such person ever lived here?"

The fur dealer said, "Three days ago, a group of young rogues, together with a few well-known courtesans, rented this place for a feast and a gambling party. The following day they settled the account among themselves and went their own ways. As far as I know, there was nothing like Wang's playing host to a dinner party. Have you perhaps been hooked by them, sir?"

Shen then realized he had fallen into a trap set by the two impostors, who swindled him of his tea-coupons and a few thousand *liangs* of silver. Then he recalled all the happenings, his meeting with the horsemen by the side of the pond, visiting Lord Wang, staying for the dinner and joining in the gambling in the small room. The events baffled him as to whether they were a coincidence or were carefully designed. Quite confused, he said to himself, "It is terrible that I can't get a hold of these two men now! There should be some reason for these occurrences. I'll find them in a few days and ask them about this."

But in the following days he dispatched people to the two men's dwellings for inquiry. Their host had lost track of them, too, and replied, "Since they left that day, they never showed up again. Their rooms are locked. After the doors were opened, nothing was found inside, with no trace of them at all."

It became crystal clear that the series of events had been carefully plotted by Zheng and Li, the two swindlers, and even the horsemen and servant-boys had been working for them. It had taken them only one night to carry through their scheme. But their craftsmanship in fleecing Shen was extraordinary!

Tale 6

Rash Young Men Startle Lovers;
Clever Young Women Recognize Jade Toads

A scholar named Feng Laiyi, with the formal name Wubin, lived in Hangzhou. He was young and quite intelligent. Because the death of his parents left him with a little property, he remained unmarried. He had an uncle on his mother's side, a man called San with the family name of Jin. This uncle of his knew that the nephew had great promise and so he took care of Laiyi. Laiyi thus adopted his uncle's family name, Jin, as his own and entered the public school under name of Jin Laiyi. Later he passed the civil service examinations at the provincial level and became a *juren*. His friends called him Feng, but on the list of those who had passed the examinations his family name appeared as Jin. His uncle spent a huge sum to rent him a residential area with a garden on the left side of Wushan*, letting him study there with two of his friends by the name of Dou Shangwen and Dou Shangwu. The two friends were brothers, young, generous and

---

*A place inside Hangzhou.

arrogant. Feng and they were congenial friends. Later the two brothers went to Suzhou to see off a relative of theirs who was leaving for the capital city to assume an official position. Feng had passed the provincial examinations, but there would be some time before the national examinations, so he stayed alone in his residence to study.

One evening the scholar felt a bit tired after reading and went out to take a stroll in his garden. As he sauntered to the east part of the garden, he spotted a goddess-like woman standing behind a second-floor window of the neighboring building just across the garden wall. The woman also saw Feng clearly and was impressed by his youthful features. Instead of being shy, she tarried there, her eyes focused on him. Admittedly Feng couldn't take his eyes off her either. There was a long period of eye contact. Then Feng walked up and down, pretending to enjoy the chrysanthemums growing in the yard. He lingered until darkness fell, assuming flirtatious postures to attract the woman's attention. The woman called out, "Longxiang, shut the windows and doors, please." As a servant-girl emerged and closed the window, Feng made his way back to his room. He was thinking, "What a beautiful young woman that family has! I wonder who she is. I'll find out her name."

The next morning he woke but couldn't concentrate on his reading. As soon as he finished washing and dressing, he went out to the east part of the garden. He looked up, but the woman was not by the window. As he waited there, a small door around the corner of the building suddenly opened and out came a good-looking servant-girl. She came into the yard to pick some chrysanthemums.

In order to start a conversation, Feng scolded her loudly, saying, "Why does a girl come stealing plants here in the yard?"

The servant-girl spat and said, "This plot is part of our neighbor's property. You are a boorish intruder. How can you accuse me of stealing?"

Grinning broadly, Feng said, "Alright, you're not a thief, nor am I a boor. It was just a slip of the tongue. Let's both forgive and forget."

Also with a smile, the servant-girl said, "Well, if I don't forgive and forget, what damages could I claim from you?"

Feng said, "Young lady, may I know who will be wearing the blossoms you are picking?"

The girl said, "Our young lady. She's finished her washing and making-up, and is now awaiting the blossoms."

Feng asked, "Could I know her name? And where she comes from?"

The girl said, "She's called Sumei with the family name of Yang. She's not been betrothed yet."

Feng asked, "What about her parents?"

The girl said, "Her parents have died. She's currently living with her elder brother and sister-in-law. She loves peace and quiet and likes to do embroidery alone in her room up there on the second floor of our building."

Feng said, "I guess she is the one I saw yesterday standing by the window?"

"Exactly," the girl responded, "It couldn't have been anybody else."

Feng said, "Then you must be Sister Longxiang?"

The girl asked with surprise, "How did you know my name, sir?"

Feng had overheard her name being called by her young lady the day before, but he lied, saying, "I've long known that there's a young lady of superb beauty called Sumei of the Yang family living in the east part of this neighborhood. And her servant-girl, Sister Longxiang, is gentle and virtuous. I've admired you both for a long time."

Longxiang was indeed a servant of little education and limited experience. Having heard that she had a good reputation, she was happy and said, "I can't believe my incompetence should have caught your attention, sir!"

Feng replied, "Well, the ranks of an invincible general keep no weak soldier. Your beautiful young lady should be matched in the company of an equally pretty servant. Fortunately, I caught a glimpse of your young lady yesterday, and, today, I have run into you, Sister Longxiang. That is good luck bestowed on me. Sister Longxiang, could you do me a favor and arrange for an appointment so I can meet your young lady some day?"

Longxiang said, "You should know where to stop, sir. Our young lady is of honorable and noble origin, not from a loose family. We don't know who you are. Why are you so shamelessly talking about meeting her?"

Feng said, "I'm called Laiyi and my family name is Feng. I just passed the fall examinations at the provincial level this year. Currently I'm studying in this residence next door to your house. It's true your young lady is a beauty second to none. But I'm a promising scholar. My meeting with her will not humiliate her."

Longxiang said, "All of you scholars like to talk like that. It's disgusting! I don't want to continue this conversation. I'll bring the blossoms to my young lady." She then turned around and went toward her house.

Feng followed closely and, bowing slightly with hands folded in front, said, "I'm asking you for a big favor. Please send my best regards to her." Turning a deaf ear to what he had said, Longxiang went straight into the building and slammed the door closed.

Feng had to turn back. But suddenly he heard the window of the building being pushed wide open and someone uttering, "Longxiang, what are you doing down there? Come back!"

He looked up and there was the woman he had seen the day before. She had just finished her make-up and was waiting for Longxiang to bring the blossoms. She and Feng looked at each other squarely. To Feng, she looked even more beautiful than she had the day before. Sumei was also carried away by his appearance, gazing admiringly at him. Thinking that it was possible to arouse the woman's interest in him, Feng improvised a poem:

I passed many lovely nights in vain.
No one knows my secret anxiety.
My love is nigh but barriers are high —
So I wear myself down in pain.

On hearing the chanting, Sumei realized it was aimed at her. However, she didn't know who he was nor did she think she could make inquiries about him. As she paused aimlessly, Longxiang came in with the handful of chrysanthemum blossoms and set them in her hair.

Longxiang asked her, "Sister, do you see that young boaster over there in the garden?"

Sumei said with a wave of her hand, "He's hanging around there. Lower your voice, or he may hear what you are saying."

The servant replied, "No, I'm making a point of letting him hear what I'm saying. What a shameless piece of trash!"

Sumei asked, "Who is he? Why do you say he's shameless? Tell me why you think so."

Longxiang recounted, "I was picking blossoms in the yard. He popped up from nowhere and accused me of stealing them. I gave him a rebuff. Then he asked me for whom I was gathering the blossoms. I told him they were for you, sister. After I mentioned your name, it's strange that he said my name is Longxiang. He also said he had heard your good name long before and had even learned something about me as your servant. He then said he spotted you by chance yesterday, and now he wanted to see you personally some day. Then I cursed him again for his rudeness as a stranger. So he told me his name is Feng Laiyi. He passed this year's examinations at the provincial level. He's studying in that residence next door to us. I was not really interested in what he had said. He bowed and begged me to give you his best regards. He also said you're a beauty and he's a scholar. Don't you think he's shameful?"

Sumei replied, "Don't speak so loudly. I think he's a young scholar, well-read and proud of himself. It's alright that you didn't listen to him, but you'd better not hurt him with harsh words."

Longxiang said, "Okay, if you don't want to slight him, I'm going to get him over here and you can talk to him personally."

Sumei said, "You smart aleck. What a sharp tongue you have! Will it be appropriate for me to see him?" They went downstairs as their conversation continued.

Feng heard their voices but couldn't catch exactly what they had said. However, he was sure they were talking about him and so he felt nervous and excited. He lingered for a few more moments and didn't go back to his study until the two women dropped from sight.

In the days that followed that he could hardly focus his attention on his reading, and lost his appetite. Each day he snooped around along the east walls of his garden, and occasionally spotted Sumei up by the window. Sumei also lost her head in a surge of longing for him. Each day she would emerge a few times at the window on the second floor. If Feng showed up by chance, they would cast eyes at each another though words were not exchanged, and their glances brought home their respective feelings and intentions. Sumei made sure Longxiang went to the yard a couple of times every day, pretending to pick blossoms while keeping track of Feng's routine.

Longxiang could read Sumei's mind. At the same time she was interested in Feng's shyness. Therefore, she decided to act as the mediator between the two lovers. From time to time she would come to Feng's place and deliver some messages. She told him that her young lady had taken a liking to him.

Feng said, "I discerned her affection but we're separated by distance, she being upstairs out there and me being downstairs here. It's hard to communicate my sentiments."

Longxiang told him, "Why not write a letter to her, sir?"

Excited, Feng asked, "Can she read and write?"

Longxiang replied, "She loves to compose poetry and poetic prose, not to speak of reading and writing."

Feng said, "Alright, I'm going to write down a poem and let you take it to her. I'll wait and see how she responds." He put his feelings on paper and had Longxiang take it to Sumei.

Longxiang slipped the paper into her sleeve and returned home. Seeing Longxiang return smiling, Sumei asked, "What did you talk about in his study? What makes you so happy?"

Longxiang answered, "It's funny that he didn't talk to me when I was there, but kept writing something on a sheet of paper. I took the opportunity, when he didn't notice, to snatch the paper away and come back with it. Sister, please read it and see what he wrote."

Sumei took the paper and read it. "It's a poem," she said. "I think the truth is that he asked you to bring it to me. But you lied!"

Longxiang said, "To be frank, he did ask me to take it to you. I can't read or write, so it doesn't make any sense to me. I was afraid I might be blamed for something offensive in it so I had to make up a story."

Sumei said, "I'm not going to blame you for anything. But the scholar is proud of himself. If I do not answer him, he may think I have failed to get his message and will keep bugging me with his writing. I won't write any poem in reply to him so as to show my learning. I will just put down some simple words to let him know what's on my mind."

Longxiang started to prepare ink by rubbing an ink stick on an ink slab and then she put a piece of colorful writing paper on the table. Sumei was unquestionably well educated. She picked up the writing brush and started to write without composing a draft. The letter read:

Since time immemorial, it's been crucial that a virtuous girl sets high value on chastity while a courageous woman loves a bright mind. Both kinds of women are considered to be commendable, though they have different moral standards. But fearing that one might acquaint herself with a treacherous lover, and give herself up to flattery and insincere promises it is better to be virtuous than courageous. I live next-door to you and we've seen each other a few times. But whether we'll eventually end up in a union is completely up to you. Please stop writing your high-sounding pieces. It is nothing but shallow and flirtatious. I'm making this reply because it contains all that I have on my mind.

She sealed the letter and gave it to Longxiang, who was to take it to Feng the following day.

Feng was glad to see Longxiang arrive. He said to her, "Here you are, Sister Longxiang. Did you deliver my letter to your young lady?"

Longxiang put on a serious expression and said, "That letter of yours got me into a trap!"

Feng said, "Good sister, what problem did it bring to you?"

Longxiang said, "When she heard that I had brought a letter from you, my young lady flew into rage saying, 'Whose letter are you bringing to me? I'm a maiden. Am I supposed to keep up a correspondence with a man?' She made to hit me."

Feng said, "If she thinks I'm a stranger and shouldn't exchange letters with me, why did she look at me steadily from her second-floor window? She's the one who has stirred up trouble. Why did she beat you?"

Longxiang said, "I did not go so far as to fight with her. I replied to her, 'I'm not educated. How can I know what's written in the letter? If you really take it seriously, sister, please send it back to him. What's the point of getting mad?' Thus I averted a beating."

Feng said, "What an irrelevant remark! But if she didn't read the letter and is sending it back to me, what's the point of my writing it? It must have ruined my plans!"

Longxiang said, "I've no idea whether your plans are ruined or not. Here's the returned letter for you. Go ahead and read it." She slipped the letter out of her sleeve and tossed it on the floor.

Feng picked it up. It was not the one he wrote. He then knew that Longxiang was teasing him. With a grin he said, "I said your young lady couldn't steel her heart to blame me. This must be good news from her."

After reading the letter, he was overjoyed. "What a foresightful woman," he said, stamping his feet. "She's in love with me but worried about my loyalty. That's why she's taking a wait-and-see attitude. Now I should give her something as proof of my faithfulness and write another letter expressing my true feelings so as to let her schedule a meeting. Sister Longxiang, I must bother you once more to take it to her. Otherwise, it will just be a waste of our time to keep this correspondence and phony talk going on, and it will leave me in suspense."

Longxiang said, "I will help you all the way. Hurry up and give it to me. I'll take care to deliver it."

Feng opened his suitcase and took out a jade paperweight in the shape of a toad, which had been presented to him earlier that year by his uncle, Jin, in celebration of his winning of a scholarly honor. It was a valuable antique, exquisitely designed. Now he decided to present it to Sumei as a token of his true love. He then wrote a letter and concluded it with the words, "Feng Laiyi, a humble scholar graced by your love, presents this to Sumei, Your Ladyship."

Feng sealed the letter and gave it to Longxiang, along with the jade paperweight. He said to her, "Our future lifelong happy marriage will hinge on your delivery of these two things. Would you please take special care to do this and bring me back a reply?"

Longxiang said, "Stop telling me to use special care. I am eager to let you two become a couple. If you talk directly face to face, no letter-exchanging will burden me."

Feng said, "You're right, good sister. I will be grateful forever if you can do this favor for me." Longxiang smiled and left.

Back home, Longxiang said to Sumei, "Master Feng read your letter and said a lot in praise about your insight. He has sent you a reply letter and a piece of jade." Sumei took that jade paperweight of the toad, a lovely shining antique.

She smiled and said, "Is this for me? But let me read the letter first." Her reading down the sheet brought a little flush to her cheeks as she nodded slightly in pleasure. She sank into thought until she came to the words, "a humble scholar appreciating the love of Sumei, Your Ladyship," sprang into view. She said with a smile, "What an interesting scholar! Who is in love with you?" Longxiang said, "Well, sister, if you don't love him, why not turn down his wooing and never let him contact you again? But since you've kept in touch with him, how can he remain detached?"

Laughing, Sumei said, "What a character you are, girl, as interesting as he is! Listen, I've something to talk to you about. I indeed have some affections toward him, to be frank. Now that he has given me this jade paperweight of a toad as proof of his loyalty and has asked me to schedule an appointment with him, what should I do?"

Longxiang said, "Sister, if you don't want to do anything about it, your love is in vain. Why do you want to keep him in suspense and ruin an otherwise possible happy marriage?"

Sumei said, "But I fear a young man such as him tends to be infatuated for a moment and then turns his love toward someone else in the future. If that happened, what could I do?"

Longxiang replied, "I can't guarantee this for you, sister. But the problem is that you want to quit your relation with him even though you love him. You want to go further with a date, but you're suspicious of his faithfulness. That is a dilemma. I wonder whether you might want to meet him once and see what kind of character he is. If he's sincere, you can wring a vow out of him. Then you can play it by ear later and make your own decision about the issue. But if he's not honest, forget about it and never talk to him again."

Sumei said, "That's a good idea. I'm going to write him. Since tonight is the fifteenth of the lunar month and there is a full moon, I'll meet him in his study." She put down a few words on a piece of paper and slid her gold ring off her finger to give him as a gift in reply to Feng's jade paperweight of a toad. She sent Longxiang away with these to his place.

With this errand, Longxiang ran into Feng's garden. She paused and thought to herself, "A date tonight! That'll be an easy gain for that bastard! I'm not going to tell him directly."

As she entered his room, Feng was looking at the paper-patched window with a blank stare. He sprang to his feet when Longxiang walked in. "Good sister, what's the news about the matter I've been concerned about all day?" He asked.

Longxiang replied, "Stop talking about the news! She was sick of your rashness in asking for an appointment. What an easy thing you thought to obtain! Her mood changed. She tore up the letter. That jade paperweight of a toad tumbled to pieces, too."

Feng was stunned, "Really? What can I do then? How long will I have wait to talk to her? This has made a wreck of my life!"

Longxiang said, "Take it easy. Take it easy. I've something good to talk to you about."

Feng became delighted and said, "Come on and tell me about it."

Longxiang said, "How conceited you are, simply shouting, 'Tell me about it! Tell me about it!' Don't you think you should apologize first for your rashness?"

Feng said with an obsequious smile, "Alright, good sister. It is my fault." He fell down on his knees and continued, "My dear sister, I'm begging you. Please let me know about it."

Longxiang pulled him up and said, "Don't be brazen. Get up and listen. My young lady was not willing to meet you at first. But I kept pushing her until she agreed to see you some day."

Feng asked, "When?"

Longxiang said, smiling, "Next year."

Feng said, "Next year? It's going to be one year from now? I'll die waiting."

Longxiang said, "Well, I'll not be held responsible for your death and pay for it with my own death. But someone would definitely hate to see you die. Here's a good prescription for your mental sickness." She took out the gold ring and letter and handed them to Feng, saying, "You may die in rejoicing rather than in lovesickness!"

Feng took the two things and opened the letter, which read:

Our correspondence falls short of our desire to express our true feelings. I suggest we hold an evening appointment to obtain a clearer understanding of each other. Though I will not hit you with a shuttle, *You mustn't be a seducer of your neighbor. This is going to be of vital importance to our lives and needs to be on the basis of a pledge of love. So I am sending you my ring as a token of my sincerity. My word is as precious as gold and I am as good as my word. We should keep away from superficiality and deceitfulness.*

And a poem was attached:

From capture by a lover's strings I refrain
But my mate, a flute player, I'll entertain.
Let a toad jade be messenger of good intent,
Tonight's sky awash with moonlight will be brilliant.

---

*This refers to an anecdote of a man who tried to lure his neighbor's beautiful daughter. The angry girl hit him with the shuttle from her loom and knocked out his two teeth.

Feng understood this was an appointment with him for that evening. Reeling in rapture, he turned to Longxiang, "This is a tremendous help you've given me. What can I do for you in return?"

Longxiang said, "Quit talking trash! Since you have this date tonight, don't let anybody hang around here and mess things up."

Feng said, "I've only two roommates who left on a business tour long ago. A meal deliverer brings my food each day from my uncle's place. But he won't stay. He's not supposed to come here otherwise unless needed. For the rest of the day, I'm pretty much alone. Don't worry about that. However, I hope your young lady won't change her mind right before our meeting."

Longxiang said, "Please rest assured. You can count on me. I guarantee you a beautiful rendezvous." Longxiang then departed.

Feng was in a very excited state, anxiously awaiting the arrival of the evening.

Sumei couldn't sit still, either. She was like a child lighting firecrackers — she was delighted and at the same time a bit nervous. She wanted to talk to Longxiang once she returned about the arrangements for the meeting. At this point, Longxiang came back and said to her, "The young man was overjoyed to see your writing. I myself was better off when he thanked me on his knees."

Sumei said, "He is such an ardent lover, I feel embarrassed. How can I go to see him tonight?"

Longxiang said, "You have made a promise, so you cannot trifle with it."

Sumei said, "What kind of fuss will there be if I cancel the appointment?"

Longxiang replied, "You'll be alright in that case. But I promised him you would be there. If you don't keep the appointment, I will be thought of as a liar. He may die as a result and will haunt me in the infernal world."

Sumei said, "You only care about your after-life, but not about my marriage!"

Longxiang said, "Your marriage? Don't hesitate any more. Make up your mind and marry him. That's it."

Sumei said, "All right, I'll keep the appointment. But I'll wait until my brother and sister-in-law turn in."

The evening arrived before the conversation was over. A full moon was slowly unveiled against the clear night sky. Longxiang went to the master's living quarters and came back to Sumei after awhile, telling her, "The master and mistress finished their dinner and then I attended to them as they retired. Now we can leave. We'd better not light lamps. We'll sneak out through that small door around the corner of the building and find our way there in the moonlight. How about that?"

Sumei said, "Alright, you lead the way and I'll follow you in case someone is trailing us."

They then set out stealthily as planned to Feng's dwelling. Pointing forward, Longxiang said, "Do you see that lit-up room? That's his study." Sumei stopped in front of the room.

Meanwhile, Feng was nervously waiting as the evening dragged on. He paced in and out of the room a couple of times before he settled by the window for a breath. At the sound of footsteps close to his room, he shot out of the door.

"Here's my young lady, sir," Longxiang muttered. "Come on and greet her."

Seeing that Sumei was as beautiful as a goddess, Feng dropped to his knees and said, "It is good fortune that has brought you here to see me. I cannot repay your kindness even with my life!"

Sumei flushed with embarrassment. She propped him up and said, "I don't deserve this, sir. Please calm down."

Holding her sleeve, Feng said, "It's not appropriate to talk here, miss. Please come on in."

Once Sumei entered the room, Longxiang said from the outside, "I'm leaving, sister."

Sumei said, "No, please stick around, Longxiang."

Feng said, "I think you'd better let her go so she can get her business done at home."

Then Sumei said to her, "You may go home, Longxiang. Check to see if everything is alright and come back here."

Longxiang said, "Okay, please shut the door, Mr. Feng."

After Longxiang left, Feng shut the door. He turned around and swept her into his arms, saying, "It has almost killed me to have the burden of thinking about you when you were not in front of me, my sweet! Now that I have you with me I am willing to die with happiness!" So saying, he reached for her chest and started to undo her garment.

Sumei said, holding his hands, "Don't behave in such a rush, sir. Let's voice our positions clearly before we make love."

Feng said, "Well, we've made our affection toward each other crystal clear. At this moment, what else should we talk about?"

As he was saying this, Feng pushed her toward the bed. Sumei, resisted by firmly placing her feet on the floor. She said, "It is vitally important matter for our whole lives. How can I take it so lightly? Whatever you do, you should at least swear an oath saying you will ever remain faithful to me."

As he kept pushing, Feng mumbled, "If I turn faithless, let bad fortune strike me in the future!" He was so ardent and kept uttering words of endearment that Sumei started to waver in her resolve, submitting to his will.

As they were about to fall into bed, a roar came from outside the gate of the garden, followed by a thunderous knocking at the gate. Feng was taken by surprise as he was in a hurry to complete his business. He said, "That's weird! Who is knocking at the gate at this time of the night? I don't think they're coming for me. Don't worry, miss. The door is shut, and nothing will happen. Let's get into bed. No matter what they yell out there, we won't care."

Sumei was anxious, saying, "No, I'm afraid not. I'd better leave."

In desperation, Feng held her tightly in his arms, saying, "Do you really want to quit this? You're going to kill me!" Overcome with lust and with no thought of the consequences, Feng didn't care what was happening outside. He took off Sumei's underwear. As he was about to proceed the door of the gate gave way to a kick, due to the wear of many years' use, and let the people in. They marched, shouting, to Feng's study.

Feng realized they were coming to his room and said anxiously, "Strange! They sound as though they are the Dou brothers. When did they return? Why are they coming at this time? What lousy luck I have! What should I do?" He let go of Sumei, and said, "I'm going to prop something against the door. Please blow out the candle and keep quiet." Panic-stricken, Sumei blew out the light while tying up her pants. She trembled in the dark and held her breath.

Feng tiptoed to the door. He gently pulled over a bench and set it against the door. Then he came back to soothe Sumei. Then a voice rose along with pounding on the door. "Open up please, Brother Feng!" Feng asked, his utterance filled with trepidation, "Who, who, who is it?"

A softer voice answered, "I'm Dou Shangwen, your younger brother."

Then another one shouted loudly, "I'm your brother Dou Shangwu. We've not seen you for two months. We just got back today. It's a nice evening with a beautiful moon. Open up and come on out, please. Let's go and have a drink, alright?"

Feng answered, "I'm sorry, it's late. I've already turned in. I don't want to get up. Would you like to come back and have fun tomorrow?"

Elder Brother Dou said, "In fact our dwelling's not far from yours and we can have a nice chat there. I thought you might have bedded down, and would refuse to come if I sent someone for you. So we brothers have made a special trip to get you. Hurry up, please."

Feng said, "It's a rather late hour, and the wind is chilly. I may catch a cold once I leave the warm quilt. So I really don't want to rise. Please leave me alone. I appreciate your kindness very much."

Elder Brother Dou asked, "What's happening to you tonight, Brother? You used to like fooling around with friends." Younger Brother Dou chimed in, "Drinking in the moonlight is a great delight and one should jump for it even if he's in bed, without any fear of catching cold."

Feng said, "Tonight I'm really not in the mood. I would sorely appreciate it if you would show some understanding." Younger Brother Dou said, "Do you mean to send us back home tonight disappointed? If you don't want to get out of bed, we're going to knock the door open. Don't blame us for being rude then!"

Feng was truly desperate, figuring, "If they do storm in, what should I do?" He then muttered under his breath to Sumei, "If they force their way into the room, they will discover what we are doing. Please go and hide behind the bed over there, miss. I'm going to answer the door and send them away."

Sumei whispered in his ear, "Be quick. I want to get out of here. If things get messed up, what can we do?"

After she settled down in the dark, Feng removed the bench and opened the door. Seeing the two brothers waiting outside, he latched the door behind him before greeting them. Then he said, "I don't have a stove inside to keep warm, brothers. I'm sorry, we should go and talk for a while somewhere else."

The two brothers said, "What to talk about! We've got dinner ready at our place. Come on and let's go to our home. We can party and gamble until dawn."

Feng replied, "I'm sorry, but I am not in the mood to go. Please spare me."

The two brothers said, "But we're in high spirits now and don't care what you say. We'll pull you over there."

They started to drag Feng away. Their servants also came to their help, pushing and pulling. Cursing himself because of his bad luck, Feng had to swallow his disappointment and give in.

Meanwhile, Sumei, her heart pounding violently, shivered with fright at the back of the room, full of regret over what she had done. As the noise died away, she heaved a sigh of relief and stepped to the front of the bed. She adjusted her dress and stuck out her head to look out of the door. Nobody was outside. She decided, "It's rather late. I'd better go home instead of waiting for him here." She pulled at the door, not knowing it was latched from the outside. As she gave a harder pull, she put forth too much strength that two pieces of her long fingernail were chipped off. She wanted to go home but couldn't get out of the room. She wanted to call "Longxiang" but she knew the servant-girl was at home at that moment and wouldn't hear her call. Between a rock and a hard place, she was restless and desperate for help. It became well past midnight, and Sumei couldn't sit still. As she didn't see any sign of Feng her anxiety gave way to a rage. She said to herself, "What happened? Did Feng go on a drinking spree and forget about me completely?" Thinking better of this, she said, "He didn't want to go in the first place. It must be those rowdy friends of his who have held him up." Nervously, she fidgeted about. Gradually sleepiness began to creep upon her and she couldn't stop yawning. She would like to have lain down but the thought of being in someone else's bed assured her she would feel uncomfortable sleeping in it. Besides, with something on her mind, how could she fall asleep? Finally she sat down and wrote a poem:

Why should an affectionate lass
A fair night in solitude pass?
Seeing embroidered bedding, she's embarrassed
And lies down in gloomy mood, fully dressed.

A sudden gust of weird wind
Breaks her sweet dream.
She finds herself in a secluded fairyland
In the bright and dewy moonbeam.

As she finished her writing, dawn broke with roosters crowing.

Longxiang woke up, figuring, "My young lady and Feng must have had a good time by now. It's still early. I should go and bring her back. Otherwise, as people get up later on, she will be discovered and in trouble." She opened the corner door of the building and walked gently on the dew-seeped grass toward Feng's study. Seeing the door was latched, she was perplexed, saying to herself, "Who latched the door from outside? It's strange!"

Inside Sumei heard her murmur and said, "Is it Longxiang?"

Longxiang replied, "Yes, it's me, Sister."

Sumei said, "Come on and open the door."

On entering the room, Longxiang saw Sumei sitting there with her clothes on. She was surprised and asked, "Why did you wake up so early?"

Sumei said, "It's not that I woke up early. In fact I stayed awake the whole night!"

Longxiang asked, "Why did you not go to sleep? Where's Feng?"

With a sigh, Sumei said, "It turned out to be bad luck! Just as we started to talk, a batch of rowdy friends of his broke into the yard and wanted to take him with them to a party in the moonlight. He tried to hold the door shut, but they forced their way in. So he had to give up and left with them. He's not come back yet, and the door was latched. I couldn't get out, nor did I feel easy when I was seated. The night was hell for me! I'm glad you've come. Let's hurry and go back home."

Longxiang said, "How could this happen? But if you still want to see Feng, would you like to wait a little longer since it's time he should be coming back home?"

As tears welled up in her eyes, Sumei sighed and said, "Forget it. Let's go." They then went home.

Feng had been dragged away by the two thoughtless brothers, and had to drink with them for half a night. He couldn't rest for even one minute. He wanted to quit drinking, only to find the two brothers pressed him to have two more bowls of wine. Though sick of it, he pretended to be in a good mood for fear of revealing any of his inner thoughts. He hoped the party would be over soon. But the two brothers, young as they were, wouldn't stop once they had started. The more they drank, the more they enjoyed drinking. Feng felt helpless until the east put on a morning sheen. The two brothers were now entirely drunk and the party broke up. Feng had watched the amount of wine he consumed, so he was only a little intoxicated. After taking leave of the two brothers, he tottered unsteadily on his way back home. Once in his garden, he saw the door to his study was open.

He dashed to it, shouting, "Sister! Sister!" Not a soul was there! The thought of Sumei being there the night before and now not being able to see her infuriated him, and brought tears to his eyes as he slapped the table and benches in drunkenness. He swore at the brothers, saying, "Damn you, Dou brothers. You've ruined me! I've worked like hell to get a chance last night. But before I could make it, you screwed it up. I wonder how much effort I'll have to go through to obtain another chance. The problem is that she might have been frightened and will not come again. What can I do about it then?" He dropped into bed in frustration.

He slept until sunset. Then he hurried to the east side of the garden and saw that the windows of the building were shut. Then he went to the building and pushed at the corner door but it was locked. With no one around to turn to for inquiry, he strolled back home in dismay.

Earlier, Sumei had returned to her room, agitated. She said to Longxiang, "I should be careful in future and never behave like this again." Longxiang replied, "I doubt you'll be able to keep your word, Sister."

Sumei said, "You wait and see. I've resolved to keep my word."

Longxiang said, "But I think it's too late."

Sumei said, "How do you know it's too late?"

Longxiang answered, "Because you've lost your virginity."

Sumei said, "How do you know that happened? As soon as you turned around and left last night, those people broke in. We didn't have chance to exchange a few words. How could we have time to do anything like that?"

Longxiang said, "If that's true, he will not let go of this business easily. It will certainly drive him crazy. If he goes out of him mind because of this, should we be held responsible? I think you should make another try tonight."

Sumei said, "If I meet him tonight, you should stay outside the room, waiting and watching to make sure no one is around. Then everything would be alright."

A smile of scorn sprang onto Longxiang's face. "Why do you smile?" asked Sumei.

Longxiang replied, "I thought it was interesting, Sister. You said you had resolved to keep your word never to do this again."

As they were talking about another meeting for that night, a servant-girl of Sumei's brother emerged and said to them, "Old Lady Feng has come for a visit." Sumei's grandmother on her mother's side had married into the family of Feng and lived inside the Qiantang Gate. Though widowed, this grandmother led a relatively affluent life and ran a pawnshop in front her house. Knowing she was wealthy, the local women of low status, like matchmakers, fortune-tellers or nuns, all curried favor with her. She had had only one daughter, Sumei's mother, who had married into the family of Yang. Sumei's father and mother had both died when she was young so Sumei had to live with her brother and sister-in-law. That Sumei had not yet been betrothed weighed on the grandmother's mind. One day the old lady had discussed her granddaughter's marriage with a woman matchmaker. The matchmaker had said, "If you marry her as the sister of her brother, Master Yang, people will not show much respect or think highly of her. You must marry her as your granddaughter and you should also take the marital gifts at your home. That will draw the attention of privileged families." The grandmother had nodded her approval. Then she had decided her granddaughter was a grown-up and so should be back with her. She came in a sedan chair and had another empty sedan chair with her as she made her way to Sumei's place.

Sumei met her grandmother and listened to the old lady's account of her intentions. Sumei was somewhat startled and raised an excuse, saying, "If I'm going to your place, I'll join you in two days after getting things ready. Would you please go back home first?"

The grandmother said, "Do you have many affairs to order? I'll wait here and then we can leave together."

Longxiang threw in her words, "I think it's appropriate to pick a lucky day for the departure."

The grandmother said, "I did. Today's an auspicious date. Let's go today."

Sumei felt sorry for herself and whispered in Longxiang's ear, "What should we say to that gentleman?"

Longxiang replied, "As long as the grandmother is here waiting, you'll not be able to leave and meet him even for another two days. I think you should go with your grandmother now. I'll let him know about this and see to it that we'll have another chance later on."

Frustrated, Sumei left with her grandmother. That's why Feng didn't see her in the house that day. Later he was told that the old lady had taken her away. Sorely upset, he stamped his feet and let out sighs, wondering when she could come back there to meet him.

As he sat in his residence distressed, a servant of his uncle, Jin, came to take him back to his uncle's home for the forthcoming imperial examinations in the capital city. The servant, named Jin Wang told Feng, "Please pack all your book boxes and suitcases and come home. You won't be coming back here in future."

Without uttering a response, Feng contemplated, "This means that was the last possible meeting with Sumei. I lost the chance and didn't know we would have to part from each other so soon. Will there ever be another opportunity to see her in the future? She's so affectionate with me. How can I stop missing her?" As he looked across the wall to the east, tears began to roll down his cheeks. He left, downhearted. His uncle met him at his home with everything lined up for his journey to the capital, including his traveling expenses. After a send-off dinner, Feng departed in the company of Jin Wang.

One day when the idling uncle was at home, a woman came to sell pearls and jade. She talked to him about a girl of the family of Feng living inside the Qiantang Gate. She said the girl was beautiful and well-learned and not yet betrothed. The uncle asked for the signs of the girl's birth time and then had a fortune-teller compare those with the ones for his nephew. The fortune-teller told him, "Their fates match perfectly. Their marriage will be filled with honor and wealth and will last throughout their lives."

The uncle was overjoyed and sent a woman matchmaker to deliver the proposal. The grandmother of Sumei learned that Jin was a rich man in the area. She approved of the marriage at once and sent someone to inform her nephew, Yang. After that a favorable date was chosen for the formal ceremony of betrothal in a cheerful atmosphere.

Sumei, however, had her mind on Feng. She became quite upset at the news of her betrothal to the family of Jin. Unable to air her complaint, she wept incessantly in front of Longxiang. Longxiang tried to console her by saying, "Marriages are predestined. If you had been predestined to marry Feng, you two would have been a happy couple. You two had such a good chance of being together that night, but you didn't make it. This shows that you were not destined to be a match.

But it's good that nothing happened between you two that night. Otherwise, how could you handle the situation of being betrothed to another man today?"

Sumei said, "What are you talking about! Though I didn't physically combine with him that night, we had some intimate moments together. I have become his. I've been planning to wait in distress until the day when I can see him again. If they want to marry me to somebody else, in desperation as the deadline draws near, I will take my own life in order to show him my love in return. How can I reject him?"

Longxiang said, "You're very faithful to him, sister. But how can you see him again?"

Sumei said, "I think he's currently taking the imperial examinations in the capital city. If we're still linked by a predestined marriage, he'll come back home looking for me, after passing the examinations. By that time I'll leave my grandmother for home and meet him. He should have become honored and rich at that time. There will still be some possibility of reversing the marriage situation. If that opportunity fails me, I will see him for the last time and die in contentment."

Longxiang remarked, "What you said is correct, sister. You should be patient and wait. Take it easy and relax. Otherwise people may read your mind and begin to talk."

Meanwhile, Feng had arrived in the capital city. He came in at the top in the imperial examinations and won the title of *jinshi*. Now a famous scholar, he was appointed to be a judge in the city of Fuzhou in Fujian Province. He meditated, "I'll visit home on my way to my official post. To fulfill a marriage is as easy as turning my hand over. I'm glad that I have found my intended one. The title of *jinshi* is not worth mentioning."

As he was about to pack and leave, a servant sent by his uncle arrived with the message, "Your betrothal to a young lady has been concluded at home. We welcome you back home to get married."

Astonished, Feng asked, "What are you saying? What a lady am I betrothed to?"

The servant answered, "It's a woman from the family of Feng inside Qiantang Gate. It's said she's beautiful and well-learned." Feng scowled and said, "My uncle is mindless! Did he check as to my intentions? Why did he handle my betrothal in such a hurry?"

The servant and Jin Wang, Feng's traveling companion, were confused. They said, "Old master did this out of good motivations. Why are you unhappy about this marriage arrangement?"

Feng said, "You know nothing about this. Leave the matter with me." Then a cloud of dismay arose to hang over his mind.

Feng decided to leave for home and see what would happen, low-spirited as he was. As he sent the servant back to inform the uncle of his forthcoming arrival, he took leave of the capital city and departed on the journey.

On learning that his nephew was on his way home, Jin decided on an auspicious date for the nuptial. He went to the house of Feng and presented the family with a generous gift, including gowns and hairpins. He added one more gift, a white jade paperweight of a toad. The paperweight of the toad originally came in pairs. But he had given one of them to his nephew. Now he was giving the other, in view of making a perfect gift for the new couple. He asked the matchmaker to deliver the gift to the Feng family and ant told them, "The young gentleman of the Jin family has succeeded in passing the imperial examinations. He's on his way home for the marriage." The Sumei's grandmother was very happy, and so, too, were relatives and friends who remarked in praise, "Sumei is good-looking and she has such good luck as well." Congratulations kept coming in. But Sumei was heavy-hearted and shut herself up in the room, letting out one sigh after another in discouragement.

Longxiang came over and said to her, "Did you see the gifts they sent here, sister?"

Sumei said, "No, I'm not in the mood."

Longxiang said, "It's such coincidence, you know. I heard the gentleman who won the title of *jinshi* and is going to marry you is the nephew of the family of Jin. I remember Feng once talked about his uncle who has the family name of Jin. I wonder whether this gentleman is Feng!"

Sumei said, "How could that happen?"

Longxiang replied, "But I saw among the gifts something like your paperweight. It's a jade paperweight of toad, exactly the same as the one Feng gave you. If they don't come from the same family, how could the two jade toad paperweights happen to be so similar?"

Sumei said, "Where's that jade toad paperweight? Could you bring it to me?"

Longxiang said, "Yes, sister. I thought there must be a story about the toad. So I told them you wanted to look at it as an excuse and brought it here."

She took it out of her sleeve. Sumei took it and looked closely at it. It did look familiar. Then she untied the one she wore from her arm and put the two together. Of exactly the same design, they matched perfectly as a pair. Tears began to drop as she recalled her past relations with Feng. She said, "If it's true, our predestined marriage bond has not been cut off! As if a shattered mirror can be patched again and a split pair of hairpins can also come together. But I don't understand why they sent these gifts in the name of Jin instead of Feng. We should find out what's happened. I just want to make sure he's the right person."

Longxiang asked, "What will you do if he's the right man and what if he's not?"

Sumei said, "If he's the one, I will be very happy, of course. If it's another man, I'll hang myself right before the wedding, as I told you before."

Longxiang then said, "I've an idea."

"Tell me about it," Sumei urged her.

Longxiang said, "On the day of the wedding, the matchmaker will go to the man's family with the message of the bride's readiness to leave home. I will go there with her, posing as her daughter. I will make sure the man is the right person. Then I'll come back to let you know."

Sumei said, "That's a good idea. I hope there's no mistake. It will be the happiest thing in my life."

Longxiang said, "I hope so, too. It seems it is he." They settled on Longxiang's plan.

Feng arrived at Jin's home a couple of days later. On the day for the wedding that Jin had chosen, Sumei's grandmother sent the matchmaker to inform the bridegroom's family of the bride's coming. Longxiang caught up with the matchmaker as she made her way and said to her, "I want to go with you to have a look at the bridegroom. If someone is curious about it, please say I'm your daughter coming with you."

The matchmaker replied, "I certainly do not deserve the good fortune of having you as my daughter. Just come with me. Don't worry about it. By the way, I've a question to ask you, Sister."

Longxiang asked, "What question?"

The matchmaker said, "Your young lady's going to get married and become a lady. This is the happiest thing that could happen to her. But why there is no sign of happiness on her face? She's murmuring all the time. She seems unhappy. What's happened to her?"

Longxiang said, "You've no idea. She made up her mind at an early age to have a perfect husband. But now her grandmother made this choice of marriage for her without consulting her. She doesn't know if the bridegroom is good. For this she's worried, that's why she's not happy."

The matchmaker said, "The bridegroom is a government official. Why is she worried about him?"

Longxiang replied, "To live together, he should be a good husband. What's so good about being a government official? By the way, do you know his family name, madam?"

The matchmaker said, "Of course, it's Jin, I know definitely."

Longxiang said, "I heard this nephew of Jin originally did not have Jin as his family name. Do you know anything about that?"

The matchmaker replied, "I know he's Jin's nephew. People call him Master Jin. But his original family name is an uncommon one and I don't remember it. I've forgotten it."

Longxiang asked, "Is it Feng?"

Nodding her head, the matchmaker replied, "Yes, it is that strange name." Almost assured that the bridegroom was that scholar, Longxiang was secretly delighted.

As they reached the house of Jin, Longxiang said to the matchmaker, "Please go inside first, Madam. I'll stick around here outside for a little while."

The matchmaker said, "Alright." She entered the room and talked to Feng about the wedding. Meanwhile Longxiang saw, from outside, that it was none other than Feng. She jumped for joy, saying, "Wonderful! Wonderful!"

She purposely showed her face at the window to give him a full view of herself. Feng, on noticing her, asked the matchmaker, "Is that girl with you?"

The matchmaker answered, "Yes, sir. She's my daughter."

Suspecting the girl he saw was Longxiang, Feng ask the matchmaker go in and have some tea and food and he walked out of the room, only to see that it was indeed Longxiang. He asked her, "Why are you here? Where's your sister?"

Longxiang answered, "Why are you still concerned about her? Go and get ready for your wedding."

Feng responded, "Sister Longxiang, let Heaven strike me dead if I've ever stopped thinking about her since we were scattered that other day! But I didn't know we would be separated for so long and there was no way of getting contact with her. Later I was lucky to win the title of *jinshi* in the capital city. As I was about to leave for home, my uncle sent me a message about his arrangement for this marriage of me to the family of Feng. At this point, I could do nothing but accept it. Do you think I would do this of my own free will?"

Longxiang purposefully taunted him, saying, "It's too late to talk about that. But our young lady's love has gone in vain. She's been sad and wept all the time."

Wiping tears from his face, Feng said, "Let me get today's business over with, and then I'll make another appointment with your lady and talk to her in detail. I will then die content. But where's she now? Did she get a chance to go back home?"

Intending to carry the fun further, Longxiang said, "She's betrothed, too."

Feng asked, "To which family?"

Longxiang replied, "It's said that it's a Jin family in town. Someone in that family just won the title of *jinshi*."

Feng said, "You're talking nonsense! There couldn't be another *jinshi* with a family name Jin in town. I'm the only one, no one else."

Longxiang asked, "At what time did you adopt the name of Jin?"

Feng said, "That is my uncle's family name. My family name was listed as Jin, not Feng, on the list of winners in the examinations."

With a grin, Longxiang said, "This is weird. It's caused a great deal of anxiety for us!"

Feng said, "Therefore, I'm going to marry your lady. Is that correct? But why did she use the family name of Feng?"

Longxiang said, "Our young lady is the granddaughter of the Feng's family. We let her be known in public as the daughter of that family in spite of her family name. In fact, she is a Yang."

Feng said, "After that day of separation, I learned from your neighbor she had been taken to her grandmother's home. Was it the

Feng's family?"

Longxiang said, "Exactly!"

"I can't believe this!" Feng said. "I wonder if you've made up the story to tease me since you knew I would marry somebody else?"

Longxiang took out the two jade paperweights from her sleeve and said, "Look, here are two paperweights that make up a pair. One of them is the one you gave our lady as a gift. The other one is an extra piece your family added to the betrothal gifts. Look at them. Do you still have doubts?"

Feng said, "Wow, I just can't believe what's happened. This is the happiest thing that's happened to me in my life!"

Longxiang said, "You're joyful, sir. But our lady is still sobbing at home."

Feng said, "If I were not the bridegroom, what would she do?"

Longxiang said, "Well, after she saw the jade paperweight and heard the bridegroom was from the Jin's family, she had an inkling, too. She sent me here to check. She said if it was not you, she would commit suicide. I'm going to hurry back to let her know. After washing and making-up, she'll be ready to see you. She'll be in heaven, too."

Feng then said, "One more thing. She's been so anxious that she may think you're calming her down with a story and it won't set her mind at ease. Take this ring with you and show it to her. It's the one she gave me. She'll believe what you say, all right?"

Longxiang said, "That's a good idea, sir." Feng slid the ring off his finger and handed it to her. As Longxiang left, he told the band of musicians to get ready and had dinner set up. Soon he would be leaving to bring his bride home.

Longxiang ran back to tell Sumei, "It is he, sister! It is he!"

Sumei said, "Are you sure?"

Longxiang said, "If you don't believe me, look at this ring!" As she said this, she handed the ring to Sumei and told her, "He slid it from his finger in front of me and asked me to bring it to you as proof of his identity."

Sumei smiled and said, "It's incredible! Tell me what he said to you."

Longxiang said, "He said he had never stopped thinking about you since you were separated from one another that day. After he was appointed a government official, he intended to fulfill his union with you. But his uncle arranged his marriage without consulting him. He didn't know that he would marry you and was rather upset about it."

Sumei said, "Since he didn't know who the bride was, what did he say he would do after the marriage?"

Longxiang replied, "He said he would manage to see you once after the marriage to let you know about his love for you. Then he could die without regrets. As he said this, tears came down from his cheeks. I saw he was sincere and so I told him the truth. He was overjoyed!"

Then Sumei said, "But he didn't know I had made up my mind to marry him and would take my life if I couldn't do so. He might simply believe I had slighted my love and given myself to somebody else. What can I do?"

Longxiang said, "I told him everything about your intentions and your saying that if the bridegroom was somebody else, you would die on the day of wedding. He became very worried. He feared that when I came back to tell you the truth, you might be doubtful, thinking I made up the story in order to get you into the sedan chair for the marriage. So he gave me this ring of his as verification."

Sumei asked, "How did he carry the ring?"

Longxiang said, "He took the ring from his finger. It shows he indeed has you on his mind." Now Sumei was relieved.

Shortly thereafter, music was played and drums beaten, while the bridegroom emerged dressed in full regalia to get his bride. Sumei stepped into the sedan chair, followed by her grandmother in a second one. Jin San met them at his home and then the wedding banquet began. The newlyweds entered their bedroom after the feast. Needless to say, the new couple was a perfect pair.

The next day witnessed a visit by Sumei's brother and sister-in-law and the two brothers of the Dou's with their congratulations. The sight of the Dou brothers brought the incident of the earlier night to the mind of Feng, who let go a smile. He thought, "Fortunately our marriage is a predestined one, so we've at last united. Otherwise, that night's experience would have been a disaster for me!" Reluctant to give voice to his inner thoughts, he was content with his secret joy. Later in their life, he occasionally talked with Sumei about that experience of fright that they still found hard to live down.

In retrospect, one finds the world is full of amusing occurrences. If Feng and Sumei had been doomed to be strangers to one another throughout life, they would have had their respective uneventful life scenarios. Since they were to become husband and wife, why should they have experienced the setback in the study? Suppose the Dou brothers had come a moment later and Feng would have achieved his end! On the other hand, if Sumei had not gone to her grandmother's home, she would have been able to have a date with Feng the next day. But all the happenings took place punctually then and there to hinder them! Later on as neither of them were prepared for the union, they became husband and wife due to a betrothal that seemed to be unwanted to both of them. All these were deliberately schemed by Heaven!

Tale 7

Five Tigers Cunningly Plot a Family Dispute;
Big Brother Mo Wisely Shatters a Sinister Scheme

During the reign of Shaoxing [1131-1163] in the Song Dynasty, a wealthy old man by the name of Mo, lived Wuxing [present-day Wuxing County, Zhejiang Province]. He and his wife had two sons and three grandsons. Brought up as the prodigal son of rich stock, Mo was naturally lascivious. Since his youth he had been obsessed with the idea of obtaining concubines and buying girl servants for himself. Due to his affluent family background, his adulthood provided him with the financial ability to afford many concubines and to maintain a sizable corps of girls. His wild wishes went uncurbed except for the fact that he had an overbearing and shrewish wife. Do you think she could go easy on her husband's lustfulness when he was young? Now as Mo grew old and raised his sons and grandsons, he simply gave up carrying on love affairs.

At close to seventy years of age, Mo wanted a girl servant to give him a massage before bedtime every night. His wife cared little about her husband's request, knowing that her husband was old, and the assigned eighteen-year-old girl servant, called Shuang He, who used to serving the wife, was compliant and virtuous. But as old as Mo was, his sexual desires were still active. He seized this opportunity to satisfy his lust by fondling Shuang He as she rubbed his back and limbs. Accepting these sexual advances with no complaints and recognizing her subordinate status, Shuang He even enjoyed being the target of his lechery, as she had reached puberty and felt urges. As their two states of mind chimed perfectly, they made love. There is a song that describes such old boys carrying on such secret love affairs:

> *The old man is as lustful as in his youthful days;*
> *He pesters any young lady who comes his way.*
> *But, alas! love-making gives him away —*
> *He rubs his wrinkled face against chubby cheeks*
> *And presses his white beard on ruby lips.*
> *The worst of all, when combat draws near*
> *He is too weak to raise his spear.*

After a few more sessions of love-making, their intimate relations gradually became known. But nobody in the family uttered a word of this in front of the mistress, due to her shrewishness, and even the sons and sisters-in-law hid the disgrace for the old master. However, things evolved against their wishes. The girl gradually grew thick eyebrows, swollen breasts and a swelling belly. She also kept throwing up. At first she thought she was sick. But after something started wriggling inside her, she knew she was expecting.

"For shame!" she said to the old master in a worried manner. "You have made me pregnant and you'll be embarrassed because of this. Your wife is jealous. I doubt she'll let it go once she finds out. I'll fall to my doom!" As she said this, tears streamed down her cheeks.

The old master tried to calm her down. "Don't worry," he said. "I know how to deal with her." But he thought to himself, there's no joking about this. I enjoyed myself at that time with no thought of the consequences of making her pregnant. If my wife learns about it, she'll definitely abuse the girl. The girl may be killed. But even if she survives, I'll be in disgrace, the oldest of a family with grandsons, who has committed this shameful act and turned the family upside down. I'd better marry the girl off now and let her give birth to a baby in somebody else's home. That'll help me for the time being. After thus making up his mind, he talked to Shuang He about the idea. Shuang He readily agreed, desiring to leave the bitchy mistress and to live with a young husband. What else could she hope for? She felt a little easier.

So Mo took the opportunity to say something to his wife against Shuang He, suggesting that they sell her to somebody. The mistress had thought about dispensing with the girl, too, feeling uncomfortable with the girl's attractive figure and mature posture. On the basis of a matchmaker's advice, Shuang He was married to Zhu San, a man in his late twenties who was honest and handsome. He sold starch noodles by Flower Chamber Bridge in the town. A capable husband and a good-looking wife, they were a well-matched couple. Intending to get the girl out of sight, Mo didn't haggle over the betrothal gifts from the bridegroom, while Zhu San was blissful, taking this marriage as a good deal, although he was ignorant of his bride's pregnancy.

But by and by things began revealing themselves. So Shuang He told her husband, "I've gotten this baby by my old master. To hide our affair from the mistress, he married me to you and promised to take care of the child throughout its life. Please be sure not to breathe a word about it so as not to incur trouble. We may depend upon him in future for financial assistance. Trust me — I'll behave and live with you for the rest of my life."

A businessman, Zhu San hankered only after petty profits and cared nothing else. Besides, he was familiar with the fact that almost no young lady who had worked as a serving girl for a wealthy family came out of it still a virgin. Furthermore, the initial joy marriage offered so overwhelmed him that he swallowed this humiliation and dropped the matter.

Five months after their marriage, a baby boy was born. Shuang He sent a secret message to Master Mo about her birth. Since the girl had been married off under pressure, the old master was concerned about her. Knowing the baby boy was his son, he sent two shoulder-poles of rice and several strings of coins in secret to Shuang He's place as a token of his financial support for the boy. Later, a steady flow of jewelry and clothing for the mother and son went to the starch-noodle seller's family. Owing on his wife, Zhu San became better off.

As the boy grew up, Mo kept secretly providing him with all living necessities. But the old man had to be content with keeping his blood ties with the boy from the public. The boy adopted Zhu San's family name and, later, at the age of about ten, became an assistant in his business in the market. However, gossip never failed to circulate and his origin was something known to the neighbors. Even Mo's sons and daughters-in-law got the general idea that the old master was raising a bastard outside of his house. But they never broached the subject, acting as if nothing had happened. Meanwhile the mistress also became suspicious. But the boy was not around the family and no one ventured to talk to her about the issue. So she had to let the matter take its own course. Before long, Mo died a sudden death because of disease. The whole family became busy with funeral arrangements.

There was a group of ruffians living in the town. They were good-for-nothings who set their minds to prying into others' business and living on gains obtained by taking advantage of others. Among them were Song Li, nicknamed Iron-piercing Bug, Zhang Chao, nicknamed Hamster, Niu San, nicknamed Oblique-eyed Tiger, Zhou Bing, nicknamed Learned Judge in Hell, Tramp Wang, nicknamed Night-owl, and a few others without real names, totaling about ten.

All day long they did nothing but snoop into other people's affairs and inquire about someone's privacy, stirring up trouble and teaming up for their personal gain. The five ring-leaders had gone to the temple of Marshal Zhao.* There they had sworn an oath of alliance by smearing the blood of a sacrifice. Most of them took Zhao as their family name to show their loyalty. So they called themselves the Five Tigers of the Family Zhao. They went wherever there was a sign of making a profit, according to clues provided by any one of them. They worked in collaboration and shared the gains. The fact that Mo was the true father of the son of the starch-noodle seller Zhu San was no news to these racketeers. Now, having learned that Mo had died, they gathered in consultation.

"Here's a big deal for us!" one of them said. "That old guy left behind him a huge legacy. The mistress had only two sons to inherit that wealth of two-hundred thousand or three-hundred thousand strings of coins. Let's go to Zhu San and talk him into seizing a share of the legacy for his son, tens of thousands at least. We should get paid for our help and then be a lot better off than we are now. If he is not successful in bargaining with the family, let him sue them and we'll do our best to help him. We can rest assured that we will come by some money eventually, a lot more than what we make by staying idle and doing nothing every day."

They all jumped with joy at the idea. "Wonderful! Wonderful!"

Iron-piercing Bug said, "Let's first go and see what that bitch of his thinks about it. We'll wheedle her into this business."

The rest said in chorus, "Exactly." They then left for Zhu San's place.

These five men used to be regular customers of Zhu San, often picking up snacks of starch noodles from his stall as they waited daily by the entrance to the local government office. Spotting the five of

---

*Marshal Zhao, by the name of Zhao Gongming, is the legendary god of wealth.

them making their way toward his store, Zhu San greeted them with a hand-cupped salute, asking, "What instructions will you give me?"

Oblique-eyed Tiger replied, "Please get your wife out here. I've something to inform her."

Zhu San asked, "What's up, sir?"

Night-owl butted in, "Her ex-master died."

Rushing out of the room, Shuang He broke into tears. "I overheard people talking about his death just a little while ago," she said, "I couldn't believe it. Now that you gentlemen are reporting the same thing, I'm convinced." Weeping, she turned to her husband, "Our pivotal source of livelihood is gone. We're going to suffer."

Hamster, however, replied, "What are you talking about? It is the beginning of your prosperous life!"

The group said in unison, "That's right. We brothers are bringing you a fortune today."

Taken aback, the couple asked, "How?"

Iron-piercing Bug then said, "Your son is a descendant of Mo. The old guy left a huge legacy, including a large block of real estate. Your son legally deserves a portion of it. Why not go there and claim your part? If they turn you down, take them to court. You may have to spend a certain sum, but just hang on. If your son still can't make it, ask the court to do a blood test* to prove his relationship. They can't beat that!"

The couple replied, "Well, that's true and we understand. The problem is that once we get involved with the court, it will not be for us to wind up the matter. An old saying goes, 'It's sagacious for the poor to shun facing the rich in conflict.' A lawsuit calls for a huge amount of money. How can we compete with Mo's family in this regard? Eventually we may go broke. That would be something we

---

*An ancient legal-medical examination based on a belief that the blood of a direct-line descendent would seep into his or her parent's bone if it was dropped on it, while the blood of a non-direct descendent would not.

would hate to see. In addition, people like us depend on labor for a living. We can't stop working even for one day. How can we take energy and time out to do things like that?"

Iron-piercing Bug said, "Yes, you need to think about that. You will need money and manpower for a lawsuit. Let's make a deal. We brothers will do our best to work for you in dealing with the court. The lawsuit costs are a problem. But you have to venture a small amount of capital if want to make a huge profit. So we five will each offer one hundred *liang* of silver for you to use. You just write us a receipt for the loan of one thousand *liang* of silver with 100% interest. Later on, after you win the court case and obtain the property, you'll simply return the loan to us with the payment of the interest, which is fairly reasonable. In terms of a reward for our help, you two may decide on whatever you consider appropriate to give us. Since it'll be an unexpected windfall, I'm sure you will be quite generous about the matter by that time."

Zhu San and his wife agreed to the proposal, saying, "Certainly, we would appreciate it very much, gentlemen. But what we should do to begin with?"

Iron-piercing Bug responded, "Don't worry about that. We'll take care of everything. Just write us a receipt for the loan and the matter is decided."

Zhu San did as he was told. A loan receipt was written with his signature on it. His son was also required to sign it. The men then took the receipt, saying, "We're taking off now. We'll scrape the loan together today and be back tomorrow to get down to business."

Seeing them off, the couple said, "We'll be counting on you, gentlemen."

Then Shuang He said to her husband, "I wonder whether they're serious about what they said. Can we act according to their plan?"

Zhu San answered, "Well, it won't cost us a single coin. We'll just wait and see what they do. Just do what seems to be practical. Who can tell we're not going to benefit. But they'll pay for what's needed and we'll reap whatever gain this lawsuit brings. What else can we expect as a deal?"

"But I don't think we should have written them a loan receipt," Shuang He said.

"We're an impoverished family of three," Zhu San replied, "and all our property doesn't amount to anything. What could they do to us with that receipt of a loan, if we fail in the court case? But if we obtain the property as expected, we won't mind giving them a certain sum as a reward. Besides, would they have lent us the money without a receipt? With something tangible in hand, they'll be assured and will go all out to work for us."

"Why did they ask our little boy to sign on it, too?" asked Shuang He.

Zhu San said, "Why not? The whole business is for the boy. It doesn't matter anyway. We'll just wait and see how they are going to work it out."

After the five men left the Zhus they said to one another, laughing, "We've aroused their fantasies for riches! Now since we told such a lie, where can we go to rake up that amount of money?" They had a discussion.

"Do you think we meant what we said and will work for their gain at our expense?" Iron-piercing Bug replied. "No! It will just be a piece of cake for me to handle. Look. It'll cost us nothing."

The rest said, "Tell us what's on your mind."

Iron-piercing Bug explained, "I only need a bolt of coarse sack-cloth to make a suit of mourning apparel. Let that lad of theirs wear it and go to attend the funeral rites at the Mo's home as a son of the dead master. That'll certainly stir up a dispute between the mother and her sons. Then our only expense will be just a piece of paper on which we'll file the form for a lawsuit. That'll be our capital of the five hundred *liang* of silver."

The other four cheered. "Bravo!" they shouted. "Don't tarry. Please go and get it right now!"

Iron-piercing Bug left. He managed to find a piece of coarse sack-cloth and took it to a tailor, who made a suit of mourning apparel. With this in hand, Iron-piercing Bug said, "Here's our capital." The five men then made their way to Zhu San's home.

Zhu San and his wife greeted them, asking, "What are you going to do?"

Iron-piercing Bug said, "Bring your son out. I've got something for him to do."

Shuang He brought the boy out and said to him, "Here are a few uncles who will help you claim your share of property from your father's legacy. Please do what you're told."

Young and innocent as he was, the boy said, "Since he was my father, I deserve part of his property. But I'm a little boy. I don't know what to say to get it."

Iron-piercing Bug replied, "You don't need to say anything. You simply wear this suit of mourning apparel and follow us to the Mo's home. You'll walk directly into the mourning hall. In front of the casket, you'll break into crying and then make four kowtows. After that, you'll turn around and get out of there. Don't say anything if you're spoken to. Once you get outside, we'll be waiting for you in the teahouse to the left of their home. This should be an easy thing for you to do."

Zhu San asked, "What's the point of his doing this?"

The others replied, "This is meant to send a message to them. After he gets home, your son will go to court the next day and present the lawsuit. We'll make arrangements to assist him. He's so young that the government officials will be compassionate. They won't be hard to him. In addition, he has the solid ground that he is related to the old master by blood ties. Just do what we've said. You can be assured of achieving your share of the fortune."

Zhu San turned to his wife, "I think what they've said is thoughtful and well planned. Let our son do as they've arranged. There won't be any problem."

The little boy agreed, saying, "I'll do it. I really want to see the picture of my father, mourn him and pay my homage to him."

Shuang He tearfully replied, "You're right, my clever boy."

Zhu San said, "I think I should stay away. If you gentlemen go with him, nothing will go wrong. So I'll leave the boy with you. I'll go to the market and attend to my business. In the evening when I get back, I should be able to hear what happened from you."

As Zhu San left, the five men and the little boy made their way to the house of the Mos. They went into a teahouse nearby and ordered some tea. Then the men told the boy, "See that gate hung with a mourning board and strips of satin? That's your old man's home. Go inside and do as we told you." They then helped him to put on the mourning apparel.

With nothing else but their words in mind, the boy strode through the gate and straight into the mourning hall. He fell on his knees in front of the altar table and started crying, as any boy of his age would naturally behave in such a situation. His cries aroused attention throughout the house. The family members, thinking another mourner must have arrived, gathered in the mourning hall. In front of them was the little boy dressed as a son in mourning, a boy who kept calling out, "My father! My father!" Astonished, the family members couldn't make head or tail of the sight. "What does this mean?" they asked each other.

The sudden commotion of the boy's mourning also caught the attention of the mistress. Rage immediately rose inside her. Vicious as she was, she shouted, "What's brought this wildcat here, making such weird howls!"

It was Big Brother who deciphered the puzzle. He said to his mother, "Don't behave rashly, please. This is not something we can trifle with. I think someone is trying to take advantage of my father's death in order to prey on us. If we fall into the trap, our family fortune will be further split. Only if you do as I arrange will a calamity be avoided." His words curbed the mistress's fury, and her yells dropped to silence. She calmly observed the boy.

Out there in the mourning hall, the boy was performing four kowtows with tears in his eyes. As he pulled himself onto his feet to leave, Big Brother rushed out and held him, saying, "I think you're the son of Zhu that sells starch noodles by the Flower Chamber Bridge. Is that correct?"

The boy answered, "Exactly."

Big Brother then said, "Since you've come to claim your blood relation to your father, it's only natural for you to also meet your mother. Come with me."

He pulled the boy behind the mourning drapes and, pointing to the mistress, said to him, "Here's your own mother. Come on and show your reverence to her." The unprepared mistress, in compliance, hurriedly received the boy's reverence. Then Big Brother pointed to himself and said, "I'm your elder brother. You must also do obeisance to me." After that he let the boy make further kowtows to his second elder brother and two sisters-in-law in sequence. Finally, he introduced the boy to his two sons and one son from his younger brother, the three of them standing in a row as required, by saying, "These are your nephews. You should receive their reverence."

The formalities now over, the boy turned around and began to walk toward the door again. But Big Brother said, "Where are you going, boy? Now you're my brother. Our father is dead and you should stay here to go through the mourning ceremony with us. Here's your home. Where are you heading?"

He then led the boy into his room and said to his wife, "Please comb the hair for your younger brother-in-law. Strip off his untidy clothes and dress him in some neat ones. From now on he's one of us."

The kindness Big Brother displayed delighted the boy. Yet he felt a little uneasy and wanted to leave, since what he saw around him were only strange faces and he was not sure of his real mother's intention. Big Brother read his mind and sent for Shuang He with the words, "I've something important to talk over with you."

Upon receiving this message, Shuang He knew the matter related to her son. As she had originally planned to make a trip of mourning to the Mo's home, she slipped into a set of mourning attire and raced there. In the mourning hall, she cried and kowtowed. Then Big Brother said to her, "Your son came this morning and we identified each other as brothers. He'll stay with us to observe the period of mourning for our father. Later he'll receive his share of the property. Don't worry about that. Besides, we'll continue to send you the amount of food and clothing each month that you received in the past from my father. Nothing will change in that regard because of your son's ties with us. However, please don't come here unless it is absolutely necessary. You have a husband. It's wise not to raise gossip and disgrace your son. From now on, your son belongs to our family and he'll adopt the family name of Mo. He won't go to your house anymore. Please talk to your son briefly and then leave."

Shuang He was overjoyed and said, "I'm very pleased that you've made such arrangements in agreement with the intentions of the late master. I'll burn incense and light candles to express my profound gratitude." Then she went inside to meet the mistress and the two sisters-in-law and expressed her thanks to them. The mistress had to hold back her resentment, and things went smoothly.

Before leaving, Shuang He said to her son, "Stay here and behave yourself on good terms with the mistress, brothers and sisters-in-law. Now you're well placed here, and I'm at ease. On the basis of your big brother's suggestion, I won't come to see you very often. You should stay here for the mourning period of forty-nine days and then come over to see us." The meeting with his mother and his mother's words soothed the boy. Shuang He left joyously to tell her husband about what had transpired.

In the meantime, the Five Tigers waited in the teahouse ready to file the lawsuit once the boy got away from the Mo family. They had already composed a written statement for the law-suit. Hours passed and the boy didn't emerge. As afternoon yielded to evening, there was still no sign of him. They became suspicious.

"Did we somehow miss seeing him while we were talking to each other so that he went straight back home?" one of them asked.

Another rushed to Zhu San's place and found out that, "The boy's not back home yet but his mother was summoned to the Mo's family." As this word reached the men, confusion turned to agitation, and they became restless as if they were ants jumping on a hot pan.

Then another one went to check with the Zhu family and brought back the word, "Shuang He's back home, very happy. She said, 'My son's been kept there as one of their family members'." This news exploded in their minds like a few buckets of icy water dumped on flames. It sent shudders down their arms.

"Damn! Such a stupid family we have to deal with!" they shouted. "Do we really want to see that little son of bitch make off with the gain after we've put in so much work?"

However, Iron-piercing Bug said, "Hold on now! We surely won't let him off with the gain. Nor shall we willingly give up."

The rest asked, "What can we do at this point?"

Iron-piercing Bug said, "We arrived at an agreement with them that once they obtain the property, they must give us a thousand *liang* of silver as payment. I've the receipt with me. It's in Zhu San's handwriting."

The rest said, "But they've given up the court case and we didn't do anything for them in terms of help. It's not appropriate to claim that payment from Zhu San. Even if we decide to do so, we can't expect to get anything of him because he's too poor."

Iron-piercing Bug said, "Well, I had the boy sign the receipt, too. Now we have to count on whoever offers a butt of attack. Let's wait for a few days and ask the boy to pay us. If he rejects us, we'll sue him. He's a rich boy now. I'm sure he will fear going to court against us. He'll send somebody to us to resolve the dispute and redeem the receipt. Now do you think we've made a futile effort?"

The rest roared, "A terrific idea! No wonder you're called Iron-piercing Bug. What a smart person you are!"

Iron-piercing Bug added, "One more thing. We should take our time. First, we got this receipt only a few days ago. If we sue him now, the court will be suspicious. Second, the Mo's family just admitted his kinship and it'll take some time before the division of property takes place among the brothers. So the boy's not yet in a position to pay us. That can only be done in half a year or more."

The group said, "Exactly. Hang onto the receipt. Let's be patient." Then they scattered.

At that moment, the mistress, still nursing her resentment, complained to her eldest son, Big Brother, saying, "Why did you so readily identify with that son of bitch?"

The son answered, "We're a well-known wealthy family. How can we avoid being the target of envy after the death of my father? The little boy is indeed a son by my father. If we refuse to recognize his kinship, some rascals will take him as a pawn and launch an endless course of lawsuits against us. By then the government officials would take advantage of the situation to blackmail us. Relatives and friends would not let us go without being skinned. Besides, the court would be another source of drainage on our wealth in terms of bribery. We can't beat that. Who knows what kind of wretched state our family might end up in! Actually the dispute would eventually be traced back to its origin and we would not be able to avoid giving up a share of our property to the boy. Given that possibility, why should we let some outsiders benefit? That's why I decided to accept the boy into our home, smashing those people's wild dreams. Don't you agree?" His explanation convinced his mother and nothing more was said in the family about the issue.

Peace continued for a time and then a mob broke in one day, demanding to see the third little master. These men were stopped by an inquiry as to their business. A yell broke out among them: "We want to talk to Zhu San's step-son!"

The unpleasant remark brought out Big Brother as the five ringleaders swaggered into the hall, greeting him and asking, "Is your little brother in?"

Big Brother said, "Yes, he's at home, gentlemen. May I know what your business is?"

The five men said, "He owes us some money and we're coming to get it."

Big Brother said, "Sorry, I know nothing of it. I'll bring him out."

Big Brother then went inside and told this to his little brother. The boy emerged, confused, only to find the Five Tigers waiting there. His greeting to them met with the men's shouts, "What have you been doing, Little Master? We sent you here some time ago. Now you're rich and we are wondering whether you still remember us?"

The boy said, "The family asked me to stay here. I was held up and couldn't go home."

The five men said, "But since you're rich now, it's time for you to pay back to us at one thousand *liang* of silver."

"Sorry," the boy replied, " I've no knowledge about that money."

The five men said, "That amount was loaned to your step-father, Zhu San. But it was for you and the receipt bears your signature as well."

The boy said, "Yes, I know we talked about the suing expenses that day. So we wrote a loan receipt to you. But we gave up the idea of going through the lawsuit and didn't use any of the loan. Why do I owe you money?"

The men flared up "We've the receipt with us," they said. "Are you going to disown it?" As Big Brother heard this cry and came out, the Five Tigers said him, "Your little brother got a loan of one thousand *liang* of silver from us at Zhu San's place. But he's repudiating it now."

Big Brother said, "He's still a little kid. I don't see why he would have borrowed such a huge sum?"

The boy said to his brother, "Don't believe what they are saying, Big Brother."

The Five Tigers replied, "All right. We've the receipt. Let's go to court." And out they stalked.

The Big Brother then turned to the boy, "What's this all about?"

The boy replied, "At first they urged my mother to go to court. She said we had no money. Then they said, 'Just write a receipt. We'll give you the loan.' Then they led me here. You took me in. We didn't proceed with the lawsuit. Why are they now asking me for the money?"

Big Brother said, "Damn those gangsters! Fortunately we didn't play into their hands. Now they hold the written statement. They won't let go of the issue and will unquestionably sue us. But, when you have to appear in court, simply tell the truth as you did just now. The judge should be clear-minded and not let a little boy such as you pay them the money. Don't worry. Let's wait and see."

The next day, the Five Tigers filed a lawsuit with the court against Zhu San and the Third Brother Mo on a charge of repudiating the debt of one thousand *liang* of silver. Officials arrived at the Mo's home to take the accused. After consultation, Big Brother and Second Brother decided to compose an appeal for their little brother, recounting the details of the issue and offering themselves as witnesses. The three brothers then made their way to the court.

The magistrate of the prefecture was named Tang Tuan. He was a capable and intelligent official. When the accusers and defendants came he called the Five Tigers in the court and asked them, "What's Zhu San to you? And for what purpose did he get such a huge loan from you?"

Iron-piercing Bug answered, "Zhu San said he needed the loan to buy his son some real estate."

The magistrate turned to Zhu San, "What would you do with this huge sum?"

Zhu San replied, "I'm a petty businessman selling starch noodles. My deals seldom amount to a sum. I had no reason to get such a great loan."

Iron-piercing Bug said, "Look at the receipt he wrote for us. We five each loaned him and the Third Brother of Mo two hundred *liang* of silver."

The receipt was then handed over to the magistrate. The magistrate took a look at it and asked Zhu San, "Did you write this?"

Zhu San said, "Yes. I wrote it but never got the loan."

Iron-piercing Bug said, "He wrote it but Third Brother Mo took the silver."

As the magistrate called Third Brother Mo, the boy answered and stepped forward. The magistrate was surprised to see a little boy about ten years old appear before him. He asked, "What could a little boy like you do with so much money?"

Before the boy could reply, words rolled out of Iron-piercing Bug's mouth. "His father, Zhu San, wrote the receipt and used the money to buy him some land. Now the boy owns a large piece of land."

The magistrate said, "I don't quite understand why the father's family name is Zhu, while his son's is Mo?"

Zhu San replied, "To let you know the truth, this boy is in fact a son by the late master, Mo, and my wife. His mother was later married to me. So his family name is Mo. These men urged him to seize a share of the real estate that the old master left behind. They coaxed me into writing them a receipt for a loan from them for the expense of bringing a court suit. But it turned out that, as the boy went to the Mo's family, the mistress and the two brothers identified him as a member of their family and decided to give him his deserved part of the property. Thus the dispute dissolved without any lawsuit. Why else would we have needed that loan? But now they're showing that receipt and asking for payment of the loan. Do you think we should pay them the money?"

The magistrate asked the boy and obtained the same account. The magistrate then nodded his understanding. "I'm getting the picture," he said. Then he asked Big Brother, "Tell me why you took back your little brother after the master's death?"

Big Brother said, "Racketeers around town usually raise disputes out of peaceful lives and stir up trouble out of nothing for their own profit. Fortunately I took the boy back into our family immediately after he came — that's why these men are not satisfied and are bringing us to court today. If I hesitated that day and a lawsuit was brought up, these racketeers would have achieved their treacherous objective. By then what I would have lost would not simply be a sum of one thousand *liang* of silver. Our damages would have been multifold."

All smiles, the magistrate said, "Excellent! What remarkable moral courage and wisdom you've displayed! I admire you. The five plaintiffs are not likely to be lenders of one thousand *liang* of silver and Zhu San not likely to be a loan receiver either. Now we've got to the bottom of the story. What treachery! Without Big Brother's control of the situation, these rascals would have made a fortune."

Then he picked up his brush and dashed off his verdict:

A gain of one thousand liang *of silver hinges on the receipt of a loan. Who would lend Zhu San in utter destitution this huge loan? And what purpose would Mo, an infant have for this great sum of money? After a thorough investigation has been conducted, the truth has surfaced that the mystery originated in a scheme of vice. Song Li procured a deed aiming at a gain. Big Brother Mo values fraternity and dissolved an otherwise brotherly dispute. The schemers, dismayed in their miscalculation, turned to the scrape of paper as a last resort. The evil plot is to be severely punished and the receipt should be destroyed at once.*

Then a punishment of thirty floggings was meted out to each one of Five Tigers. They each received another twenty cudgel thrashings on the back in compliance with the law regarding their manipulation of the innocent by fomenting ill will and cheating. Finally, with their faces tattooed, they were sent to a remote border area to perform military service.

The town of Wuxing were happy for the removal of the Five Tigers. To commend Big Brother Mo the magistrate of the prefecture rewarded the Mo family with a horizontal board on which the characters inscribed were, "A Family of Filial Dedication and Virtue," and they were given a waiver of the forthcoming corvee. Now the mistress of the Mo family fully comprehended her elder son's initial wisdom. It is indeed a lesson to be remembered by those who get involved in a dispute with their brothers and intend to file a lawsuit with the help of outsiders.

Tale 8

Lord Man Deserts His Benefactor Spouse; Jiao Wenji Wreaks Vengeance After Death

Once in the Song Dynasty [960-1279] there was a deputy minister of foreign and ethnic affairs whose family name was Man. Because he did not come to an honorable end, his full name has now been tossed into oblivion, and he is known simply as Deputy Minister Man. Before he raised to his position, he was addressed as Master Man. He came from a well-known aristocratic family in the area south of the Huaihe River, a family graced by many high-ranking officials in each generation — his uncle, Man Gui by name was currently working as deputy director of the Privy Council — and kinsmen of the family were scattered throughout the capital city. They were all honest persons. But Master Man was a different character. A handsome youth with scholastic achievements, he was ambitious, conceited and free of conventions, never doubting his capability to make a successful career of his learning in the future. After his parents died in his childhood, he led a carefree life, spending his days composing poems on subjects such as snow, wind, plants and the moon, and traveling freely far and wide. As his family fortune was thus squandered, he had little left for marriage. His relatives gradually turned away from him, but he still maintained his style of living. Having learned that a friend of his father now held a government position in the city of Chang'an, he decided that he might turn to this official for an improvement in his living conditions. So he packed his things and set off on a journey to that city. But upon his arrival, he was told that the official had lost his tenure due to neglecting his duties and had departed. Master Man therefore had to turn back.

Being a thoughtless young man, Man had anticipated nothing but that this acquaintance would supply everything to meet his financial needs. Now he had lost ground and his money was all gone. On his way back, he stopped at Zhongmu County near the city of Kaifeng, where one of his clansmen served as a clerk in government. He decided to call on the relative and obtain some money to cover the cost for the rest of his homeward journey. However this relative barely survived on a meager income in his modest business, so the most he could do to help Man was to give him just a string of coins. Man found this sum only enough to pay for his room and board in the town, with almost nothing left to cover his trip home. It was the twelfth month. Man mused that if he went home with no coins to jingle in his pockets, he would not be able to tide over the hard time before the new year. He thus decided to stay in the area and pick up some odd jobs to do, and to return home after the holiday season. He started trekking westwards instead of eastwards, thinking that a couple of his friends holding government positions in the Guanzhong* region might be of some help.

As he reached the county of Fengxiang, he was caught in a

---

*Guanzhong, literally meaning "among passes," refers to the area along the Weishui River in Shaanxi Province.

snowstorm that lasted three days. His plight is depicted by these lines:

While my horse balks in snow gathering around a pass,
I ask the towering mountains in mist, where my home is.

Snowed in at a small inn for days on end, Man couldn't pay the inn-
keeper for his meals. So the latter stopped feeding him. A thought
came into Man's mind, "I'm from a respected family and well learned.
Obtaining a position is for me as easy as picking up a blade of grass.
Since my star hasn't risen yet, I ramble everywhere. Who could
recognize me as a minister-to-be in adversity? I would greatly
appreciate it if someone came to my rescue right now, but company
and success go hand in hand. Should I really expect sympathy at this
point of my life?" Sadness overwhelmed him and he broke into crying.

An old man next door was disturbed and came over to ask, "Who's
crying here?" The old man was dressed this way:

He wore a sheepskin coat with a fox-fur cap sitting on his head;
a faint intoxication caused a flush over his face with a burgundy
complexion; he emerged in white with snow-dotted gray hair
and beard; he looked like a poet on donkey back; or a scholar in
a leisure boat in a snowy night.

"Who's crying there?" the old man asked a waiter.

The waiter replied, "It's a scholar. He's been snowed in here for a
few days, unable to pay for his meals. It's been snowing and he can't
continue on his journey. Because he can't pay, we stopped providing
him with food. I think he's crying because of his hunger."

The old man then said, "One can do a favor to others anywhere and
secure blessing from God. Since he's a scholar, please give him some
food on my account. I'll pay the bill."

The waiter replied, "I see, sir," and brought a dinner to Man, saying to him, "Sir, here's your dinner. Dalang order me to serve you this."

Man, of course, asked, "Who's Dalang?"

The old man came over and said to him, "It's me."

Man hurriedly paid him courtesy, "We haven't met each other before. Why are you so generous?"

The old man replied, "My family name is Jiao. I live next door to this inn. It's snowing heavily. I was staying inside with my daughter, having a drink of warm wine to keep away the cold when I heard someone crying. It didn't sound like a laborer, so I came over to take a look. The inn manager told me that you are a scholar snowed in here. I respect refined upbringing. I could not bear watching a learned man suffer from hunger so I had the dinner brought to you. This suburban inn has nothing special with which to treat you. Besides, in such freezing weather, you need a few drinks to keep warm. Please stay here and I will send a servant to bring you some wine."

Man was delighted, saying, "I'm stranded on my journey. I've never met you before, and so it's very kind of you to treat me with such generosity and care. Your hospitality is really too much for me."

Jiao Dalang responded, "You look a cut above the ordinary. It's now merely a time of difficulty in your life, and I'm sure you'll be successful in future. I'm a native and should play the host. Please rest at ease. So long as you stay here I'll take care of everything. Don't worry about your journey until the weather clears up."

Man said, "I feel deeply indebted to you."

Then Jiao Dalang inquired about Man's name and native town, and left. Man was joyous about his good luck. "I didn't realize I might meet such a generous person in my desperate situation."

As he was wallowing in glee, a servant-boy came up with four dishes, four plates of tidbits and a pot of wine. He said to Man, "Dalang asked me to bring this food to you, master." Man thanked the boy and put the dishes on the table. The boy left.

Taking sips of the wine, Man asked the waiter, "Who is Jiao Dalang, and why is he so hospitable?"

The waiter answered, "He's a magnate. He's kind and upright and never fails to come to the rescue of the poor. He's particularly interested in making friends with learned persons, and he shows special treatment toward them. He loves to drink. If you can drink with him to his heart's content, he will be even more intimate with you."

Man said, "So he must be rich?"

The waiter replied, "He has some property. But I can't say he's very rich. He's just a generous person. You're lucky to have run into him. I don't think he will mind your staying here a few more days."

Man then asked, "Could you take me to his home when the snow lets up?"

The waiter said, "My pleasure."

A moment later, the servant-boy came back to clean up, bringing to the waiter Jiao Dalang's message, "Please let Man have whatever food he needs here and come to our home to fetch more wine for him." The waiter nodded in agreement and supplied the things accordingly. Man was profoundly grateful.

The following day it was clear and sunny. Master Man wanted to depart, but he had no money on him. Besides, he thought he should call on Jiao Dalang to express his gratitude. He also anticipated an offer of funds, from such a noble man to cover his need for traveling expenses. This exemplifies the prevalent saying, "Give someone an inch and they'll take a mile." As the waiter led the way, Man made straight for Jiao Dalang's place. The old man rose to greet him joyfully.

Man dropped to his knees and expressed his thanks, "I deeply appreciate your kindness in assisting me in my time of difficulty. I will absolutely put myself at your disposal should you need my services in the future."

Jiao Dalang replied, "Mine is not an affluent family. But I saw you were in a wretched state. It's out of my sense of duty that as host I offered you some help, nothing much. How could I deserve your services as payment in future?"

Man replied, "I'm going to take the imperial court examinations soon. It will be my responsibility to pay for your kindness once I'm successfully established in my career."

Dalang said, "All right. But it's close to the end of the year. I wonder where you're going now?" Man said, "I failed to find an acquaintance of mine as I had originally planned. I had spent all the money I had brought with me. I felt too ashamed to go home. Then I changed mind and decided go to the Guanzhong region so that I could turn to a couple of my friends there. I didn't know, as I was bogged down here, that I was to have such good luck in encountering you. The eve of the new year is around the corner, and to continue my planned journey now looks rather bleak. This's just like the saying, 'A traveler finds himself stranded in an isolated area.' It's hopeless. I think I'd better stay at the inn until after the holiday season."

Dalang said, "But the inn is not a place for you to spend the new year. Please stay at my place for a few days, if you don't mind my modest abode. I would like to have the pleasure of company over meals and tea. You may schedule your trip for after the holiday season. What do you think of that?"

Man said, "I was a lot of bother to you when staying at the inn. I'm afraid that my moving into your home will cause more inconvenience. You've treated me with great benevolence and I feel sorry that I may not be able to return your kindness later."

Dalang responded, "All men are brothers. Further more you're a learned man, full of promise. Once you make a name for yourself in future and still remember me, an old man living in the remote country, I will be quite satisfied. Why, I wonder, are you showing so much reserve and courtesy?"

Dalang was, in fact, a person who enjoyed a social life. He took to Man and did his best to accommodate him because of the young man's good-looks, civilized conduct and eloquent speech. Man was lucky to strike up the acquaintance of such a good man.

The waiter from the inn brought over his baggage, and Dalang had dinner with Man that evening. The guest talked eloquently and drank profusely in high spirits, with no sign of intoxication, while the host enjoyed the dinner, feeling sorry that he had had few chances of pleasure like this in the past. When they were tired, a room was arranged for Man to retire.

Dalang had an eighteen-year-old daughter named Wenji, who was without compare both in beauty and intelligence. The father would not marry her off to an ordinary person. He wanted to find her a husband in the local area, who, refined and literate, would come and live with his daughter so that he himself might be taken care of in his later years. However, his civil social position never attracted the attention of influential families in terms of marriage, and mediocre young men from wealthy families were beneath his notice. Therefore his choice of marriage for his daughter was a dilemma to him, and the years flashed past until Wenji was grown-up. Now, with enough knowledge of love and marriage, the girl paid attention to whichever young men came into her sight. But most of the visitors to her house were commonplace, none of them capturing her fancy. When she learned her father had brought a scholar home from the nearby inn, she fidgeted in her room, hoping to catch a glimpse of him.

Man's appearance and manner were impressive and her passion was somewhat stirred. This was partly Dalang's fault. It was generous of him to help Man in his time of need, but Dalang should have given the young man some money for traveling expenses and sent him on his journey. Because Dalang was a widower, living with his unmarried daughter, why should he go out of his way to accommodate Man at his home? Admittedly, Dalang loved drinking with friends and, interested in Man's personality, was glad to treat him well. But it never struck Dalang that his guest might not be honest. Man took advantage of his host's hospitality and respect for learning, putting on an air of arrogance. He also had the thought in mind that, because the old man had a beautiful daughter, he might be fortunate enough to marry the woman. Man found it hard to get this idea across. So he waited as the days went by, and his plan for going to the Guanzhong region was thrown into oblivion.

Dalang indulged in daily drinking, unwatchful against his guest. The attraction that Man and Wenji showed to one another gradually grew into a passionate love and they carried on with each other behind the old man's back. But their frequent contact eventually revealed their affair to others. Occasionally their behavior caught Dalang's attention, as suspicion rose in him. Attention produces understanding. At the beginning of his stay, Master Man had easy and free talks with Dalang each day over wine. As Dalang became skeptical later, Master Man was absent-minded and confusingly verbose, certainly not the person he had been earlier.

One day Dalang went out on an excuse and came back half a day later. He found Man asleep from tipsiness in his study. A gust of wind caught the young man's garments, revealing underneath a reddish dress like something a lady usually wore. Dalang stepped forward to take a closer look. It was indeed his daughter's dress, over which dangled a sachet with the design of a couple of mandarin ducks on it, embroidered by his daughter.

Astonished, the old man let out a cry, "This is odd! He must have had her!"

Awakened, Man got up and hastily adjusted his clothing. His face became a ghastly white, knowing Dalang had seen the dress he had on. "Where did you get the dress you're wearing, master?" asked Dalang.

Understanding that he could not deny what he wore Man quickly made up a story by saying, "I didn't have enough clothing and couldn't bear the cold. So I went to see your daughter, hoping to borrow some used clothes of yours. But she offered me one of her own. I felt the cold and didn't hesitate to take it and wear it underneath my garments."

Dalang replied, "If you needed clothing, you should have talked to me about the matter. How can you find it decent to have personal contact with a young lady in her maidenhood? My daughter is disgraceful!"

Thus said, he marched toward the inside of the house. A servant-girl, called Qing Xiang, was going out at that moment and bumped into him. Dalang grabbed her and said, "Tell me everything about your young lady's relation with that scholar and I'll spare you a flogging!"

Qing Xiang was quite scared. She stammered around for a cover-up, and then said, "I haven't seen anything about that."

Dalang became irritated. "Don't fool me!" he shouted. "I saw her dress on him."

Knowing she was in a dilemma, the servant-girl, still not telling the whole story, said, "The young lady saw that you treated him with respect, so she showed courtesy each time she met him. When he told her he felt cold today, she loaned him one of her dresses. They didn't talk about anything else."

Dalang then said, "Is it decent conduct for a young lady to lend a man one of her gowns? I was out this morning, but, when I came back, I found the young man smelling of alcohol. Where did he get the drinks?"

Qing Xiang hemmed and hawed. "I really have no idea," she said.

Dalang shouted, "Bullshit! Did he have anywhere else to go for a drink? He told me just now about it. You'd better tell me the truth, or I'll beat you to death!" With no way out, Qing Xiang had to make a clean breast of the matter.

Rage rose in Dalang. He trembled and cried, "What a good-for-nothing! And she had an affair with a stranger. What shall I do next?"

Qing Xiang said, "My young lady took the chance while you were away to set up food and drink. She asked the scholar to take an oath that they would get married and be faithful through the rest of their lives. They drank together. Then my young lady took off her dress and gave that and a sachet to him as souvenirs."

Dalang howled, "How shameful they are!" Then, with a sigh, he muttered, "It's all my fault for being hospitable. I can blame nobody else." He walked out with his hands clasped behind his back.

Meanwhile, seeing that her father was questioning Qing Xiang, Wenji knew something had gone wrong. She secretly overheard Qing Xiang's thorough account of the story. She was frightened. When Qing Xiang came into her room Wenji knew that her father had left.

Wenji pulled herself together and said to Qing Xiang, "Now that my father knows everything, what can I do? I would rather die!"

Qing Xiang consoled her by saying, "Don't worry. I saw your father sigh, blaming himself. I guess he does not wholly object to your love."

Wenji asked, "How do you know?"

Qing Xiang replied, "He has held Man in high esteem. If he should throw him out, he will offend the scholar and the hospitality he has showed will be reversed. And where would that leave you, his daughter? I think the master is going to talk to Man. If he makes sure that he is not married, he may unite you."

"I hope this is true," Wenji said.

Exactly as Qing Xiang predicted, Dalang shuffled out contemplatively. Then he turned around and made his way into Man's study. "Do you have a wife at home?" he asked Man sternly.

Shivering in panic, Man murmured in reply, "I've been a vagabond and never got married."

Dalang said, "You're educated and should know the code of decent conduct. I didn't know you before, but I felt sympathetic after seeing you in trouble and away from home. I did my best to help you. But what a despicable thing you have done, destroying my daughter's reputation! That's something utterly beyond a gentleman's conduct!"

With a deep sense of shame, Man fell to his knees and kowtowed.

"I'm terribly guilty of the offense against you. I feel an immense gratitude for what you have done for me. But I was driven by my passion and committed an injury to you. If you pardon me this time, I will dedicate myself to you in return and never forget your kindness for the rest of my life."

Dalang sighed and said, "Well, since what is done cannot be undone, I should take the blame in that I didn't bring up my daughter with good morals so she has been disgraced. Since you have had an affair with her, how can I marry her off to someone else? I suggest that you move into my home and stay with us as my son-in-law, if you don't mind the distance from your native place. I will be satisfied to have someone taking care of me in my advanced years."

Dalang's words filled Man with boundless joy, as if a special amnesty had been granted to a criminal. He dropped to his knees for another kowtow, swearing, "I couldn't pay for your benevolence even with my life. My parents are dead and I'm single. I'll be willing to serve you for the rest of my life. I will go nowhere."

Dalang said, "That's easier said than done, I'm afraid. I wonder whether you'll become unfaithful later on."

Man said, "Your daughter and I are deeply in love. We took an oath. If I turn out to be disloyal, let me die a wretched death!"

Seeing that he was sincere, Dalang had to be content with what he had promised. A date for the marriage was picked at random and a feast was held to celebrate the union of the young couple. The marriage can be depicted as follows:

The bride in new silk attire arranged;
In draped bed none of their parts were strange.
Though the lady was made honest after conduct amiss
The wedding night was spent in no less bliss.

Man and Wenji were overjoyed that their initial secret infatuation had burgeoned into a happy marriage. Wenji said to Man, "At first I saw my father respected you, and out of admiration for you I gave up my virginity at the risk of dishonoring myself. After my father learned about our love, I didn't think we could go on any further, and death would be my only choice. Fortunately, my father backed down and granted our marriage. Now I'm very happy that I narrowly escaped death. You mustn't forget this."

"I was nothing but a vagrant," Man said. "But your father treated me as if I were an old friend, providing me with food and clothing, with far more than I can ever repay. Then you didn't frown upon me, but loved me deeply so that we could get married. This is the double kindness I've received. If I were to become treacherous, I should not be considered human." Naturally, they grew more passionate.

Man, not occupied, read day and night, hoping to sit the next imperial court examinations. Dalang was pleased that he had gotten a worthy son-in-law, and a life of harmony ensued.

In the spring two years later, notices were issued that the imperial court examinations were to be conducted at the capital city. Man expressed to his father-in-law his desire to participate in the examinations. Dalang agreed and gathered a sum of money for his traveling expenses before he sent his son-in-law off on the journey. Leaving his father-in-law and wife behind, Man reached the capital city, took the examinations and passed them with flying colors. Soon after, he and other successful examinees had an audience with the emperor. Man, missing his wife and realizing that it would take some time before he received the formal appointment to a government position, thought to himself, "It's not a long distance to Fengxiang. My white civil robe has been replaced by a green official one. Why not take the time to go home and be together with them for a celebration!" Now tended by servants, Man called on them to do the packing and he departed at once. In a few days he was at the gate of Dalang's house.

Dalang had received a message about his son-in-law's imminent arrival, and he busied himself the whole day with preparations for a welcoming homecoming. With the beat of drums and the playing of music, Man strode into the house in his green robe with a white skirt*. As soon as he met his father-in-law, he fell to his knees to make four kowtows before him. He didn't pull himself up immediately, but instead uttered his words of appreciation.

"I owe my present-day success to your help," he said. "If I had been left alone and penniless at that inn, I would have been dead long ago and would never have achieved such wealth and honor." Then he started kowtowing again.

Dalang raised him up, replying, "Your talent deserves this grace. Don't mention my help. You had adversity in those days like any virtuous person often undergoes. You've graced me a great deal with your return in honor." Then Man met Wenji formally with an exchange of compliments.

Neighbors thronged around the house to see Man. Some said, "Jiao has a keen eye for virtuous person and he is benevolent to others. This is indeed a reward he deserves. And his daughter benefits from a good husband, too."

The sarcastic remark, however, was, "It's said the girl had an affair with the man before marriage."

Another person responded, "Dalang had the idea in his mind that he would marry his daughter to this young man. That's why he let him stay with them. It doesn't matter if they had an affair. They have become husband and wife anyway and so the disgrace is erased. She will be a ranking lady. What more can you say about them?"

Amid the gossip came a number of people leading sheep and shouldering jugs of wine, most of them close neighbors and relatives presenting their congratulations to Dalang. Then Dalang was lifted up

---

*The emperor would customerly grant a white skirt to each of the successful examinees when he saw them.

and raised above the heads of others. He felt quite proud.

He threw a party for his son-in-law, inviting a few close kinsmen and friends for company. The next day another party was held for those sending their congratulations. The celebrations continued for about ten days, with relatives and neighbors treated in succession. It cost Dalang a lot of money but he felt exactly as the saying goes, "One spends generously at a time of bliss." At the same time, Man and Wenji enjoyed happy moments of love. Even Qing Xiang received attention and respect for her services in the past.

As the husband and wife, now in their glory, spent their days making merry, Dalang, in all his kindness, had gone on a spending spree and his expenses kept climbing. He counted on the wealth of his daughter and son-in-law to keep him for the rest of his life, so he spared nothing in delighting the young couple. Man was a person who always enjoyed himself at others' expense. As the appointment to of government position drew near, Man was about to leave. Dalang believed that in order to be appointed to a choice position Man needed to present the appointer with some gifts. So Dalang sold the best part of his real estate and scraped together an impressive sum of silver for the use of his son-in-law. This fundraising consumed almost all the possessions that Dalang had, since he was not a rich man in the first place. However, he was at ease, anticipating a recovery after his son-in-law's appointment to a government position.

As Man was leaving, Wenji said to him, "We're deeply in love. Before you left for the imperial court examinations, I suffered a lot from the sadness of parting from you. But I knew we were expecting something good from your trip so I was not too depressed. It's different this time. Though you have passed the exams and will assume office, I have a strange sense of foreboding in seeing you off. Do you think there's going to be bad luck for us?"

Man replied, "I'm going to take office as one of the top winners in the imperial court examinations. I should be assigned one of the best government positions. As soon as that is done, I will come back to fetch you and your father. We'll go to live there with untold wealth and high honors. All this is guaranteed and won't take long. Why are you talking about bad luck? Don't worry about it."

Wenji said, "I know this. However, I have a strange feeling and can't hold back the shedding of tears. I don't know why."

Man said, "Well, I think it's because you're aware of the forthcoming loneliness following the revels and my departure."

Wenji agreed, "Maybe you're right." They didn't stop talking intimately in this way, but reassured one another of their love until dawn. The next day saw Man packing his clothes, taking leave of his wife and father-in-law, and setting off with his servant on his journey to the capital city for his assumption of office. Dalang and Wenji comforted each other as they started straightening up their own things in the hope that they would be sent for in the days to come so as to join Man in his tenure of office.

Upon his arrival in the capital city, Man was appointed to be the director of the county of Linhai. As he scheduled his departure and got ready to return to the county of Fengxiang to pick up his wife and father-in-law, a man stalked into his room, addressing a greeting to him.

"Hello, my young brother," the man said. "I couldn't find you anywhere. But you're here!"

Looking up, Man recognized that he was one of his cousins in their large clan. Man rose to welcome him. The man said, "In the last years, you've been away from home traveling around. You didn't send any message home but kept our whole family in suspense. Then you suddenly emerged from nowhere in the capital city and stunned the world with your fame. Our entire family was overjoyed. Your uncle, the Deputy Director of the Privy Council, saw your name on the list of winners in the exams and sent people to bring you back home. But you were nowhere to be found. Now that you're appointed to an official

position, you should take time off and come home to see us. I came
here for some business and I'm done now. So I have rented a boat
down there at the bank of the Bianhe River, with my belongings
thrown into it. I've been looking for you. Since you've gotten
everything ready, let's go home together and meet our kinsmen before
your departure for your office."

Man's mind was on Fengxiang and not on his old home. His
cousin's words ran against his will, but he didn't want to make this
clear. So he gave a perfunctory reply, "I've other business to tend to,
Brother. I can't go home right now."

His cousin said, "You're kidding! Look at your packed baggage.
You're ready to take off. Where are you going if you don't return
home?"

Man said, "I received very generous treatment from a man during
time of difficulty. I'm now going west to express my gratitude to him."

His cousin responded, "You are a newly appointed official and are
not rich yet. You need money to buy gifts for your friend. You should
take your time to do that after you assume office. Besides, you can
stop at home on your way east to the place of your office. Why are you
taking the opposite direction and going instead to the west?"

At this point, Man should have told his cousin the truth and
expressed his regrets for being unable to return home, and the latter
might have shown some understanding. However, not experienced in
such situations, Man kept his own counsel, equivocating this way and
that, and refusing to change his mind no matter how much his cousin
pushed him. Then flaring up, his cousin swore, "What a shallow,
irrational bum you are! Should one be content with staying away from
home, after making a name for himself, forgetting all about his family
members, relatives and close neighbors? If you feel pushed to do that,
that's fine. But won't you come back and pay tribute at the grave of
your parents? Let's talk to people and see whether your conduct is
acceptable or not." His cousin's forceful rebuke brought a flush of

shame to the cheeks of Man, who found himself unable, and afraid as well, to a reply. Seeing that Man was thus silenced, his cousin called the servants to move Man's carry-on suitcase onto the waiting boat, regardless of his protests.

Unable to stop him, Man figured, "I've been away from home quite a long time. I was a wretch when I left home. It's not unsuitable for me to go back home now with honor. And I don't think it will be of grave consequence if I go home before I return to Fengxiang." Then he turned to his cousin, "Okay, I will go home with you." However, this trip brought a result that:

While the green-robed youth was bound to new conjugal ties;
The dark-haired beauty was left in eternal hopeless waiting.

Man went back home with his cousin. His impression of the relatives and neighbors, most of them flatterers, struck him quite differently than it had before. But he was satisfied with the change in his life. He went straight to see his uncle, Man Gui, who was now not only high on the social ladder as a retired deputy director of the Privy Council but was also the patriarch for the whole clan. Seeing his nephew return with honor, the uncle was delighted.

"You've been away from home all these years." the uncle said. "I thought you must have settled somewhere else and I never expected you would finally pull through, passed the imperial examinations and come back home with the appointment to a government position. You truly have done our family credit."

Man made a lot of modest remarks. His uncle continued, "I've one more thing to talk over with you. Your parents died long ago and you missed the prime of youth for marriage. Now that you're established with fame, the first priority should be your marriage. The other day when I saw your name on the list of winners in the imperial court exams, I began thinking about this matter. I have heard that the second daughter of Zhu Congjian, a senior official working in the capital city, is beautiful and intelligent. I sent a matchmaker to talk to him about his daughter marrying you and he granted the betrothal. It's going to be a wonderful marriage for you. I know the director of Linhai county has not been relieved of his position yet. You'll have plenty of time before you have to be there to replace him in office. I think you should get married first and then leave with your wife for your new position. Don't you think that's a good idea?"

His uncle's words took Man aback and, for a while, he found himself completely tongue-tied. If Man had known what was what, he would have told his uncle everything about his predicament and happy encounter with Dalang in Fengxiang and made the clear-cut statement, "I'm sorry but I got married long ago and should be faithful to my wife. I request you terminate this betrothal with the Zhus." If he had displayed such resolution, his uncle would not have pushed any further. However, Man would not give tongue to his early vagabond experience and marriage in Fengxiang as if it was a disgrace. He simply equivocated his disagreement.

Then his uncle said again, "I see you are finding it hard to make up your mind. Are you worried about the lack of a satisfactory arrangement for the marriage on my part? I sent betrothal gifts to the girl's family the other day. You can count on me for the rest of marriage expenses. You just get ready to be the bridegroom."

Man replied, "I'm much obliged for your hospitality. But I think I need more time to think about this marriage."

His uncle put on a grave look and said, "Now everything's ready. What else do you want to think about!" His uncle's harsh voice and stern face silenced Man, and he withdrew from the room in submission.

Back in his own room, Man became lost in contemplation. If I yield to my uncle's demand, he thought to himself what should I do about the kind treatment I received from Wenji and her father? But if I reject this arranged marriage, I will not only hurt my uncle's feelings by ignoring his good intentions, but I will hardly be able to speak out my refusal in front of him, given his pride. Admittedly, this will be a good match for me in terms of marriage and it will cost me nothing. I shouldn't let this chance slip away. Being married to two women at the same time is not uncommon among government officials. But the problem is that I would be tied to both women. If I let Wenji be my first lady because I married her first, the young lady from the Zhus, the descendant of a noble family, will surely refuse to stoop to a position beneath Wenji. That would be a tough nut to crack. He wrestled with such thoughts in a gloomy mood for days on end without solution.

Then Man's frivolous personality began to take a grip over him, as he succumbed to the allure of the fact that Miss Zhu was a good-looking lady from a family of high social position and that the marriage would demand of him no money. But he was still a little conscience-stricken over the thought of his indebtedness to Wenji and her father. The struggle in his mind lingered on for a time before he came to a decision. A person usually acts rationally on his or her initial idea and chances are they will do something good in the end. But if one haggles over his losses and gains, some vicious ideas tend to arise. Man continued to be obsessed with the idea of marriage for two more days before he made up his mind. As he figured it: "At first I had an affair with Wenji and so she can be counted at most as one of my loves. Though we got married later, our union was not completed through appropriate ceremonies. I'm now a government official and deserve someone of privileged origin to be my life partner. Since the Jiaos are no more than ordinary townsfolk, humble in their social position, is Dalang's daughter suitable to receive the honor of an imperial appointment in the future and of being my wife for the rest of my life? I'll marry Zhu's daughter for the moment. If Wenji comes to see me later on, I'll use gentle words to persuade her into marrying to someone else. If she wants to stay with me, I'll have to keep her. But then she can't refuse to be my concubine." With this idea in mind, Man went to his uncle to let him know his decision.

His uncle chose an auspicious date and went to the house of the Zhus with greetings, and accepted the bride. The Zhus regarded the marriage as an important occasion, given the fact that they were not an ordinary family and their son-in-law was a newly appointed official. The dowry was comprehensive and well prepared. Brought up in an official household, the bride was well known for her beauty, and equally admirable for her morals, proper speech and diligence in housework. Man was overjoyed, and thoughts of his connection with Fengxiang seldom again surfaced in his mind.

The match was perfect in terms of social status, age and appearance and the couple indulged in obsessive love. Now Man was bothered with regrets over his former marriage to Wenji. Occasionally those memories of the past slid into his mind and stung for some moments. Therefore, he took out the garment and sachet Wenji had given him and, steeling his heart, set fire to them in front of his new wife in an attempt to sever his links with his previous marriage.

As his wife was curious about what he was doing, he briefly recounted to her his marriage with Wenji, and then said, "That's my misfortune. Now I'm married to you. Don't mention that any more."

A virtuous woman, his wife said in response, "Since you and she went through hard times together, you shouldn't forget about her once you're prosperous. I'm not one of those jealous wives. If you have a chance someday to bring her here, let her stay with us. I don't mind."

However, as Man had broken the oath he took with Wenji, he didn't want to see her again in case he would face a disgraceful and difficult situation. How could he go even further now to bring Wenji to live with them? Besides, he feared that Zhu might be humiliated if Wenji was brought there. So he rejected Zhu's proposal. "I appreciate your kindness, madam," he replied, "But she's from lowly origins. If she hears nothing from me for some time, she will surely marry someone else. Don't worry about it, please." After that the matter was never brought up again.

At first Man was ill at ease with his ignoble motives. He feared that Wenji might come to see him some day. But his anxiety gradually turned to joy as nothing happened for a long time. An old saying goes: "One's strong sense of filial respect for one's older generations fades away with each passing day." Gradually the burden fell from his mind. With his new wife, he went to Linhai County and took office. In the ten years that followed, his term of office was pleasantly renewed four or five times. His wife Zhu was also twice granted an imperial reward. He was finally promoted to be a deputy minister and took charge of the administration of the prefecture of Qizhou.

Man's living quarters in Qizhou were spacious, providing the whole family with pleasant housing. Three days after their arrival in Qizhou, the family was well settled and his wife wanted to go out into the backyard for a stroll. So Man accompanied her with a few family relatives and close servant-girls, about ten of them in total, leaving the rest of his retinue behind. They walked at a leisurely pace. Then a small door to a small yard on the right came into the view. Man pushed the door open and his trespass startled a servant-girl in a black dress in this small yard. The girl dashed off and he chased after her, but she vanished instantly behind a ragged door-curtain. As Man drew near to the place, a woman emerged from behind the door-curtain. A close look at her assured him that it was none other than Wenji from Fengxiang.

Man had long loathed the idea of meeting her because of his guilty conscience. The sudden encounter put him in a panic. Wenji grabbed him and said, sobbing, "You devil! You've been away for ten years and you forgot our mutual love. What a hard-hearted person you are!"

Man was so frightened the idea never crossed his mind that he should ask her where she had come from. He simply muttered an explanation, "I didn't forget you. When I got back home, my uncle forced me to marry a woman he had betrothed me to. I tried to reject him, but in vain. I had to yield to his will. I'm sorry I didn't have an opportunity to come to see you."

Wenji said, "I knew what happened to you. Don't speak of it any more. But my father has died and our real estate is gone, leaving me and Qing Xiang with nothing and nobody to turn to. We could not keep body and soul together so we traveled thousands of *li* to come here and see you. We arrived here a few days ago and the gate-keeper would not let us in. We pleaded time and again until, finally, were allowed to stay in this empty room in the yard. I'm glad we have met here. Now I'm poor and have nowhere to go. Since you've gotten a perfect match, I would like to serve you and your wife as your concubine so I will be able to live with you for the rest of my life. I won't try to find out the rights and wrongs of the past. I will drop it." As she said this, her sobbing was incessant. Then she tossed herself into his arms and broke into a bitter wail. Qing Xiang came out and joined her in her grief.

Man was quite touched and shed tears also. For fear that they might be seen by others, he quickly comforted her, saying, "It is my fault. Please stop crying. I won't forget that I owe you. Fortunately my wife is kind and virtuous. There won't be any problem if you don't mind being a concubine. Please wait here and let me talk to her."

Aware of the quagmire he was in, Man had to go to his wife Zhu and say to her, "I told you about the woman from the family of Jiao in Fengxiang. I thought she had probably married somebody else, for I had heard nothing about her for years. However, after her father's death, she has managed to track me down here, along with a servant-girl. If I don't take them, they won't have any place to go. What should I do about them?"

Zhu replied, "I told you before that you should bring her here and let her stay with us. But you wouldn't listen to me, and thus put them in this miserable state. How can you send them away? Please bring them here — I want to see them."

Man said, "I know you're virtuous."

He then went back through the door in the yard and told Wenji what she had said. Turning to Qing Xiang, Wenji said, "I'm so glad we've finally got a place to stay." They followed him into the main yard to meet his wife.

After an exchange of greetings, Wenji said, "I appreciate much your kindness in allowing us to stay, Madam. I would like to serve you, by doing things like making the beds."

The wife responded, "What are you talking about. We should treat each other as sisters." Then she led the two of them into the house, had a nice bedroom cleaned up for them, and had Qing Xiang live in the same room and attend Wenji. Wenji swallowed her pride and acted without complaint, while Man's wife Zhu treated her with great compassion and tenderness. Thus the days went by in peace and harmony.

After a certain time in office, Man's guilty conscience still gripped his mind, keeping him from spending a night in Wenji's room with her. One evening, however, he returned home a little intoxicated. Dim candlelight shone light from Wenji's room. This brought back to his mind those intimate days in the past that he had spent with her. He seemed encouraged and heedless under the effects of alcohol as he reeled inside and stood in front of Wenji. Both Wenji and Qing Xiang were delighted and helped him into bed.

When his wife Zhu learned about this, a smile sprang to her face and she said, "It's been some time since they came here. He should spend a few nights with her." She turned in alone that night.

The following morning the whole family arose, but there was no stirring in Wenji's room, though it was well into the day. Remarks were traded among the amused household.

"See, they haven't seen each other for ten years. Who knows how long they are going to cuddle with one another in bed! They're not up yet at this time of the day! Even Qing Xiang must have been bored listening to them. But it's weird that she has not woken up, either."

An experienced person, said, "They must have talked to each other about their lives during the past ten years until well after midnight. They probably went to sleep at dawn." The flurry of speculation lasted for a while as the room remained silent.

Man's wife Zhu had finished her washing-up. The quietness of Wenji's room puzzled her as well, and so she said, "At this late hour of the morning, he should rise. Should he forget about his duties observing the morning court office?" She went to Wenji's room with a servant-girl and heard nothing from inside. A push on the door failed to open it, since it was bolted from inside.

Others said, "He usually wakes up early in the morning and attends to his official routine. But today, it's outrageous that he sleeps so late. We may as well remind him of the time."

Someone gently knocked on the door and called out. There was no response. The force of his knocking and calls gradually increased until he was smashing at the door and yelling out. But the room remained dead silent. He then said to Zhu, "This is really unusual! We can't wait until he wakes up. If Your Ladyship will give us permission, we will knock down one side of the wall and go inside for a look. Later, when His Lordship gets angry about the mess, we will depend on Your Ladyship to take responsibility."

Zhu said, "Alright, go ahead. I'll take the blame." At once a group of servants started forcing a way through the wall. In a moment a big piece of the wall tumbled down and they swarmed inside. What they saw in the room struck them dumb.

People saw Man laying on his back on the floor, his mouth and nose bleeding. They drew close and touched him. His body warmth was gone, revealing he had died hours before. No one else was in the room, including Wenji and Qing Xiang. The bedding was the only thing left there. They hurried out and led the wife in. The scene frightened her out of her wits and she instantly burst into tears.

A moment later she stopped crying and said, "Such a bizarre happening is inconceivable! Can it be that the two of them killed my husband and fled in the night?"

The servants answered, "No. All gates were locked tight and no one could have gone out. In addition, this room was locked from the inside. How could they have made their way out?"

Zhu said, "You're right. Then I wonder if the two women who stayed here with us for many days were not just two ghosts?" She couldn't make head or tail of the events. Word started to spread about Man's sudden and violent death, and arrangements were made for his funeral.

That evening, the wife withdrew in grief to her bedroom. As she was about to get into bed, Wenji showed her face from behind the bed. She came forward and said, "Don't be sad, Madam. Your husband received generous treatment from my family, but he betrayed our trust later on. He left and never came back to us. Our whole family suffered greatly as we awaited his return. Later I died of grief and then deep grief also took my father's life, which was followed by Qing Xiang's death. We went to the underworld and reported the wrong done to us. With permission granted to us, we came and took his life in order to avenge the ten-year injustice we had received. I'm going to the underworld now to reason with him to his face. I appreciate your kindness, Madam, and won't disturb you. I'm here to say good-bye to you."

Before the wife had a chance to say anything to her, a blast of cold air filled the room and she awoke shuddering. She realized Wenji and Qing Xiang were indeed two ghosts who had taken Man's life to Hell to judge about the rights and wrongs of the matter.

The wife had long known about Man's unfaithfulness toward Wenji. After his death, she held no grudge, but escorted his casket to his native town. Unquestionably, the rest of her life was devoid of all the comforts she would have enjoyed otherwise, due to Man's sinfulness. Reflecting upon Man's deeds, the reader should be clear about whether it is acceptable for a man to betray his wife.

Tale 9

A Senseless Young Master Squanders His Fortune in Liberal Donations;
The Virtuous Father-in-law Plots to Bring Him Back to a Sensible Life

A young man with the family name of Yao lived in the prefecture of Wenzhou in Zhejiang Province. His father used to be the Minister of the Ministry of War, and his father-in-law, Shangguan, also held a high government position. The Yao family was rich, with an enormous amount of wealth and a great deal of property that covered one hundred *li* across and encompassed many cultivated fields, orchards, gardens, ponds, hills, woods, streams and lakes. Since his parents had died and he had no brothers, the young master was in charge of the family affairs. His wife was submissive, unmindful of anything beyond her threshold. The young master followed his inclinations and developed a wasteful way of life, taking it for granted that he had an inexhaustible supply of wealth. A few rogues with whom he kept company, flattered and abetted him by saying, "Heroes either in the past or now do no manual labor, but spend lavishly. Their reputations for chivalry reside in their scorn of materialism and denial of a frugal existence." Young and vain, this young master took their words as good advice and kept them in mind. If he saw a man who cared about his business transactions in terms of profit and kept his living on a budget, he would frown and take him to be a contemptible person beneath his notice.

He hated learning and had no interest in pursuing any career. Therefore when he met with scholars, he would feel ill at ease. Painfully uncomfortable, he would skulk away at once. However, he could not tear himself away, even for one day, from a bunch of loafers, who were constantly joking, jabbering, making sharp-tongued remarks and seeking favors. Another group of people who delighted him were valiant, brawny fellows, interested only in flexing their muscles, practicing fist-fighting, admiring confrontations of might, and bragging of themselves as heroes. Associating with them made the young master talk eloquently and walk briskly. He felt comfortable only with these two groups of people. They introduced him to other acquaintances of their stripe. So this company of town idlers and young scoundrels gathering around him grew rapidly. They did their best to convince him of their dedication to his service by showing off and flattering him in an attempt to depend upon him for a living. To achieve his reputation of generosity, the young master received them all, asking them no questions about their individual backgrounds. Wherever he went, more than one hundred of such hangers-on kept company with him. These men were not only on the young master's payroll but they took the young master's supply of staples back to their homes according to the size of their own families — staples such as monthly rations of clothing and grain. Seeing them carrying this booty away from his house, the young master was complaisant.

The young master loved horse-riding and hunting. So a fine steed and strong bow were two prizes he sought. One day one of his men would tell him about a well-known horse on which had been placed a price of one thousand *liang* of silver, and which could run a few hundred *li* each day. Immediately the young master would give him that amount of money and let him purchase it, bidding him not to haggle over the price. When the horse was brought in front of him, so long as horse had a nicer hide and a bit taller body than usual, he would take it a good deal. If someone said it was not worth the payment, that annoyed the young master. He would be pleased only if everyone said it was a good buy. Knowing his personality, people would throng to the front, praising him over any purchase he made. This was also true about his accumulation of strong bows.

His friends developed a sense of understanding and flattering. And in this way they helped him purchase about twenty fine steeds and forty strong bows. The young master picked out the best horse for himself, letting the rest be shared among his friends. He often scheduled horse-riding tours and raced with his men in different directions, riding on his horse and holding his bow. He would designate a place as their destination, rewarding whoever got there first and penalizing whoever came in last. The rewards were distributed at the young master's expense and the penalty was nothing more than a drink of wine as a fine. If the young master beat them all, everybody was fined with a drink, which was followed by a presentation of a large vessel of wine to the young lord himself in celebration. Sometimes, the group broke into a few hunting platoons trekking different trails and in no time at all joined at one junction. The purpose was to see who could obtain the largest catch, and the rewards and fines were allotted exactly the same way as they were in the horse-riding. These games were conducted purely for fun. One such game would cost the young master a big sum in covering the food, drink and prizes.

Sometimes the participants galloped several abreast and trotted heedlessly into fields, crushing a farmer's crops, frightening the cattle away, or causing other damage. As the young master was nice and liberal-minded, his men would goad him on by saying, "It's better for a touring young master to make them eager to see you than to generate grudges among local subjects. If we damage their crops, it's our fault and they would fear seeing us come again. Only when we pay them double their loss, they will feel they got the better of you and thus welcome your return."

The young master would nod in complete agreement, and say, "This is an insightful idea indeed!" He would then ask them to estimate the damage, saying, "Better calculate the cost amply and make a handsome payment. Don't hurt them."

His men would make secret agreement with the local people that they would share the compensation. So the calculation of the cost usually came to seven or eight times the actual loss. The young master would immediately pay the money, never checking the amount his men had calculated. During his hunting trips this became a common expenditure.

Two of his companions were particularly intimate with the young master and in his favor. One of these was a literary hack called Jia Qingfu and the other an instructor in *gongfu* (martial arts) called Zhao Nengwu. Whenever the young master went the two men, one brainy and the other brawny, followed like a shadow. Any suggestion made to the young master, without the cooperation of these two men, would come to no avail, even though numerous words were showered on the master daily in flattering, prodding and coaxing. With one of the two men working hand in glove, the young master usually spent generously to the benefit of his followers.

One day when the young master was on a hunting trip, a startled hare shot out in a sprint. He whipped his horse in chase and shot two arrows, but he missed it. Just at this juncture his men caught up and Zhao Nengwu knocked down the hare with one shot. The young master laughed, clapping his hands. They had come a long way from home in hunting the hare before they realized that hunger was preying on them. Looking around, they saw they were in a wild place, which, with beautiful scenery of hills and streams, lacked any tavern or restaurant. Jia Qingfu and some other young men who were participating in the hunt soon arrived. They all admired the surroundings.

"What a nice location!" they said. "We should have a drink here." The young master felt encouraged. Turning around, he asked the men to check the money they had brought with them. They had enough silver and copper coins, but the problem was that they had no place to buy food and drink.

Zhao Nengwu said, "Why do you say we don't have things to eat? We have something in front of us."

The rest asked, "What's it?"

Zhao Nengwu answered, "Just now we shot a hare. Let's set up a fire and roast it. Then our master should have enough food to go with his drink."

Jia Qingfu cut in with the remark, "For drink, we can send someone with a fine horse to get wine. A village is just five to seven *li* away from here. But I don't think one such trip can bring back enough wine to satisfy our craving for spirits."

The young master said, "Well, it will be good to obtain whatever you can get."

As they conversed, they saw a group of people, old and young, approaching with some things in their hands. These people greeted the young master and said, "We're countryfolk, sir. We have never met a distinguished master before. It's a rare occasion today that you, young Lord, have honored us with your presence here. We have scraped together some modest food and drink, things such as fruit, chickens, millet, homemade wine and edible wild herbs. We're now presenting them to your followers for picnic."

Hearing about food and drink, the young master was excited. He turned his head and said to his men, "I can't believe this coincidence that some people have such inspiration in the world!"

Jia Qingfu and the rest remarked, with applause, "It's simply due to the fact that you, master, are a man of good fortune so that you can have the food and drink brought to you with divine assistance." They dismounted from their horses and sat down on the ground.

Then the villagers said, "Since your young Lord doesn't frown upon our coarse supply, why not come to our home and sit down to eat and drink. We've chairs and tables there. It doesn't look good for you to dine out here in this wilderness."

The group responded, "Exactly! You certainly know what to do."

With the villagers respectfully leading the way, the companions helped the young master walk to a thatched cottage, which, though lacking space, was neat and clean. Then a table and chairs were brought out. One steady, old chair was chosen as the seat for the young master. The rest of his companions took seats too, some on chairs, some on stools and still others on a rice-threshing rack pulled out from somewhere. Sitting in a circle, they ate and reveled, as the host family was kept busy supplying the table.

Then Jia Qingfu called out, "Please bring more wine here. We want to have a good time. Our master won't let you down in terms of payment." The host family kept bringing out and warming the home-brewed wine for the guests. The young master and his men ate and drank their fill until they were unable to sit straight. As the saying goes, "The hunger are not particular about food, the thirsty are not particular about drink," so it is universally true that hungry and thirsty people find their food and drink tasty. The party was now in high spirits so they decided that the dinner was the best feast they had ever had, despite the rough food, fat chicken meat and stale alcohol.

The young master was very pleased. His men all said to him, "This warm host deserves a double reward."

The young lord agreed, saying, "Surely he does." He let Jia Qingfu come up with an estimate of the cost, and the latter, only too familiar with what he usually did, gave a higher figure than necessary. The young master wanted to pay the host three times that figure. The young master's manager and the rest of the men took one third of the payment, behind the young master's back, before handing the remainder to the host. How could the host family be unhappy as it was reaping such a great interest on their investment?

So all the members of the family turned out to express their gratitude in front of the young master, as he mounted his horse to leave. This added to the rapture in the young master's heart. So he observed, "Look, how cordial these people are!"

Zhao Nengwu rejoined, "They're not only hospitable, they are courteous as well." The young master therefore bade his followers to give them even more of a reward.

The manager galloped up and inquired, "How much do you want to reward them, sir?" The young master let him check the amount of money left in his silver sack. The manager opened it and saw several *liang* of silver inside, in no less than one thousand bits.

Then the young master said, "Let them take all of it. Why bother to count it?" He lifted the sack with his hand and dumped all the pieces of silver onto the ground. The sack was then empty. Seeing the silver dropping all over the place, the members of the host family dashed forward to collect it, jostling and shoving one another in neglect of their filial respect for the old and custodial care of the young. The quickest one picked up a big piece of silver and then swooped down for a second, while no sooner had the slowest one retrieved a piece than it was grabbed away by a quicker hand. The old host picked one piece of silver, holding it tightly and trying to keep his tattering body steady before he slipped twice on the ground.

The young master with his men burst into laughter and applause, saying, "This is the funniest thing we've ever come across!" Though the trip resulted in a large expenditure, the young master enjoyed showing off his generosity. The host family was paid amply for their labor.

This news soon got around the local area. The other villagers felt shame over the fact that they didn't have the good luck to run into the young master. After that, someone would always come to inquire about the young master's itinerary whenever he planned to go out on tour, and welcoming countryfolk would line the road carrying jugs of wine and pots of food wherever he rode. In each place the local people would flatter him profusely, while he would repay their hospitality handsomely, usually with a modest remark, "The payment is too paltry for the hospitality." Inciting him on, his companions would say, "They're mere country people, sir. But they accommodated you with the best of their possessions, treating you more honorably than they would the emperor. If you fail to pay them substantially, how will you be able to encourage them?" The young master would answer, "Exactly!" So rewards were added to the payments, while the payments steadily increased. Actually this was a trap contrived by his companions together with the local people. Jia Qingfu and Zhao Nengwu at the head of them first planned the itinerary and made arrangements in advance. That's why the young master would be warmly entertained wherever he went. Then they would share the gains and work for more profit the next time.

Among the young master's kinfolk, there was one man called Zhang San. He found it shameful that the young master spent his wealth so extravagantly. He remembered how the young master's father, the late Minister of the Ministry of War, lived. So he advised the young master one time when he met him, saying, "Your father had a wealth of property. But he did not achieve it merely through receiving a regular government salary. As a matter of fact, most of his income came from his strict budget and calculated expenditures. I personally saw that he rose early in the morning and turned in late at night, working with an abacus, weigh-scale, account books and other things. If someone owed him even a tiny amount of money, he would argue with a stern face until he was given his due. Occasionally he snapped up a small bargain. Then I saw his joy was tremendous. Therefore the legacy of wealth he left you was hard come by. Now your wasteful expenditures are worlds apart from your father's frugality."

The young master flushed with embarrassment. Before he could make a reply, some of his companions, led by Jia Qingfu and Zhao Nengwu, yelled, "How can you speak to our young master about such a narrow-minded style of living! The young master is a hero known in the region. How can he be particular about gain or loss of wealth? Besides, one's family fortune is granted by Heaven, rather than being achieved through one's effort. Don't you know that Li Bai* wrote a line of poetry which reads, 'I was born to fulfill a heavenly designated mission, and gold dissipated will come again.' What the late father of the young master did only shows his miserliness, which certainly was a flaw. Our young master does not follow in his path but gives up the convention. This demonstrates our master's unrestricted and chivalrous character. This can never make sense to a country bumpkin!"

These words helped the young master regain his confidence and feel a lot easier. Meanwhile, Zhang San realized that the young master was in these knaves' pocket and wouldn't listen to any good advice. So he never brought up the subject again.

The young master was manipulated this way for a few years and eventually all his wealth drained away. He began to use grain as currency, grain which had been collected in his granaries over the years. He would either sell some grain for some silver or pay with grain in kind or borrow silver at the time of purchase and pay it back after the fall harvest. But this tight budgeting bothered him. Seeing that the young master's property remained intact, his companions decided, "The young master still has a lot left for us to desire."

---

*Li Bai (AD 701-762), a famous poet.

After discussions with Jia and Zhao, they came to see the young master and made a suggestion, saying, "Here's a good idea, sir, to remove your worries about money."

Too eager for a way out of the difficulties, the young master asked quickly, "What is it?"

Those men gesticulated as they replied, "You own a great deal of land crisscrossed with paths that take up half of the county's area. It's pity that you've no idea how much of the land you've never even been to. In the past when your household was at the peak of prosperity, it often received plots of land from local farmers as a token of their respect, or from rich families by way of gifts. So the lands were not necessarily all obtained through purchases. Even some of the purchased land was obtained after deductions of interest and debts owed to your family. Actually, a few of the landowners were impoverished, with no inheritors left behind them, and had to turn the land over to your family for little payment. Therefore your land largely lies waste now. Only a small part of it is being farmed. Without renting out the land, you currently don't receive interest. But you need money and grain at this point. If you don't make arrangements to get rid of the land now, it's going to be a problem for you in the future. The land is nothing but trash to you now. It would be quite useful for the peasants to till it. If you were to let farmers take the land, wouldn't you turn your trash into silver? Besides, you will save money and grain."

The young master rejoined, "Yes, I really hate dealing with issues regarding money and grain. If I can get them out of my way and come by some silver as a result, that will be something worth doing."

After that, whenever there was need of money, the young master simply wrote out a sales contract for a certain plot of land. Usually the potential land-buyer desired the bargain but would feign reluctance saying he would rather receive some other things instead. The men surrounding the young master would then talk the land-buyer into accepting it. At such moments the young master often felt uneasy and worried about the buyer's refusal to take the land until the contract was accepted. If a rich man was interested in a given fertile plot of the young master's land, he would inform Jia Qingfu and Zhao Nengwu in secret. The two men would lead the young master on a detour to the rich man's home, using hunting as the excuse. The host often happily gave the young master a special treat of dinner, and sometimes he would let his wife come and entertain the young master. Some land-seekers even kept prostitutes at home to pose as their wives, women who would make eyes at the young master. The motive behind such arrangements was not totally unknown to the young master, but he responded with tacit approval, feeling proud of himself. Toward the end of each dinner, the young master would be asked to make payment with a titled deed. The young master was not good at handwriting. So a good writer among his men would do the writing, while another one calculated the cost of the dinner and still another located the lot of land in the account book. After this was done, all that was left for the young master to do was to sign his name on the paper. He knew nothing about the location and quality of the land. When told to sign the paper, he quickly did so. Occasionally, the calculation of the cost of the land would be more than the expense for the dinner, so a couple of *liang* of silver would be given to the young master to cover the difference, which delighted him greatly.

As such transactions took place frequently, signing such papers became a bore for him. Then the young master spoke to Jia Qingfu, saying, "I don't need to handle silver any more, but now just give them a written paper. That's easy and I feel relieved. However, I still have to bother with the signing my name on the deeds, and I'm tired of it."

Zhao Nengwu echoed, "We have no problem in wielding the lance and stave. But using the brush-pen, if you want us to, is really an achievement way above us."

Jia Qingfu said, "I've an idea that will save labor."

The young master inquired, "What is that?"

Jia Qingfu answered, "We can cut printing blocks containing those words, leaving blanks for the year and month. Then we can print a hundred copies and keep them with us. When you need to use one, just put in the amount of land to be sold and then fill in the blanks with the year and month. To simplify your signing process, we can even cut your name into a seal. Then you will be able to print your name instead of signing it at the time of need. Won't that save you labor?"

The young master replied, "Absolutely right! But I still have one thing to worry about. If I give up my property so lavishly through block printing, people with petty sophistication may laugh at me. How can I put a lot of effort into explaining the matter to them one by one? I have improvised a doggerel and I'm going to have it cut into the printing blocks, too, and print it at the end of the document. When they read it, they will know I'm broad-minded, not despiteful like them."

Jia Qingfu asked, "What's your doggerel?"

The young master said, "Let me read it. You can put it down." It goes like this:

The land stands for ages, but not the landlords,
So why should I keep expense records?
Where are those wealthy and powerful in past?
Even the imperial dynasties have turned to dust!
Fortune goes lightly — equally light it will come.
Having none of it is as good as having some.
Ridicule me for wasting a legacy on whim,
And I will laugh at you for living in a vain dream.

As he finished saying this, he had someone write it down. Jia Qingfu commended him, saying, "See, you're a highly accomplished poet, sir. Who will doubt that you will be able to achieve fame and wealth sooner or later in future? On the contrary, the land is nothing to be worried about. Since you put down a poem on the contract, your good reputation will increase with each distributed sheet."

The young master was overjoyed and immediately ordered that over ten copies be printed each day. These were to be kept by Jia Qingfu and Zhao Nengwu. When payment was needed on any of the subsequent tours, they took out one copy, put down a few words and put the seal on it, and thus a contract for the land was made and given out. The young master smiled and said, "It has really simplified the business! I don't need to touch the brush any more. Wonderful! Wonderful!" When some of his men wanted to obtain a plot of land for themselves, they simply filled in the form with whatever words needed to put in and put the master's seal on it stealthily. As time elapsed, the young master never worried, knowing the daily cost was just a few sheets of paper. But he was ignorant of the fact that his land was being quickly nibbled away. He enjoyed himself until all the land was lost, the provision of food and grain ceased, and the printing facilities and contract forms were untended. Without a supply of food, he called his followers, and asked them why they didn't sell some land to get his daily supply, only to get the reply that he had became landless.

Seeing that financial troubles now weighed down the young master, some of his men, those who had fleeced him out of land and built up their own family fortune, gradually deserted him. But Jia Qingfu and Zhao Nengwu remained, though they, too, had enriched their own families with full jugs and vessels of supply at home. Believing that, as a proverb went, a skinny camel still gives a thousand *jin* of meat, they hung on. Then they talked the young master into selling his large house and made money for themselves as brokers in the deal. Later they went on with their wheedling and purchased a small house for the young master and made money out of the transaction for themselves as well. After he moved into the new house, they told the young master the house needed renovation. So they discussed with him the remodeling costs in terms of purchasing timbers and rocks, out of which they profited. The house soon assumed an impressive appearance but the young master was short of money again.

The young master thought to himself, "I don't have many dependents right now so there is no need to keep these horses." Then the two men took charge of selling the horses. However, the price dropped to one or two-tenths of the original cost. The young master asked, "Why has the price come down so much?"

The two men answered, "Well, they've been ridden and run quite a distance so the price has definitely dropped." The young master did not explore the matter further because he had gotten for the moment something to spend. At first he had two or three fine horses left for his use; later on as he did not need to reward anyone and had a far smaller platoon of followers, and thus the issue of hunting sank into oblivion, even the two or three horses were of no use. Furthermore, horse-tending took labor and skill. Eventually, Jia Qingfu and Zhao Nengwu found an opportunity to sell them, but it was not a good price and, in addition, not all the earnings reached the hands of the young master. Now the two men shifted their attention to the young master's house that he had purchased only recently. The earlier renovation of the new house had turned out to be a waste, and, since its sale was urgent, the original price was the best the young master could obtain. With the new house gone, renting became a necessity. Due to the lack of space in the rented house, his remaining possessions, most of them of little value, were sold at half price or given away as trash.

After the young master moved in the rented house, Jia Qingfu and Zhao Nengwu soon disappeared and didn't show up again. His only companion was his wife. When he led a gay life, his wife had advised him a number of times against his extravagant spending. Not only did the young lord turn a deaf ear to her words but squabbles over the matter erupted periodically. Knowing that her warnings did not help, she had to let the matter take its own course. His wife, of course, was also of an upper-class background. She depended upon others for her living, not caring about the future, so she had never put aside a sum for herself. So when the young master was rich, she was well off; when her husband was in poverty, she was too. Hence they lived in the rented house on the money they earned from the sale of their house.

At intervals the young master wandered the streets and bumped into some of his former followers, who were all now well-dressed and surrounded by their own followers. For the first a couple of times they exchanged greetings with the young master, showing a minimum of courtesy. Later, they would hurry past, shielding their faces. Finally on any encounter with their former master, they would march forward without greeting him.

One morning the young master stumbled across Zhao Nengwu, who said to him, "Did you have your breakfast, sir?"

The young master replied, "No, not yet. I'm going to buy some refreshments."

Zhao Nengwu replied, "Since you want to have some refreshments, why not come to my home and have a taste of something I have cooked."

The young master then followed him to his home and Zhao Nengwu said, "I killed a stray dog last night and made of it a very tender in stew. I'm going to share it with you." He brought out the steaming dog meat and the two then devoured it instantly. After this hearty meal, the young master returned home, thinking Zhao Nengwu was a good man. Whenever he became bored, he went to Zhao Nengwu's place. But later the warmth cooled off, and Zhao Nengwu also shunned the young master. Jia Qingfu sometimes met his former patron, too. He would pretend to be all smiles. When the young master was led to his home, a cup of fine green tea would be the best treat given him. Jia Qingfu would let the young master have a taste of his tea and then talk empty words. He would also sit cross-legged, playing a piece of music on his vertical bamboo flute. That was a show of his respect. He did not even bother to buy the young master some scanty food for little cost, which would have somewhat subdued the guest's hunger. The young master had to leave unsatisfied. No one else paid any attention to him.

The young master's father-in-law, Shangguan, was man of good sense. At the beginning when the young master happily squandered his properties, the father-in-law used to come and advise him against his style of living. But later, seeing the young man had no intention of changing his ways, the father-in-law backed off, figuring he would wait until the young master wastefully spent all his possessions and suffered a great deal so that he would realize how senseless his life was. Therefore the old man did not put forth a further word of admonishment when the young man was wealthy, nor did he give him a hand when financial plight tormented him, as if he had nothing to do with his son-in-law at all. When the young master ran out of money, food and clothing and had nothing in his house for sale, he hit upon the stupid idea, after long meditation, of selling his wife. He decided that would save a mouth to feed and give him some money as well. Though he did not express this thought out of fear of his father-in-law, the signs of it began to show in spite of himself. Shangguan read his son-in-law's mind from the very beginning, and thought to himself, "I should do something before he makes such a rash move. I'll let him fall into my trap and then wait and see." So he summoned Zhang San, the one who had advised the young master before, and asked him to be a disguised envoy and talk to the young master. Zhang San went on the mission accordingly.

The young master felt ashamed of the fact that he had turned a deaf ear to Zhang San's earlier advice and had thus sunk to such depths of hopelessness. Zhang San said, "Do you now realize that what I said to you in the past was wise advice?"

The young master rejoined, "I now feel sorry for myself."

Zhang San said, "I heard that you're having a rough time and want to dispose of your wife. Is that true?"

With flushing cheeks, the young master replied, "We got married in our early years, so how could I have made such a casual remark?

However, I'm at the end of my resources and have nothing with which to feed the two of us. I thought that, instead of letting her die of hunger, I might send her to a good family. On the one hand, I will then only have myself to feed. On the other, she will be well placed in someone else's home instead of suffering from hunger with me. I hate to say this, but that idea did cross my mind."

Zhang San then said, "If you're serious about it, would you be willing to let me be the matchmaker?"

The young master said, "That would be fine. But do you have any idea as to what interested family there might be?"

Zhang San said, "Yes, someone did ask me to keep my eyes open regarding this matter. That's why I came to talk to you."

The young master said, "The problem is how can I shamelessly bring up the matter in front of my father-in-law, even if someone wants to take her?"

Zhang San said, "I have come to let you know that your father-in-law has learned about your squandering your property and he is worried about your wife's life in the days to come. He has the same idea of remarrying her. But it would look disgraceful if she left your house and went straight into somebody else's home. So your father-in-law wants to bring her back to his house and let her stay there while waiting for the selection of a choice marriage partner. At that time I will be the matchmaker. After the marriage, I'll quietly bring the dowry to you. That will keep your reputation unharmed. What do you think of that, sir?"

The young master said, "That's a very good idea, despite the hassle. That'll spare me needless embarrassment in parting with her. Since my father-in-law is making arrangements about this, it's inappropriate for me to go and see him now. But where do you think I should go to pick up information about her marriage?"

Zhang San said, "You just come to my home and check with me. After she goes to your father-in-law's house, the marriage should be settled speedily. I will send you word. Please don't worry."

The young master said, "Then I will keep this from my wife and simply wait until my father-in-law sends people here to take her back home."

Zhang San said, "Exactly." Then they parted.

Soon Shangguan sent people to bring his daughter home. A few days later, Zhang San came to see the young master and said, "The marriage is done."

The young master asked, "Who married her?"

Zhang San said, "A rich man, whose family is also Yao."

The young master said, "If he's rich, the dowry should be plentiful?"

Zhang San said, "They said it's her second marriage at middle age and so they would not pay more. After I highly praised her kindness and competence, they gave forty *liang* of silver. From now on you should lead a simple and budgeted life. Don't be wasteful. Otherwise you won't have anything more."

The young master received the silver and was overjoyed, expressing his thanks repeatedly. Zhang San said, "Since you've gotten some silver, you can't expect to see your wife anymore now that she has married into a rich family. I wonder why you're so happy?"

The young master explained, "Well, it's better than that we both die of hunger. Now she is going to have a good life and I'm better off with the silver. Why should I be unhappy?" It so happened that the father-in-law wanted to play this trick of taking his daughter back home for fear of the young master's selling of her. He gave him this silver secretly to support him financially. The old man would now wait and see what the young master would do with the silver.

With the silver in hand, the young master didn't need to stint on his expenditures. But how long could he continue in this way? Besides, he had been unable to keep his head above water in terms of a number of unpaid bills for housing and food. Therefore his spending of the silver did not last long before he relapsed into destitution. As he saw he had nothing for sale but himself, the thought of selling himself tangled his mind. He believed he might make money on the sale and have something to eat. But who would be willing to purchase a young master like him? Besides, he was a single man now, as useless as a stick too long for firewood and too short for a door-prop. Who would want to buy trash like him? Brushing aside embarrassment, he sought assistance for the sale of himself. When this news soon reached Shangguan, he took out a few *liang* of silver as payment for the young master and had a farmhand sign a contract to purchase him, and keep him on one of his manors.

The farmhand, posing as host of the manor, said to the young master, "You're not of humble stock so you have been better paid. But now you're one of my men and should be at my disposal. You should be able to sustain hard work and be obedient. I won't take you unless you accept these terms."

The young master figured that when he was rich, he had tens of servants at home. They usually got fed and idled about every day. He wondered what kind of hard work and rough time this man could have for him? So he agreed readily, saying, "That's fine, sir. Since I have been sold to you as your slave, I'll do whatever I'm told to do." At first the young master did no work but just ate whatever he was offered. He thought his sale to this family was a bargain. However, a couple of days later, the host imposed a daily work quota on him. He had to cut firewood in the morning, shoulder jugs of water during the day, and husk grain with a pestle and mortar and winnow away the chaff in the evening. He was exhausted with aches and pains all over his body, but he was given no breaks at all. When he paused for a breath, the farmer would threaten to beat him with a cudgel. He was not be able to bear it anymore. He stayed for less than ten days and then ran away. As required by Shangguan, the farmhand did not pursue him and waited to see how he would make a living.

The young master was on the run with no definite place to go. He was hungry, and seeing that beggars who got alms had something to eat, he swallowed his pride and begged for food. After a few days of independent wandering, he joined a platoon of beggars. But his sense of dignity nagged at him, reminding him of his happy days in the past. Then he composed a long song. He sang the song to the melody of "The Fall of Lotus Flowers," as he rambled down the street begging. The song went like this:

> They say time, like a shuttle, flies fast;
> I say time can pass in different ways.
> I was envied in my glorious past,
> But I have wasted my happy days.
> Today, alas! My riches are all spent.
> Each moment to me is never-ending torment.
> I used to ride a strong horse, wear fur coat and cap tall
> And see an army of millions march at my call.
> The shouting hunters, encircling, scared forest elves into fleeing;
> Villagers welcomed and treated me as if I were a heavenly being.
> Now my gold is gone, so my friends have left.
> With hares gone, like old arrows on the shelf, I'm bereft.
> I haven't a bowl of gruel in the day nor sleep all night long,
> I wander in the streets singing a vagabond song.
> Who can bear a fall from paradise to an infernal state?
> I should not blame my parents, nor blame fate.
> Had I foreseen this dire hour of need,
> I wouldn't have befriended men of greed.
> Now helpless, I advise you all:
> Take a lesson from my downfall.

Shangguan learned that his son-in-law was reduced to street beggary so he sent someone to ask the young master's fellow beggars to insult him, rob him of the food he had obtained through begging, and leave him alone. Therefore the young master suffered a great deal more from hunger. But whenever he showed signs of resistance, his fellow beggars would threaten him by saying, "If you dare to rough us up, we will go and tell your owner about you!" That made him panic and run away. But he still had to live on the streets. He underwent all the bitter experiences of suffering from cold, hunger and worry that life had to offer.

Meanwhile, Shangguan decided that the young man had had enough. So he let his daughter move into a large residence and had a small room close to the back gate of its yard cleaned up, with some simple bedding put inside. Then he asked Zhang San to find the young master.

Accordingly Zhang San spoke to the young master, saying, "How did you fall into such a miserable state so soon after my matchmaking for your wife?"

The young master answered, "Such a miserable state? That's not all of it. I have to endure those beggars' bullying as well!"

Zhang San said, "But you're from a family of noble origin. How can you tolerate those beggars' bullying? I know you are not afraid of them, but you fear seeing your owner. You are lucky your owner hasn't found you. Otherwise you would be sent to jail. If he were to take you to court for seizing the money from selling yourself, the rest of your life would be ruined!"

The young master replied, "Now I've no way to survive but have to put myself at fate's mercy. I'll die sooner or later and won't see you again. You did the matchmaking and helped marry off my wife. How are things with her these days?" He then started crying.

Zhang San said, "That's something I wanted to talk to you about. Your wife is currently the mistress of a rich family with broad social relations, as imposing as yours were years ago. Recently they asked me to find them a doorkeeper for the back of their yard. I'd like to introduce you to them. Your job will be just to open the gate in the morning and shut it in the evening, nothing else. You will enjoy plenty of free time and meals. How would you like the job?"

The young master said, "If you can help me get this job, the kindness you've shown me will be as great as that of my parents."

Zhang San said, "There's one thing you've got to bear in mind, however. Your wife is now the mistress of the household — your boss. It will bring shame to her if it becomes known that you were formerly married to her. So keep your mouth shut on that matter, or you will lose the job."

The young master said, "Life changes. Now she's up there in heaven and I'm down here as a doorkeeper for her. It's my good fortune that I will not die from starvation and have my body cast in a ditch in the wilderness. I will be pretty happy with my state and not brag about anything."

Zhang San said, "All right, then come with me and I'll help you get the job."

The young master accompanied him and waited outside the gate of the residence. It took a long time before Zhang San came out and said to him, "Everything is in order. Come on in with me, please."

He led the young master to the room at the rear of the mansion. The room was roughly furnished with a new bed and bed-drapes. For some time the young master had spent nights in the open, experiencing the harshest forms of life. He was overwhelmed at the cleanness and tidiness of the room and household necessities.

He asked in surprise, "Who lives in this room?"

Zhang San replied, "It's for the doorkeeper, and now it's your room."

The young master was delighted since the room seemed like paradise to him. Zhang San then warned him, "Your mistress is wealthy and has an army of pretty servants. She wants you to take care of the back gate. You should simply stay here and enjoy your light job. The master of the family and your mistress may go in and out of their rooms at the front gate. You should not snoop about. She would feel disgraced if she met you. Don't step outside your gate. If you run into your former owner, you'll not be able to stay here any more." He repeated the warning several more times and then left.

The young master had been through hard living, so he now acted with particular caution. On the one hand, he feared losing this job, and on the other, he dared not give away his identity and create trouble were he to stumble across his former owner. Thus he kept to himself inside the room and stayed there for more than two months.

Shanguan learned that the mind of his son-in-law had become sensible, and so he sent a man one day to bring an envelope to him with a silver reward sealed inside and to tell him, "The mistress is having her birthday celebration, rewarding all the servants. She said you did a good job in watching the gate, so she rewards you one *qian* of silver. You may use it to buy yourself some wine."

The young master took it, realizing the day was indeed his former wife's birthday anniversary. He recalled that when his family fortune was at its zenith, he often had invited a host of guests to come and present their congratulations, and to enjoy drinks during the birthday celebration. But now he was an employee of somebody else. Tears began rolling down his cheeks. He wrapped up the silver, reluctant to spend it.

A few days later a man came and said to him, "The mistress wants to talk to you in her room."

Surprised, the young master murmured, "Zhang San told me the other day that she would feel ashamed if she met me, and he asked me to keep my identity from others. Why is she now asking me to see her? How can I go and see her at this point?"

But he was in no position to turn down her request. So he followed the man through to the main room of the house. He saw her sitting there with the dignified bearing of the mistress. The young master hung his head in shame.

The wife spoke to him, saying "I heard about a doorkeeper with the family name of Yao, but I didn't realize it was you. You're from a wealthy house. How have you become a doorkeeper working for my house?"

The young master, with a shameful face, could not utter a word in reply. The woman continued, "Since you're doing well at doorkeeping, here's an envelope containing a reward for you. You may use it to purchase some clothes."

A servant-girl handed him the reward. He accepted it with thanks. Then the mistress had him led back to his small room at the back gate. In his room, he opened the envelope and found five *qian* of silver inside. He was joyous and wrapped them together with the silver equivalent to one string of cash that he had received on the mistress's birthday, and put these away. But some of his fellow servants came and tried to coax him to spend the newly received reward on drinks. He turned them down.

Not giving up, they said, "Okay, perhaps it will cost him too much. We should throw in our share, making it half-and-half."

The young master held his money tightly in his hand, replying, "There's no easy money. I will put this to good use later. I don't want to be a prodigal 'good fellow' any more." They found him unyielding, and so they all left.

At dusk one day, a servant-girl came and said to him, "The mistress wants to talk to you in her room about things of the past."

Refusing to meet the request, the young master said, "It's not an appropriate time for me to talk to her in the evening. I'm here to keep the door secure. If something happens, they will fire me and throw me out onto the street. I will then definitely die. I think I should stay here in the room. Please go back and tell the mistress that I don't dare to enter her quarters."

In the meantime, Shangguan sent men to check on the young master periodically and learned of the change in him after his undergoing so much hardship. So Shangguan asked Zhang San to visit the young master again. Meeting Zhang San, the young master expressed his deep gratitude for the former's recommendation of him for the job.

Zhang San asked him, "How do you find life here?" The young master said, "I won't need to worry about my food and clothing anymore until death as long as I live in this room. I owe you a debt for doing me this favor. Without your help, I might have died long ago somewhere. However, I have one thing on my mind: I think it shameful to earn easy food and idle away time as I do. I feel sorry for myself. I've saved some money and never want to spend it. You're a good man. Please teach me a way to earn interest on the money, or teach me a trade so as to make the rest of my life more meaningful."

Zhang San replied, "Alas, when did you learn to value time and property?"

With a grin, the young master rejoined, "It took long time to learn this. But now it's too late."

Zhang San said, "I have come to you with a message that one of your relatives wishes to see you."

The young master replied, "I've sunk so low that none of my relatives cares about me anymore. Who wants to see me now?"

Zhang San said, "There is one. Come with me."

Zhang San led him into the parlor. A man, with a stately hat on his head and elegantly attired, emerged and walked up with measured, haughty strides. The young master saw it was his former father-in-law, Shangguan.

"Aha!" the young master let out a shrill cry, turned pale and tried to leave. Zhang San darted up and grabbed him, saying, "That's your father-in-law. Where are you going?"

The young master answered, "How can I have the courage to face him?"

"Why not?" Zhang San said. "He is your father-in-law."

The young master replied, "I sold my wife. How can he still be my father-in-law?"

Zhang San said, "He has learned that you have become sensible, so he wants to let you and his daughter renew your marriage."

The young master said, "His daughter is the mistress of the family I'm serving. Does he have another daughter to marry off?"

Zhang San said, "I did the matchmaking to sell your wife before. But now I'm doing the matchmaking to return your wife to you."

The young master asked, "How can you do that?"

Zhang San said, "You stupid idiot! How could a privileged family remarry their daughter? In those days your father-in-law had feared you might behave recklessly and so he sent his men to bring your wife back home. But he told you that she remarried. You're now living in one of your father-in-law's residences. Because he was afraid that you might die of hunger and cold on the streets, he asked me to make arrangements to bring you to that room as the doorkeeper. Now that you've completely discarded your former way of life, I've been sent here to let you know what's really happened and to prepare you for a reunion with your wife. The whole course of developments has been in the control of your father-in-law, with his good intentions of making you turn over a new leaf in life."

The young master now said, "No wonder I've been living in the room for such a long time, knowing there was a mistress of the family, but never seeing the master. I was rather compliant with your request and didn't inquire about anything. I didn't know something like this was happening. How amazing that my father-in-law went out of his way to help me!"

Zhang San said, "Why not go up and give him your greetings?"

He led the young master forward by holding his hand, while Shangguan came toward him and remarked, "Have you made up your mind to remember your suffering and relinquish your former style of living?"

Shamefully at a loss for words, the young master dropped to his knees and burst into crying.

Shangguan said, "Since you now hate your stupid behavior of the past, I will give you and your wife this residence and one hundred *mu* of land so that you can make a living. But if you slip back into your former way of life, I'll throw you out and never let you see your wife again."

Crying, the young master said, "I've suffered a lot and received tremendous benevolence from you. If I fail to mend my ways sincerely, I will sink into a state so worthless swine and dogs will be more valued!"

Then Shangguan led him into another room to meet his daughter. The husband and wife flung themselves onto each other's arms and cried. Then they talked to each other and came out to express their thanks to Zhang San.

The young master said to Zhang San, as the latter was about to leave, "I've one more thing to worry about. If my former owner finds me, what should I do?"

Zhang San replied, "There is no such an owner. Your enslavement was organized by your father-in-law! If you can manage your household, you needn't worry about anything."

Then the young master felt easy. As the host, he lived with his wife in the residence, enjoying a life of adequate food and clothing, which was earned through diligent work and careful budgeting, although his life was not as abundant as it had been in his early years. With painful recollections of the past lingering in his mind, the young master refused to allow a single loafer into his place anymore.

As the news of the young master's renewal of family life reached Jia Qingfu and Zhao Nengwu, the two men with some of their fellows visited their former companion. The young master came out and said to them, "My life is fine and I want to be left alone. I don't want to associate with you anymore."

At this Jia Qingfu broached such subjects as the playing of music, and Zhao Nengwu talked about someone's fine horse, another man's strong bow, and some places that had many birds and wild animals. The young master simply gave a cold sneer and made this remark after their monologues were finished, "If you two brothers find someone like I used to be, please come and let me know, so we can go together and fleece him." The two men felt snubbed and beat a hasty retreat in disappointment.

When Shangguan learned that those men had come to bother the young master again, he sued them. A thorough legal investigation into their doings was conducted. A large part of land they had seized illegally was confiscated and returned to the young master. The young master's property thus grew larger. The husband and wife lived a happy life till death. The moral of the tale lies in the fact that the young master led a prodigal way of life simply due to his lack of life experience of hardship. It is highly significant that children of a rich family should go through difficulties and suffering in their lives, and they should use caution in dealing with their followers as well.

Tale 10

Tea-and-wine Master Xu Kidnaps the Bride Amid Wedding Festivities; Zheng Ruizhu Utters Her Grievances Ending an Unsettled Case

In the county of Jiading of the prefecture of Suzhou, Zhili Province [today's Jiangsu Province] there lived a family named Zheng, who maintained a brokerage profession on a small scale. The family had a daughter called Ruizhu, whose extraordinary beauty brought such shame to the natural world that it made fish sink, wild geese alight, the moon grow dim and flowers fade to obscurity. She was betrothed to a man of the same county, called Xie Sanlang, and she awaited the time to be married. A fortunate date of the month was chosen, and the family of Xie prepared to come and carry her away in marriage. Three days before that date, Ruizhu needed her hair styled. Her father decided to bring in a hairdresser. The local convention at that time was that an ordinary family with a daughter to be married usually hired a man to do the make-up.

There was a young man called Xu Da, who was indecent, vicious and full of lust. He had set him mind on finding out which families had pretty girls. To satisfy his desire to ogle such pretty young ladies, he made a special effort to learn the trade of hairdressing so that he could be allowed into the rooms of women. He also went through training to work as a Tea-and-wine Master so that he could leer at the brides. What was a Tea-and-wine Master? He was a master of ceremony. At the wedding ceremony the master usually stood aside calling out, "Please have some tea," and "Please have some wine." That was why he was called "Tea-and-wine Master." Xu Da did these two kinds of work, which provided him with access to women. The Zhengs asked him to do the make-up for their daughter, Ruizhu.

Xu Da arrived with combs and other tools, and went straight into the room of Ruizhu. He had never seen the girl before. Now he had the chance to work on her face. The sight of her beauty filled him with lust. While working on her hair, he turned and bent, sending lecherous glances toward her. His body, like a snowman near fire, was half-melted. If there had been no other people around at that moment, he would have cuddled and touched her for awhile. Ruizhu's father, seeing all this, realized that he was evilly motivated. No sooner had Xu Da finished than he ordered him out of the room.

Xu Da was fully aroused, and returned home with the girl constantly on his mind. Knowing that she was marrying into the family of Xie, he managed to obtain a job working as the Tea-and-wine Master on the day of Ruizhu's wedding. On that day, Zheng Ruizhu's father took his daughter to the bridegroom's home and saw that the master of ceremony coming out to greet them was none other than Xu Da, who had styled his daughter's hair a couple of days before. He was surprised, saying to himself, "I didn't know he would also be here!" As the bride rose from the sedan chair and greetings were exchanged, Xu Da struggled for glimpses of her, thinking of nothing else. The ritual calls he uttered as the Tea-and-wine Master became mumbled and muddled. As a result the ceremony proceeded in utter disorder. At

Xu's confusing order the bride made many greetings until the wedding ceremony was over and the bride retired to her bedroom.

The next item on the agenda was to entertain the relatives and friends with a wedding feast. The family of Xie, not very rich, was short-handed. So Xie, the father, and Xie Sanlang, the bridegroom, had to be in the main room with the merrymaking guests. Back in the kitchen, the mother personally directed two woman servants in fixing drinks of wine. A couple of men looked after the party. They were always in a rush. Xu Da was supposed to perform the rite proceedings, but when the guests were all seated awaiting his calls of "please have your soup" and "please have your drink," there was no sign of him. After two or three trips were made delivering soup to the guests, the host himself had to replace Xu Da in the performance of rite. Toward the end of the feast, they saw Xu Da come out from behind to make a few calls. As the party was about to be dismissed, Old Man Xie, having become unhappy with this Tea-and-wine Master's demeanor, wanted to call him in for a scolding, but Xu Da was nowhere to be found. The manager of the ceremony said, "He went to the front a moment ago."

Old Man Xie said, "Why did we hire such an irresponsible person? How negligent he is!" He could not wait any longer for the Tea-and-wine Master to come and perform the rites, and so he had to express his thanks to the guests personally.

Meanwhile Xie Sanlang went to his new bedroom, but he did not find his bride there. Thinking she might have gone to sleep, he lifted the bed-drapes only to discover an empty bed. Looking around, he still found no sign of her. He rushed to the kitchen and asked the people there where she might be. They shouted at him, "We've been busy here with kitchen work. After the wedding ceremony, the bride was alone in her room. Why are you coming to ask us?"

Sanlang called the house retainers and together they searched everywhere in the house. As they came to the rear gate of the house, they found it locked. Then they went back to the hall and told everybody there about the strange turn of events. The whole family became most distressed.

The house retainer said, "This Tea-and-wine Master has not been an honest one. When he was making the ritual calls, he was absentminded and his eyes were fastened on the bride. And he failed to show up twice this evening. Now he's even disappeared. Did he work out some plan and steal the bride?"

Old Man Zheng said, "The Tea-and-wine Master was not decent. The other day when my daughter needed her hair styled, it was he who came and did the work. I noticed his despicable behavior. I loathed him. I was surprised that you had hired him as the Tea-and-wine Master."

One servant who came with the family of Zheng said, "He originally was a good-for-nothing street ruffian. He only learned hairdressing and directing nuptial routines not long ago, so that he could spend his days bluffing his way around. I think there must be some reason he has vanished. He can't get far. Let's go and hunt for him."

The house retainers of the family of Xie said, "If he kidnapped the bride from her room, he must have had to take her out through the rear gate. A moment ago we saw that the rear gate was well locked, he must have come back to secure it from the inside. That is clear. And that is why he showed up the last time we saw him. He must have gone outside the front gate and into the rear alley. That's why we don't see him now. It's unquestionable that he took her."

The bridegrooms family had torches available in the house. With torches lit, the servants of the two families and their masters, totaling about ten persons, each with a torch in hand, opened the rear gate and hurried down the alley. It turned out that this alley behind Xie's house was straight without curves or forks. The torches illuminated the alley as clearly as if it were broad daylight. Three men could be seen walking ahead a little distance away. Later two of them were gone, leaving the last one on the road. The group hurried to catch up with him. Under the torch light, they could see that it was indeed the Tea-and-wine Master Xu. They asked him, "Why are you out here?"

Xu Da answered, "I've some business to attend to, so I left for home without staying through to the end of the party."

The men asked, "Since you wanted to go home, why didn't you let the host know? Aside from this, you were not seen at the party for quite awhile tonight, but you're now here in the alley walking. Are you really heading home? You'd better tell us the truth. Where did you take the bride to?"

Xu Da spoke evasively, saying, "The bride should be in your home. Am I, a Tea-and-wine Master, supposed to look after her?"

The men struck and shoved him, yelling, "Bring this villain home and torture him to make him tell us the truth!"

They escorted him back to the Xies' home. The host, the bride's father and the bridegroom interrogated him for awhile, but Xu Da categorically denied any knowledge of the bride's whereabouts.

Then they said, "Such a hardened, deceptive bag of shit! He won't yield anything to our interrogation today. Fasten him to a post, and take him to the county office tomorrow. Will he refuse to tell the truth to the authorities as well?" So they tied him up and waited until the next day. At the time the most disappointed one was Xie Sanlang.

Surrounding Xu Da, the men babbled and prattled all night, some intimidating him and others trying to persuade him. How could they get any sleep? Xu Da simply remained silent on the matter.

Soon it was well into the morning. The father and son and the family of Xie told the servants to take Xu Da, with a written complaint, to the county office for prosecution. Upon hearing the accusation, the county magistrate was shocked and said, "Did such a thing really happen?"

Then he questioned Xu Da. The magistrate asked, "Where did you take Zheng Ruizhu to?"

Xu Da replied, "I was the Tea-and-wine Master at the wedding. I was in charge of the performance of rites. How can I know where the bride is?"

Then Old Man Xie recounted the story of how Xu Da had left without saying good-bye and how he had been caught in the alley later that night. The county magistrate shouted loudly, "Torture him!"

Though a rogue, Xu Da was weak-willed and could not stand the torture. He equivocated with a few words at first and then yielded to the physical pain by saying, "When doing the hairdressing the other day, I was attracted to girl's beauty and began to harbor an evil plan. After I learned that she was to be married to the family of Xie, I decided to get the job of Tea-and-wine Master at the wedding. I and another two men plotted in advance that they would wait outside the rear gate in the evening. As the bride completed her wedding rituals and the feast began in the main room, I went inside and saw that the bride was sitting alone in the room. I lied to her by telling her that she had other wedding rites to perform. So she came out with me. She didn't know her way in the house and so I led her to the rear gate and pushed her out to the two men waiting there. The bride wanted to cry out but I quickly locked the rear gate and came back to the front. I went out the front gate, ran to the alley at the back of the house and caught up with the two men. As we were about to make off, we saw torches flashing behind us. We knew we were being pursued. The two men left me in desperation and ran away. I had the bride with me and so I couldn't get away. It happened that there was a dry well by the roadside. I hastily lifted her up and dropped her into the well. But I was caught by the men and brought here in front of you. The bride is still in the well. That's all I can tell you."

The county magistrate asked him, "But why did you not tell the truth in their home?"

Xu Da answered, "I thought I could get away with it, and later I could take her out of the well to enjoy her. But now I couldn't bear the torture and had to tell the truth."

The county magistrate had his words recorded. Then he told a runner to escort Xu Da, with the two families of Zheng and Xie, to the well, saying, "Go to the well to check on his words and report back to me at once."

The group of people arrived at the well. Old Man Zheng looked down into it. It was pitch-dark and quiet at the bottom. Thinking that his daughter might have died by now, he grabbed Xu Da and dealt him a few sound blows, saying, "You killed my daughter. You must pay with your life!"

The rest stopped him by saying, "Let's get her body out first. Stop beating him. The law will mete out his punishment." But Old Man Zheng was frantic and vengeful. He began to bite Xu Da and would not let go of his flesh. Xu Da screamed painfully like a pig being slaughtered.

Meanwhile, Old Man Xie told the servants get a bamboo basket and a rope ready. Someone had to go down into the well. A brave soul from among the servants fastened the rope around his body and slid down to the bottom. He found no water there but touched something with his hand. It was indeed a human body lying on the ground. He pushed at it, but it remained motionless. He lifted it up with his arms and put it into the basket, which was pulled up out of the well. The men were shocked to see that it was not the bride at all, but a thickly-bearded man with blood all over his body and his head split open. They were stunned.

Old Man Zheng gave Xu Da another slap, saying, "What do you have to say about this?" However the sight also frightened Xu Da out of his wits.

Old Man Xie said, "What the hell is this bizarre thing?" Then he called to the man down in the well, "Is there anybody else down there?"

The man answered, "Nobody else. Please get me out of here."

They threw down the rope and pulled him out. Then they asked him, "What else did you see down there?"

He replied, "Only rocks. It's a dry well. I picked up that person in the dark, but I didn't know whether it was alive or dead. Is it the bride?"

The men told him, "No, it's a dead man with beard, not the bride at all. Look, it's over there."

Then the runner said, "Don't waste time talking nonsense! Let's go back and report to the county magistrate. I think this guy is the only source for locating the bride's whereabouts."

Old Man Zheng and Old Man Xie said, "Exactly!" So they left someone to take care of the body and the rest of them went back with the runner to report to the county magistrate.

The county magistrate said to Xu Da, "You told us that you dropped Zheng Ruizhu into the well. Now we find it's a man's body instead. Tell me where Zheng Ruizhu is and where this man's body came from?"

Xu Da answered, "I saw people coming in pursuit. It is true that I pushed the bride into the well. But now it's become a man's body. I'm confused too."

The country magistrate asked, "You summoned two fellows to work with you. What are their names? They must be tied in with this matter."

Xu Da replied, "One of them is called Zhang Yin and the other, Li Mao." The county magistrate wrote down the names and addresses and sent men to arrest them. To capture the two was as easy as picking up a turtle bottled in a jar. As they were brought in, each was placed in a leg-clamp.

They immediately confessed. "Xu Da asked us to wait outside the rear gate that night," they said. "Later we saw him push the bride out. We carried her on our backs and started to run. He came up from behind. As we were getting away, we saw torches blazing away behind us and men clamoring. We were scared so we left the bride with Xu Da and fled in desperation. As to what happened afterwards, we have no idea." Then they turned to Xu Da and asked, "Where did you take the bride to? Why don't you give her up now? We have to bear punishment for you!" Xu Da couldn't say anything.

The county magistrate, pointing to Xu Da, said, "You slippery slave are the only source of the truth!" Then he called loudly, "Torture him again!"

Xu Da cried supplicatingly, "I deserve death." He told his story again up to the part where he dropped the bride into the well, but he could not go any further.

The county magistrate then asked the fathers of the two families and the matchmaker to visit their neighbors and make a thorough investigation. Those neighbors who were asked had no knowledge of the incident, so they provided no clues, and were unable to identify the dead body. The county magistrate posted a notice announcing the finding of an unidentified body, but no one emerged to claim it. The families of Zheng and Xie offered a prize from their own money for anyone who could give a clue about Zheng Ruizhu's whereabouts, and the county magistrate prepared notices for them. But no news emerged. Unable to close the case, the county magistrate threw Xu Da into jail and took him out every five days for further interrogation. Xie Sanlang was worried and kept pushing for action. The county magistrate did his best but still couldn't force any additional information out of Xu Da, even after repeated floggings. Xu Da had begun with sinister motives but now ended up in a quandary, hopelessly unable to free himself from suffering. So he lived in trepidation through the cycle of five-day thrashings. The case lingered on with neither any clue for further action nor any way of solving it. We will now leave it for the moment.

As for Zheng Ruizhu, when she was taken by Xu Da that night to the back gate of the house, she was handed over to the other two men.

Seeing the gate was bolted, she realized she had fallen into the hands of villains. She wanted to yell for help, but since she had just married into the family, she didn't yet know any of their names and so couldn't call to them. She hastily let out two shouts of "Help!" but these raised no attention. The two men carried her on their backs and raced away. She was terrified. Then they suddenly saw that they were being chased from behind. They set her on the ground and fled. Xu Da then grabbed her and put her down the well. It was dry at the bottom and not deep. She stumbled but was not injured. She heard people talking and yelling outside the well and realized they were from her own family looking for her. The torches lit up the area, shedding some light into the well. Zheng Ruizhu cried "Help!" at the top of her voice. However the men had by now seized Xu Da who kept squalling so loudly, no one could hear her. The bride had a soft voice and was down in a well, so her cries were drowned out. A moment later the men took Xu Da away and their talking and yelling gradually died down in the distance. Zheng Ruizhu lost hope and burst into weeping.

Later as the day began to dawn. Zheng Ruizhu thought to herself, "There should be someone up there coming and going by now." So she shouted "Help!" several times, and then broke into howling again. It happened that there were indeed two men passing by the well. Because of their coming:

A traveler became a ghost deep down in a well;
A bride was made a stranger's wife away from home.

The two men were traveling merchants from the Qixian County in Kaifeng Prefecture, Henan Province. One was called Zhao Shen and the other, Qian Si. They had joined forces by putting their money together and had come to the region of Suzhou and Songjiang to do business. After obtaining a huge profit, they were now leaving for home. As they accidentally passed by this place, they heard the shouting and weeping coming from inside the well. They walked over to the mouth of the well and looked down. In the bright daylight, they faintly saw a woman in the well. Then they called, "Who are you down there?"

The answer came up, "I'm a bride kidnapped by some bandits. They threw me down here. Please help me out. You'll surely get a huge reward once I'm back home."

The two men then talked to each other. "The old saying goes," they said, "'saving a life is a deed more meritorious than building a seven-tiered Buddhist pagoda.' In addition it's a woman. How can she get out by herself? Without help, she will definitely die. It's our good luck to happen upon her. We've got a long rope in our baggage. Let's go down and get her out."

Zhao Shen said, "I'm skinny and light. Let me go down."

Qian Si said, "I'm fat and heavy, not fit for this kind of work. I'll stay up here and pull the end of the rope, expending some physical labor." That was the beginning of Zhao Shen's doom. He was delighted at the sight of a woman. Rubbing his fists and rolling up his sleeves, he tied the rope around his waist and then held onto it with both hands. With one foot stepping on one end of the rope, Qian Si clutched the rope in his hands and slowly let Zhao Shen slide down. As Zhao Shen reached the bottom, he could see there was no water there.

He relaxed and said to Zheng Ruizhu, "Let me get you out."

Zheng Ruizhu replied, "I deeply appreciate your kindness."

Then Zhao Shen untied the rope from his waist and tied it around hers the same way he had for himself. He said to her, "Don't panic. Just hold the rope tightly in your hands and the man up there will hoist you up. The rope has been tied fast and you won't slip. Once you're out, pull me up." Eager to get out, Zheng Ruizhu summoned up her courage and grasped the rope. At the mouth of the well, Qian Si could see the rope getting tight and knew that someone was hanging at the other end of it. So he made one strenuous effort after another and pulled her out. Then he saw in front of him a young lady in dazzling attire:

Despite the disheveled hair and displaced hairpins
She was the beauty second to none;
Unexpectedly she rose from the well,
As if emerging from the palace of the Dragon King.

A person should keep away from selfish desires. If such a desire seizes one's mind, the person may commit an atrocious crime. Originally Qian Si and Zhao Shen had agreed to save the woman. That was a worthy motive. After the woman was pulled out of the well and turned out to be a beauty, the idea of seizing all the gain flashed into Qian Si's mind. He thought to himself, if Zhao Shen gets out of the well, he will surely want to take a share of the profit. Then I can't expect to enjoy the young lady all by myself. Besides, he has plenty of money in his bag. His life is now in my hands. If I kill him, this young lady and his money will both be mine.

As these sinful thoughts turned in his mind, he heard a shout coming from inside the well, "Why don't you toss down the rope?"

Qian Si hardened his heart and said aloud, "Kill him!" Then he picked up a big rock by the side of the well and flung it in, shouting, "Get him!" Alas, Zhao Shen had anxiously been waiting for the rope to come down, but he never thought it would be a rock thrown down instead. With no preparation to dodge it, he was hit on the skull. His skull was shattered and he was killed immediately.

After Zheng Ruizhu was rescued, she adjusted her clothes and pulled herself together. But when she saw what Qian Si had done, her heart leaped into her mouth and she mumbled repeatedly, "May Buddha preserve me!"

Qian Si said to her, "Don't worry. He is my foe. That's why I coaxed him into going down and then killed him."

Zheng Ruizhu thought to herself, "Your foe but my savior!" However she dared not express her feelings. She begged Qian Si to take her back home.

He responded, "What a daydream! I went out of my way to get you out of the well. Now you're mine. I come from Kaifeng in Henan Province. Come with me to my home and be my wife. You'll enjoy plenty of wealth. Come on, let's go!" Zheng Ruizhu was completely at a loss. She couldn't tell where the road led to and whether it was close or faraway from home. With no one around that she knew, she didn't know what to do next. But Qian Si pushed her by saying, "If you reject me, I'll throw you down into the well again and kill you with a rock, too! Did you see what happened to that man?" Zheng Ruizhu in great fear and, unable to do otherwise, was led away by him. It was exactly:

No sooner than she got free of lechers' jaws
Did she fall into a lecher's claws.
Knowing he was not a man with whom to consort
She only followed him as the last resort.

On the way Qian Si told Zheng Ruizhu, "Once we're home and you meet my family members, say to them that you're from Suzhou. If people ask about Zhao Shen, the dead man, tell them that he's still in Suzhou."

A few days later, they arrived in Qian Si's home in the Qixian County. Zheng Ruizhu was surprised to find out that Qian Si had a wife by the name of Wan, with the pet name Chonger. A vicious woman, Chonger showed her true nature immediately after meeting Zheng Ruizhu. She bullied Ruizhu in every way she could. She stripped Zheng Ruizhu of her jewels and the clothes she wore and had her put on a coarse dress. She made her carry out all the harsh household chores alone. When Ruizhu failed to meet any requirement, a beating ensued. Zheng Ruizhu said, "I'm not married to your family. You didn't pay any silver to get me here. I was brought here by force. Why are you beating me so cruelly?" Wan Chonger didn't listen to her complaints. She didn't even bother to find out Ruizhu's background. Chonger assumed that she was a concubine and so she was subjected to jealousy and cruelty.

Wan Chonger had a reputation for high-handedness and the other women in her neighborhood all criticized her for it. A woman living nearby often felt indignant on Ruizhu's behalf, seeing Chonger beat Zheng Ruizhu so ferociously. One day a woman neighbor overheard Zheng Ruizhu's complaints. "The girl is not married," she mused, "nor was she bought. Then she must have been abducted. Such a wicked deed has ruined someone's daughter!" She kept this in mind.

Sometime later Qian Si was out for business and Zheng Ruizhu came to her home to borrow a bucket with which to fetch water. The neighbor woman stayed her for awhile. The neighbor asked Ruizhu, "I can see that you come from a decent family. But why did your parents marry you off so far from home and let you suffer such cruelty?"

Zheng Ruizhu wept and said, "How could my parents have married me here?"

So the woman asked, "Then how have you come here?"

Zheng Ruizhu told the story of her betrothal to the family of Xie, her abduction at the wedding night and being flung into the well.

The neighbor asked, "Was it because Qian Si saved you from the well that you came with him?"

Zheng Ruizhu replied, "No, it was another man who went down into the well and saved my life. What a bad fortune that man had! He thought that once I got out he would be pulled up with the rope. Nobody could have known that Qian Si would be so treacherous and cruel. He threw a big rock into the well and killed that man. Then he dragged me away by force. At that moment I was lost. I also feared he would kill me. Besides, he told me that I would be his wife after I came to his home. I really didn't know that I would sink into such a wretched state and suffer from such cruelty!"

The neighbor woman said, "Originally Qian Si went with a Zhao from our neighbor village on a business tour. But Zhao hasn't come back till today. The Zhaos asked your man about Zhao's whereabouts and got the reply that he was still in Suzhou. The Zhao family took Qian Si's words for granted. Now on the basis of what you just told me, I believe that the man who went down into the well to save you and later got killed must have been Zhao. Young lady, why not report this happening to the government office so that you will be sent back home and be able to free yourself from such suffering?"

Zheng Ruizhu replied, "I'm afraid that, since I came here with him, I may bear the responsibility for an offense as well."

The neighbor said, "No, you're a woman who was kidnapped. What offense did you commit? I'm going to let the Zhao family know about this. They will definitely sue the murderer. Then I'll write a statement for you so you can take it to the government office. As long as you tell truth, I can guarantee you'll be free of accusation and able to go back to your family."

Zheng Ruizhu said, "If that's the case, I will be able to renew my decent life."

When they agreed to this, the neighbor woman left to tell the Zhaos. At the same time as the family of Zhao filed a lawsuit, Zheng Ruizhu turned in her statement to the county government. The Qixian county magistrate questioned Zheng Ruizhu about her statement and then sent runners to arrest Qian Si and bring him to the court. Qian Si gave an evasive answer to the court's questioning, but Zheng Ruizhu offered irrefutable details that dashed Qian Si's elusive attempts.

Qian Si cursed Zheng Ruizhu, "I saved your life. But you're damning me in return!"

Zheng Ruizhu said, "That man saved my life. Why did you kill him?"

Qian Si was thus silenced. The Zhao family requested that the murderer pay with his own life.

The county magistrate said, "The murder is admitted, but it is based on verbal statements only, without any evidence of a body. So the case can't be settled. The murder was committed in Jiading county, and Zheng Ruizhu comes from that county. That is where the dead body is, too. What I can do here is to record all oral statements and send them together with persons concerned to Jiading County. There the law case can be concluded."

Then he had Qian Si flogged with thirty strokes and shut behind bars. Zheng Ruizhu was released on a surety bond completed on her behalf by the woman neighbor. Zheng Ruizhu was happy that she was able to leave that brutal Wan Chonger. The county magistrate established a lawsuit file, signed the order to escort the prisoner on a long journey, and sent this group of concerned persons to Jiading County of Suzhou prefecture.

The day that the group arrived in Jiading was the day scheduled for the regular interrogation of Xu Da. As the Jiading County magistrate had Xu Da brought into court, the runner from Qixian of the Kaifeng Prefecture handed in the lawsuit file. The Jiading County magistrate at once had called out the names listed in the file. When the roll-call got down to the name of Zheng Ruizhu, she answered. Looking up, Xu Da realized she was the one who had disappeared, the one he had seen clearly when doing her hair.

He shouted loudly, "She's exactly the one my life hinges on! I've no idea how many beatings I've received because of you. Where have you come from? You're not a ghost, are you?"

On hearing this, the county magistrate asked Xu Da, "How do you know this woman?"

Xu Da replied, "This is the bride who was in the well. Now you needn't torture your slave for her whereabouts."

The county magistrate was astonished, saying, "What a strange thing!" So he called Zheng Ruizhu to the front and questioned her closely. Zheng Ruizhu retold her story in detail. Then the county magistrate went over the lawsuit file and came to the conclusion that the dead body in the well was that of Zhao Shen who was deliberately killed by Qian Si.

He ordered that Zhao Shen's body be brought in and examined by the coroner. The coroner's verdict showed that a fractured skull, caused by the striking of a rock, had led to the death of the man. Thus the county magistrate convicted Qian Si of a capital crime. Xu Da was involved in the abduction, and the one who initiated the plot, although it eventually failed. So a three-year imprisonment was given to him. Zhang Yin and Li Mao, his accomplices, were flogged with a stick in the light of their individual offenses. The judge said that Zheng Ruizhu suffered from misfortune and, with a verdict of innocence, should be returned in marriage to her husband, Xie Sanlang. Zhao Shen's body could be claimed and buried by his family members. After the burial, which took place away from his native province, the family was allowed to leave for home.

The verdict having been delivered, the county magistrate said with smile, "If they had not solved the case there in Qixian and sent these two persons here, this unsettled legal matter would have never been closed."

The news circulated quickly in Jiading. Poor Xie Sanlang, who lost his bride on their wedding night and did not get her back until then, but she was no longer a virgin. Two human lives were lost in the event. All the bad fortune originated in a man's styling hair for a girl. Hence a strict watch on outsider men should be maintained.

Tale 11

A Muddle-headed Instructor is Mistreated by His Pampered Daughters; A Once Poor Scholar Finances His Teacher for a Happy Old Age

There was a scholar living on a government stipend in the area of Qianlou, near Taihu Lake, in the prefecture of Huzhou in Zhejiang Province. He was named Gao Guang and his formal name was Yuxi. Honest, upright and old-fashioned, he had three daughters who were married. His wife was dead and he had no son. But he did have a nephew called Gao Wenming, who lived away from him and was quite wealthy. Gao Yuxi lived in a house that had been handed down to him from earlier generations. In fact his nephew was entitled to part of the estate — however, since he earned a great deal of money he thought he deserved better housing, given the fact that the old house was crumbling and repairs would not be easy. Therefore the nephew bought a good house and lived separately from his uncle. In terms of the rights of succession, Gao Yuxi's property should go to his nephew after his death since he had no son. But Gao Yuxi purposely avoided mentioning this matter. Besides Gao Yuxi naturally was partial to his three flesh-and-blood daughters. Some of his savings from teaching and other earnings were gradually given to them. Later, on the official recommendation of the imperial court, he was granted a teaching position in Feixian county of Shandong Province. Afterwards he moved to Yizhou and he was promoted to be the governor of Dongchang Prefecture. After two or three terms in office, he returned home with savings of more than four or five hundred *liang* of silver. Reader, you should know that usually a humble person with one or two *liang* of silver tends to pose as someone in the possession of ten *liang*. In addition, most people are shortsighted and prone to gossip about others. The mere sight of a suitcase a little heavier than usual sets tongues wagging, with people guessing that there are possibly thousands of *liang* of silver in it. Some even pin down an exact figure as if they have personally seen and weighed the silver. Admittedly this is a typical provincial sentiment. When Gao Yuxi came back home with some earnings, word spread that he had brought back a fortune of thousands.

Having learned that their father was now rich, the three daughters came and competed with one another in currying favor with him. Gao Yuxi was delighted and said to himself, "Though I lack a son, my daughters please me a great deal. My life should be alright in my later years." But, on second thought, he said, "I've collected some savings over these years and have no one to share them with. Why not give some to my daughters? After they have received the money, they will show even more filial respect toward me." So thinking, he took out three hundred *liang* of silver and divided it equally among his three daughters. His daughters were overjoyed and grateful at first, but later when they learned their father had more money that he had kept from them they became unsatisfied.

Desiring more, they said to one another, "Who knows to whom he will give the rest of his huge amount of money?" Although they constantly thought of this, they said nothing about it to him for fear of offending him. But they did not stop flattering him. Meanwhile Gao Wenming paid regular visits to his uncle and Gao Yuxi showed due respect in treating his nephew. He also gave his nephew a little sum of money out of his government stipend or a few gifts. But considering that his nephew hospitably welcomed his uncle back home, the gifts could merely offset the entertainment. The nephew possessed a large enough fortune, so he had no craving for his uncle's money.

As the few days of excitement ended, the daughters took off for their homes. The old man was left alone in the run-down house. He felt abandoned. Each of the three daughters had said, "I'm going to bring our father back to my home." They had vied with one another, while Yuxi smiled and said, "Don't argue about this. I'll surely see you a great deal. I think I'll go to live with each of you in turn." After they left, Gao Yuxi stayed at home for two days, feeling quite lonely. The boredom annoyed him and so he packed and made his way to his eldest daughter's place. Later the second eldest daughter and youngest daughter both sent for him. Gao Yuxi arrived at their homes in due order. The daughters even grumbled about his coming too late and staying too short. In a couple of days one of the others would come to take him.

Gao Yuxi's went through two rounds of stays with his daughters, who showed kindness and reluctance at parting from him. Gao Yuxi figured, "All in all I have no son. I'm aged and weak, and have no wife or concubine to support. Why do I have to live by myself? Now that I have the three daughters accommodating me by turns, I should be well taken care of for the rest of my life. But I feel uneasy about depending on them. When I returned home I gave each of them one hundred *liang* of silver, from which they have spent some on me. Why not let them know that I will divide the rest of my money equally among them and they should take turns in supporting me. I'll be free of cares, living with this one for a time and another one for a time. It'll save me trips to purchase firewood and rice, hard things for me to do in old age. That will make my life a lot easier."

When he told his daughters this, they couldn't agree more, and said to him, "It is a daughter's duty to support her father. We couldn't complain even if you were to give us nothing." Gao Yuxi was overjoyed. He went back to his home and moved suitcases and wooden boxes containing his belongings to his daughters' homes. He rummaged through his belongings and came up with more than three hundred *liang* of silver. With an air of generosity, he distributed one hundred *liang* to each family, leaving little for himself. The daughters were, of course, delighted at receiving the money.

After that Gao Yuxi lived with each daughter in due succession and never returned to his own home. The house, which had been passed down from earlier generations, stood empty for quite a long time and started to collapse. Since it was not one man's property, it could not be sold. His daughters persuaded him that since there were useful materials in the broken-down house he should tear down some of the rooms and bring useful things back to them. Gao Yuxi saw no reason to go back to his own home, and so he agreed. Making sure about what his sons-in-law needed for renovations, he went back to his house and carried various construction materials to their homes. One family took away a roof beam at one point and another family seized a post at another. Even the rafters and planks were pulled off the pig sty. Bit by bit most things were taken away. His nephew, not petty-minded, did not compete with the daughters in seizing bits of the property. Soon the house had been demolished and turned into nothing.

In the beginning, when he still possessed his fortune, Gao Yuxi felt comfortable living with each of his sons-in-law's families. Later, when he had nothing more to give, he found himself lacking freedom and convenience in doing things. Like an ordinary elder, he normally maintained a nature of partiality, finding fault over trifles and causing distress in the family. When offended by anything, he would grumble harshly, "I'm living on my own, not a dependent yet." Such words kept rolling out of his mouth as he stayed with one family after another.

Gradually he became disliked in the three families of his sons-in-law. Furthermore, as nothing he owned remained to be desired, much of the former warmth left his daughters. Though they restrained themselves from throwing him out, they were eager for him to go to the next family so that they might have a few days of peace. Previously, usually a few days ahead of the schedule, Gao Yuxi would be picked up by the next family. But now, the next family often did not come even after the scheduled time had passed, in hopes that he would stay longer with the current family. Seeing that no one came to pick him up, Gao Yuxi would have to stay a couple of more days. Then comments arose in the family, such as, "Your time for staying with us is over. Why don't you leave for my sister's home?" Sometimes the words would carry a feeling of fury like: "You divided your money equally among our three families. I didn't take it alone!" Gao Yuxi found those scraps of complaint unbearable. As one family hurt his feelings, he uttered complaints to the other two families. But the sisters had inherited the same temperament from the same mother. They all showed their true nature as time went on. Whenever he grumbled against one of his daughters, the other two would come to her defense. His sons-in-law unquestionably sided with their wives, and their mediation over the disputes bore apparent ridicule of and blame against him. Gao Yuxi was driven beyond forbearance. Thus he incessantly squabbled on pointless matters, and the peace of the families was shattered. He became a disgusting old man to them, being pushed back and forth among them for years. As a result he had no dependable place for living, despite the fact that he stayed in three homes in turn.

Reader, from the perspective of the daughters and sons-in-law, the old man lacked reason and sense, and he was loathsome. But, in terms of justice, he had given away all his savings and counted upon the three families for a living. It would therefore have been reasonable for the daughters to show certain understanding toward him. However such is human nature that one takes from others for granted but regards anyone who uses some of his money as an enemy. As well, there were always issues that could be hardly settled fairly in terms of the obligations for each family. If the old man wanted to entertain a guest, the daughter with whom he was staying had to play host. She would moan, "Why should I be host?" She might accept the responsibility verbally, but not wholeheartedly, and she would put the matter off day after day until the time he could leave for the next family. As he mentioned the matter to this family, they would say, "You should have performed this in their home when you stayed with them. Why are you making a point of doing it here in my family?" So the daughter would turn him down and in the end the old man had to give up his plan. How could the old man treat each business in an absolutely fair way so that each of the three families felt satisfied? Hence nothing was ever completed. How could the old man rest at ease? However, this was a natural outcome in terms of human nature. He should not have pampered his daughters by giving away his money — but now, as he was obligated to them, how could he feel free? He should be a bit more submissive — but since he had divided the money among them he wasn't willing to be treated that way. He also thought about taking leave of them so as to avoid further insults — but as he had neither money nor a home, he was in a dilemma. He could not maintain his dignity nor move out. The idea of going to talk to his nephew was not good either, since he had given his nephew nothing in the past. He believed his current plight would only raise ridicule and he had no face to see his nephew.

He turned the matter over in his mind again and again and ruefully talked to himself, saying, "Because I didn't raise a son, I'm suffering today! I have three daughters, but they are ungrateful and don't have their hearts in the right place toward me." Feeling particularly sad, he walked into an old temple with tears in his eyes, and sat down. As he recalled and regretted, his rage became greater and greater. Finally he lay down on the ground and cried. Suddenly the idea struck him that, "I've been a scholar all my life, but now I'm old and in a rotten state. What meaning does life hold to me? I'd better cry and tell my grievances in front of the Boddhisattva, and then commit suicide here!"

An old saying goes, "Coincidence makes up the soul of a tale." As Gao Yuxi wept sadly, his nephew Gao Wenming happened to pass by outside on his way back from collecting his debts. His boat was sailing along the river bank when he heard somebody weeping inside the temple. Instinctively he could not uncaringly go past. He pricked up his ears and realized that it sounded like his uncle crying. Then he said to himself, "Be the man my uncle or not, the crying sounds strange. I'm going to take a look." He told the boatman stop sculling and, as the bow hit the shore, sprang out.

He entered the temple and shouted, "Who's crying here?" As both parties looked at each other, they were stunned. Gao Wenming said, "I thought it might be you, Uncle. Why are you crying here?"

Seeing his nephew, Gao Yuxi became more sorrowful. Gao Wenming tried to calm him down, "Uncle, you're old and should refrain from grief. Otherwise you'll harm your health. Please tell me who has hurt your feelings and made you feel so sad?"

Gao Yuxi replied, "It's a shame to talk about this. I was stupid in counting on my daughters alone. I gave them all my savings, withholding no money for my future. Now they have all turned their backs on me! It so infuriated me that I cried here. I was going to vent my grief to the deities before I commit suicide. I didn't know I would meet you here. I feel ashamed."

Gao Wenming said, "Why are you so narrow-minded, Uncle? The sisters are behaving from a female perspective. Don't take it seriously!"

Gao Yuxi said, "I would rather die here than go back to any of their homes."

Gao Wenming said, "It's up to you, uncle, to stay with them or not. It's certainly not the matter for suicide."

Gao Yuxi said, "I'm homeless now. How can I continue to live?" Gao Wenming said, "I'm not prosperous, but I would certainly have no problem in supporting you. Why are you talking like this?"

Gao Yuxi said, "In the past I never granted any favor to you. All my property went to them. Now I'm broke. How could I trouble you?"

"We're flesh-and-blood kin," Gao Wenming said. "Don't talk about troubling."

Gao Yuxi said, "Even if you're kind to me, your wife will not like to have me in your home. I've had the experience of paying dearly for cold treatment. Besides, not to mention that I have nothing other than myself!"

Gao Wenming replied, "I'm a man and won't let a woman take charge! Moreover, my wife is very righteous and reasonable. She won't behave like that, I'm sure. Come on, Uncle, and follow me to my home. Don't hesitate. Come aboard the boat, please." Before the old man could make a reply Gao Wenming grabbed his uncle's sleeve and dragged him onto the boat. He shipped the old man home.

Gao Wenming stepped into his house first and told his wife about his uncle's sorrow and intention of suicide. His wife was shocked and said, "Where's he now?"

Gao Wenming answered, "I brought him back by boat."

She said, "Though the old man is poor and miserable, we should take him into our home to keep the dignity of the Gao family. Otherwise we would be ridiculed by others."

Not quite sure about his wife's sincerity, Gao Wenming made an intentional remark, saying, "It's true that he's useless. But we have some geese in the pen. Let him tend them during the day so that he won't be totally dependent."

His wife replied, "What are you talking about? To feed one more mouth won't break us. Even if he does nothing, we're of one family and he's not somebody else! It's outrageous for a nephew to let his uncle tend geese at home. Don't talk any more. Go and show him in."

"If you think its all right," Gao Wenming said, "I'm going to bring him in. Please go and fix food and drink for us." Then Gao Wenming strode down to the boat and got his uncle. They came into the main room and took seats while dinner was brought. Still lost in deep sorrow, Gao Yuxi told his nephew one or two more of his grievances, tears dropping from his eyes, as Gao Wenming tried to calm him down. Thus they began to live together.

The news reached his daughters. They understood their father's hurt, but were pleased for his staying away from them. Occasionally they sent someone to present greetings to the old man but none of them expressed any intention of bringing him back their homes. Gao Yuxi, odd and stubborn, would not have gone to them even if invited.

As the New Year was around the corner, the daughters hypocritically sent a message that they would come to get their father for the holiday. Their verbal expression was followed by no sincere action. Gao Yuxi's reply was a "no". The daughters didn't push the matter any more.

Gao Wenming said to him, "It's absolutely right that you should spend the New Year in my home so that you can worship our ancestors. If you were in any of your daughter's homes, they would have the pictures of their husband's ancestors on display and you would find it inconvenient to do what you want."*

"Exactly," Gao Yuxi said, "I've two old suitcases with two robes in them, plus an old black gauze cap. They are at the home of my eldest

---

*It was a convention that pictures of the ancestors of each family were put up over the New Year of lunar calendar for a period starting from the New Year's eve.

daughter. We can send someone to get them and then I'll be able to wear them when I worship the ancestors."

Gao Wenming said, "Yes, Uncle. You need them. I'll write a note and have someone go and get them."

So a man was sent to the eldest daughter's home to get these things. The eldest daughter's family was fearful that the old nuisance might come again. Seeing the man who had come to take the outfit, they understood that he would be spending the New Year in his nephew's home. They immediately returned the old suitcases as if they were burning paper money to expel an evil spirit.* Gao Yuxi received his outfit and realized that he would not be allowed to go back to his daughter's home. So he set his heart on spending the New Year with his nephew.

In general, low-ranking officials in retirement liked to wear their red glittering outfits on special occasions. This offered them a lot of pleasure. At the Spring Festival Gao Yuxi wore his outfit and worshipped his ancestors. His nephew, with his wife, kowtowed to the uncle in respect. The whole family was immersed in harmony. The old man thought this was much better than staying in somebody else's home. However, Gao Yuxi often felt guilty over the fact that he had given his nephew nothing before and was now living off his nephew's family. He expressed his willingness to tend the geese, only to be turned down by his nephew.

One day as Gao Yuxi was sitting idly, a man in a runner's attire came and said to him, with one hand cupped in another, "Sir, I have an inquiry. Is there an old man called Gao Yuxi around here?"

Gao Yuxi said, "Why are you looking for him?"

The runner replied, "I've been asking directions all the way and am told he lives here. I'd like to see him and talk to him about something

---

*People in ancient times had the superstitious belief that burning paper money would drive away evil spirits.

urgent."

Gao Yuxi said, "He is old and useless. What business do you want to talk to him about?"

The runner said, "Lord Li is the imperial inspector of Fujian Province. He's from Yizhou in Shandong Province and used to be one of Gao Yuxi's students. The imperial inspector has made a detour on his way to his office to visit Gao Yuxi. He's inquired about him for two days."

Gao Yuxi smiled and said, "I'm Gao Guang."

The runner said, "Really?"

Pointing to the wall, Gao Yuxi said, "If you doubt it, look at my worn gauze cap."

The runner realized that what he said was true and replied, "I'm sorry for my rough manners." He turned to go.

Gao Yuxi said, "Can you tell me the name of this Lord Li from Shandong?"

The runner answered his name was so and so. Gao Yuxi thought for a moment and then said, "It's turned out to be that man!"

The runner said, "Please get ready, sir. He's running out of patience. I'm going to report to him and he'll be here in no time." With the good news, the runner left in happiness.

Gao Yuxi called for his nephew and told him about this. Gao Wenming said, "This is going to be something significant. An important person's visit should be good luck for you. How did you get to know him, Uncle?"

Gao Yuxi said, "When I worked as an instructor in Yizhou, he was a new scholar in the school. His family was poor and couldn't afford the present to be given to his teacher on the first meeting. More than half a year passed, and he was still unable to come and present me with gifts. Two of my colleagues urged me to issue a summons and force him to come. I didn't do it. Later I found out that he was indeed very poor. So I summoned him in front of me and told him I had decided to waive his presentation of gifts. My colleagues saw what I did and they were not in a position to take anything from him either. I noticed that though the new student was poor and humble, he appeared dignified and good-looking. I asked about his family and learned that his family was too poor to pay for lighting expenses. Hence I gave him some money, and praised him a great deal to others. That helped him acquire a tutorship in a well-paid private school the following year. When I worked in Dongchang, I recommended him to the prefecture school. Since I returned home I've heard nothing of him. Later I heard that he had passed the highest imperial examinations, but I did not know where he held office after that. I'm old and not interested in world affairs. I didn't care about things and did not bother to inquire as to his whereabouts. But I'm glad that he's still kept my kindness toward him in mind and has found his way here to see me."

"He's really a good man." Gao Wenming said.

As they talked, an uproar arose outside. A big boat was pulling in to shore, and people turned out and have a look. Gao Wenming stepped out and saw a man racing toward the house with a red note. Gao Wenming accepted it. Gao Yuxi hastily put on his ancient outfit and ran out to welcome the guest. As the cabin-door opened, out stalked an imperial official, who appeared imposing and neat. The sight was like this:

He was in glittering attire, brocaded
Which awed the public into withdrawal;
As he mounted the horse, he set out to rid the world of evils;
When his chariot halted, the earth and mountains shuddered.
An ivory table he held was as white as frost, a token of justice;
His complexion, clear and stern, struck all misdoers with terror.
If not for a student's gratitude to his teacher,
How could he have deigned to visit such a wild shelter?

Imperial Inspector Li met with Gao Yuxi and, all smiles, kept calling him "my teacher," as they cupped their hands in greeting each other. When they headed for Gao's lodging, Imperial Inspector Li paused, unwilling to walk ahead. He urged Gao Yuxi to walk first. This left the latter gasping for breath. Since Imperial Inspector Li persisted, Gao Yuxi had to yield to his courtesy and, with a lift of his sleeve, made steps first. When they came to the main room, Imperial Inspector Li had a rug spread out on the floor and made four kowtows to Gao Yuxi for his past generous help. Gao Yuxi returned the salute repeatedly. Then a gift note was presented containing a sum of twelve *liang* of silver. Gao Yuxi accepted it. As chairs were arranged for people to sit, the imperial inspector made a point of not taking the seat of honor, so they were reconciled to taking seats on the left and right sides facing each other. Still the imperial inspector would not sit down until Gao Yuxi's seat on the right was lifted a little higher than his.

In speaking of Gao Yuxi's past financial support, the imperial inspector showed his deep appreciation, saying, "Since I passed the examinations by luck, I've been thinking about returning your kindness every moment of each day. Now I'm fortunate to have this chance to be going by way of your province to my appointed office. I've detoured to come here to see you. I'm surprised to see that your residence is in such an outlying area."

Gao Yuxi replied, "It's my shame! My shame! How could I say I have my residence? It's my nephew's. I'm just seeking temporary lodging here."

The imperial inspector said, "I thought you had a house of your own, teacher."

Gao Yuxi said, "I miscalculated and lost my inherited house. Now I have nowhere to stay but here."

He started to choke up. The old man's tears quickly welled up in his eyes and streamed down his cheeks. Feeling sympathy for him, the imperial inspector said, "Be a little patient, teacher. When I go to my office I'll find a way to settle you down."

Gao Yuxi said, "If you are so kind to me, I'll cherish your kindness till death."

The imperial inspector said, "As soon as I arrive at my post, I'll send men to take you there." Their talk continued for some time before the imperial inspector took his leave.

Gao Yuxi saw him off and watched as the boat moved away. He then opened the pack and had a look at the silver he had received, and said to Gao Wenming, "Take the silver as my payment for the expenses of my living here."

Gao Wenming replied, "What are you talking about? It's my duty to support you, Uncle. Please keep it for your own use later on."

Gao Yuxi said, "I've been troubling you a lot. I feel uneasy. I had nothing to give you in the past and now have to live in shame. I got the silver from my student. How can I keep it for myself after I have cost you so much? If you refuse to accept it, I won't feel comfortable about living here any more."

Unable to turn him down, Gao Wenming said, "If that's the case, I'll take half of it. Please keep the rest." Gao Yuxi agreed and they each took six *liang*.

The imperial inspector's visit raised a flurry of discussion across the region around Taihu Lake. Talk circulated for days and eventually reached Gao Yuxi's daughters. They heard that the nephew of their father had gotten half of the silver he received. One of them said resentfully, "His nephew had his family honored and he got silver as well!" Another one said, "His silver is not much and won't last long. Don't envy him. We're better-off, free of that disgusting old trash. He won't have any more imperial inspectors coming to give him silver." Thus their muttering continued.

In the meantime, Imperial Inspector Li arrived in Fujian Province, went on extensive tours of inspection, rid the province of evils and executed criminals. His performance was vigorous and swift, and his enforcement of the law was strict. He had outlaws brought to justice no matter what their background was. Three months later, he sent a runner on business to Huzhou. At the same time he gave the runner a letter to be delivered to Gao Yuxi, asking that Gao come to his government office and including an initial gift of twelve *liang* of silver to cover the old man's expenses for the journey. The runner was told to come back with Gao Yuxi after completing his business. Upon receiving this letter, Gao Yuxi talked to Gao Wenming and they decided that they would go together. They packed and set off with the runner, who had finished his business and come to pick them up. The journey cost Gao Yuxi little since the runner paid the expenses. In less than twenty days they were in the capital of Fujian Province.

At that moment the imperial inspector was on an inspection tour in Zhangzhou. The runner went to him and reported, "Master Gao is here." Immediately the imperial inspector ordered that he be provided with temporary lodging and then he personally went to meet him in a sedan chair. At their meeting the imperial inspector ordered his attendants to clear out, then they talked a great deal in privacy. After his return to his office, the imperial inspector sent another gift of silver to Gao Yuxi to cover the expenses of his return journey. Then he had two tables of food prepared for the old man and they ate and talked until midnight. Seeing the tremendous respect and hospitality that the imperial inspector showed to Gao Yuxi, who else would not show due respect to the guest? Government officials of prefectures and counties all came to present their gifts and flattering remarks poured down on him. Local officials, high and low, were not slow in showing their respect in hopes that the inspector might give them favorable treatment. All of this made the old teacher feel elated. Many people came to request favors from him: some asked him to help them get a commendation; some hoped to be released from the indictment on their offenses; some wanted to be exempted from punishment; some desired to obtain a waiver on the demand for returning money they had received as bribes. The imperial inspector made secret arrangements with his favorites of prefectures and counties that, as he finished his inspection in this area and went to the capital of the province or to the area of Wuyi, they should bind the records of the matters entrusted in sealed envelopes and send them to him. He would grant all those requests.

Gao Yuxi stayed for half a year until the imperial inspector left to report back on his mission. Gao Yuxi packed for leaving. He counted his total acquisitions to be worth more than two thousand *liang* of silver. Other numerous things he received included local products, and cloth. That was a huge gain, three or four times the salary he had received as a government official years before. The uncle and nephew were overwhelmed with joy. They shipped the gifts home and moved them into the house. As neighbors learned that Gao Yuxi had returned with a fortune obtained from the imperial inspector in Fujian Province, they came out to watch. They saw piles of heavy suitcases. Word got around, "What a large wealth he's brought back home!"

After the three daughters learned of this, they sent men to present their regards and a message inviting the old man to come to live with them. Gao Yuxi sneered. He figured to himself, "They see that I'm rich now, and so they pretend to be affectionate!" A few more invitations arrived, but he made the point that he would not go.

As the daughters learned that their father had turned them down, they scheduled a time to go together to Gao Wenming's place and visit their father. All smiles, they said to him, "We don't know how we have hurt your feelings, Father, so that you don't want to come and live with us. Now we're coming personally to invite you. Please come and stay some time with each of us."

Gao Yuxi said with a grin, "Many thanks! Many thanks! I bothered you a lot before. This time I'll be sensible and won't go to your places again!"

Then the daughters competed in saying, "We're one family anyway,

Father. Why do you so loathe us?"

Gao Yuxi lost his patience. He rose and entered his inner room. A short time later he emerged with three packs of silver in his hands, each containing ten *liang*. He gave one pack to each of the daughters and said, "Here's a gift from me, an old man. I won't bother you any more. You needn't come to pester me, either."

He then pulled out a note, handed it to Gao Wenming, and showed it to his daughters. They pressed forward to take a look at it. It read:

When I was poor, my nephew alone took me in and looked after me; now I have a fat purse and do not want outsiders to harbor any wild wishes; I have given all I had saved during my government career to my three daughters; this legacy is to go to my nephew; this paper should be my testimony.

Some of the daughters could read between lines. As they understood what it said, they became infuriated and felt snubbed. Disappointed, they picked up their packages and left for home.

Gao Yuxi decided to give all his possessions to his nephew. But Gao Wenming would not accept them, saying, "You should keep them for yourself for your later life. Otherwise you might get into trouble again and need the support of others, as in the past."

Gao Yuxi replied, "You took me in the past when I had nothing. Now that I want to give you my property, will you treat me badly instead? I'm an old man, frank and outspoken. I don't need any long-term plan. Accept this property and we will live as one family. I will feel comfortable that way. Don't fuss over what's yours and what's mine." Gao Wenming could not decline any more but accepted the property. In the years that followed, he did his best to support his uncle, meeting all his requests and making his life happy. Gao Yuxi never again went to his daughters' homes. He lived and died in his nephew's house, leaving all his possessions with Gao Wenming. The feeling of endearment Gao Wenming showed for his uncle was eventually rewarded.

Tale 12

A Rich Man Encounters a Headless Female Body;
An Assistant Prefect Clears up Two Unsettled Cases

It is said that there was a rich man, whose family name was Cheng in Huizhou Prefecture, Zhili Province, during the period of Chenghua [1465-1488] in our [Ming] Dynasty. According to local convention, a rich man was usually called "the Chaofeng". This had been the form of address applied to high-ranking government officials in the Song Dynasty. It was just as a rich man was then addressed as Esquire, as a means of showing respect. Cheng the Chaofeng possessed immense wealth. And, as the old saying goes, "Easy circumstances breed lewd thoughts," he was only interested in women. If he saw a woman of certain attraction, he would go to great lengths to seduce her. He didn't care how much it might cost, so long as his desire could be met. Thus his expenditures ran high, but the number of women he lured was large as well. An old proverb also says, "Heaven brings misfortune to the lecherous." A person driven by a constant desire for lechery will commit inconceivable deeds, which will eventually lead to the destruction of family and reputation. Regrets usually come after the ruin. Let's, however, leave this subject for later treatment.

A wine-seller called Brother Li Fang, lived in the town of Yanzi in Huizhou. His wife née Chen, was full of charm and attraction. The Chaofeng lusted after her and hung around the tavern all day long, talking to the husband and wife in the guise of buying drinks. Though he gradually achieved familiar terms with them, Chen was righteous and left no chance for him to seduce her. The Chaofeng thought to himself, "In this world, no one can withstand the temptation of money. Brother Li Fang and his wife are poor. I will go for high stakes by throwing a huge sum of money at them. Will she not be hooked then? Seeking her favors with her in secret is not as good as a deal made in the open."

One day he asked Brother Li Fang, "How much do you make each year by selling wine?"

Brother Li Fang replied, "Even with your kindness, it is good luck if my wife and I are able to barely survive in this trade."

The Chaofeng then said, "Do you have anything left after the deduction of your costs every year?"

Brother Li Fang said, "If I have one or two *liang* of silver, I keep it as capital for future business. But we're operating on a shoe-string right now. How can we expect to make a profit?"

The Chaofeng asked, "If someone would lend you five or ten *liang* of silver as capital, would you take it?"

Brother Li Fang said, "If I had five or ten *liang* of silver, I would open a prosperous tavern. Then we would be able to feed ourselves and make some profit every year as well. But where could I obtain such a huge loan? Even if someone loaned us some money, we would be in debt and have to pay the interest. I think it's less risky to keep this small business."

The Chaofeng then said, "I think you're an honest person. If you will do me a favor, I will give you twenty or thirty *liang*. It doesn't make much difference to me."

Brother Li Fang said, "The cost of twenty or thirty *liang* might be nothing to you, but that amount would benefit me for the rest of my life! Why would you be willing to do that?"

The Chaofeng replied, "I would, if you should be kind to me."

Brother Li Fang said, "Please tell me how I can be of service to you."

With a smile, the Chaofeng said, "I'm interested in something in your home. It won't cost you anything. I will just check it out and return it to you after I use it. If you agree, I'll give you thirty *liang* at once."

Brother Li Fang asked, "What do I have in my home that you can make use of, and after you use it, you will return it to me, something that will cost me nothing? Why should I get paid so much money by you?"

The Chaofeng laughed and said, "I doubt that you would like me to use it. If you would, your wife might not. You'd better talk to your wife today. I'll be back tomorrow with the silver to see whether we can make a deal. I am just giving you a hint today and can't say anything more about it explicitly." Still laughing he left.

Brother Li Fang told his wife about the matter that evening. "I wonder what it is in our home that he's interested in," he said. After a few seconds of thought, Chen said, "You're taken in by his round-about way of talking! If he wants to borrow some object from us and will return it after the use, the most valuable thing you possess, cannot deserve such great sum. He must have been calculating on me. You're a man. Make sense of it. Don't let him deceive you."

Brother Li Fang laughed and said, "How could that be true?"

The following day the Chaofeng came as promised with a pack of silver, and said to Brother Li Fang, "Here's the silver. I have it ready for you. Now it's up to you to make a decision." The Chaofeng opened the pack and showed him the silver shining brightly.

Brother Li Fang was then tempted and said, "Please tell me directly what you need so I can lend it to you."

The Chaofeng said, "You're a sensible man. Do you really want me to make it explicit? Just think, what you possess in your home is so valuable!"

Brother Li Fang said, "I just can't figure it out. I don't have anything worth more than ten *liang* except the bodies of me and my wife."

The Chaofeng laughed and said, "Exactly. Who talked about anything incorporeal?"

Brother Li Fang flushed with shame, saying, "You're kidding. How can you make such a joke?"

The Chaofeng said, "I'm not kidding. I'm paying ready money for an article on hand. If you agree, we'll make a deal. Otherwise I'm only making an offer. How can I push you?" Then he started to gather up the silver.

An old saying goes, "A drink of wine makes one blush and shining gold leads one to evil." Seeing that the Chaofeng was about to pick up his silver, Brother Li Fang stared in silent hesitation. The Chaofeng read his mind. So he took out an ingot of silver, more than three *liang* in weight, stuck it into Brother Li Fang's sleeve and said, "Take this first as a sample. You'll get ten ingots like this one. You two may give thought to the matter."

Brother Li Fang took the silver with much hesitation. The Chaofeng was rather composed in his usual sophistication, knowing that Brother Li Fang's touching of the silver was a sign of success. So he said, "I've got to go and will be back later to get your word."

Brother Li Fang entered his room and said to his wife, "You guessed right yesterday. What he wants is exactly what you said. I taunted him and he felt embarrassed. So he gave this ingot to me as an apology. I've kept it."

Chen then said, "It would have been better if you had not taken the silver. Since you took it, he may take it a sign of your approval. How can he give up his lecherous desire?"

Brother Li Fang said, "I was at a loss for words when I took it. Before he left, he said, 'If I'm satisfied, I won't mind giving you ten of these.' I figured, we toil a whole year and can't make a few *liang* of silver. He intends to spend a great deal of money on you. We may as well take advantage of his desire and satisfy him a little bit so that we can later get a big sum of silver from him. It's a lot easier money than what we make out of each bargain we reach with a customer."

Then Brother Li Fang set the silver on the table. Chen picked it up and looked at it, saying, "You're a man. Does the mere sight of this make you willing to let your wife have a lover?"

Brother Li Fang said, "It's not the matter of willingness. But it's rare that a rich man comes to us to ask for a favor. Let's bear the momentary pain of shame and have lasting wealth. We're not an illustrious family. In the topsy-turvy world of today, even if we keep a clean record, you can't expect someone to build a memorial archway for us. We may follow the trend."

Chen said, "It sounds alright. But it's rather humiliating for me to lure him."

Brother Li Fang said, "Anyway he will pay for everything. I'll play the host by inviting him to come in for a drink in the evening. Then I'll leave you alone by going outside. When he arrives, tell him that I am out and will be back shortly. If you have a drink with him, he will certainly make advances toward you. You may see the chance and yield to him. When I get back, it will be over. We'll obtain a lot money from him with ease!"

Chen said, "It's too humiliating. I can't do it."

Brother Li Fang said, "The Chaofeng is no stranger to us. Why do you feel ashamed? You'll be the host in drinking with him. You don't need to go outside to solicit him. You just see what he does and says, and then behave accordingly. It's certainly not something embarrassing." Chen heard this and saw that nothing too much was demanded of her. So she agreed.

Brother Li Fang made arrangements as the host and went to the Chaofeng's place with the invitation, saying, "I appreciate your kindness in not detesting me. I've got some wine ready in my humble home. You're invited to have a chat with me this evening. Please come." Seeing this, the Chaofeng was quite happy. He said to himself, "Everyone wavers at sight of gains! He must have talked his wife into agreement. Since he is inviting me for tonight, I'll surely be able to make it with her." So he impatiently waited for the evening appointment to arrive.

It is universally true that success involves set-backs. That evening the Chaofeng joyously sauntered out into the street. He stumbled into another rich man called Wang, who seized him by his sleeve and asked him to go with him to see a newly arrived whore called Wang Dashe. As Wang urged him to go, the Chaofeng turned the invitation down by making an excuse that he was busy.

Wang asked, "What business do you have?" The Chaofeng was flustered and couldn't make up a plausible story. Seeing that he could not come up with a good reason, Wang said, "If you have nothing to do, why do you spoil the fun by declining my offer?" Ignoring the Chaofeng's reluctance, he and a few of his young fellows shoved the Chaofeng to come along with them. After they got there, Wang became interested in the whore, so he paid the price, played the host and decided to spend the night with her. The Chaofeng felt restless at being held up there. After he downed a couple of drinks, he fled. It was about midnight. Brother Li Fang had gone to the home of one of his friends on an excuse. The Chaofeng rushed to Li's tavern. Seeing the door was ajar, he understood she was there waiting. He entered and locked the gate. The rooms in the tavern were not large. Looking through the door, he saw the gleam of candlelight in the main room and a table loaded with food and wine. All was dead silence. He walked into the room and found no one inside. As he picked up a light from the table and took a close look around, he uttered a scream. "Horrible!"

These on the floor he saw a pool of blood in which a headless body of a woman rested. He was stunned by the scene, his teeth chattering in trepidation. He dashed to open the gate and raced back home. Shaking all over, he couldn't squat or stand still. His heart pounded against his ribs. He was sure that he had invited disaster upon himself. We will leave him with his terror for now.

In the meantime, Brother Li Fang stayed in his friend's home until well after midnight. Reckoning that the business between his wife and the Chaofeng must be over, he began to stroll back home to have a drink. As he got there, he noticed that the gate to his store was open. "That Chaofeng is careless," he thought, "He was having an affair but did not bolt the gate." Li Fang went into the room and found no sign of the Chaofeng but there was a body on the floor with no head. A closer look at the clothes assured him that it was his wife. He was startled and yelled out, "What happened?! What happened?!" He sobbed and wondered, "My wife was willing to receive him. But what could she have said to hurt the Chaofeng so that he would kill her? I must find him and take revenge!" He cleaned up the mess, locked the gate and ran to the Chaofeng's place.

The Chaofeng, still unable to make sense of the murder, heard a knock on his door. He could tell it was Brother Li Fang so he opened the door, hoping to find out from him what had happened. Brother Li Fang seized him and began questioning, "What a horrible thing you did! Why did you kill my wife?"

The Chaofeng replied, "When I arrived in your place, I didn't see anybody. I only found your wife on the floor, murdered. Why do you say I killed her?"

Brother Li Fang said, "Who else, if it was not you?"

The Chaofeng said, "I loved your wife. If she had been with me, I would have never had enough intimacy with her. Why would I have turned out to be so cruel as to kill her? You have to look into this matter thoroughly. Don't accuse me rashly."

Brother Li Fang said, "My wife and I had a peaceful life before, you stirred up all this trouble. Now you have killed her. On whom do you want to shift the responsibility? Let's go to court. You must give me back my wife!" They kept shouting at each other until it was well into the next morning. Then, as they wrangled, they went to the government office.

Having learned that this was a murder, the prefect accepted the lawsuit and assigned Assistant Prefect Wang to investigate the case. Assistant Prefect Wang accompanied the complainant and the accused to Li's store to examine the body. The examination showed that it was a woman's body. She was killed with a knife and her head was missing. The Assistant Prefect ordered the local authorities to have the body laid into a container and put away, and then he brought the complainant and the accused back to his office. He first let Brother Li Fang tell his side of the story. Brother Li Fang said, "I'm Li Fang and my wife was Chen. We have made a living by keeping a tavern. This man Cheng was attracted to my wife and sneaked into my house on the excuse of buying wine while I was away, and then he intended to rape her. My wife must have refused him, so he killed her."

The Assistant Prefect turned to the Chaofeng and asked how he would explain this. The Chaofeng said, "The husband and wife ran the tavern and I was a regular customer. Li invited me to have a drink in his home yesterday. I got there late because I was held up by other business. I didn't see Li in his home but only found his wife on the floor dead. I was frightened and ran back home. I had nothing to do with the murder."

The Assistant Prefect said, "He said you went there to buy wine as an excuse and tried to rape her. But you said you were invited. If he invited you as the host, why was he not at home? It appears that you are a rapist!"

The Chaofeng said, "He did invite me. So I went there. Now he's here. You can question him about it. He can't deny it."

"I did invite him," Li Fang said, "but he went there before I got back home, and raped and killed my wife."

Assistant Prefect Wang asked, "Since you invited him, why were you not at home when he went there and committed rape and murder? You must both be concealing some details from me!" The Assistant Prefect had cramps brought out and put them both on rack. That turned them into truth tellers.

Brother Li Fang now said, "In fact, Cheng fancied my wife and promised me some silver, requesting a drink with my wife. I was driven by the desire for money and reluctantly agreed. It's true that I asked him to come and have a drink. As I knew that I would be in his way, I left home for awhile. When I got back, I was surprised to find that he had killed my wife and had fled home."

The Chaofeng said, "I admit I was interested in his wife and plotted to seduce her. He did grant my request and invited me for a drink. Why would I have changed my mind and killed her? In reality when I arrived there, his wife was already dead. I was shocked and ran back home. I had nothing to do with it."

The Assistant Prefect then said, "Li Fang played host in name, but pandered in actuality. When Cheng got there, the woman rejected him and so he killed her on the spot. That's obvious. It is despicable to seduce the wife of somebody else. Cheng should pay with his own life."

The Chaofeng said, "It is my fault to harbor wild desires at sight of a beautiful woman. As for the murder, I'm indeed ignorant. Furthermore, the husband and wife talked and agreed on the arrangement of asking me to come and have a drink. Even if his wife had been reluctant, I would have certainly taken time to plead with her. Why would I have gone to such an extreme as to kill her?"

Assistant Prefect Wang abhorred Cheng's lust as the source of the crime and wouldn't listen to him any more. He thought of sentencing him on the capital crime of rape and homicide, but the woman's head was missing from her body and no murder weapon had been found at the scene. The case lacked enough evidence to be concluded. The Assistant Prefect thus demanded that the Chaofeng come up with the head by a certain deadline.

After the deadline was renewed several times, however, the Chaofeng still presented no clue as to the whereabouts of the missing head. He pleaded, "Even if I had been refused in a rape attempt and killed her, what's the use for me to keep the chopped head? There is no reason for me to be subject to interrogation now!"

Finding his words reasonable, Assistant Prefect Wang began to suspect that the killer might be another man. So he ordered that both Cheng and Brother Li Fang be detained in jail and had their neighbors rounded up in court for investigation. The neighbors all said, "Li and Cheng were a seller and customer in frequent contact. We've never heard about any adultery between them. As for Cheng, he's married, and it's likely that he has committed seduction. But we've never seen him behave brutally. He might not have been involved in the murder."

The Assistant Prefect then said, "If he's not the murderer, you local people must be familiar with the Li family. Then you know something about Li's foes. Is there anything suspicious that you can tell me about?"

The neighbors said, "Li Fang ran his tavern every day and didn't have any foes. He and his wife were good people and never bickered with others. We can't figure out who committed the murder that night. It's really a puzzle for us neighbors."

The Assistant Prefect said, "You should go around and make inquiries about it."

With that demand placed on them, the neighbors were about to leave when one elder stepped forward and said, "On the basis of my humble guess, there is a man who might be the murderer."

The Assistant Prefect asked, "Who?"

The elder said, "There was a wandering monk from far away in our place. He beat his clapper and cried for alms every night for more than a month. After the murder of Li's wife, I didn't hear his voice any more. Is it just a coincidence that he left right after the murder? Furthermore, I never heard about anyone ever giving him alms. Would he have been satisfied before he left? That is something suspicious."

The Assistant Prefect said, "It is wandering monks' nature to commit atrocities. Your doubt is not groundless. But where can we hunt for him?"

The old man said, "When a high reward is offered, brave fellows will come forward. You can summon that Cheng, your lordship, and let him know the situation. His family is wealthy and will surely be willing to offer a handsome reward for the capture of the real criminal. I don't think the monk has gone too far away. He should be somewhere in the vicinity. It won't be hard to find him."

The Assistant Prefect agreed. The Chaofeng was brought out from jail and told what the old man had said. The Chaofeng said, "This thread gives me a chance of living. I only hope my lord will take charge of this matter, issue a wide-search dispatch and assign a few arrest-runners to launch a large-scale hunt. I'm willing to make an offer of a reward and pay the money upon receiving information about the murder."

The Assistant Prefect immediately selected a few arrest-runners. The Chaofeng asked someone to invite the arrest-runners to see him and he first gave them ten *liang* of silver as their traveling expenses, and put aside thirty *liang* as a reward, which would be handed to them upon the capture of the monk. The runners agreed to this and set off.

The arrest-runners had many colleagues and they were well informed. They never failed in whatever they set out to do. With the knowledge of Cheng's rich family background plus the generous reward, they spared no effort in accomplishing their mission. In less than a year the monk was discovered in the prefecture of Ningguo, begging on the street at night and retiring in an old temple. The runners had taken a local man with them, and he identified the monk as the one who once begged in the town of Yanzi.

The arrest-runners discussed the matter among themselves. "He's the man for sure," they deliberated. "But we don't know whether he's the murderer or not. Even if he is, we can't arrest him without any evidence. We will have to use strategy to get him." They decided to find a woman's garment and let a younger runner wear it. He was to go with them in disguise into an ambush in a wood next to the sole path by which one could go from the street to the old temple.

They kept watch there until midnight when the monk was seen walking along the path alone, with his clapper in hand. In the woods the arresting runner in the disguise of a woman muttered, "Monk, give me back my head!"

The monk was taken aback. He came to a stop and vaguely caught sight in the darkness of a woman in red. Fear gripped him immediately. Another such utterance rose right after the first. "Monk, give me back my head!" Then the phrase became a steady repetition.

The monk shivered in dread, replying, "Isn't your head on the rack of the store three doors up from your house? Don't importune me!"

The arrest-runners in ambush knew by this that the monk was undoubtedly the murderer. With a whistle, they sprang out, seized him and tied him up, shouting, "Bald villain! You committed murder in the town of Yanzi, but have hidden yourself here!" A solid beating subdued the monk. The monk was taken back to the prefecture court.

The Assistant Prefect asked the arrest-runners how they had captured the man. They recounted the trap set with the disguise of a woman, the monk's panic and release of the truth, and their final capture of him. The monk was brought in. He knew that his crime was discovered and he could not get off, and so he confessed, "I killed the woman."

The Assistant Prefect asked, "What rancor was between you and her?"

The monk rejoined, "I didn't have rancor against her. That night I howled for alms and went by the house and saw the gate open, so I stole inside, hoping to steal something. Then I was surprised to see that the candles were lit brightly and a beautiful woman was standing by the bed in dazzling attire. I just couldn't hold back my urges. So I clasped her in my arms, attempting to have sex with her. But she desperately resisted. In a fit of anger, I pulled out my knife and killed her. I picked up the severed head and ran out. Then I thought, 'Why do I need this head?' So I put it on the rack in the store three doors up the road. I was angry that she had not yielded to my request but felt released after I killed her. During that very night I fled there. Now I've been arrested. I should pay with my life, and have nothing else to say."

The Assistant Prefect issued a summons and had the manager of the store brought into court, and asked him, "The monk confessed that there was a human head on your shelf. Where is it now?"

The manager answered, "Yes, there was a human head there. When I saw it in the morning, I was afraid I would become a suspect in a murder. So I took it to Zhao Da's family, about ten doors further up the road, and hung it on a tree outside his house. I have no idea what happened after that."

The Assistant Prefect sent some men with the store manage to bring Zhao Da to the court. Zhao Da said, "That morning I saw a head hanging on the tree. I was shocked and was going to report this to the government office, but I feared I might be involved in a legal case so I buried it in my back garden."

The Assistant Prefect asked, "Is it still there?"

Zhao Da said, "I thought that it might someday be useful as a piece of evidence, so I marked a small shrub on the spot. How can it not be there?"

The Assistant Prefect said, "I doubt what you've said is true. I must go there to take a look for myself."

The Assistant Prefect rode in a sedan chair to Zhao Da's home, with Zhao Da leading the way. As they reached the back garden, Zhao Da pointed to a spot and said, "It's underneath there."

The Assistant Prefect had his men dig up the ground. As soon as some earth was removed, a human head rolled out. It was caked with mud. The followers called out, "Here it is!"

The Assistant Prefect then said, "The woman's body is complete today."

The followers flicked away some of the dirt and looked more closely. They were shocked, saying, "It is strange! How could the woman be wearing a beard?"

The head was presented to the Assistant Prefect and he saw:

the eyes were closed, mouth shut; the neck bore knife wounds and a beard covered the chin. Can a skull perform magic and turn a woman's head into a man's?

Assistant Prefect Wang screamed, "This is a man's head, not a woman's. Its mysterious appearance shows that there are other hidden facts behind the scenes!" He shouted, "Lock up Zhao Da!" But Zhao Da had run out the moment he had seen that the unearthed head was not that of a woman.

Assistant Prefect Wang went into the main room of Zhao Da's house and had a table placed there as his desk. He took a seat and summoned Zhao Da's wife in front of him for interrogation. Zhao Da's wife, unable to cover the matter up, had to confess, "Ten years ago Zhao Da had a foe surnamed Ma, who he killed. He brought his head home and buried it here."

The Assistant Prefect asked, "Zhao Da was here a moment ago. Where's he now?"

His wife said, "He saw the head dug up and knew that his murder was out. So he fled without even telling me where he was going."

Assistant Prefect Wang said, "It was only moments ago. He must have gone to the home of one of his relatives. He can't be far away. Be quick to tell me the address of all your relatives."

The wife feared torture and had to say, "We have a son-in-law surnamed Jiang, who works as clerk in the prefecture government office. I think he must have gone to his place." The Assistant Prefect at once sent runners with Zhao Da's wife to the home of Jiang. The Assistant Prefect waited at Zhao Da's house.

Meanwhile Jiang, as a government official, knew the consequence of compliance with the law. When his father-in-law Zhao Da came to his home and said his murder had been discovered and he had to hide himself in his place, Jiang feared that he himself might become involved in the case. So he rejected Zhao Da and told him to find another place to hide. Zhao Da couldn't think of any place to go, and, as he hesitated, the runners arrived with his wife. Jiang found himself caught in trouble. Eager to free himself, Jiang couldn't do anything but turn Zhao Da over to the runners. Zhao Da was brought back to his own home. On the way, his wife said to him, "The lord questioned me and I told him everything. You should confess as well, to avoid torture."

Accordingly, Zhao Da confessed everything to the Assistant Prefect. During further questioning by the Assistant Prefect, Zhao Da said, "This Ma had a long-term feud with me. One day I ran into him on a trail in the hills. That day I had an ax with me for chopping brushwood, so I killed him with it. I thought that if I left some traces behind the murder would be discovered. Therefore, I stripped the body of clothing and chopped off the head. Then I set fire to the clothing and buried the head in my back garden. The family of Ma found later him missing and inquired about him. They heard a dead body had been found in the hills. The body had no head, so they could not identify it. It's been long time since the family of Ma has mentioned the matter. I buried Ma's head about ten *chi* away from the spot where the woman's head is buried. Because a head had been buried in my back garden, I feared it might be discovered. So I planted a shrub as a mark when I buried the woman's head. The two spots were some distance apart so I didn't flinch to have people dig out the woman's head without revealing Ma's head. But it happened that Ma's head was dug out first. This is a debt I owed in my previous life and I'm doomed to pay it back now. If I had known the result in advance, I would never have told about the burial of the woman's head."

The Assistant Prefect asked, "Where's the woman's head now?"

Zhao Da said, "It should be there. There's no mistake."

The Assistant Prefect took him to the back garden and had his followers dig again on the same spot. As expected, another head was unearthed. It was identified as the woman's head. The Assistant Prefect laughed and said, "The examination of one murder has led to the solution to two. That must be the will of Heaven!"

Zhao Da was chained, the two heads were brought into court, and a summons was sent to the family of Ma for identification of the head. Only then did the son of the Ma, ten years after his father disappeared, find proof that his father had been murdered. The son then filed a make-up indictment, and the Assistant Prefect passed it. The family of Ma was allowed to take the head back home to bury it. Brother Li Fang was called in to identify the other head, which was indeed his wife's. The monk and Zhao Da were each flogged thirty times and sentenced to death. Since the Chaofeng had committed the crime of paying for a seduction, which led to the murder of the woman, so he was sentenced to imprisonment, but was allowed to redeem himself by paying a sum. The offense of Brother Li Fang resided in his taking money for his wife's adultery, so he was sentenced to the penalty of a cudgel beating. According to the verdict, the Chaofeng had to pay Brother Li Fang six *liang* of silver for the burying expenses for Li's wife. The manager of the store, three doors from Brother Li Fang's house, would have been sentenced for his crime of transporting the head, but he actually received a verdict of not guilty. The reason for this was that Zhao Da was to be executed for his murder as well as his burial of the transported head, so justice was already done as if at the request of Heaven.

Assistant Prefect Wang's thorough examination concluded two unsettled murders. His performance was reported to higher levels of government, widely commended and has since become a popular and admirable story. It is interesting to note that the Chaofeng started with the desire to seduce a woman, but ended in a failure to obtain her, which caused her meaningless death, his own suffering from fright, his more-than-one-year imprisonment and his fine of one hundred *liang* of silver. The lesson for him was severe. Chen would not have met her violent death if she had stuck to her own will, regardless of her husband's plan. As for the discovery of Zhao Da's murder, on the basis of Chen's death, which was committed long before with almost no possibility of being resolved, it demonstrated a deliberate arrangement of Heaven. The moral is crystal clear that no evil deed is doable.

Tale 13

Zhang Funiang Resolves to Stay Unmarried for
Integrity;
Zhu Tianxi Takes a Long Journey to Identify a Name

This tale is about a government official from Suzhou in the period of Chunxi [1174-1190] during the Song Dynasty. He was called Zhu Quan, styled Jingxian, and became the director of the Department of Tea and Horses* in (present-day) Sichuan Province. He had a son by name of Zhu Xun, who was twenty and betrothed to a woman from the renowned Fan family of Suzhou. But, before he was married, the young man followed his father to his office. The young man was in his prime, full of vigor. He found life in his father's residence boring. Unable to curb his desires, he asked someone to talk to his father on his behalf, to request that he be allowed to take a concubine first.

Jingxian said, "I wonder whether there's such a rite that allows one

---

*The Department of Tea and Horses, an administrative organ in charge of trade of tea and horses with ethnic minorities, was set up during the Song Dynasty in northwest and southwest regions of China.

to take a concubine before a wife."

The son answered, "No, there certainly is not. But I am right now thousands of *li* away from home. To rid myself of loneliness, I have to go against convention. When I marry a wife in future, there will be nothing wrong in dismissing the concubine."

Jingxian said, "That sounds alright, but you will find it hard to part from the concubine once you become intimate with her."

The young man said, "A man is as good as his word. Why should it be hard to break off with her?" Jingxian then granted his son's request.

The young man asked an able runner called Hu Hong to seek out a concubine for him. Hu Hong learned that a Zhang in Chengdu had a daughter named Funiang, who was beautiful and genteel. He told the young man about her. The young master presented a gift of fifty *liang* of silver to take the girl as his concubine. Funiang and the young man were about same age, so the young couple had boundless pleasure in living together. They spent a year in mutual attachment.

The father of the family of Fan in Suzhou became concerned over the waste of youth in his grown-up daughter and would-be son-in-law, who was living so distant from her with his office-holding father, because there was no sign of his return in the foreseeable future. So the father prepared a dowry and set off with his daughter to go to Sichuan for the marriage. As they got close to the border of Sichuan, a messenger was dispatched to inform the young man of the Zhu family of their imminent arrival. After learning of the young master having taken a concubine one year earlier, Fan stopped their journey and sent a letter to Zhu Jingxian, saying:

It is always acceptable to take a concubine after marriage, but where does the moral system allow a concubine to come before the wife? Now my daughter is on the way for her marriage along with her dowry. The concubine must be disposed of before the marriage can be completed.

Reader, it is preposterous for a man to take a concubine before marriage, though it is common that a man takes concubines. But since a concubine, in this case, had already been obtained, it would be realistic to make clear the wife's superior status and to warn the concubine that she mustn't take her advantage of earlier arrival so as to bring the family life into harmony. However, all women are jealous. A woman can't stand hearing the word "concubine." A concubine is a thorn in the flesh which should be pulled out. Who could talk the bride into tolerating a concubine? A prudent father should speak to his daughter with reason, saying, "Though the concubine is humble, she's from a good family; since she has given herself to my son, she will be willing to serve him for the rest of her life. How can we mistreat her by renouncing her? Besides, to force her into a marriage with someone else is not completely an act of righteousness. In view of the present condition, I suggest that you take a noble-minded stance and treat her with generosity, which will eventually earn you a reputation of virtue. The concubine will undoubtedly be satisfied with her inferior family standing. Isn't that the good way to solve the problem?" If he had said so, the girl to be married might not have gone to such great lengths to get what she had wanted, even though she was consumed by jealousy. The father of the girl, however, would act only in the interest of his daughter and made no attempt at reconciliation, certainly unmindful of what trouble might arise in the young master's family.

Zhu Jingxian received the letter and said to his son, "At the very beginning, I talked to you about the possible consequences of your taking a concubine. Now your father-in-law blames us in his letter. We cannot counter him. He's requesting that you dispose of your concubine before your marriage to his daughter. Your wife has been escorted to the border of our region and will not come to meet you until you give a satisfactory answer. I think we will have to meet their request."

The young man could not bear to tear himself away from his concubine. However, he had made the promise earlier to get rid of the concubine upon his marriage. Now his father was pushing him and his father-in-law was awaiting an immediate reply of compliance. If he refused, his marriage would be impossible. He was in a predicament, feeling greatly dismayed. He told Zhang Funiang about his state of mind.

The concubine rejoined, "It would be all right if originally your family had not taken me as your concubine. Now that you have taken me into your house and I did not commit any offense. It's not fair for you to throw me out now because of your marriage. On the other hand, you can rest assured that I will show respect and courtesy in serving your wife once she moves into the family. Why do you have to drive me out?"

The young man said, "I am by no means willing to let you go. I promised my father at the time of your coming that, when I formally married, you would be sent back home. Now my father is urging me to make good my word. My father-in-law and his daughter are currently waiting on the border, waiting for me to send you away before the marriage is completed. I'm in a dilemma."

Zhang Funiang said, "I'm without privileges and at your disposal. If you resolve to get rid of me, how can I refuse to leave and stop your wife from coming into marriage? However, something has happened to me that keeps me from leaving you now."

The young man asked, "What's happened to you?"

Zhang Funiang said, "I'm expecting. It is an offspring of yours. If I go home now, I'll give birth to a child later. Since the child is yours, how can you deny it a place in your family? If you eventually decide to take the child home, it would be better for me stay here right now."

The young man said, "If you stay, the Fan family will reject the marriage. That will ruin my whole life. Besides, even if my wife is forced to accept you into the family, you can't expect to be treated well by her in future. If you're resented all the time, that'll make your life miserable. You'd better leave for home now. I'm assuring you that I'll talk to my wife and get you back sometime after the marriage."

Funiang was silent. This is exactly the scenario that:

One should not choose to be a woman if a choice is available;
Otherwise one chooses to give up the choice of life to someone else.

Funiang was unwilling to leave, but the young man's father insisted on sending her away and the young man would not turn down his future father-in-law's request for a marriage. Unable to reverse the course of the matter, Funiang sobbed sadly and left for home.

At once the family of Zhu sent a message to the family of Fan. The future father-in-law then renewed the journey with his daughter. A trip of several days and nights brought them to the office of Zhu. A date was picked and the marriage was completed. The young master was indeed a man by nature and his feeling was an inconstant as the dew drops rolling on a leaf. The newlyweds were in marital bliss, utterly ignoring the sadness-stricken Zhang Funiang. It seemed to them all right that the concubine was absent.

The following year, Zhu Jingxian's term of office expired. The central government sent a ranking official, named Wang Wo, as his successor and summoned Zhu Jingxian back to the capital city. Zhu Jingxian decided to leave in the eighth month. Funiang, close to giving birth, sent a message asking to be taken to Suzhou. Zhu Jingxian said, "She should be with us since she's pregnant. But it will be an annoyance if she gives birth on the journey. If she has the child before our departure, we'll take her with us. Let's see what fortune befalls her."

Funiang sent in a few more messages pleading, "What I've said is that I was one of your family before. I moved out only for the sake of the arrival of the young master's wife. I see no reason for us to break off. Besides, the baby I'm carrying is the young master's. How can you be at ease being rid of it? It's only rational for you to take me along with you back to your native place no matter whether I give birth before or after the departure, because I'm intrinsically part of your family." As a ranking official, Zhu Jingxian fell short of words to argue with the woman. So he talked to his wife, and they went together to try to persuade their daughter-in-law into taking Funiang back and bringing her along with them.

The young wife had learned of this problem earlier from her husband. Now her father-in-law brought it up again putting more pressure on her. Being from a civilized family, she was quite sensible, and finding it irrational to haggle over the matter, she made herself ready to receive Funiang into the family. However,

the change in weather is beyond man's ken;
the fortune or misfortune is at Fate's whim.

The young man was a womanizer. In his early years, he had been impatient to wait until marriage and had taken a concubine. As a result, Zhang Funiang was victimized and abandoned. Was the young master truly a lecher? His marriage with Fan witnessed his continuous unrestrained indulgence in sex. After Zhang Funiang had left, a fresh eruption of passion plunged him into insatiable acts with his newlywed. Consequently he contracted consumption, spitting blood and running fever at night. The doctor warned him of the danger of continued sexual indulgence.

Jingxian talked with his wife, who said, "Our son's sick. We will have to let him and his wife sleep separately. If Zhang Funiang joins him now, that will add oil to the flames. I think we should leave Zhang Funiang here instead of taking her along with us. It's a shame that she's going to give birth. Since the baby is of our descent, no matter whether it's a boy or girl, it's hard to leave it."

Jingxian said, "Our son and daughter-in-law are pretty young. If our son gets back his health, we won't need to worry about obtaining grandsons. It's a good time now to desert Zhang Funiang before she has the baby. Otherwise she may give birth anytime later with us, and it would be difficult to renounce her at that time. We can use the inconvenience of childbirth on the journey as an excuse. If we can't talk her round, make a promise that we will bring her to join us in the future." After making up their minds, they firmly turned down Zhang Funiang and left Chengdu for Suzhou.

Left behind, Zhang Funiang wept many times. She waited on herself attentively before the day of birth. Forty days after the departure of the family of Zhu, she gave birth to a baby boy. To her mind, the boy would sooner or later go back to the family Zhu. For the present, she named him Ji'er, meaning living temporarily away from home, and she raised him in her home in Sichuan. With her son, she would rather live in poverty than remarry, ignoring whatever her parents and neighbors said about her. A rough life of twisting hemp threads and mending clothes for others kept her and the son alive. Under her care, the boy grew up to be handsome with chiseled features. Among his peers, he always stood at the head, addressing himself as a "government official" and bossing others around in loftiness. At age seven or eight, Funiang sent him to school. He had a retentive memory and was quick to learn the Confucian classics by heart. His intelligence placed such high hopes in Funiang's mind that her confidence was further strengthened in remaining single with her son, unmindful whether the Zhus would acknowledge the boy's legitimate identity.

As Funiang spent her days with her son in Sichuan, the family of Zhu, after returning to Suzhou, tens of thousands of *li* away, had no contact with her. Two years later, the young master failed to recover from his illness and died. His wife had been married to him for four years, but had slept separately from him for the last two. She had had no children. Zhu Jingxian had the young master as his only son, and his death left the family without progeny.

Zhu Jingxian scarcely benefited from the honor and wealth his government career had brought him. He had to attend to his aged mother and widowed daughter-in-law. The lack of grandchildren rendered his later years depressing. A few years following the death of his son his mother died. Jingxian sank deeper into grief. By now he had completely forgotten the pregnant concubine his son had left behind years before, as if ages had elapsed.

One old saying goes, "A tale counts on coincidence." Wang Wo, the succeeding director of the Department of Tea and Horses in Sichuan, learned of the grief his immediate predecessor, Zhu Jingxian, sustained over the death of his mother, and sent a runner with brocade to offer condolences.

Who was this runner? He was the competent runner Hu Hong, who the young master had entrusted with the concubine-seeking task and who had obtained Zhang Funiang as a result. Hu Hong took a ride on the boat of Zou Gui, a patrol runner going to Suzhou on business, and came to the home of Zhu Jingxian. After accepting the gift, Zhu Jingxian asked him about former happenings in Sichuan. Hu Hong answered all questions in full detail. Zhu Jingxian had been in desolation for a time. Now seeing his former subordinate, he liked to chatter about experiences of the past. His sadness faded.

While staying at Zhu's place for some time, Hu Hong talked a great deal with members of the host family. Seeing their present state, he said to one servant, "The young master died so young. It's a shame. He left no son behind. Will the family adopt a son as heir?"

The servant replied, "Adoption is inevitable. But after all it is not the family's blood and flesh. How can he feel deeply attached to the family? So our old master has not mentioned this matter yet."

Hu Hong then said, "If the young master left one offspring, how would your old master like that?"

The servant replied, "He would surely be overjoyed. But how could that have happened?"

Hu Hong said, "Well, there's a possibility. But I wonder whether your old master is serious about the matter."

Confused and interested, the servant asked, "What do you mean?"

Hu Hong said, "Do you remember that the young master once took a concubine?"

"Yes," the servant said, "he did. But, after his marriage, he sent the concubine back home."

Hu Hong then said, "But she gave birth to a son."

The servant said, "So she remarried and gave birth. What does her son have to do with our family?"

Hu Hong replied, "You've wronged her! She has never remarried. The truth is the seed was planted in your family!"

The servant said, "I doubt what you've said. You had better talk to my old master."

The servant told Zhu Jingxian what Hu Hong had said. Zhu Jingxian recalled that when he left his position Zhang Funiang was going to give birth and had begged to be taken back with them to Suzhou. He realized that their family would have a child born in an alien place. Now the news that the child was a boy both surprised and delighted him. He hastily called Hu Hong for further inquiry.

Hu Hong said, "I didn't know how you would react to this matter, so I didn't bring it up."

Zhu Jingxian said, "Tell me about the young master's concubine. What happened to her?"

Hu Hong said, "To tell you the truth, I helped the young master attain the concubine, so I know everything about her. She was expecting when sent back home by the young master. She gave birth to a son forty days after your departure."

Zhu Jingxian asked, "Where's the boy now?"

Hu Hong replied, "This little master is very handsome and bright. He's good at learning. Now he and his mother, both of them, are living together."

Zhu Jingxian asked, "Did this woman not remarry?"

Hu Hong answered, "I feel sorry for her. She's lived on a tight budget by mending clothes, and she has managed to support her son in school. She refused to marry. Her parents often tried to persuade her in this regard, and some neighbors have wanted to marry her. Even I myself hoped to make a little money by playing a matchmaker for her. But she has stood firm and no one has been able to talk her round. When she saw that her son was an excellent student, she became still more resolute."

Zhu Jingxian said, "If that is the case, my family name will be carried on. How happy I am! But are you sure what you've said is true?"

Hu Hong answered, "I used to be your inferior, an honest man, not a liar. Furthermore, I handled the business concerning this woman from the very beginning and know every detail of it. How could anything be wrong?"

Zhu Jingxian said, "It sounds believable. But the heir of my family is no trifle. They're tens of thousands of *li* away from here, and I'm not sure of the situation. You're only a servant. How can I venture on something I've obtained by word of mouth only from you?"

Hu Hong said, "If you don't believe me, you can double-check with Zou Gui, a patrol runner and also one of your old inferiors. I came here with him in his boat."

Zhu Jingxian decided that the news was not groundless and thus he really wanted to make sure. So he sent for Zou. Seeing himself called by his former superior, Patrol Runner Zou did not delay in completing a visiting card and soon arrived. At Zhu Jingxian's inquiry about the matter, he recounted Zhang Funiang's resolution to remain unmarried and to educate her son, and he described her son's extraordinary features and talents. His narrative fitted Hu Hong's story perfectly. Zhu Jingxian went into raptures. He went inside to tell his wife and daughter-in-law. The whole house was in great happiness, saying, "If this is true, we're seeing the hope of survival in an impasse. Congratulations to our ancestors!"

Zhu Jingxian ordered a dinner to be prepared for the patrol runner and then talked to him about bringing the mother and son to Suzhou. Patrol Runner Zou said, "It's going to be a long journey, and it will be hard for her and her son, woman and boy, to trek over the rough roads. Without substantial help, they cannot make it. Since I'm finished with my business here, and am going back pretty soon, you can take advantage of my return trip by writing a letter to the authorities there and providing the traveling expenses. I will do my best to bring mother and son here. Arrangements like this should be safe."

Jingxian said, "That is the shrewd vision of experience. I'm going to write two letters, one to Minister Liu of the Department of the Military and Security and another to Wang Wo, director of the Department of Tea and Horses, requesting that they make arrangements for the journey and make sure that the mother and son will be alright on the way here. As for their packing and departure, I have to entrust that you and Hu Hong will take care of everything. I will appreciate it very much, and you will be rewarded later."

Zou said, "This is a way that Hu Hong and I can return the kindness you showed us in the past. How could we treat slightly the mission to bring the young master here? Please compose the letters, my kind master. I'll take off soon."

Zhu Jingxian started to write the letter, which read as follows:

I, Zhu Quan, an unblessed man, have lost my mother and son. I have no grandson. During my tenure in office in Sichuan years ago, my son had a concubine called Zhang, and left her behind pregnant. Now according to the reports of Zou Gui, one of my former patrols, and Hu Hong, one of my former runners, she gave birth to a boy and the boy is now eight years old. The deserted offspring in an alien land reveals my family's slim line of descent. I mean to let the mother and son come here to join us. However, the journey is not easy for them. I am presenting this request for your assistance in their travel by boat and carriage so that we can have a family reunion and maintain the succession of our family name. My gratitude is beyond expression.

Zhu Quan reporting

He prepared two copies of the letter and gave them to Patrol Runner Zou. At the same time he rewarded Hu Hong and extended his gratitude for the gift that Wang Wo sent to him in terms of the condolences on the death of his mother. In addition he gave the two men adequate money for traveling and made repeated requests regarding their mission before they departed. Zhu Jingxian thought that, with the help of the local authorities and his old subordinates, everything would be alright, so the whole family settled down to patiently wait.

Patrol Runner Zou and Hu Hong made their way back to Sichuan. Zou took the letter to Minister Liu. Hu Hong reported to Wang on his completion of business and presented the note of thanks and letter from Zhu Jingxian. Wang asked Hu Hong about the business concerned in the letter. Hu answered in detail. Then Wang told Hu Hong, "Go and tell the mother and son about this and let them prepare for the trip. Then report back to me. I'll make sure they get on the road soon."

With this charge, Hu Hong made directly to see Zhang Funiang, telling her of his business trip to Suzhou regarding condolences on the death of Zhu Jingxian's mother. Funiang eagerly inquired for news about the young master and the rest of the family. Hu Hong told her, "The young master died five or six years ago."

Zhang Funiang broke into tears. Then she asked about what happened after his death. Hu Hong said, "Without issue from the young master, the old master was despairing day and night. I touched upon the subject of your life with your son, your discipline of your son regarding education and your resolution to remain single. Master Zhu was not convinced until he double-checked with Patrol Runner Zou. Then he was delighted. He wrote two letters, asking Minister Liu and Lord Wang to make arrangements for your trip to Suzhou. I have just came back from meeting with Lord Wang and he told me to let you know that you should get ready for the trip. You and the little master should be on your way soon."

Years before, Zhang Funiang had wanted to go with the family back to Suzhou, but was rejected. She had had to stay in Sichuan and led a rough and unmarried life. Now the family was bringing her to Suzhou, just as a falling leaf finally finds its settling place at the roots of the tree. How could she help but get excited? She expressed her thanks for Hu Hong's bringing the message, and then told her son to pack for the trip that was being arranged by Wang Wo.

Wang Wo met with Minister Liu and discussed Zhu Jingxian's recovery of the grandson. They said to each other, "It will be a happy family reunion for Zhu Jingxian. We should do our best to help him."

It happened that a *jinshi* called Feng Zhenwu was about to depart for Lin'an via Suzhou by boat. His boat was spacious enough for a few more passengers. Having learned of this, Wang Wo reported the matter to Minister Liu, and then they separately sent letters to the *jinshi*. With two ranking officials looking into this minor business of requesting a ride for two extra boat passengers, how could the *jinshi* refuse? Accordingly, he told the boatman to partition the cabin and to clean it up. Minister Liu and Wang Wo presented Zhang Funiang and her son with traveling funds, tea, dried fruit and silver, and asked Patrol Runner Zou and Hu Hong to take care of them as they departed on their way. Hu Hong was ordered to escort the mother and son to

Suzhou.

Zhang Funiang said good-bye to her own family and got aboard the *jinshi* boat. Knowing that they were the dependents of a high official and it was a special mission from Minister Liu and Director Wang, the *jinshi* showed no negligence in taking care of them all the way.

Meanwhile, Zhu Jingxian was waiting anxiously at home as if a rainfall was expected in a land of long drought. One day the imperial court announced that they would hold a ceremony of rites south of the capital city to grant privileges to one son of each government official or the grandson if the son was not available. Zhu Jingxian wanted to register his grandson, who had not yet arrived though men had been sent to bring him from Sichuan. If he waited until his grandson arrived, this good chance to receive the imperial privileges would slip away. He decided he would enter a name now and have the ceremony later after his grandson arrived. With this plan in mind, he only needed to write down a name for his grandson in the book to be sent to the imperial court. He pondered, "What name should I give him?"

That whole night he tossed and turned, but could not come up with a satisfactory name. Next morning an idea struck him, "I'll soon receive my grandson by Zhang Funiang. It is a great fortune that has fallen from heaven on me after years of despair. Is it perhaps Heaven's bestowal? *The Books of Songs* says, 'Heaven bestows a huge fortune on you.' Let me name my grandson Tianxi. That name implies Heaven's granting of my grandson and carries a touch of classic elegance. Wonderful!" So he put down the name Zhu Tianxi for his grandson in the book that was to be sent to the Department of Rites. After the privileges were granted, he waited for the arrival of his grandson to receive the post.

Before long, Hu Hong reported his arrival. He presented to Zhu Jingxian the two letters from Minister Liu and Wang Wo and said, "The two masters provided the traveling funds. Zhang and the little master rode in the boat of the *jinshi* Feng and are now waiting down on the river bank."

Zhu Jingxian was delighted and was about to go out to meet them. Then the *jinshi* entered with a note of greeting. He said, "Minister Liu and Wang gave me this mission and I have brought your grandson and his mother by boat. It's good luck that they have arrived here safe and sound." Then Zhu Jingxian expressed many thanks to the *jinshi* and went out to meet the mother and son.

Zhang Funiang led her son, Ji'er, up to meet his grandfather and aunt. The calling up of memories of the old days brought tears to all the family. The little master was taken to meet every member of the family, which was in great happiness. Zhu Jingxian asked Zhang Funiang, "Does my grandson have a name?"

Funiang answered, "He has a pet name, Ji'er. Two years ago when I sent him to school, the teacher gave him the name, Tianxi."

Stunned, Zhu Jingxian said, "I had a request from the Department of Rites for the name of my grandson not long ago, a name that could be used at the reception for granting imperial privileges. I thought for a whole night and finally decided on the name Tianxi. I put it down in the book and sent it in. I couldn't have known that you had obtained exactly the same name two years before and tens of thousands of *li* away from here! It must have been predestined by Heaven. What an extraordinary miracle!" The whole family was amazed.

Zhu Jingxian's sudden recovery of his grandson from Sichuan was news in its own right. The grandson had acquired the same name in two different places, and now had come home to attend a ceremony for receiving imperial privileges. This fact added more amazement. The event circulated as a tale of admiration. Later Zhu Tianxi achieved a high government position due to his reception of imperial privileges. Zhang Funiang also received the imperial conferment of title. It was a reward for her moral integrity and strict upbringing of her son.

Tale 14

Yang Chouma Asks to Be Thrashed; A Rich Man Is Frightened

During the Song Dynasty [960-1279], in Jiangyuan of Shu Prefecture [present-day Sichuan Province], there was a remarkable man called Yang Wangcai, with the formal name Xilu. No one knew how he, as a little boy, had met a supernatural man, acquired a magic book and learned extraordinary skills from him. At seven or eight, he showed some of his magic tricks at school. Often he summoned a group of school-children around him and made them dance, babbling away and improvising acts of entertainment. He simply mumbled something and those village kids would dance to his beat, as if they were following a teacher's instructions, offering an amusing spectacle. After each performance, the children never could explain what he had done. One day one of his schoolmates had hundreds of coins in his bamboo-woven suitcase. No one knew he had the money. Yang asked him to lend him some. The student told him that he had no money to lend.

Yang then counted on his fingers and said, "You have so many hundred, so many ten and so many coins in your bamboo-woven book box. Why do you say you don't have money?" The rest students didn't believe him. They opened the student's box and found that exact amount of cash inside. Then word got around that the boy from the Yang family possessed magic powers. As he grew older, his looks became ugly and threatening, and he had ghostly eyes. But his predictions were accurate, so people from far and wide came to him to have their fortunes told, and he never failed them. Because of his ability in forecasting horoscopes and prophecy, he obtained a nickname, Yang Chouma.* His prophecies always came true no matter whether they concerned the present or future, the regular or irregular. Here are some examples.

There was a big tree to the south of his house, the leafy branches and twigs of which shaded a huge circular area tens of yards in diameter. One day he posted a notice on his door saying, "Please stay away from here and make a detour during the first three hours tomorrow afternoon. There may be a strange disaster." A man spotted it and soon word spread that, "Chouma has a notice on his door." At once a crowd gathered to look, and because everyone had heard of Chouma's mysterious powers, they believed in his prophecy and warned one another about the danger of walking past his door during the specified time the next day. Exactly at that time the following day, the tree fell, completely blocking the road in front of the house and destroying some of the buildings along the street. This was Yang Chouma's work of enchantment. He thought the happening might hurt some uninformed pedestrians, so he had offered the warning in advance. If someone had been ignorant of the impending disaster and had wandered through the street at that time, they could not have avoided being struck and crushed like a meat pie, as if hit by the

---

*"Chou" means fortune-telling and "ma" is the heavenly horse, whose movements determines people's fortune or misfortune.

Monkey King's golden cudgel as described in the popular novel *Journey to the West.* *

Yang was also a street vendor of fine silks and brocade. Often a customer would purchase a piece of silk eleven or twelve yards long from him, the price being determined by the length of silk. If the customer bargained with him, expecting to bring down the price a little, Yang never haggled. But after the transaction, when the customer measured the silk again trying to calculate the cost, he would be shocked to discover that the amount of his purchase was exactly as the price he had paid. Even if you measured the silk to be tens of yards, it would turn out but a few yards, since the money you had paid was the price of this length.

Yang Chouma once rode on a fine mule to visit a friend. He dismounted at the house and tied the mule on a post inside the yard. The host and guest talked over tea. After tea, Chouma excused himself to go out for awhile, leaving his mule behind. The mule had neighed and pawed the ground when it first arrived with Chouma, but now it was quiet. As time passed, Yang did not return and then the mule became silent and started to shrink. The host was stunned. He took a close look only to find that the mule was made of paper.

Another time the department of military and security affairs in Sichuan urgently needed to examine a file, which had been misplaced thirty years before. They could not locate it. The clerk working in the department was frustrated for days. Then a man said to him, "Why not go ask Yang Chouma? He knows everything." The clerk went to Yang for help. Yang Chouma told him that it was in a certain pile, which was stacked in a certain cabinet of a certain room. The clerk followed his instructions and quickly located the file.

One day he was visited by Monk Chen from Meishan. Another local

---

*A Chinese novel written by Wu Cheng'en (c. 1500-1582). The Monkey King is a hero of the novel, who wields a magic cudgel to subdue monsters.

guest was also at the meeting. This guest had a horse that looked rather imposing with a black body and white nose.

Seeing this horse, Yang Chouma said to the guest, "Your horse is not good for riding, sir. You'd better give it to me. If you keep it for riding, misfortune will surely befall you."

The guest became angry and rebuked him, saying, "Why do you bluff me? Do you want to rob me of my horse? I paid thousands of coins for this horse and have not ridden it much. How can I simply let you take it away?"

Chouma laughed and said, "I'm sincere in my desire to help you steer clear of a terrible catastrophe. If you don't believe me, you will experience ill luck. Here we have Monk Chen as a witness. On the 20th of the fifth month, next year, you will meet your doom because of some old grudge in your former life. Keep this in mind: don't go to the stable to fodder the horse that day, and you will need to protect your left side of your chest as well. If you survive that day, we may have chance to see each other again."

The guest thought his warning was absurd and offensive. His rage ran high, so he ignored his words and left. By the specified day the following year, the guest had completely forgotten about the warning. As he went to feed his horse, the horse suddenly pounced, kicking its feet wildly and knocking his owner to the ground. With the man lying there, the horse stamped forcefully on the left side of his chest and broke all his ribs. The man let out a yell and made a few more gasps before he breathed his last. Monk Chen learned of this and was, of course, shocked. He told everyone he met that he saw with his own eyes that Yang Chouma could predict accurately.

Prime Minister Yu was called back from his mission in the prefectures of Jing and Xiang to the capital city. His son, Gongliang, sent a letter to Yang Chouma for a prediction as to his father's next assignment. Chouma replied in his letter,

"He may go, or not, to Sutai, but he will be appointed concurrent minister of justice fifteen days after he arrives in Sutai."

At that time the government position was called minister of justice and Sutai had no position of concurrent minister of justice. Prime Minister Yu doubted what Chouma said. Later he was indeed sent to the work in Sutai. Fifteen days after his arrival, he was appointed concurrent minister of justice under the Privy Council as Yang Chouma had predicted. Because another official, called Qian Chuhe, had been appointed minister of justice before Yu's appointment, he was appointed to the concurrent position, which fitted Chouma's prediction perfectly.

An old private school instructor called Guan Qisun was urged by one of his colleagues, who had heard about Yang Chouma's supernatural powers, to send a servant to get an account of his fortune. Yang Chouma had foreknowledge the servant's arrival and told his wife, "Go and fix dinner. A servant from the family of Guan is coming. We have to entertain him."

His wife cooked the dinner accordingly. When the food was ready, the servant arrived. Before he stepped up to the door, Yang Chouma emerged to meet him, saying with a smile, "Have you come all the way on behalf of somebody else rather than for yourself?"

The servant was astonished and said, "You're as omniscient as a god, sir!" Yang's wife attended him with food. Chouma wrote a letter of reply telling the fortune and sent the servant off.

Yang Chouma's wife, whose first name was Su, was not an ordinary woman either. With common looks, she had once been a prostitute. However, she had put on such airs that she usually shunned receiving clients. When people passed her house, she would comment, "This one is good, but that one is bad. This one will prosper, while that one will go broke. This one will get through to be something eventually, but that one may never see the end of his current state." She appeared as a fortune-teller sitting in a tent and meting out accounts by judging a person's complexion. However, she never made explicit predictions in front of the people concerned. Yet behind a customer's back she might say one or two sentences that never failed to come true. Thus her reputation reached far and wide, drawing crowds that included government officials and dependents of celebrities riding in carriages. She was attracted to some of the visitors and let them stay the night. Those who were on familiar terms with her wanted to marry her, but she spoke her mind, saying, "None of the people I've seen can be my husband."

Later she met Yang Chouma whose terrible looks caught her fancy. She then said, "Here comes my husband!" Similarly Yang Chouma's impression of her struck a note of intimacy. He said, "I didn't know my wife could be found here!" Agreeable conversations ensued. Therefore Yang Chouma married her. It was a perfect marriage like that of Peach Blossom Girl and Duke Zhou.* Since then the two meted out even more accurate prophecies concerning the fortune and misfortune of human and ghosts.

After the marriage, Yang Chouma's reputation rose even higher. His visitors, princes and nobles, could be satisfied now, even if he was not in, by enlisting the clairvoyant services of his wife who was equally gratifying.

One day Yang Chouma walked in the town of the prefecture where two runners, Zhang Qian and Li Wan, greeted him. Yang grabbed both of them and dragged them out of the office building. He said to them, "Please honor me with your presence at my home. I have something important about which to talk with you two."

The two men were mediators in the government office. Guessing

---

*A popular story about a strategic contest and marriage between a girl called Peach Blossom Girl and a fortune-teller called Duke Zhou.

that it would be some kind of rewarding business, they instantly agreed to follow him. Yang Chouma said, "Would you please bring your penalty cudgels with you?"

Zhang Qian and Li Wan asked, "What's the point of bringing the cudgel to your house? Do you want us to beat somebody?"

Chouma replied, "You'll have use of them. It'll be clear once you're there." Knowing Chouma was a man of bizarre behavior, the two men figured that perhaps he did have some business for them to do. So they each picked up a cudgel and went to his home.

Once there, Chouma took out thirty thousand coins and gave them to the two men. Zhang Qian and Li Wan said, "What sort of business do you want us to do, sir? Why should we get paid before doing anything for you?"

Chouma said, "Only after you accept this little pay will I be comfortable enough to tell you what I want you to do."

The two men said, "Please tell us what the business is, and we will definitely do our best to accomplish it."

Chouma went to the inner room and called out his wife to meet the two runners. Zhang Qian and Li Wan, unable to make out his meaning, thought, "Why is he bringing his wife out?" They were confused but said nothing.

Chouma and his wife then each picked up one of the cudgels and handed it to the two men. Chouma said, "I have nothing particular for you to do, but a simple request that you beat my wife and me each with twenty cudgel strokes. I will appreciate considerably your kindness." Stunned, the two men said, "What are you talking about?"

Chouma answered, "Don't mind, please. Just do as I say. I'll be grateful for your help."

Zhang Qian and Li Wan said, "Tell us why you want to do this."

Chouma answered, "We deserve this cudgeling torture now. So I asked you government runners to come to my house to complete the business. It will save us public disgrace in future. You're doing us a favor now."

Zhang Qian and Li Wan said, "Absurd! Absurd! We absolutely cannot do it!"

Chouma and his wife sighed and said, "Since you've made up your minds not to beat us now, we're doomed to adversity and can't find a way out. Anyway, please accept the money as you're already here."

The two men said, "Your reward makes no sense."

Chouma said, "Please take it. Later we will have chance to appreciate your kindness."

Zhang Qian and Li Wan made a perfunctory refusal but clutched the money, for government runners had an insatiable appetite for money just as a fly feeds on blood. They thanked him by saying, "We appreciate your kindness in giving us such a handsome gift. An old saying goes, 'The young have no right to turn down a reward from the old.' Please don't hesitate to let us know if you need us in future. We'll make every effort to work for you." Having gotten paid without having to perform any service, they left in joy.

The worship of gods was a routine business for Yang Chouma. He usually set up six seats at home. Leaving the two seats vacant on the east side, he and his wife often took the two seats of honor on the west, and gave the last two to a Buddhist monk and a Taoist priest as invited guests. At that time there was speculation as to what gods he might worship, for he did not believe in Buddhism or Taoism. The suspicion of his weird practices gave rise to the accusation that he upheld heresy, with which he "misguided the public" and so "deserved capital punishment". An indictment was submitted to the prefecture governor. The governor permitted the filing of a lawsuit. Runners were sent to arrest him and his wife. The two were put behind bars without trial.

The jailers had heard about Chouma's supernatural abilities and feared his retaliation, so they did not fasten him with shackles but made a point of playing up to him. But they were anxious because he might make an escape with his magic powers. Chouma recognized their apprehension and said to them, "Take it easy, sirs. I'm fine. My wife and I should receive punishment. Our ill fate is doomed, so we can't escape it but will meet it with easy minds."

One jailer said, "You have magic powers. Why didn't you use them to keep off destruction instead of coming to meet it?"

Chouma rejoined, "This evil force holds sway and we can't flee. After undergoing the punishment, we should be able to attain divine enlightenment." His words put the jailers at ease. In the days that followed he stayed in prison, compliant and free of his powers.

The prefecture magistrate sent him to Judge Yang Chen for trial. Judge Yang knew Chouma was a man of supernatural abilities and hoped to protect him. In order to put on a show for the public, Judge Yang brought Chouma into court for interrogation. Facing the judge directly, Chouma disregarded the accusation and said, "You've got an uncle. Have you heard anything from him recently? It's a shame, it's a shame!" Ignorant of what he was talking about, the judge made no reply. At that moment a man arrived from Chengdu, bringing news of the death of the judge's uncle. The judge was enormously surprised, and withdrew with admiration for this extraordinary man.

At the time the judge's daughter was afflicted with a lingering disease. She used prescription of a doctor named Chen which showed no effect. The judge called Chouma into court, planning to ask him for help. Before the judge could utter a word, Chouma said, "Your daughter has been sick for a long time, sir, and the use of doctor Chen's medicine is fruitless. Stopping taking it. She is plagued by a small snake on the hackberry tree in your back yard. I'm now in prison, unable to subdue the snake, nor can I use my magic powers. As soon as I receive a cudgel punishment, I'll cure the disease. Don't worry, please."

The judge told his wife about this, and his wife said, "It does seem that this may be the cause of our daughter's disease. One day she spotted a small snake winding up the hackberry tree in the back yard.

After that she fell into a deep trance and contracted the disease. Since this man seems to know the cause of her sickness and is able to cure her, he must possess a way of doing it. You should let him out of prison immediately and ask him to treat our daughter."

With the idea of releasing him, the judge altered the charge against Chouma, and issued a verdict that Chouma did not originally want to misguide the public, so it was not a capital crime; what he did was to spread absurd fortune-telling accounts studded with sorcery. Chouma was interrogated and unable to deny this. The sentence was punishment by cudgel. The verdict was reported to the prefecture magistrate. On the basis of law, the magistrate made a final decision that Chouma and his wife should each receive twenty strokes of a cudgel thrashing on the buttocks. The runners who were to carry out the thrashing were none other than Zhang Qian and Li Wan, the two runners whom Chouma had called to his home and given money to days before. The two men wanted to return Chouma's generosity and admired his foresight so they performed a perfunctory thrashing, just to show the act of law enforcement. Chouma and his wife had foreseen their time of adversity, and the flogging was merciful. Thus they bore it easily.

Chouma went back home after the punishment. He at once drew a figure, wrote a few words on it, wrapped it up in an envelope and sent it to the office of the judge as a token of gratitude. The judge opened it and saw that it was a figure for him to hang on the tree. Along with it was a slip of red paper with characters that said, "Your family will have good tidings next year." The judge tentatively hung the figure on the tree, and then his daughter regained her health. The judge wondered whether the prophecy would also come true. The following year, the judge and his three brothers all passed the imperial examinations or obtained promotions.

Chouma's preternatural actions were numerous. But his reception of the cudgel thrashing was the most remarkable. He had the prescience of going through such an ordeal, but asked the two runners to flog him so as to keep off the misfortune. Though the two runners had refused to meet his request, they were predetermined to carry out the order of punishment.

The exceptional powers and apocalyptic speech of Chouma earned him awe and admiration. However there was a rich man, a long-term friend of his, who was supposed to be kind and generous but was in fact a little conceited and skeptical about Chouma's abilities. One day Chouma happened to need twenty thousand pieces of cash for a certain business transaction, but he did not have the sum with him at the moment. He thought to himself, let me trouble him. He went to see the rich man to get a loan from him. The rich man was not happy about his request.

Reader, the rich are stingy in general and consider money as important as life. They treasure it and are parsimonious in regard to it, so that the god of money is inspired and accumulates riches for them. If one irritates the god of money by squandering riches, then money does not come steadily to them. So frugality makes the rich, while the rich have to be frugal.

Just as "a mention of money breaks off relations," the rich man, though a friend of Chouma's, in fact was no more than a good-weather friend. Seeing Yang Chouma ask a loan, he started to calculate. He figured that because Chouma was a fortune-teller, he envied the rich man's wealth and wanted to rob him of his money. He thought that if he lent Chouma the money, chances were it would be gone forever. Besides, in view of their friendship, he couldn't ask for payment of interest even if the principal could be regained. Furthermore, Chouma might develop the habit of borrowing money from him, so this dangerous precedent should not be set.

Therefore, the rich man replied to Chouma, "I'm sorry but I'm currently short of funds also. I can't meet your demand."

Seeing that the rich man was turning him down, Chouma broke into laughter and said, "Well, I made a courteous request, but you rejected me. All right, I'm going to let you have some pangs of fright. You'll soon know more about my powers and be too eager to give me the sum."

The rich man was satisfied that he had rejected Chouma. One day at dusk he sat resting in his study. Suddenly there was a knock on the door. He rose and opened it, and a woman slipped in. With a frown, she curtsied and said, "I live next door. My husband has gotten drunk and abused me. I can't bear it. It's midnight now, and I can't go anywhere for refuge. It's good to have you as a neighbor. I'd like to stay in your house for the night. Before dawn, I'll go back home and see to it that my husband awakes from his drunkenness."

Seeing that she was graceful and elegant, the rich man thought to himself, "It's midnight and there's nobody around. I'll let her stay and sleep with me. She said she would leave before dawn. Who will know what I've done tonight?"

Thus he promptly replied, "I appreciate your kindness in not overlooking me, madam. You can stay with me for the night and go home tomorrow morning. No one will know about it." The woman readily agreed. Smiling, she undressed herself, got into bed and slept together with him.

After their love-making, they were weary and fell into a deep sleep. Before dawn, the rich man awoke and figured that someone might see them together at daybreak, so he quickly called to the woman to get up. He called her a couple of times and gave a few shoves, but there was no answer and the body remained motionless. He was puzzled at this and the strong, unbearable stench of blood that rose up into his nose. He got up, lit a candle and went back to the bed for a closer look. "Owww!" he yelled.

What he saw was the woman's body, chopped into three parts, with blood streaming all over the place and a hot, offensive smell all around. It looked like a homicide. The rich man shuddered, thinking, "Did her husband come last night and kill her? But why didn't I get injured? I know I was exhausted last night after two rounds of love-making, and slept soundly. But how could I not have been disturbed in the slightest when she was so cruelly killed at my side? Now this has happened, and the body is on the blood-smeared bed. Pretty soon it'll be daylight and her husband will surely come here to look for her, the body will definitely be discovered. I could try to cover it up, but how can I completely clean it up? This is a horrible calamity for me! I can't shake it off unless I have the help of Yang Chouma. He's powerful with his sorcery. He can produce a magic trick to free me of it. I've got to rush right now and talk to him!"

In desperation, the rich man tottered in the dark toward Chouma's place. He raced to the door and pounded on it with all his might, narrowly avoiding injury to his hands. Yang Chouma uttered a reply from inside, "Who is it out there?"

The rich man, catching his breath, said, "It's me. It's me! Please be quick and open the door. I've got something urgent to discuss with you."

Knowing it was the rich man, Chouma did not hurry to open the door but chided him casually, "We've been good friends, and should come to each other's help in times of need. The other day when I wanted to borrow some money from you, you turned me down. Now it's night time. What can I do for you?"

The rich man said, "That was my fault, sir, and we can talk about that later. But do hurry up and let me in now."

Chouma slowly opened the door. The rich man fell on his knees, tears in his eyes, and said, "Please help me, sir. I'm involved in a disaster!"

Chouma asked, "What sort of business makes you so frantic?"

The rich man said, "You don't know, sir, that at dusk yesterday a neighbor woman came to ask me to put her up for the night. I did wrong to let her stay. It is strange that she was killed during the night by somebody. Now her body is in my home. This is a catastrophe that has fallen out of the clear sky. I'm begging you to apply your powers to save my life."

Chouma said, "That is very easy, but you rejected my request when I needed your help. Why should I help you now?"

The rich man said, "Friend, for the sake of our long-term relationship. It was my mistake to offend you when you were in need of money. If you save my life now, I will never refuse to lend you money in the future."

Chouma laughed and said, "Don't worry, then. I'm going to draw you a figure. You should put it up in your bedroom and shut the door. Don't let anybody know about it. The next day when you open the door, the body will be gone."

The rich man said, "Don't kid me, sir. If I open the door the next morning and nothing has changed, it will kill me."

Chouma said, "Nonsense! If that were true, my figure would have no power at all. How could I then continue with my trade? Besides, you're my old friend. Why would I make a fool of you? Go and do as I told you, and everything should be alright."

The rich man said, "If you help me this time, I will give you a million pieces of cash as a token of my gratitude."

Chouma laughed and said, "Why so much? I only need the twenty thousand sum I originally wanted to borrow. That'll be enough."

The rich man said, "I'll be more than willing to give you that."

Chouma then picked up a brush and drew a magic figure. The rich man slipped it into his sleeve and raced out. He was lucky to return home before dawn. He frantically posted the figure in his room and then reeled out, shutting the door behind him. He stood outside, his teeth grinding incessantly and his heart in his mouth. He stayed there until it was broad daylight. He didn't dare to open the door but peeped through a crack in it. The mess was gone. So he entered the room and saw that his bedding was neat and clean, free of blood stains. There was no sign of the dead body. With a sigh of relief, he became happy. Then he took twenty thousand pieces of cash and went to Chouma's home, with his servant following behind carrying wine and food, to extend his thanks.

Chouma said, "I only wanted to borrow twenty thousand pieces of cash from you, and that's all. Why do you bother to bring me wine and food?"

The rich man replied, "Your skills were extraordinarily powerful, and I appreciate your kindness in saving my life. I would like to present more as a token of my gratitude, but you insisted that you only want twenty thousand pieces of cash. You did me a huge favor. This modest gift of wine and food is far from enough to repay your kindness. I'd like to have dinner with you while we entertain ourselves a little today."

Chouma said, "Well, I should like to have a drink with you, but my house lacks space and I have visitors arriving and leaving all the time during the day. That will disturb our fun in drinking. Why not take this dinner to some place out of town tomorrow so we can enjoy ourselves there?"

The rich man said, "Absolutely right. But please keep the wine and food for yourself today. I'll bring some money with me tomorrow, so we can go to the country and have a good time there together."

Chouma replied, "Many thanks, many thanks." Hence Chouma accepted the wine and food, and the rich man left.

The following day the rich man came with an invitation for a meal. Chouma went with him out of town. A trip of a few *li* brought them to a quiet refreshing place where a tavern was located with a streamer flapping in the breeze. Chouma said, "It's nice and clean here. Let's have a drink."

The rich man told the servant to set down the gift basket on the table, as he, with Chouma, walked in and took seats facing each other. He called the tavern-keeper to bring out the best wine available. A waitress emerged with a wine pot in one hand, and walked up to them. Glancing up, the rich man was astounded. It was the woman who had asked him for accommodation and was later murdered. There was no mistake about it. The only difference was that she looked like she had recently recovered from an illness. The woman also stared at the rich man, nonplused and ruminating over some puzzle.

The rich man was confused and said to her, "We don't know each other. Why are you gazing me?"

The woman replied, "To be frank, I had a dream the night before last that I was invited to a house. I entered a nice study and a young man asked me to stay. That young man looked like you. So I was curious."

The rich man said, "What happened after that?"

The woman rejoined, "After midnight I woke up. My body felt pinched, and then I found that blood was flowing profusely out of me. I'm still feeble now. I never had such a sickness before. I've no idea what happened to me."

Yang Chouma said nothing but laughed inwardly. The rich man realized that it was a trick Chouma had played on them, but he felt too embarrassed to say so. The fantasy of his intimacy with the woman that night lingered with him. He gave a generous reward to the woman and told her to get some medicine to help her recover. Yang Chouma also slipped a sheet of paper with a figure on it out of his sleeve, and, with a smile, gave it to the woman, saying, "Post this on your bed, madam, and you won't have that kind of odd dream any more. You'll be fully recovered soon." The woman expressed her thanks.

The two men left the tavern. The rich man grumbled to Yang Chouma, "I didn't know how that terrible incident could have taken place the other night. Now I know it was a trick you played on me. You frightened me and caused this woman to become sick. It was not the right thing to do."

Chouma said, "I was bringing her soul over to bewitch you. If you had held on to your integrity, would you have been so terrified? It was your fault to be tempted with thoughts of seduction! How could you, then, have avoided the fright?"

The rich man laughed and said, "When this beauty came to my room at midnight, how could I hold on? Though terrified later that night, I enjoyed myself the first half of the evening. Now I beg you to bring her to me once again so we keep up our affection. That way I would even more appreciate your kindness and thank you with much payment."

Chouma said, "This woman was somewhat connected to you by fate, so I was able to bring her soul to you. But I cannot perform such magic rashly. If I do, don't I fear the punishment of the gods? You owed me a debt of twenty thousand coins in the previous life, so I played this trick. If I had not done so, you would never have lent me the money. I told you that I only needed twenty thousand. I have no use for anything beyond that sum. I don't want any more of your money, and you should reject those fantasies." The rich man was then compliant and admired of Chouma's extraordinary powers.

Later, Chouma maintained his fortune-telling business in Chengdu, but nobody knew where he died. Whatever magical arts one possesses, one's life is in the hands of fate.

Tale 15

You Use-me Lustily Revels with Confined Women; Minister Yang Sinisterly Castrates His Literary Hack

During the Song Dynasty, Yang Jian, a minister of the imperial military department, abused his power, encouraged favoritism, defied the law, and enjoyed sensual pleasures with an army of concubines, the second largest in number at that time, only a little fewer than those of Prime Minister Cai Jing. One day Minister Yang wanted to visit his family tombs in the city of Zhengzhou. He took with him a few of his favorite concubines, and the connected nurses and maid servants. Left behind were the older concubines, the young who were inexperienced in flattering their master, those physically fragile, and those undergoing a period of menstruation so as not to be fit for travel, plus a host of nurses and servants, totaling about fifty or sixty women. Being a suspicious and jealous man, Yang had the women tightly guarded under lock and key inside the inner quarters, some distance away from the main entrance to the mansion. Seals of paper strips with red characters were posted on the inner gate. A hole was hollowed in the wall of the verandah beside the inner gate, and a revolving wheel was mounted inside the hole in order for the old housekeeper to supply food from outside to the inmates. The housekeeper, surnamed Li, stayed in the main courtyard keeping watch. At night he supervised a patrol of men beating gongs and clappers through to dawn, which struck anyone with awe who wanted to peep into the mansion.

Among those concubines who remained in the mansion a few were rather attractive. They were the minister's most favorite ones. They were Fair-moon, Jade-beauty, Sweet-smile and Fine-flower. With their group of servant-girls, they lived in tedious confinement, having nothing to do except play bone dice, hold plant competitions, ride on a swing, and kick a feather-stuffed ball. These games quickly became tiresome. What else could they do to while away the hours? Even if they managed to fill the hours of the day, how could they kill the boredom of the night?

Jade-beauty was originally the wife of a jade craftsman in the capital city. She was intelligent, full of charms, and had some close friends and a fame in the capital. On one occasion, Minister Yang had caught sight of her and used his power to take her home. Particularly attracted to her, he ranked her as his seventh lady. Her name indicated her appearance of jade-like beauty and grace. Among her female peers, she stuck out because of her wisdom and sexual appetite. Even when the minister was at home, she often tried to smuggle in a young man for fun. Now the minister was away and life had become restricted and dull. How could she endure the tickle of her lustful fantasizes?

The minister had a literary hack, surnamed You and styled Use-me, a profligate young man who was poor at learning but versed in calligraphy. He was used to doing secretarial and bookkeeping work. In his late twenties, You Use-me looked handsome. As boys, he and the minister had been lovers. He was humorous, considerate and easy to get along with so he won the favor of the minister, who kept him as an assistant for meeting guests. When the minister departed for Zhengzhou, he was left behind so as to avoid any traveling hassle with the large number of concubines. He stayed in the outer quarters of the mansion. You Use-me had a good friend, called Fang Wude, who had been a schoolmate of his. You Use-me often went to have a drink with Fang Wude, when not engaged in business in the minister's residence. Now with the absence of the minister, You Use-me was quite bored. He took strolls with Fang Wude during the day and at night they often stayed in a brothel or at his study.

Jade-beauty found it hard to while away her nights, so she called a favorite servant named Ruxia to go to bed with her. Jade-beauty told Ruxia obscene stories. In the heat of story-telling, she took out an artificial male organ, tied it around her waist and performed a love-making act.

Ruxia got excited and asked her mistress, "How do you find this in comparison with a real man?"

Jade-beauty said, "Well, it quenches my desire for the moment. But it's far from a real one. Making love with a man is a lot more exciting!"

Ruxia said, "If a man is so desirable, it's shame that one idles about outside this yard."

Jade-beauty asked, "Are you talking about You Use-me?"

Ruxia said, "Of course."

Jade-beauty then said, "He's the favorite employee of the minister. He's handsome. I often glance at him out there and I am filled with amorous feelings."

Ruxia said, "If we could bring him inside, wouldn't that be wonderful?"

Jade-beauty replied, "He spends the day idling away his time, but the wall is high. How could we make him fly over it?"

Ruxia said, "I am saying this for fun. Of course he can't enter our mansion."

"Let me think about it," Jade-beauty said. "Definitely I want to get him here!"

Ruxia then said, "Outside the backyard wall stands his study. Let's wake up early tomorrow and explore the area. If you come up with a good idea and bring him in, we can all enjoy ourselves."

Jade-beauty laughed and replied, "I've not got hold of him yet, but you're already thinking of sharing him with me, aren't you?"

Ruxia said, "You'd better not begrudge us. We servants will then be highly motivated and give you a hand in obtaining him."

Jade-beauty then said, "You're right."

The night passed without event. The next morning, after washing and dressing, Jade-beauty and Ruxia went into the backyard to pick flowers. Walking past the swing and exploring the area, they spotted a rope hung high from the swing framework. With a grin, Jade-beauty said, "We can use it!"

A tree-pruning ladder was leaning against a huge rock. Jade-beauty called to Ruxia. "Look, look! We now have these two things here. We can do something about the wall."

Ruxia asked, "What's your idea?"

Jade-beauty said, "Let's go to the wall and figure out a way."

Ruxia led Jade-beauty to the side of two parasol trees, and said, pointing forward, "Outside this wall is You Use-me's study."

Jade-beauty examined the trees and then said, "I think we can get him in here tonight. It won't be difficult."

Ruxia replied, "Tell me what idea you have, madam."

Jade-beauty said, "Let's move that ladder quietly over here and lean it against the tree. You can climb the ladder and get high up into those tree branches. Then you should be able to call outside across the wall."

Ruxia said, "It won't be hard to get up on the tree and talk to him over the wall, but the problem is one of how we can pull him up to the top of the wall."

Jade-beauty said, "I'm going to fasten a few boards at the ends with the swing rope, one foot apart. Gathering them up, you have a bundle, and spreading them out, you get something that looks like a ladder.

After we schedule a time with him, you can go up into the tree branches with the ladder and fasten one end of the rope tightly onto a sturdy fork in the tree. Then you can throw the bundle of boards across the wall. That will give him a rope ladder. It will be strong enough to hold several men, let alone himself!"

Ruxia said, "Excellent, excellent! Come on and let's do it right now to see whether it works or not." She joyously raced into the room and grabbed about ten small boards and gave them to Jade-beauty.

Jade-beauty asked her to untie the swing rope and fasten the boards, and then she said to Ruxia, "Get the ladder and lean it against the tree. You can climb to the top and take a look to see whether you're able to make yourself heard outside. If nobody is around, you can go down outside and contact him."

Accordingly, Ruxia set up the ladder, sprightly ascended into the tree branches, and looked around outside. It happened that You Use-me and Fang Wude had just returned after staying out the whole night for merrymaking. As You Use-me was about to enter his study, Ruxia laughed and called out, pointing to him, "Is that Master You over there?"

You Use-me heard the sound and raised his head. He saw a girl talking to him, and recognized that she was Ruxia. How could he, a young man, remain emotionally unaroused? So he asked, "Young lady, were you talking to me?"

Ruxia wanted to flirt and answered, "You're coming back early in the morning, sir. Did you go somewhere last night?"

You Use-me said, "I couldn't stand the loneliness. So I stay out for the night."

Ruxia said, "Look here inside. Every of us is lonely. Why not come in and join us? Then we'll all not be lonely."

You Use-me said, "I don't have wings. How can I fly in?"

Ruxia replied, "If you want to come in, I've got an idea. You won't need to fly."

You Use-me bowed low with hands clasped in front of him and said, "I appreciate your kindness, sister. Please let me know your idea."

Ruxia said, "I'm going to tell the mistress. Please come here this evening for instructions." Then she slid down the tree.

You Use-me, puzzled by Ruxia's words, wondered which mistress it was. He thought to himself, what good luck I have! But how will I be able to go in? I'll have to come and see this evening. He only wished the sun would set fast.

Let's leave him waiting there for the moment, and return to Jade-beauty, who stood inside the yard listening to each word of Ruxia's conversation with You Use-me. She become quite excited, and, before Ruxia reported to her, joyfully returned to her room.

Ruxia said to her, "We're not going to be bored this night."

Jade-beauty responded, "If he's timid, he will withdraw. Things happen that way."

But Ruxia replied, "He looked so anxious to get inside just now that he made a big bow to me. How could he be timid? You just get ready for fun tonight, madam." Jade-beauty restrained her joy at this news.

As dark drew near, Jade-beauty and Ruxia went into the backyard again. They walked to the ladder and Ruxia quickly mounted the tree. She gave out a loud cough over the wall, where You Use-me was sneaking about in the falling dusk. Hearing someone cough, he looked up and saw Ruxia up in the tree.

He said, "Good sister, I'm running out of patience! Tell me how to get inside!"

Ruxia said, "Just a moment. I'll take you in."

Climbing down the ladder, Ruxia told Jade-beauty, "He's been there waiting pretty long."

Jade-beauty said, "Hurry up and let him come in."

Ruxia picked up the rope and boards that had been fixed earlier. Tucking them under her arm, she clambered up the ladder and tied the ends of the rope to the tree fork. With a shout of "go," she tossed out the bundle of rope and boards. The rope ladder hung across the wall outside. You Use-me, waiting outside, suddenly saw the rope ladder descending. Overjoyed, he tentatively set his foot on it to make sure that it would hold him steady. Then he climbed the boards with his hands holding onto the rope, and, step by step, ascended to the top of the wall. Ruxia descended from the tree, crying, "He's here! He's here!" Meanwhile, fearing the initial embarrassment of a meeting, Jade-beauty had moved away to the side of the rock on which she sat, waiting.

Having gotten on top of the wall, You Use-me used the ladder to slide down the other side. He sprang forward and locked Ruxia against his chest, saying, "Sister, you did me a great favor. I'm dying with joy!"

Ruxia spat at him and said, "It's shameful! Don't do this with me. Go and see the mistress now."

You Use-me asked, "Which mistress?"

Ruxia replied, "The seventh lady, Jade-beauty."

You Use-me then said, "Is she the one who is well known for her beauty in the capital city?"

Ruxia said, "Who else?"

You Use-me said, "Humble as I am, how can I be so imprudent as to meet her?"

"It's she who has wanted to see you," Ruxia said. "She thought up this idea to get you inside. Why are you so shy?"

"If so, the bliss is far more than I can deserve," said You Use-me.

Ruxia said, "Stop pretending to be modest. Go get your good luck! But, don't forget that it was me who first introduced you to her."

You Use-me said, "I dare not forget your kindness. I'll requite it with my body."

They walked, talking, to where Jade-beauty was sitting. Ruxia said, "Here's Master You, Madam."

With a deep bow, You Use-me smiled and said, "I'm a worldly

being. How could I have ever expected to meet you, a goddess, in my life? I appreciate your kindness in thinking about me. I suppose my ancestors must have accumulated enormous meritorious deeds."

Jade-beauty said, "I used to stay in my abode. Occasionally I caught glimpses of you at the feasts held by the minister. I've been admiring your impressive deportment for a long time. Now the minister is not in and I feel lonely, and so I'm inviting you to come to my room for a chat. If you honor my request with your agreement, that will be my good luck."

You Use-me said, "You've stooped to see me, Madam. How could I dare turn you down? However, if the minister learns about our meeting, it will not be an ordinary offense."

Jade-beauty said, "He is muddle-headed and doesn't have many informers working for him. In addition, the way you got in is known to no one else. Don't worry about it. Let's go to my room."

With Ruxia leading the way, they walked arm in arm. You Use-me was thrilled at this moment, totally uncaring of the grave consequences that might arise in the future. He quietly followed Jade-beauty to her room.

It was completely dark now, and silence reigned everywhere in the residence. Ruxia brought wine and food, and they drank to each other. Lost in each other's gaze, they traded terms of endearment. After three drinks were downed, they found their urges burning. They cuddled as they lurched into the drape-hung bed. The ensuing enjoyment was beyond narration.

The love-making done, You Use-me said, "I've long admired your reputation for beauty. Today I've gotten the great fortune of sharing a bed with you. I won't be able to repay your kindness for the rest of my life."

Jade-beauty replied, "I aspire to romantic love. But the minister keeps close watch. It may look like I have plenty of fun all day long, but what true love can I get out of it? If you had not come to join me tonight, it would have been the loss of a good time. We should definitely do this again and again. I will die satisfied!"

You Use-me said, "Madam, you have such a jade-like enchanting body that even having a chance to touch it would be my immense good fortune. Now you've let me enjoy your body the whole night. This would not have occurred to me in my wildest fantasy. Even if it is divulged, I will die with no complaints."

As they chatted away merrily, the day was dawning. Ruxia came to the bed and urged them to rise. "You've had a good time the whole night, sir," she said. "That's enough! Get up and leave before daylight. Do you want to be late?"

You Use-me hastily slipped into his clothing. Jade-beauty hated to part from him and, grabbing his hand, assured him of a meeting the following night. She told Ruxia to send him off with the rope ladder, the same way he got inside. You Use-me came back as planned the following night. After a few nights of fun, even Ruxia rolled into their revelrous play.

Too excited to calm herself down, Jade-beauty lost her head when talking with the other ladies and, with a slip of her tongue, blurted out her nightly pastime. At first the other ladies didn't take it seriously. But they gradually grew suspicious. At night some of them tried to spy on her and picked up a few clues. Such a matter made these ladies envious, and they hoped to take advantage of the situation to enjoy themselves as well. But they still couldn't understand how a man could come and go.

One day these ladies went out in high spirits to ride on the swing. Close to its framework, they found the rope missing. They began to search while Jade-beauty and Ruxia held their tongues. On the first a couple of nights, the rope had been untied from the tree, after You Use-me departed, and returned to its original position so that its absence would not be discovered by others. Later, since the rope was needed repeatedly every night, Jade-beauty and Ruxia let down their guard and they did not bother to untie it anymore. Therefore after You Use-me departed, the rope remained hanging from the tree over the wall. The rope was now found by the ladies.

They asked, "Is that the swing rope over there? Why is it hanging from the tree by the wall?"

Sweet-smile was young and spry. With the aid of the ladder, she swiftly climbed into the tree branches. She pulled the rope up and the ladies saw that it held a bundle of boards. Surprised, they said, "Strange! Strange! Did someone come and go from here?"

Blushing, Jade-beauty remained silent. Fair-moon said, "We'd better report this to Housekeeper Li and he will tell the minister about it later on." As she said this, she hurled glances toward Jade-beauty, who was keeping her head low. Fine-flower figured out what had happened and said with laugh, "Why did you, Jade-beauty, not say anything? Do you have something on your mind? I think you'd better let us know about it. It would be wonderful for us all if you talk about it with us."

Realizing that they could keep the lid on no longer, Ruxia said to Jade-beauty, "If we don't let them know about it, they will make a scandal. The whole business for us will be ruined. Better tell them and seek their understanding."

Clapping their hands, the rest said, "Exactly, you're right, Ruxia. Come on and let us know."

Then Jade-beauty had to tell them how she had managed to let You Use-me come. Fair-moon said, "Good sister, you have enjoyed yourself behind our backs!"

Sweet-smile said, "I don't think we should talk about it anymore. Since it's now known to everybody, let's share the fun."

Fair-moon said, "I think some of us want to, and others do not. You cannot say so."

Fine-flower said, "Those who do not want to join in should help us for the sake of sisterhood."

Sweet-smile said, "You're right, aunt." The crowd dispersed laughing.

Actually Fair-moon was a close friend of Jade-beauty. She intended to join Jade-beauty in the pleasure-seeking, but talked seriously to the other ladies for show. When left alone, she went to the room of Jade-beauty and asked her, "Sister, is he coming here again tonight?"

Jade-beauty replied, "To tell you frankly, Sister, we've enjoyed each other's company so much these days, why should he stop coming?"

Fair-moon laughed and said, "Are you going to keep him to yourself, Sister?"

Jade-beauty said, "According to what you said to us just now, it seems you're not interested."

Fair-moon said, "Well, that was a general remark. I want to have a try."

Jade-beauty said, "If you're really interested, sister, I'd like to yield him to you tonight. When he arrives, I'll send him directly to your room."

Fair-moon replied, "I don't know him very well. I will be embarrassed. How can you let him come to my room directly? I think I should be a helper at your side, instead. That'll be fine with me."

Jade-beauty laughed and said, "You don't need any helper doing this kind of thing."

"I know," Fair-moon said, "but I do feel shy for the first time. I just want to have a little try in your name, Sister. Don't let him know I am with you. I'll find a way after he and I become familiar with each other."

Jade-beauty said, "All right, you just hide yourself somewhere in my room. He will get into my bed and undress himself. After I blow out the light, we can simply switch places."

Fair-moon said, "I'll need your help anyway, good sister."

Jade-beauty said, "Sure, I'll be with you." Thus they agreed.

The evening arrived. Ruxia was again sent to the backyard to toss the rope over the wall, which brought You Use-me in. Jade-beauty got him into bed and blew out the light. Then she dragged Fair-moon out from the hiding place and tucked her into the bed. Fair-moon's desire had been aroused earlier when she talked with Jade-beauty. Then in the semi-darkness, she saw You Use-me come into the room, attractive and graceful, and her passion ran wild. Before Jade-beauty had pulled her out of the hiding place, she was already out of patience and ready to jump into play. In the darkness that screened all shades of embarrassment, she slunk into the bed. You Use-me took it for granted that Jade-beauty was with him, and, with no trade of words, immediately began in the familiar way of rolling on top of her and thrusting himself into her. Driven by her sexual frenzy, Fair-moon vigorously played her part.

As they reached the peak of excitement, with their bodies rubbing against one another, You Use-me found something peculiar in the way the lady under him moved her body and limbs. The fact that he had a silent partner this time raised a further suspicions. He murmured, "Sweetie, why don't you talk to me tonight?"

Fair-moon could not utter a word. You Use-me continued to question her, and she remained silent, even holding her breath. You Use-me released the frantic shout, "Strange," and paused in the wriggling of his body.

Standing by the side of the bed, Jade-beauty heard his words and let out a laugh. She gently lifted the bed-drape and gave him a forceful slap, saying, "You idiot! What a good deal you have! Why do you keep talking? You have Fair-moon with you tonight, ten times better than me. Yet you haven't realized it."

You Use-me now realized that he was with somebody else, so he said, "I wonder who this lady is who is showing such kindness to me. I'm an ordinary man. Please forgive me for my rude behavior before greeting you."

Fair-moon then said, "Don't pretend to be courteous. Now you know it, and that's fine." Her soft voice tickled You Use-me's fancy and he was aroused in an attempt to continue with the love-making. Sunk in extreme pleasure, however, Fair-moon said, "You knew what I needed, Sister, and offered me such enjoyment!"

Having heard her words, Jade-beauty was unable to bridle her own lust. She sprang into the bed, while You Use-me was anxious to complete his part of the action but Fair-moon had reached her climax and was now exhausted. Fair-moon, after having a good time herself, yielded the position by getting up and pushing You Use-me into an embrace of Jade-beauty. You Use-me then made no delay in launching another round of battle with the second opponent.

Let us now leave them for the moment. Sweet-smile and Fine-flower, after learning of Jade-beauty's affair, were sure that You Use-me would come again that night. So they decided to talk to Fair-moon about seizing the man and sharing in the fun. After dinner, they arrived at Fair-moon's room to find her not in. Their suspicion arose.

They ran to the room of Jade-beauty and encountered Ruxia standing outside. They asked Ruxia, "Is Fair-moon in your place?"

Ruxia laughed and answered, "She's been here for some time! She's now in my mistress' bed!"

The two sisters asked, "Is she going to bed with your mistress? That will make that business impossible when the man arrives."

Ruxia said, "Why impossible? It gives more fun, in fact. The three of them can roll into work together!"

They asked, "Did that man already arrive?"

Ruxia said, "Sure. Maybe he is now tired of that in-out business!"

Sweet-smile said, "When I said we could share the fun this afternoon, Fair-moon pretended to be virtuous. But she tried her hand at it ahead of us."

Fine-flower responded, "The most high-sounding are the least to be trusted."

Sweet-smile said, "Let's intrude on them now. They can't throw us out."

Fine-flower said, "No! No! He's working on two of them and must be worn-out. How could he have enough energy left to entertain us tonight?"

She then whispered in Sweet-smile's ear, "We'd better be patient tonight and wait until tomorrow night when we can take the initiative and sweep the man into our room. What fun won't we have at that time!"

Sweet-smile said, "Exactly!" They then parted and retired to their own rooms.

The rest of the night passed without incident. The next morning You Use-me was sent back home. Ruxia came to Jade-beauty's bed and told the two ladies that Sweet-smile and Fine-flower had arrived to look for Fair-moon the night before. Fair-moon became anxious and asked, "Did they know I was here?"

Ruxia rejoined, "Why wouldn't they!"

Fair-moon said with frustration, "What can I do then? They will laugh at me."

Jade-beauty responded, consolingly, "Never mind. We will simply pull those two girls into our party. It will save us a lot worry. By then, You Use-me won't need to leave before dawn and return at night. He can just stay here. We can take turns with no worry at all. Isn't that a pretty good idea?"

Fair-moon said, "Yes, it truly is. But I will feel embarrassed when I meet them today."

Jade-beauty said, "Just do as usual today, sister. Don't say anything if they don't mention it. If they do, I'll take care of the matter."

Fair-moon's heart was thus set at rest. The fatigue of the previous night overpowered her and she didn't wake up until noon the following day. She basked in silence and personal contentment. She was a little scared that Sweet-smile and Fine-flower would broach the subject, so she tried to avoid their glances during the day. However, she didn't know that they had made up their mind not to mention the business in front of her. Hence, Jade-beauty and Fair-moon passed the day comfortably as if nothing had happened.

Night returned. Sweet-smile and Fine-flower, after consulting with each other, waited in the backyard to meet that man. Hiding some distance away, they watched the tree. Soon You Use-me came over the wall and descended down the ladder. He adjusted his turban and whisked the dirt off his clothes. As he was about to move forward, Sweet-smile jumped out, yelling, ""What a villain is this? What are you up to?"

Fine-flower dashed forward, grabbed and shouted, "Stop thief! Stop thief!"

Terrified, You Use-me stuttered and quivered, saying. "I, I, I have come here at the request of two ladies who made an appointment. Lower your voice, Sister, please."

Sweet-smile questioned him. "Are you Use-me?"

"Yes," he replied, "I surely am."

Fine-flower then said, "You seduced the two mistresses. It is not an ordinary offense! Do you want to resolve this problem in court or out of court?"

You Use-me said, "They asked me to come to them. I would not have had the courage to do that on my own. I would rather resolve it out of court instead of making it public."

Sweet-smile said, "In terms of settling it in court, you'll be turned over to Housekeeper Li and have to wait until the minister comes back to deal with you. It's bound to be a terrible punishment for you. Since you want to be treated privately, you should keep away from the two ladies tonight, but follow us quietly to our room. You'll be subject to our disposal."

A smile lit up You Use-me's face as he said, "I'm sure I'm not going to be punished in your room. I'd like to go with you." Then the three of them stealthily went into the room of Sweet-smile. Fine-flower also stayed with them. What followed was a passionate play.

Meanwhile Jade-beauty and Fair-moon waited until dusk and there was still no sign of You Use-me. They sent Ruxia with a light to meet him. Using the light, she looked around the tree and found the rope hanging on the inside of the wall. You Use-me always pulled in the rope each time he got into the yard for fear of being detected by others who might hunt him down. Later this became routine. Ruxia thus knew that You Use-me was inside the yard.

She ran back to report, "Master You has already come in. Since he's not here, where is he?"

Jade-beauty pondered the matter and said with a smile, "Okay, someone stole him."

Fair-moon said, "I guess he's with those other two." They then sent Ruxia to find out.

Ruxia first went to Fine-flower's room and found the door shut and the room quiet. She turned to go to Sweet-smile's room. There she heard laughter from inside and the groan of the bed under pressure. She knew You Use-me was in there making love. Envy sprang up in her immediately.

She sprinted back and told the two ladies, "He's indeed there, in the heat of doing that business! Let's go and harass them!"

But Fair-moon said, "No, no. They didn't disturb us last night. If we break in on them, it'll be our fault and hurt their feelings."

Jade-beauty said, "I had thought of getting them two into our game, but didn't realize they would start on their own. It fits my idea very well. We should leave them alone tonight. I have a way to cut off his retreat. Let's play a trick on them and make them frantic. Then they will join us."

"So what can we do?" Fair-moon asked.

Jade-beauty said, "Send Ruxia to untie that rope and put it away. You Use-me won't be able to get out of here tomorrow. Then we'll see how they can keep the matter from us."

Ruxia said, "Absolutely right! We first worked out this plan to get him in. How can they get him away without letting us know? Outrageous! Outrageous!"

With a lantern in hand, Ruxia raced to the backyard. She climbed into the tree and untied the rope. She then rolled the rope and boards into a bundle and carried them back to the room, shouting, "I got it down! I got it down!"

Jade-beauty said, "Hide it somewhere until tomorrow. Let's go to sleep." The two ladies retired to their own rooms and went to bed in loneliness.

In the meantime, Sweet-smile and Fine-flower thrilled to the embraces of You Use-me the whole night. They promised to meet again the following evening. They saw You Use-me off before dawn. You Use-me walked in front, followed by Sweet-smile and Fine-flower, their hair disheveled. Quietly they reached the back of the yard. As usual, You Use-me climbed the tree. But the rope ladder was not there.

Unable to get out of the yard, he descended and said, "I wonder who took the rope away? Maybe because the two ladies didn't see me last night, they figured I was elsewhere and were hurt. That's why they are making trouble for me. Where can I obtain a rope to get out now?"

Sister Sweet-smile said, "Where can we find a rope that is thick enough to hold a man and land him down outside?"

You Use-me then suggested, "I may as well go and see the two ladies and admit my fault, so we can be reconciled."

Fine-flower protested, "But we will be embarrassed."

As the three talked, they saw the two other ladies and Ruxia come into the yard. Jade-beauty and Fair-moon clapped their hands and said, laughing, "You enjoyed yourselves behind our backs. Why not let him fly out now?"

Sweet-smile replied, "Someone did it before, so we simply followed suit."

Fine-flower said, "Stop bantering. We were supposed to team up in doing things. But you two ladies took the opportunity secretly first. Therefore we did it in return. Now let's forget about the matter. Please bring out that rope so he can get out."

Jade-beauty broke into laughter and said, "I've got a question. What is the point of sending him out? Since it's known to everybody now and we all have a share in the business, why do we need to take precautions against each other, even if he stays here all day long? We can work in collaboration and have fun together."

Everyone laughed, saying, "Excellent, excellent! What you say is absolutely right!" Then Jade-beauty took You Use-me by the arm and went back toward the rooms with the other ladies.

After that, You Use-me lived inside day and night, indulged in revelry day and night, either coupling with the ladies or pairing off with the maidservants. It was an ongoing spree of lust, a steady drain on the young man's energy. He became rundown and wanted to have a recess. But how could he be allowed that privilege? Then he asked for a couple of days off to go home. However everybody begrudged him of that opportunity. Then each of them brought some nutriments at their expense in order to keep him in good condition. In fear that Housekeeper Li might inform on them later on, they gathered up a generous sum of money and bribed Li. They were unscrupulous and had run out of control. Remember:

> *Ambitions should not be completely fulfilled,*
> *While joy should be curbed within a certain boundary.*
> *As good fortune is succeeded by misfortune,*
> *The day of fall was inevitable.*

One month of gaiety ran by happily for You Use-me before the minister suddenly was reported to be coming back. The ladies and girls were awakened from their dream, not yet totally convinced of the master's returning. However, the minister's arrival was unexpectedly quick, with the residence gates and yard doors being immediately thrown open. The women flew into agitation. Two of them hastily led You Use-me to the backyard and asked him to get over the wall. As You Use-me mounted to the top of the wall, they dragged the ladder away, shouting, "Get out! Get out!" and frantically raced off, leaving him alone. Because they were in such a flurry, they forgot to fix the swing rope for him. Hence he was left on the wall with neither the rope to slide down outside nor the ladder to ascend inside. He thought to himself, "If someone comes here right now, I will be in trouble!" He wanted to leap down, but did not feel capable of doing that, given his withered body and feeble limbs. Finally he just sat on the wall shuddering in fear.

An old saying goes, "Foes are doomed to a single-handed encounter." Upon his return, the minister did nothing but walk along the yard wall, trying to detect dubious traces. As he came to the back yard, he at once noticed someone sitting on top of it. From his perch, You Use-me could see the minister clearly. In desperation You Use-me bent over the ridge. His position could be described by the phrase, "The hare shields its face only." He was able to hide his face but not his body. The minister was particularly cunning. He quickly realized something had happened relating to this man. But this was obviously tied in with his ladies, whose scandalous behavior would eventually bring down his own reputation.

So he called out, as if he were unmindful, "The wall is so high, how can a man get onto it? That man sitting on the top of it must have been haunted by evil spirits. Get a ladder and bring him down so we can see what has happened to him."

The followers brought a ladder and supported You Use-me so he could come down carefully. You Use-me had heard the minister's words clearly, and decided to take advantage of the minister's apparent confusion by pretending to be muddled. Therefore the men had to pull and shove the reeling You Use-me in front of the minister.

The minister recognized him and said, "You are You Use-me, aren't you? Why do you look so pitiful? You must have been bewitched by ghosts." With his eyes shut tightly, You Use-me held his tongue. Then the minister sent for a priest from the Monastery of Divine Happiness to dispel the evil spirits haunting him.

No one dared slight the minister's command. Thus, shortly thereafter, a priest arrived. The minister asked him to examine You Use-me. The priest said, "He's bewitched." Then, with a sword in hand, he chanted incantations, sprayed a mouthful of pure water over him and said, "All right. He is all right."

You Use-me opened his eyes and asked, "Why am I here?"

The minister said, "What happened to you just now?"

You Use-me made up a story. "Last night I was sitting alone in my study. In the dim light I saw five generals glitteringly attired with colorful hats on their heads. They told me to go with them to the heavenly palace to transcribe something. I was scared by their strange looks and desperately trapped there. They had some followers pick me up and carry me into the air. Frantically I grabbed the twigs of the tree shouting, 'I work for Minister Yang. You should not be so rude!' After hearing the name of Minister Yang, they let me go. I dropped and lost consciousness. I didn't realize I was in front of you. When did you return? Where is this place?"

Some men told him, "You were bewitched by ghosts and moments ago were sitting on the wall. The minister asked us to bring you down. It's the backyard here."

The minister then asked, "What monsters was he speaking about?"

The priest replied, "According to what he has described, it must have been the Ghosts of Five Accomplishments, who saw him staying alone, so they wanted to extort some gains by plaguing him. I will give him an amulet. Post it in the room and present the sacrificial meat, food and drinks, so as to ease the concern of gods. Things should be alright soon."

The minister told his followers on duty to do so accordingly and sent the priest away. As he was supported back to his room for a rest, You Use-me mused, "What good luck I have! The most horrible destruction has been avoided!"

You Use-me's extravagant acts of sex had considerably undermined his constitution. Now he went through a period of rest and recuperation from the so-called haunting experience of ghosts. In ten days, he had gradually recovered, young as he was. He went to see the minister to express his thanks.

"Without your prompt rescue in sending for the priest," he said, "I would have been virtually wretched in the hell of evil spirits, and probably would have even died."

The minister put up a show of gladness and responded. "I'm glad you're back to health," he said. "I haven't seen you for a long time, and now you're recovered from sickness. Let's have some food and drink together."

The minister ordered that wine be brought, and then they started to drink and play drinking games. It was a friendly, pleasant get-together. You Use-me played it by ear, responding to and flattering the minister. At dinner, You Use-me brought up the subject of his encounter with the ghosts in order to detect the minister's mind.

But the minister said, "You were left alone in a solitary room, so the ghosts attacked you. It was my fault."

The load was thus off You Use-me's mind, and he, with silent gladness, mused, "He is absolutely ignorant of what I did. But it's shame that I don't know when I will be able to join those pretty ladies again. Maybe I will have to meet them only in my dreams for the rest of my life." After that, sitting in his study, he often sank into recollections of the ladies in the still of the night. But he heaved a sigh of relief, overjoyed at his good luck in keeping the minister unaware of his affairs.

The minister, however, was not what he appeared to be. When he saw You Use-me sitting on the wall he was nine-tenths convinced that something had gone wrong. One day the minister ventured into Jade-beauty's room and found the rope there. It was the rope that the ladies had used for the ladder, but later untied from the tree and left in the closet of the room, forgetting that they needed to put it away. The minister pondered, "This is exactly what they used to get the man inside." Then he ordered that Ruxia be tortured. She couldn't bear the pain and confessed everything. The minister made a follow-up examination and obtained a clear picture of the happening. But he revealed nothing that was in his mind. Instead he treated You Use-me even better than usual. It is true that:

With a dagger held behind his back,
He gave a smile that preceded a fatal blow;
If you choose to tickle a tiger,
You should be clear about what you may end up with.

One day the minister summoned You Use-me for drink and brought him into his inner study. They drank happily for awhile and then two singing girls were called to entertain them with songs and offer them wine in turn. The sight of the singing girls brought back to You Use-me the memories of his love affairs with the ladies. He kept drinking in sadness until he was completely drunk. The minister then rose and left, and so did the singing concubines. Alone in his seat, You Use-me dozed off. All of a sudden four or five stout men broke into the room. They quickly tied him up. You Use-me was still drunk and mumbling away. The men set him on a bed, and one of them pulled out a sharp knife.

Reader, you may think that You Use-me was about to be killed. Killing was indeed a common practice in the house of the minister.

Besides, You Use-me's offense was so outrageous that he would ordinarily have been killed. But why would the minister have the drink with him first before killing him? It turned out that You Use-me was not supposed to die. The planned penalty was odd. The stout man slid down You Use-me's pants. Using his left hand he pulled out You Use-me's organ, and with his right hand holding the knife, cut it off. Then he removed You Use-me's two testicles. You Use-me screamed in pain and lost consciousness. The stout man at once smeared some effective pain-relieving and muscle-recovering medicine on the wound. They then untied You Use-me and left him in the room. Who were these men? They were castrators who were hired whenever a castration was needed. Although the minister hated You Use-me for the seduction of the ladies, he liked him for his quick wit and easy-going manners. Therefore he called these men to castrate him instead of having him killed. Because the man to be castrated needed to be kept out of the wind for health reasons, the business was done in the inner study, which was called by an old phrase "The Silkworm House." The minister ordered servants to take care of You Use-me as he recovered and to prescribe methods and diet without hurting his health.

You Use-me suffered enormous pain, but eventually recovered due to the attentive treatment. He now realized that the minister had learned of his affair and for this reason had ordered the cruel punishment. He could not complain to anyone and had to bear the insult. He felt fortunate for having survived. In about ten days, he struggled to get up and wash his face with hot water. A few beard hairs dropped from his lower chin into the basin. He at once took a mirror and saw in it the complete look of eunuch. Looking down under his belly, he saw a big scar there, with his penis nowhere to be seen. He reached to feel that part, while tears streamed down his cheeks.

After his castration, the minister smiled at You Use-me each time he met him, and treated him with even more kindness. He led him into the rooms of his concubines and let him chat with them, for You Use-me had lost that part of his anatomy and thus no longer posed any concern to the minister. In fact he became a target of ridicule.

At first Fair-moon, Jade-beauty and the other ladies who had had affairs with him were rather sympathetic whenever they talked of those old days. Later they regarded him as useless, for his looks aroused their passion which only had to be repressed thereafter. You Use-me said to his former lovers, "After the return of the minister, I thought I would never see you ladies again. I didn't know that I would be seeing you now from time to time, but as a useless person. Shameful! Shameful!"

After that, You Use-me stayed in the inner yard and seldom went out. In addition, his bare chin and feminine voice, those attributes of a eunuch, made him afraid to meet friends. So he dared not stroll in the street at all. His close friend, Fang Wude, did not see him for half a year, and once went to the home of the minister to inquire about him. The common reply, as required by the minister, was, "He died."

One day the minister took his concubines with him on a tour to the Temple of Xiangguo, and You Use-me went along too. As You Use-me walked alone into the Pavilion of Mercy, he ran into Fang Wude. Fang was puzzled at the sight of a man who looked like You Use-me but whose facial skin was unusual. Fang had heard that You Use-me was dead, so he dared not to greet the man, but walked away instead. You Use-me recognized Fang Wude and called to him immediately.

"Wude, Wude," he said, "why don't you recognize your old friend?" Then Fang Wude knew it was indeed You Use-me. He came up to greet him.

You Use-me clasped the hands of his old friend, tears rolling down his cheeks. Fang Wude said to him, "I've not seen you for ages. Why are you so sad?"

You Use-me replied, "I'm stupid and had a terrible misfortune. It is a long story!" Then he told his friend about his experience and said, "I had a brief revelry but suffered a horrible torture!"

He cried incessantly. Fang Wude said, "Your extravagant enjoyment incurred this disaster. It is over now. Forget about it. Later you should come out periodically to see your friends and have a good time."

You Use-me said, "How can I meet my friends after such a disgrace? I will stay alone in order to keep a lingering, shameful life."

With a deep sigh, Fang Wude left. Later he learned that You Use-me lived in sorrow and died shortly after in the house of the minister. It was the payment he received for his lustful indulgence. Later Fang Wude often warned young lechers by telling them about You Use-me.

Reader, the young should behave cautiously on the one hand. On the other, though the minister took revenge by cruelly torturing You Use-me, his wives and concubines had been enjoyed by the young man. It is a lesson to be learned by the rich, who like to keep a large number of women for themselves.

Tale 16

Mother Reproaches Daughter for a Suspected Affair; Youth Takes Wife from a Mistaken Lawsuit

It is said that there was a seventeen-year-old young master living in Wusong with the family name of Sun, who, was the offspring of a Confucian family and very handsome. Residing a few doors away was a widow with the family name of Fang, who, at an early age, had been married into the family of Jia. Her husband, however, had died and left her with a daughter named Runniang. The girl was also seventeen. She was extremely attractive. With no man at home, the mother and daughter had to hire a servant-boy to do the chores. Due to lack of hands, the mother and daughter had to do some work in public. Neighbors admired the beauty of the daughter. Sun, a student of the same age, often saw Runniang from a distance and they traded amorous glances, but they kept silent about their affection for each other. Mother Fang was cunning, cruel and hard to deal with. She watched her daughter closely, following her about all day long and shutting her in her room before dusk fell. Though attracted to Sun, Jia Runniang had to bear the pain of being unable to express her feelings. Each day Sun paced around in front of her house, like a shuttle going to and fro, with infatuation burning but having no chance to be with her. Fortunately Mother Fang took a fancy to the young man and occasionally invited him into their home for tea and a chat, which gave the young man opportunities to exchange a few words with Runniang. Worried about her mother's suspicions, Runniang remained restrained. As time passed, Sun grew desperate, but he could do nothing.

One day Jia Runniang, dressed in a pink garment, was doing embroidery work by the window. Sun came along. Seeing nobody around, he spoke to her in a flirting manner. Jia Runniang kept silent for fear of being seen by her mother. Sun then teased her several more times.

Rather worried, Jia Runniang said quietly to him, "What are you up to here in broad daylight?"

After hearing this, Sun walked away, thinking to himself, "What she said makes some sense. If she does not want me to be around here during the day, does she mean that I should come at night instead? Probably I will be able to see her at night."

When evening arrived, he came again and stood before her house where the door was shut. Suddenly the door creaked open. A little nervous, the young man stepped backward. Someone slipped out and could be faintly seen wearing a pink garment. Delighted, Sun began to follow. The person walked into the walled latrine and Sun went in also.

Embracing the person, he said, "Sweet sister, thinking of you is killing me! You drove me off this morning. Now we're here at night. What are you going to do with me?"

Spittle shot out of the person's mouth, and the person swore, "You little rascal! Who did you think I was?"

It turned out that this was Mother Fang rather than Jia Runniang. She had gone out to fetch the chamber-pot from the outdoor latrine that evening after she had slipped into the pink garment her daughter had just taken off. Sun took her for Jia Runniang because he had expected Runniang to come out and the pink dress had assured him that it was her. Besides, in the dim light both women looked alike. When he heard her yell, he was shocked and realized he had hugged the wrong person. He quickly disappeared.

Mother Fang trembled in embarrassment and rage. With chamber pot in hand, she said to herself, "What that little son of bitch said was strange. It must have something to do with my daughter. Probably they had an appointment, but he took me for her by mistake. I guess that is the reason."

She furiously marched into her daughter's room and cried, "That son of bitch from the family of Sun is waiting outside for you. You better go out and see him."

Jia Runniang, not knowing what had happened, said, "I don't understand what family of Sun you're talking about."

Mother Fang said, "You slut, you have brought him here, but you're pretending to know nothing!"

Jia Runniang felt wronged and said, "How can you say that? I was sitting here and did nothing with anybody. You've insulted me!"

Mother Fang said, "I went out just now. That son of bitch chased me and called me sister. Didn't he take me for you? What a shameless person you are! You should go and die!"

Unable to clear herself, Jia Runniang cried, "This is a terrible wrong you're doing to me! How could I know anything about it?"

Mother Fang said, "Even if you had a hundred mouths, you could not convince me of your good name. If you had behaved yourself, why would he be bold enough to get fresh with me?"

Mother Fang was hard to get along with and annoyingly garrulous when offended. Jia Runniang wanted to defend herself, but knew she was silently in love with the young master, so she was in no position to give a forceful argument. However, she felt injured and remained silent on the basis that she had done nothing of the kind. As she weighed the matter, tears gushed out of her eyes. She thought, "Now my mother will keep a closer watch on me. He will be too embarrassed to stop in and I will lose the opportunity of continuing my relationship with him. Besides, I cannot bear this disgrace and her taunts. I would rather die and meet him in the great beyond!" She wept until midnight. Mother Fang went to sleep, having become worn out by her fit of fury. Runniang rose and hung herself from a crossbeam using her silk girdle.

Mother Fang awoke the next morning. She again gave vent to her anger of the night before and swore at her daughter, "You're capable of soliciting at night, but you're not up at such a late hour in the morning. Why are you still clinging to your bed, you lazy bones." She prattled in this way as she dressed herself. Having received no response, she called out, "Did you hear me? Are you unhappy with your mother's words?" She angrily slid off the bed. Then she found her daughter hanging from the beam, as if on a swing. She screamed, "Calamity!" She quickly untied the girl, who had stopped breathing, her mouth was capped with the white foam of saliva.

Terrified, grieving and regretful, she held her daughter in her arms and set her on the bed. Hitting her own chest and stamping her feet, the mother wept. After awhile, she paused and said bitterly, "Her death was caused by that little rogue! I will surely make him pay for it with his life. Otherwise I will never be able to live down this disgrace." Then she thought, "If that little rogue gets word of this, he will go into hiding. I should summon him here before he learns of it. I will lock him up and sue him. He can't flee." She sent the boy servant to bring Sun without telling him anything else.

The young man had been rather frustrated by what had happened the previous evening. After he received the message from Mother Fang, he became flustered, thinking to himself, "Why is she asking me to come? Is she going to throw a fit in front of me?" Yet as an old neighbor, he found it hard to turn her down. So he followed the servant-boy to go to see Mother Fang, with a look of shame on his face.

Putting on a smile, Mother Fang said to him, "You were rash last night. Did you take me for my daughter?"

Blushing, Sun was tongue-tied. Mother Fang said, "Our two families are of the same social status. If you love my daughter, just let me know. After we trade betrothal gifts, you can marry each other. Why did you have to take to such a stealthy, ignoble line of action?"

These words delighted the young man, who wasn't aware of her trap. Then he replied, "I appreciate your kindness, Madam. I'm going to fix a humble gift and find a matchmaker."

Mother Fang said, "There's no hurry yet. Please rest assured of my words. Come on in and meet my daughter first. You can go to find the matchmaker later." This was exactly what Sun hoped to do. He joyfully followed Mother Fang into the room.

As they came to the door, Mother Fang pushed him into the room and said, "She's inside. Please go in and see her." With no other thought, Sun strode into the room. Immediately Mother Fang slammed the door closed and locked it. Through the screen board, she shouted, "Listen, you little son of bitch. You've caused the death of my daughter. The body is now on the bed and left with you. I'm going to the authorities to bring suit against you for her death because of your adultery. You're going to pay for it with your life!"

Sun was a little scared as the door slammed shut, but after hearing Mother Fang's words, he realized that she wanted to get revenge for her daughter's death. Looking ahead, he saw a person lying on the bed. Terrified, he turned to leave, but the door was firmly locked. He began to plead from inside, "Madam, I know it was my fault. Please don't go to the court. Let me out and we can talk." Outside, Mother Fang had already disappeared. She went with the servant-boy to the county government office and turned in an indictment.

How could the young and inexperienced man remain tranquil in the face of such a horrible situation? He thought to himself, "To cause a death is no ordinary crime. I will surely be sentenced to die." He sighed and said, "If I have to die, I can't do anything about it. But it's shame that, though she and I were in love, I did not even have a chance to touch her. Now she has died for me and I will have to pay with my life. Two lives will be gone. Is it something predestined by fate because of evils we committed in our former lives?"

Staring at Jia Runniang's body, he broke into tears, saying, "My sister, you were so lovely yesterday when talking to me. What has happened to make you like this today? It will be my doom!"

While in great sorrow, he glanced at Jia Runniang and saw:

Her eyes shut, but she looked alive; her slim waist resembled a hanging willow branch; her tall and upright figure suggested a lotus rising out of the water; truly she was a sleeping beauty, who awaited her talented lover.

Seeing that Jia Runniang appeared pretty and pitiful he couldn't help touching her cheek with his own and kissing her on the face. He stroked her body and was surprised to find it still soft and springy. At this he got excited with a fantasy, saying to himself, "I didn't touch her even once when she was alive. Now there's no one around. Her body is subject to my will. I will undress her and have her to fulfill my aspirations. I will not die for her in vain." So he untied her outer girdle and skirt. He then untied her pants and slid them off. Her snowy legs sprang into his sight. Sun could not repress his urges. He leaped on the top of her body and gave her a wild kiss. However, at this point Jia Runniang started to breathe and noises came out of her throat. It turned out that when Mother Fang took her down from the beam she was strangled due to the tight knot of the girdle. But she was actually not dead, with her heart beating softly. Yet she could not recover from the choking right away. Mother Fang had been impetuous, and taking her daughter for dead, she did not look further before thinking of taking revenge. She had rushed out without trying to revive her daughter. Now, after the young man had squirmed on the top of her, her breath started to come back through her nose and mouth. His wriggle inside of her also helped bring her slowly back into consciousness.

The young man was stunned at the surprising turn of events. He quickly slid off her. As he propped Jia Runniang up, she swallowed and screamed, "Ahhh!"

Her eyelids slowly opened. Seeing Sun, she said, "Am I dreaming?"

Sun replied, "Sister, you almost had me killed."

Runniang said, "Where is my mother? How did you get in here?"

Sun said, "Your mother told me you were dead and tricked me into coming here and then locked me in your room. She has now gone to the government office to sue me. I was surprised to see you wake up. Now that your mother is away and we're shut in here together, it is good luck, allowing us to do whatever we want!"

Runniang said, "Last night I could not tolerate my mother's scolding and so hung myself. I was shocked that I have come back to life today. When I saw you by my side, Brother, I thought I was in another world." Sun came over and hugged her in attempt to get affectionate.

Runniang said with embarrassment, "Yesterday my mother scolded me and swore a lot for no reason at all. If I do something with you today, she's going to get extremely angry."

Sun said, "Your mother called me here, so we should not be to blame for whatever we do here. To tell you the truth, I did something when you were unconscious. Now you needn't resist it, Sister."

Hearing these words, Runniang looked down at herself and found her girdle and skirt untied. She also felt a faint pain in her private parts. Then she realized that he had taken her. However, since she loved him, why should she stop him from doing anything to her? Hence she gave herself entirely up to his will. Sun got excited again and the two jumped at their chance for love:

> *One awoke while the other regained his thrill;*
> *It was a good match, as raging flames consume dry firewood;*
> *Passion came as a devastating storm,*
> *As the act was studded with tender and immature movements;*
> *They gave no care for any eavesdropper,*
> *They were joyous to be confined;*
> *With no need of a matchmaker, their love was natural and*
>   *intense;*
> *Their affection ran strong as water slakes one's thirst;*
> *Love gave them so much excitement*
> *They would willingly die for it and come back in another world.*

They were gratified in their love-making. Then Runniang said, "If my mother returns, what can we do?"

Sun said, "We did it. When your mother comes back, she can't split us apart. Why do you worry? What can she say since she, herself, is to blame for locking us up here?" Then they again sank head over heels in love. They guessed Mother Fang would come back soon. But she did not. As evening arrived, Runniang took a lighter from the room into the attached kitchen and started cooking for Sun, who followed her around as her helper. They were like husband and wife. Then, as evening turned to night, Mother Fang still did not return. They became courageous and gave no heed to the results of their actions, going to bed together in each other's embrace. They felt lucky and hoped that Mother Fang would not come back until the next year. Let's leave them for now.

That morning Mother Fang had raced to the county yamen and shouted her grievances. When the county magistrate let her in, she told him of her daughter's death because of seduction. The county magistrate doubted her story and said, "You have an immoral style of living in your area. Women there are cunning and vicious. Your daughter must have died of some disease, but you want to land the responsibility on your neighbor."

Mother Fang said, "My daughter was unwilling to comply with the rapist and has committed suicide. The seducer is now in my home. I am asking for you to send some men with me to bring him here. You can then interrogate him in court. If I've made up anything, I will be willing to receive punishment." Seeing that she was so sure, the county magistrate told a clerk to record her words and he then issued an arrest order.

From the beginning, the government office took advantage of Mother Fang as woman and kept asking her for money to pursue the matter, until her patience ran out. Now she was finally assigned a runner, but the runner also asked her for money before departing. Thus she was held up two or three days before she could go back home with the runner. She said to herself, "I didn't know that it would take so long to get back. That son of bitch must be reduced to a bag of bones by hunger, if not have worried to death." She let the runner take a seat in the main room. As she went to open the locked one with her key, she heard the sound of chatting and laughter. Confused, she thought to herself, "With whom can that rogue be talking?"

After opening the door, she found the two lovers sitting shoulder to shoulder and murmuring tenderly to each other. Mother Fang was stunned and rubbed her eyes before taking a closer look. She asked her daughter, "How did you come back to life?"

Sun laughed and responded, "I appreciate your kindness in giving me your dead daughter. However, I am now returning your daughter to you alive. She's mine now!"

Mother Fang was at a loss for words. For quite a while she just stood there hunting for words with which to rebuke him. Slowly she pulled herself together by saying, "Why did you commit fornication? I've sued you."

Sun replied, "I didn't do that, but you locked me up in here. I don't care now if I go to court."

Mother Fang was completely at a loss and for the moment forgot that the runner was waiting outside. The runner called anxiously, "Why don't you come out? I've got to go and report to the lord."

Mother Fang then had to come out. She told the runner what had happened and said, "My daughter committed suicide by hanging herself. That is true. It is for that reason that I brought a suit to the court. I didn't know, however, that she would later come back to life. Now what can I say to the county magistrate?"

The runner flared up, shouting, "Are you going to say that you can do whatever you want in this world? One's life and death are serious issues. You first brought the matter to court and now are denying it. Even if your father were the county magistrate, you would not be able to do things at will. It is your fault for telling a lie in the first place."

"I admit it is not true that my daughter is dead," Mother Fang said as she shoved the young man in front of the runner, "but the seduction is crystal clear. I beg you to bring him to court and I will account for the matter in full."

Sun said, "The truth is that I didn't come here of my own free will. Besides, she is not dead. I didn't commit any crime. What is the point of bringing me to court?"

However, the runner said, "You are not right. I've got an order to arrest you. It is not my business whether you are a criminal or not. You have to defend yourself in court. Since I've come, you must pay me."

Sun said, "I was confined in the room without food for days. How can I have money to give you? I don't care if you will bring me to the authorities. Mother may do what she pleases!" Finding herself in a weak position for further argument, Mother Fang had to feed the runner with a meal.

As the runner also wanted to take Runniang to court, Mother Fang requested permission that he let her daughter stay at home. The runner replied, "At first you said she was dead. If so, the body would have been examined. Since she's now alive, how can you keep her from appearing in court?"

Jia Runniang heard this and said, "If I have to be humiliated today, I might as well hang myself and die."

Not listening to them, Mother Fang kept pleading. The runner persisted, but finally, permitted her request after he accepted some gifts from her. Hence the runner, brought Sun and Mother Fang, the plaintiff, to the government office.

The county magistrate first said to Mother Fang, "Tell me how your daughter died."

Mother Fang found it hard to answer for her daughter was not dead. She had to explain, "My lord, my daughter did not in fact die."

The county magistrate said, "If she is not dead, why did you sue someone for seducing your daughter and causing her death?"

Mother Fang replied, "Originally she was dead, so I brought my suit to you. After you approved it, she surprisingly came back to life."

The county magistrate said, "What a sheer fabrication! I have long heard that the women from your area are sly and deceptive. Your daughter was alive but you reported her death. You deserve a beating!"

Mother Fang said, "Though she is not dead, the seduction is definitely true. The offender is here."

The county magistrate then called the young man before him and said to him, "Fang has sued you for seducing her daughter. What's your side of the story?"

Sun said, "I did not commit seduction at all."

The county magistrate asked, "Where were you arrested?" Sun replied, "In Fang's house."

The county magistrate said, "Then you were caught on the spot of seduction."

Sun said, "I was tricked into going into her house and locked in there. I didn't go in there by myself. Why am I accused of seducing her?"

The county magistrate then asked Mother Fang, "How did you trick him into going into your house?"

Mother Fang said, "My daughter had an affair with him. I learned of it and swore at my daughter. She hung herself and died that night. So I tricked him into going into my house and locked him in. Then I came here to sue him. But when I later got back home, my daughter had come back to life. They stayed in my house for a couple of days. Their affair became outrageous."

Sun said, "I and her daughter were neighbors and have been on good terms since childhood. We didn't have any affair before. I don't know what Fang said to her daughter that night so that she tried to commit suicide by hanging herself. After learning of her death, the mother tricked me into going into her house and locked me up. I was absolutely ignorant of what had taken place. I was frightened at the sight of her daughter's body. But she slowly opened her eyes and came back to life on the bed. I couldn't get out of the room. So I had to stay with her in the room until several days later. Now I am brought here. I didn't do anything wrong since I didn't go into her room of my own free will. Would you please, make a thorough examination of this case?"

The county magistrate laughed and said, "I think what you have said is true. Now the daughter didn't actually kill herself, but there must have been some reason for her attempted suicide."

Sun said, "That's something between them, mother and daughter. I have no idea about it."

The county magistrate called Mother Fang up and asked, "Tell me why you daughter tried to commit suicide?"

Mother Fang rejoined, "I told about it a moment ago. They had an affair."

The county magistrate asked, "How did you know they had had an affair? You would need to catch both of them at it. Did you catch them?"

Mother Fang said, "He mistakenly took me for my daughter, speaking obscenely to me. So I was suspicious of the affair they must have carried on."

The county magistrate smiled and said, "How can you base your conclusion just on suspicion? They might not have had an affair at all before, so you were wrong in your suspicion. Later she gained consciousness and stayed with him for a couple of days. It's hard to tell whether they carried on an affair or not. In addition, you shut him inside there, helping him achieve his end. It seems they are predestined to be a couple. Besides, it is extremely rare for the dead to come back to life. It must be the will of heaven. I see this young man is handsome and speaks eloquently. Don't quibble anymore, I suggest, but marry your daughter to him."

Mother Fang said, "I don't have any hatred for him. After my daughter's death, I found it hard to swallow the insult, so I wanted to make him suffer. Now that my daughter is alive, I regret bringing the suit to court. I would like to follow your instructions now, sir."

Laughing, the county magistrate said, "If you had not brought the suit to court, how would your daughter and son-in-law have had the opportunity to stay together for a couple of days?" Then he picked up a brush and wrote this verdict:

"The son from the family of Sun and the daughter from the family of Jia are a good match in appearance and age. They were suspected of carrying on an affair but it was not true. The girl was thought to be dead but she came back to life. The boy was confined in the room, but, in fact, given the chance to sleep with his love. Their union is part of a heavenly design instead of human aspirations. Their love should be maintained and their wish be fulfilled."

Then an official read the verdict to Mother Fang and Sun. They were happy, expressing their gratitude, and withdrew. Sun proceeded to prepare for his marriage with Jia Runniang on a selected date.

Tale 17

Fisherman Wang Donates a Mirror in Worship of Buddha; Two Monks Lose Their Lives for Stealing the Treasure

This story is about a fisherman called Wang Jia, who lived in Jiazhou in the Shu region [present-day Sichuan Province], during the reign of Longxing [1163-1165] of the Song Dynasty. His family, generations of fishermen, lived close to the Mingjiang River. Every day with his wife he rowed out in a boat along the river, casting out and pulling in the net. A day's catch usually provided enough food for his family. Though he took fishing as his trade, he was a good-natured person who was a faithful Buddhist. Each day he brought the fish and lobsters he caught to the market for sale. If he had more than enough left to feed his family for the day, he would give the rest of his money to monks as a donation or to beggars as alms. When Buddhist temples collected alms, he was not stingy at all in giving a few coins. His wife was familiar with his way of doing things. A submissive woman, she was an even more pious Buddhist. So she was in agreement with her husband. Though they did not prosper at their shoe-string business, their alms offering of a couple of strings of cash was a daily necessity in their lives.

One day they were rowing in the river when they saw something rippling under the water, like the sun's shadow cast in brilliance. Wang Jia said to his wife, "Do you see that? It must be something extraordinary. We should pick it up and see what it is."

He told his wife to throw out the net and, as the bow of the boat turned, pulled it up. The thing shone brightly in the net. He grinned and asked, "What kind of interesting thing is it?"

He picked it up in his hand. It was an antique mirror with a diameter of about eight inches, and it bore the engraving of a dragon and a phoenix as well as some indecipherable seal characters resembling those used for incantations. Handing it to his wife, he said, "I have heard that an antique mirror is precious. Though I don't know how much this mirror may be worth of, it must be a valuable possession. Let's take it back home and save it. Later we can show it to some expert for judgment so as to give it its due respect."

Reader, this mirror had a particular origin: it was the product of an ancient chief called Huangdi, who created it with magic powers at the auspicious moment of the day, month and year, the prime of sunshine and moonlight. On the mirror were some badges, seal characters and boxes engraved in gold. The mirror brought wealth, including gold and silver, to its location and hence it had obtained the name of a treasure-gaining mirror. Due to their benevolence and the virtuous deeds they had accumulated in former lives, Wang Jia and his wife had the good luck to obtain this magic mirror. Soon, a fortune rolled in. A sweeping of the floor gathered scraps of gold; the plowing of land led to the discovery of a silver pit; hauling in the fishing net yielded jewelry; and even gems were found inside fresh-water mussel shells when they were ripped open.

One day they were fishing in the river. They noticed two little white objects moving about on the shore as if they were chasing one another.

Wang Jia leaped onto the shore, picked them up and put them in his lap. They were two little rocks the size of the lotus seeds, clean and immaculate, shining with great beauty. He tucked them inside his sleeve and brought them back home. He put them into a small box. That night in a dream he met two beauties in white dresses. They told him they were sisters coming to wait upon him. Upon waking, he decided, "They must be the souls of the two little rocks. The rocks are indeed precious." Then he wrapped them up and fastened them to his girdle.

A few days later, a Persian visitor arrived and said to Wang Jia, "You have something valuable on you. Can I have a look?"

Wang Jia replied, "I don't think I have any such thing."

The Persian said, "I noticed a wisp of treasure rising along the shore from a distance. I tracked it here and saw it in your home. But when you came out, I saw it on you. Please show it to me. You can't lie about it."

Knowing this man was someone who could tell good from bad, Wang Jia took the rocks from his girdle and showed them to the Persian. With clicks of his tongue in admiration, the Persian said, "It's good luck to come by this sort of treasure. It's particularly hard to acquire a pair of them. I wonder if you could spare them and sell them to me."

Wang Jia replied, "I have no use for them. I'll sell them to you, if you give me a reasonable price."

The Persian was delighted at the host's agreement to sell them, and said, "This treasure does not have a definite price. I've got thirty thousand pieces of cash on me. I'll give all of that to you for the sale."

Wang Jia said, "I acquired them by accident. I have no idea what they are. You offer such a handsome price so that I can't ask for more. I only hope you will tell me why you want to purchase them?"

The Persian rejoined, "These rocks are called 'Water-clearing Stones.' If you take them with you on a sea voyage, sea water will become crystal clear no matter how muddy it is. If you put them into sea water, it will become as fresh and drinkable as lake water."

Wang Jia said, "But why do they cost so much, given that is the use for them?"

The Persian explained, "In my country we have a treasure pond in which there are plenty of marvelous treasures. But the water is muddy and full of sludge. Besides, it is poisonous. If a person goes into the pond, he's likely to die when he gets out of it. In order to obtain the treasure, one has to hire people for a huge amount of money, who are willing to go under the water at the risk of their lives. After those people die, we have to support the families they leave behind. Now a treasure-fetching person will be able to go into the water with one of these rocks on him, and the water will become clear and harmless so treasure can be scooped up at will. Don't you think such a thing is priceless?"

Wang Jia said, "Well, if that is true, why are you buying two of them instead of just one? It might be good to leave one with me."

The Persian said, "The reason that I want two of them is that they are a pair, an intrinsic whole, supplementing one another. The combination gives them long-lasting power. If they are separated, they will become shriveled and useless. That's why we can't split them."

Wang Jia realized that this Persian was fairly knowledgeable, so he brought out the antique mirror for his judgment. At the sight of it, the Persian immediately prostrated himself before the mirror with his palms together, saying, "It is not an earthly treasure. It has extraordinary powers, about which I'm not in a position to tell. Only a person who has massive good luck can come into the possession of it. Even if I had the money, I would not be courageous enough to buy it. I think I've gotten enough with the purchase of the two rocks. Please store the mirror in a safe place. Don't trifle with it." Accordingly, Wang Jia put it away carefully. He then completed the deal with the Persian on the purchase of the two rocks at the price of thirty thousand pieces of cash.

Wang Jia had become rich overnight. But he would not give up his fishing career. One evening when a storm broke, he rowed his boat homeward. He saw someone on the southern riverbank with a torch, anxiously signaling him to ferry them across the river. Knowing there was no other boat around at that time, Wang Jia decided that if he ignored the request the person would be in trouble. So he turned his boat around and rowed it against the storm in the direction of the light. It turned out to be two Taoist priests, one in yellow dress and the other in white. They climbed on board the boat and were ferried across the river.

They said to Wang Jia, "It's dark and raining hard. At this hour we can't find any lodging. If you can accommodate us tonight, we would appreciate it very much."

Being a charitable man, Wang Jia said, "My home lacks space, but, if you, masters, deign to respect me, I have thatched beds for you."

Then he fastened the boat and led the two Taoists to his home. He called his wife to prepare dinner for them, but the Taoists insisted they would not eat anything, telling him, "Please don't bring us any food. We just want to sleep." They ate nothing before they turned in on the bamboo bed.

During the night, Wang Jia and his wife heard a grating sound coming from the bamboo bed on which the Taoists slept, and then a thump as if some heavy object had dropped on the floor. The couple thought, "Could it be the visitors who have dropped to the floor? But the fall of a human should not make such a loud sound." Puzzled, Wang Jia tiptoed to the Taoists' room and found it in dead silence. He became even more baffled. He went back to his room to light a candle. Then he let out a cry, "Ah!" when he saw what the candlelight revealed. The bamboo bed was crushed and the Taoists were lying under the bed, motionless on the floor. Reaching out to feel their bodies, he became terrified, standing open-mouthed for quite a while.

What had happened? These two Taoists,

> *were deadly cold and rigidly hard; they looked human but in*
> *reality were two bodies of treasure in white and yellow colors,*
> *without which no one can make a living in the world, nor a*
> *traveler make a trip.*

Wang Jia called to his wife and said, "It is weird that the two visitors have become hard and stiff, not human beings anymore."

His wife asked, "What have they become then?"

Wang Jia said, "In the candlelight I can't see clearly. I've no idea whether they are copper, tin, gold or silver. We can't make sure until tomorrow morning."

His wife replied, "If it's something supernaturally powerful, it will not be copper or tin."

Wang Jia said, "You're right."

As the daylight gradually got brighter, they looked closely and found that the Taoist in the yellow robes was now a gold figure and the one in white a silver figure, with a total weight of about one thousand *jin*. Wang Jia and his wife were overjoyed believing this was a gift bestowed on them by Heaven. But they feared the figures might move somewhere, because they were capable of changes. They rushed out to purchase more than ten baskets of charcoal, and started to melt the figures. As a result, the yellow human figure was turned into ingots of pure gold and the white human figure, into bars of fine silver. Earlier, Wang Jia had acquired lucky treasures every day. Then the sale of the two rocks brought him a good sum of money. Now the sizable amount of gold and silver filled all his jars and urns, causing his home to be short of space.

A law-abiding man, Wang Jia had no intention of building another house, nor did he want to purchase fields despite his overnight possession of wealth. He just quit fishing and stayed at home. As the fortune continued to flow in with no effort on his part, he grew extremely rich in two years. The husband and wife could not put their wealth to use, so they became uneasy. One day Wang Jia anxiously said to his wife, "Our family has made a living by fishing for generations. A gain of one hundred pieces of cash was the most we could hope to come by in a day. We could obtain no more than that. Since we have acquired this magic mirror, fortune keeps coming in huge amounts. It is a windfall. I would have never dreamed of it. I've often wondered what kind of people we are to deserve such tremendous wealth. I guess it's outrageous in light of the heavenly laws. On the other hand, we live simply in terms of clothing and food. Why do we need this great wealth? If we continue to keep this mirror, the wealth will accumulate steadily. To my way of thinking, the treasure of the world should not go to just one family. Such accumulation is evil. We should take this mirror to the Temple of White Water on Mt. Emei* and donate as the halo of the figure of Buddha. It will be a complete virtue if we dedicate and contribute it to Buddhism forever. By doing this, we will be happy and prove our devoutness to Buddha. Do you think that is a good idea?"

His wife answered him, "It is indeed a good thing to do in terms of Buddhism. We are sensible. That is just what we should do."

So they piously abstained from eating meat for ten days and went to the temple to present the mirror. Upon learning of their arrival, Falun, the abbot of the temple, said in praise, "This is your enormous contribution to Buddhism." Wang Jia asked for a statement to be written. According to the statement, all the monks of the temple would gather to observe a three-day performance of Buddhist rites for saving the souls of the dead. The subsequent Buddhist charitable effort in collecting food and money cost Wang Jia tens of *liang* of silver. After

---

*Located west of the city of Leshan, this mountain is one of the major spiritual centers of Buddhism in China.

the performance, Wang Jia handed his mirror to the abbot and was about to leave.

Falun had heard about Wang Jia's possession of the mirror long before, but to cover up his secret thoughts he hypocritically said, "It is the most precious treasure in the world and highly valued by the gods. You've donated it to the worship of Buddha, indicating your great allegiance. How could we Buddhist monks be so blasphemous as to seize it for ourselves? Please set it in front of the statues of Buddha and prostrate yourselves in worship. Then you can leave. We will never touch it."

Wang Jia and his wife did accordingly and performed four kowtows. They then said good-bye to Falun and left for home.

It turned out that Falun was very cunning and sinister. He had learned of how Wang Jia had prospered from this mirror. Upon Wang Jia's donation of it, he began to think of some way to procure it for himself. He worried that Wang Jia might change his mind and want to claim it back, so he assured Wang Jia that he would never lay a finger on it, in order to make an easy disavowal later. After Wang Jia left, Falun took the mirror and called in an experienced mirror craftsman. He asked the craftsman to make another mirror exactly like the original, so that no one could tell the real from the fake. Falun gave the craftsman a generous reward and asked him to keep his mouth shut about the matter. Then he put the newly made mirror in front of the figure of Buddha and stored the original one away. After he thus acquired the magic mirror, gold and silver started to roll in for Falun without any effort, just as it had for Wang Jia over the last two years. He had abundant food and clothing and bought more than three hundred disciple-servants licensed by the governmental ministry of sacrifices. The temple thrived with such immense wealth.

After Wang Jia returned home he found his life becoming poorer with each passing day. Going broke does not take much time. Even though one may be free of robberies and disasters, one will find their fortune quickly fading away before they realize it if they live on their savings with no income or they fail in their business. Wang Jia had come into the possession of his wealth without effort, so his spending was generous and unthoughtful. His wealth dwindled quickly, as if the contents dropped out of a bottomless bucket. With the magic mirror gone and no new resources, Wang Jia sank from being a rich man to being a fisherman again within two years. He was then as poor as he used to be. An old saying sums it up: "It's better for a poor to get rich than for a rich to become poor."

After Wang Jia had squandered his fortune away so quickly, he mused, "Originally I was poor. After I acquired the magic mirror, I obtained a great deal of treasure each day and became rich. If I had kept the mirror at home, wealth would have kept coming in. How could I have suffered in poverty? Now I need money but the mirror is sitting in the Temple of White Water. The temple is now rather prosperous but I'm poor. This is outrageous."

He and his wife blamed each other by saying, "Why didn't you say something at that time against the idea of donating the mirror to the temple?"

Wang Jia then said, "All right, it's fine. In fact we didn't sell the mirror to the temple. We just presented it in front of Buddha for worship. We should go and tell the abbot about what has happened to us. We'll bring it back home. It was originally one of our belongings. I don't think he will turn us down. In terms of showing our Buddhist faithfulness, we will promise to bring it back to the temple once we are rich again, to add sublimity to the Buddha statues. It should not be considered unrighteous."

His wife responded, "Exactly. Why should we suffer while other people prosper. Make no delay. You should go and bring it back." They thus settled on the agreement.

The following day Wang Jia made his way to the Temple of White Water.

When he had donated his magic mirror to the temple he was a generous man; now he came back to pick it up because of his financial plight; there were rich and poor patrons who made their pilgrimages alike but some were happy while others not.

Wang Jia met the abbot Falun. He told him of the decline in the family fortune due to the loss of the magic mirror, and requested its return so as to overturn his financial plight. As he spoke, Wang Jia was somewhat worried that Falun might reject him with an excuse.

Surprisingly, Falun immediately agreed and said, "It was yours originally. Come and get it today and I will by all means return it to you. I haven't touched it because I thought you might possibly come back for it. Why should I bother to prevent its return? I'm an ordinary monk. My earthly body is not mine, let alone anything else. I've been worried that the mirror might be damaged or stolen at night. If that happened, your generosity would go for nothing and I would feel ashamed to see you again. Now that the mirror is going back to its owner, I will be able to sleep soundly, completely at ease. Why should I refuse to return it to you?"

Then he ordered the kitchen to fix a vegetarian dinner for Wang Jia. After dinner, he let Wang Jia personally go to pick up the mirror from on the statue of Buddha. Holding the mirror in his hands, Wang Jia checked it carefully and was sure that it was indeed his mirror.

Back home, Wang Jia showed it to his wife. They highly valued and treasured it in the hope that wealth would soon steadily flow in as before. However, the miracle did not happen this time, and they remained as poor as ever. Occasionally they took out the mirror. It looked as glittering as before. But it had simply lost its magic powers. Wang Jia heaved a sigh and said, "Is this because my good luck is over that the mirror won't work any more?" He never realized that the mirror was a fake.

While Wang Jia tried to fight his poverty with the false mirror, the Temple of White Water continued to prosper. People began to speculate that, "It's because the original mirror must still be in the temple." The mirror craftsman was ignorant of what was happening when he was told by Falun to make a mirror with the original one as a model. Now the mirror craftsman heard that Wang Jia had become rich with a magic mirror and then had donated it to the temple, but that the monk defrauded him of the mirror, bringing wealth to the temple and leaving Wang Jia in poverty. The truth thus dawned on the mirror craftsman. Gradually he told the story publicly, which made people despise the monk Falun. Though Wang Jia learned that he had been cheated of the magic mirror, he did not know where could he obtain evidence to prove the point. He lacked any forceful reason with which to go to the temple for argument. He had to put up with the situation and moan about his fate. His wife, feeling wronged, did not know where to turn to for justice. At the same time, Falun was happy that he had made a gain great enough for an eternal use.

Reader, you may think from this that treachery triumphs and no justice is done. But,

the more tolerant one remains, the more good luck one will gain;
while the more crafty one becomes, the more destruction one
will sustain.

Falun had procured Wang Jia's magic mirror by means of deception and had become rich. This ran against the heavenly law and naturally drew punishment.

There was a jail director named Hun Yao, who came from prefectures Han and Jia [in present-day Sichuan]. A greedy man, he learned of the prosperity of the Temple of White Water and became covetous of its wealth. Later he heard about the magic mirror that had brought the fortune, and then thought to himself, "He's an ordinary monk. It won't be difficult for me to demand a great deal of treasure from him. But even a great amount of treasure will be gone sooner or later. Besides, it will draw public attention. If I acquire his magic mirror, wealth will begin to come to me, and the mirror is small and handy." He at once sent a favorite jailer, called Song Xi, to the temple to borrow the magic mirror.

The request to borrow the magic mirror deepened Falun's secret worries. How could he meet the demand? He said, in answering to the jailer, "I'm telling you the truth, sir, that a man donated an antique mirror a few years ago, which was put on the figure of Buddha. But he took it back home long ago. I would appreciate your kindness if you would report that to the jail director."

Song Xi said, "The jail director talked to me about the mirror that you own and wanted to see it. He must have known a lot about it. How can I let him down by bringing back nothing?"

Falun said, "To be frank, I'm not in possession of it, so how can I produce it, sir?"

Song Xi said, "Even if that is true, I would not dare to tell him so. If I do, I will definitely get scolded."

Knowing Song Xi was intentionally making trouble, Falun brought out ten *liang* of silver from the temple, since he had no lack of it, and gave it to the jailer. Then Falun said, "I'll be grateful if you will take this message to the jail director for me. Here's payment for your service. I hope you will not complain about this meager amount."

At the sight of the silver, Song Xi was overjoyed and said, "To return your generosity, I'll do my best to pass on the message."

After sending the jailer off, Falun turned to a favorite disciple, called Zhen Kong, and said, "Our temple counts on this mirror to prosper. How can we let someone take it away for that will become known to everybody later? Haven't you seen how Wang Jia has become poor? Besides, if the government official borrows it and then doesn't return it, we can never retrieve it. Since we've already deceived Wang Jia about the mirror, we'll have to keep the matter from the public. From now on we'll watch the magic mirror closely and deny any knowledge of it. If they press hard to see it, we'll give them some silver and send them away."

Zhen Kong said, "Sure, how can we easily give it away to someone? We can let them take everything from the temple but not this mirror. With it, we'll be assured of prospering more." The master and disciple thus became even more watchful.

The jailer, Song Xi, went back to report to the jail director, Hun Yao. The jail director flew into rage and cried out, "How indiscreet the monk is! I, a government official, wanted to borrow something from him. But I can't believe he dared reject me!"

Song Xi explained, "He didn't say he refused to show it to you. He denies that he possesses the mirror."

The jail director said, "Nonsense! I have checked the fact that a rich man named Wang presented the mirror to the temple. The monk replaced it secretly. He gave the copy to Wang and kept the original for himself. You must have taken bribes from him so you are speaking for him. If you can't bring it here, you'll be punished with a beating!"

Song Xi panicked and said, "I'm going to talk to the monk again and make sure to wring it out of him."

The jail director said, "Go, and hurry up! Don't come back without the mirror."

Pressed, Song Xi retreated and returned to the temple. He said to the abbot, "The jail director insists that he must have the mirror. His rage makes me worry. I can't go back to see him unless I get the mirror."

Falun said, "The other day, I told you that the mirror was returned to the owner. How could I have another one?"

Song Xi said, "The jail director told me in detail that the donor Wang presented it to the temple. Later he came to pick it up and you gave him a false one and kept the original for yourself. I don't know how he learned all this. How can I tell him you haven't the mirror?"

Falun answered, "It all comes from gossips who saw our humble temple was a little bit richer and envied us. So they spread this nonsense."

Song Xi said, "But you can't reason with the jail director. Wind always comes with rain. If he got that word, there must be something of the truth in it. If you insist on denial, I think you'll have to give him something so as to satisfy him."

Falun said, "Except for the mirror, which we don't have, I can let you take anything from our humble temple. I'm not stingy. I'll follow his instructions."

Song Xi replied, "To my mind, you will have to give him one thousand *liang* of silver in order to smooth out his displeasure."

Falun said, "That sum of money is fine with us. But how can I deliver it to him?"

Song Xi said, "You can count on me. I'll have a way of delivering it."

Falun said, "Alright. I only hope that we can settle it once and for all, and not be bothered again." So he told Zhen Kong to bring out one thousand *liang* of silver and hand this to Song Xi. Then an additional thirty *liang* of silver was given to Song Xi as a token of reward.

Song Xi took the silver. He kept two hundred *liang* for himself and gave the rest — eight hundred *liang* of silver — to the jail director, telling him, "The monk indeed does not have the mirror. But he is presenting you with a gift equal to the value of the mirror."

Meanwhile Song Xi was thinking to himself, "The magic mirror may not even cost this much money. The matter should be dropped."

The jail director saw the silver and though his fury had hardly abated, mused, "In comparison with the magic mirror, the seven or eight hundred *liang* of silver are nothing. Why should they be considered a sizable amount? You bald son of bitch! The mirror was cheated from others, why should you be so penurious in showing it?

Now that he's denied possession of it, it is hard to deal with him."
Suddenly the jail director hit upon an idea. "I'm in charge of a jail for
prisoners with heavy sentences," he reasoned. "I will take this silver to
be a bribe that he sent to me, and accuse him of bribing, pulling strings
with a jail official and slandering the local government. I'll have him
brought here for intimidation and torture. I don't think he can bear it."
At once he ordered that the silver be put away in storage, and he sent
two runners to arrest Abbot Falun of the temple.

Falun saw the runners coming and realized they were after the
mirror, the unsettled business. He told Zhen Kong, "The jail director is
sending men to arrest me. He can't come up with any accusation
against me, so I should be fine. He just wants to rob me of the magic
mirror. I'll go with them and see what he says about it. I'll let him
know clearly about the situation. Then he may drop the matter. Who
knows? The other day the jailer Song Xi took the silver. Probably the
jail director desires a larger amount. If I have to make a painful
decision, we can give him another amount of silver doubling the
previous amount. His insatiable demand can't keep rising. Anyway,
you should take good care of that mirror and never let out any sign of
it."

Zhen Kong said, "Please be at ease, master. When you are at the
government office, just send word back home for whatever you need.
Regarding that thing, I'll store it in a place no one can find. No matter
what kind of people they send here, I'll give them a complete denial."

Falun bade, "Even if they come to fetch it in my name, you
shouldn't acknowledge that we have it." Thus they settled on the plan
and treated the runners. The runners, in addition, were very glad to
receive some money as pay for their business trip.

Falun was confident that he had enough money. He did not fear the
government office and marched away with the runners. After they
arrived at the government office, Director Hun held a court session. At
the sight of Falun, the director banged on the table in rage and shouted,

"I'm in charge of the jail, a government section of life and death. You, you bald knave, offered a bribe to the government office. What are you up to? Now the bribe is in the storage. You must have some evil plan. Tell the truth immediately!"

Falun said, "You sent the jailer to fetch the mirror from us. Our humble temple does not possess the mirror. The jailer asked me to offer you the silver to make up for it."

The jail director said, "That's all bullshit! How can that be true? You must have pulled strings with your money. You apparently won't tell the truth without a beating." He then told the runners to beat him. The beating brought Falun to the brink of death, and he was then thrown into jail.

Later the jail director secretly sent Song Xi to cajole Falun into telling the mirror's whereabouts. Falun made a desperate decision and said to Song Xi, "I don't have the mirror. If he wants more silver, you can go and talk to my disciple who will gave him more as a way of redeeming me."

Song Xi said, "He only wants the mirror. I don't think he will let you out after he has received more silver. But I'll talk to him first and see what he says." Song Xi went back with the monk's words. The jail director said, "I don't think I can get anything out of him by talking to him. Even a beating makes little difference. The mirror must be in the temple. I'll quietly send men to put the temple under siege, confiscate the property and rummage through everything thoroughly in the name of seizing bribes. I think we can get the mirror that way!" Thus he sent out Song Xi and four other runners at once.

Because Song Xi had received money earlier from Falun, he secretly told Falun about the jail director's intentions. Falun thought to himself, "I talked to Zhen Kong before I left the temple and he promised me that he would store the mirror in a safe place. I don't think the runners will be able to find it. They can't sweep away everything from the temple."

So he said to Song Xi, "I assure you that we don't have the mirror. It's fine with us if you sift through the trunks and boxes. My disciple is there, but I still have a request that you take care of the confiscation so that my things do not get lost. If you can do this favor for me, I'll give you a good reward after being released."

Song Xi said, "Sure, I'll do my best," and then he went with the runners to the Temple of White Water. Let's leave them for now.

Zhen Kong, Falun's disciple, was a young, lewd monk. He behaved at will with the temple's fortune. But he always felt restrained in the abbot's presence. Now Falun's absence played into Zhen Kong's hands and he was free of any scruples. An old saying goes, "One has to think of ways to dispose of money he has stolen from his master." Zhen Kong once had a number of lovers and whores. Now he lavishly gave some of the temple's treasure to each of them. Thus a large amount of wealth was gone. Then he transferred other treasures in countless numbers out of the temple and stored them in various places for himself. But he soon realized, "Once the master gets out of jail, he will look for the property. How can I keep him from knowing about it? Besides, the government investigation regarding the mirror is progressing. Soon I'll get involved, too. I will take advantage of the master's absence and make off with all the property, as well as the mirror, and go to another prefecture. I'll let my hair grow, resume a secular life, and enjoy the rest of years. Isn't that a wonderful idea?" After thus making up his mind, he sorted out the valuables at night, and prepared two shoulder-pole loads. The next day he carried one shoulder pole and hired a man to carry the other. Telling the others in the temple that he was going to save the master from imprisonment, he set out on the downhill journey.

One day later, Song Xi arrived with the four runners to search the abbot's room. The monks responded, "The abbot is currently with the government, and his major disciple is away, too, leaving an empty house behind."

One runner said, "Stop talking about that. We have come with a government order to search for stolen goods. We don't care whether you have someone in charge or not. Let's break in." They pulled down the door to the abbot's room and entered. What they saw were only heavy objects in the room, such as sturdy tables and chairs and empty trunks and baskets. There was no treasure at all. Then they dug into the floor, but still couldn't find the mirror.

Song Xi said, "The abbot told me to take care and not lose any of his things in the room. But it's an empty room. What's happened?"

The monks said, "His major disciple said he went to see the master.

Why would he strip the room before he left? Did he possibly take advantage of the opportunity and run away?" The four runners realized that something unexpected had occurred, and a longer search would not bring any better results. They scraped up the old clothes and took them with them. They asked the monks to write down a statement regarding Zhen Kong's escape and left with Song Xi to report to the jail director.

The jail director flew into rage and said, "These bald asses! They are so sly! It is obvious that the abbot opposed me by secretly letting his disciple run away." At once he ordered them to bring in Falun and give him another sound thrashing. Falun was the abbot of a temple in the mountain who had led a rich and easy life. How could he bear such severe torture? The imprisonment had pushed him to the verge of physical collapse. He had expected to be released shortly after spending some silver. Now he knew his disciple had made off with all his valuables. He was thus quite depressed. The severe beating was devastating, and made his condition worse. How could he stand it? Tossed back into jail, he had little breath left in him. That very night he died. The jail director heard of his death and let the matter drop. Falun had treacherously robbed someone of the treasure. He had finally paid for his evil deed.

Now Zhen Kong had fled the temple with the treasure he had stolen.

He did not care about his master's life. His mind was only on how to run to another place so he could enjoy himself. He picked up the things he had previously stored in other places, and put them together with those he carried out of the temple. He got a cart, set the baggage on it and set out on a run, with a man he hired to pull the cart in front. Reader, you may wonder, since the abbot had such a huge property, including silver that was heavy, how would Zhen Kong be able to load all of this into a cart? Well, during the Song Dynasty, the government issued many bills called "paper money." One string of cash equaled one bill. Ten hundred thousand strings of cash equaled ten hundred thousand bills, not heavy to carry around. Falun had silver and treasure, but he also possessed tens of hundred thousand bills. So it was easy to carry them. Zhen Kong carried the magic mirror on his person and followed the cart on the journey. He trekked in the mountains and made his way toward the county of Lizhou.

When he reached the side of the Brook of the Bamboo Man, a heavy fog developed, enveloping the road ahead. Then a godlike spirit in golden armor leaped out in front of him,

with an awe inspiring look he was more than ten feet tall;
attired in a golden suit of chain armor he held a halberd.

The godlike spirit shouted, "Where are you going? Return the magic mirror to me!" Terrified, the cart puller took flight in the direction from which he had come, going as fast as he could and wishing he might be given another pair of feet to carry him. Horrified too, Zhen Kong deserted the cart and carried the magic mirror in a wild run. He fled into a wood where a fierce tiger sprang out in a sudden gust of wind. The tiger leaped onto Zhen Kong and dragged him off. Zhen Kong had robbed his master in his greediness, for which he now paid with his life.

Wang Jia had returned home with the mirror, but the mirror did not reverse his poor financial state. Later he saw that the temple steadily thrived and he learned about the abbot's seizure of his magic mirror by a deceptive substitution. Bu he did not know how to get it back. He was kind-hearted and could just blame his bad luck. He and his wife often talked to each other about their old days when the magic mirror gave them so much treasure and joy, and they were saddened because of their present state. One night in a dream they both met a godlike spirit in gold armor, who said to them, "Your magic mirror is now by the side of the Brook of the Bamboo Man. You may go there and pick it up."

They woke up and talked to each other. Wang Jia said, "We have been thinking about the mirror, so I had such a dream."

His wife said, "It's true that we thought of it and so we dreamed about it. But the dreams should not be exactly alike. Is it possible that we've got some good luck left and the gods have come to our help with this clue? Since the location is specified, we should go and explore it."

The next day Wang Jia headed for the Brook of the Bamboo Man. He trekked through mountains and arrived at the spot. He saw a cart turned over by the roadside, which contained a huge amount of wealth, great piles of silver and countless bills worth tens of hundred thousand pieces of cash. He found no one around and thought to himself, "This is a deserted fortune. Is it bestowed on me by Heaven? I was told in the dream that the magic mirror would be located around here. I wonder whether it is in the cart or not." He raked through the contents of the cart but did not find the mirror. Then he searched about in the grass. Still there was no sign of the mirror. He smiled and said, "Though the mirror is gone, I've got this fortune, which will surely provide me with a good life. I'd better take it with me before someone arrives." He straightened out the load on the cart and pushed it to a crossroads. Then he hired a man to pull the cart back home.

Wang Jia said to his wife, "I followed the divine clue to the side of the brook. Though I did not find the mirror, a fully loaded cart was abandoned there. I waited, but no one arrived to claim it. I decided it was a heavenly bestowal and so I brought it back home." His wife saw the collection of silver and money. She unloaded it and put it away.

Wang Jia and his wife were overjoyed. But they were puzzled. "I was told in the dream that it would be the magic mirror I would find in that place. Though I've obtained this fortune, the magic mirror is still not back with me. Why? I should go there again and search more closely." Wang Jia then said to his wife, "I think I will go there tomorrow and find it."

That night Wang Jia had another dream. The same gold-armored godlike spirit appeared and said to him, "Wang Jia, don't think about the mirror anymore. The magic mirror is a heavenly treasure. Due to the kind-heartedness of you and your wife, it was ordained to come down to earth in order to help you prosper. But unexpectedly it twice fell into the hands of evil monks. Now the evil monks have been punished. The magic mirror should return to Heaven. Reject your wild dreams about it. Yesterday you acquired a cartload of wealth. That is the fortune the magic mirror gathered. It is yours now. As long as you remain kind and honest, this fortune will provide you with a prosperous life." Wang Jia awoke in a shudder. It was a dream. Wang Jia recounted the dream in detail to his wife. Knowing it was the will of heaven, they let the matter of the mirror drop. They, husband and wife, enjoyed the wealth the temple had accumulated and became rich in their native region. It was the payment they received for their benevolence.

Tale 18

Sister Mo Elopes with the Wrong Lover;
Second Brother Yang Marries His Former Mistress

Xu De, who lived in the Northern Zhili Province, worked as an assistant in the town government office. His wife, Sister Mo, was quite attractive. She loved to drink and tended to flirt with men after she became drunk. Their next-door neighbor was a lecherous young man called Second Brother Yang, who whiled away his days and did nothing to pursue a career. He carried on an affair with Sister Mo, which later became known to everyone. Though Sister Mo was also interested in other men, Second Brother Yang was the one who most caught her fancy. Moreover, Xu De was busy with his government work and often stayed away from home for a month at a time. So Second Brother Yang had plenty of opportunities to be with Sister Mo. Later they even lived together as if they were husband and wife.

Later on Xu De earned enough to ease his family budget. In time he found an occasional replacement for himself at work and so he didn't need to show up regularly at the government office. As the length of his stay at home increased, he gradually discovered his wife's affair with Second Brother Yang, which was further confirmed by his neighbors' remarks.

One day he said to Sister Mo, "We've worked hard during the first half of our lives to establish ourselves financially. Now we should be cautious and behave decently so as not to be laughed at by others."

Sister Mo replied, "Why do they laugh at us?"

Xu De answered, "The bell needs striking to toll, and the drum will not sound without beating. The only way to keep your deed secret is to not perform it at all. Who does not know what you've been doing in the neighborhood? Why have you not been honest with me on this point? I'm just giving you a warning."

With her husband talking directly about her affair, Sister Mo could no longer cover it up by showing her wifelike indulgence and ignorance of it. Though she hemmed and hawed, she understood that she had been rather unscrupulous in the affair and it was impossible to keep her husband from knowing about it. She did not deny it openly, but thought to herself, "I'm truly in love with Second Brother Yang, as intimately as if we were husband and wife. Now our affair has been discovered by my husband, who will watch me more closely. How will we be able to keep up our relationship as before? I should talk to my love. We can take some of the family property and elope together to another prefecture to live a free and happy life. That is a marvelous idea." She held on to this idea in secret.

One day when Xu De was not at home, she met Second Brother Yang and talked with him about her idea. He said, "I have nothing to worry about but myself. If you, sister, want to escape with me, I am willing to do so at any moment. The problem is that we need money to feed ourselves after we leave our homes." Sister Mo said, "I'll seize all the valuables in my household. Don't you think those things will provide us with a living for some time? After settling down in some place, we will manage to find a way to make a living one way or another."

Second Brother Yang said, "Alright. We should get prepared and decide later on the date to flee."

Sister Mo said, "I'll wait for an opportunity and schedule a date of departure with you. Don't let anybody know about it."

Second Brother Yang replied, "I understand." They did not miss the chance to make the most of being together, before they vowed to each other to carry out the plan, and then separated.

Xu De came back a few days later. Seeing that his wife seemed absent-minded and disturbed, he made inquiries and learned that her lover had been with her again. Xu De nursed his anger, thinking to himself, "When I run into him again, I will break him in two!" Sister Mo detected her husband's rage and so she sent a message to Second Brother Yang telling him, "Don't come to my home at the present time." Thus Second Brother Yang dared not to meet her in her house. Sister Mo waited while constantly thinking about her flight with her lover. She did not care about her home, and her husband became nothing but a thorn in her flesh.

When women are involved in amorous relationships, they tend to lose their minds, getting infatuated and talking wildly. With Second Brother Yang out of sight, Sister Mo was constantly tormented by thoughts of him. Discomfited, she got her husband's approval to go on an arranged trip with a few neighboring women to burn joss-sticks at the Temple of Mount Tai. Since Xu De knew his wife was not virtuous, he should not have agreed. However, he was open-hearted as all northerners were. He thought, "I've been watching her closely. I find her in a daze. Maybe she's sick. Let her go for a release of tension." According to the conventions of north China, a husband would let his wife go alone on a trip while he took care of business at home. Therefore Sister Mo set out in a sedan chair with her women friends, carrying with them sacrificial offerings such as food, wine, paper money and paper horses. But her departure was to become a turning-point in her life, as:

it was a stroke of fate that a beautiful woman would be cast into a brothel, and a bed-sharing lover would narrowly escape death in prison.

It came to pass that a tall and handsome man named Yu Sheng lived outside of Qihua Gate. Full of salacious and sinful thoughts, he observed no code of honor, but seduced many chaste and pretty ladies. He also liked to engage in immoral acts, such as procuring petty gains from others. He and Sister Mo were cousins and because of this kept close contact. Though they were attracted to one another, they had not had a chance to start an affair. However, Yu Sheng felt sorry for himself because of this, so he never let her drop from his mind. By chance he was idling about one day in front of his house when he saw several sedan chairs go by. He peered stealthily into one of them and caught a glimpse of Sister Mo as the curtain flapped open. He noticed the paper money hanging from the sedan chair and servants carrying boxes on shoulder poles. He realized that the ladies were heading for the Temple of Mount Tai to offer incense and to have a picnic with wine. He pondered, "If I go with them, I will see a lot of her, but that will be the best I can do. It will not be much fun. I won't be able do anything with her. Moreover, the other ladies are around and I will have to restrain myself from making advances. I'd better fix some food and wine here and invite her to come in for dinner on her way back home. Nobody will be suspicious. Sister Mo loves drink and fun and I know she has some amorous feelings toward me. She will never reject me. I will arouse her with wine. Then I think I can make it. Excellent! Excellent!" He ran to the market and purchased plenty of good fish, meat and hazelnuts. He then prepared these in a clean, neat fashion.

Sister Mo arrived with the ladies at the temple. After burning incense, they strolled around. Then they sat down on the ground in a wild clearing and opened the wine hamper for a picnic. The women drank moderately three or four cups of wine. But they all knew that Sister Mo was a good drinker, so they pressed her to take more. Sister Mo lightheartedly accepted their urge to drink more, downing one cup after another. After the wine was all gone, she was close to drunkenness. Darkness was starting to fall, so they cleaned up their things and got into the sedan chairs to go home.

Seeing them passing by his house, Yu Sheng raced in front of Sister Mo's sedan chair and said in greeting, "Here's my humble home, Elder Sister. I think you must be thirsty on your tour. Please come in and have some tea."

With only dim vision because of her intoxication, Sister Mo recognized Yu Sheng as her kinsman and the one with whom she had flirted a great deal before. So she immediately called for a stop. She dismounted from the sedan chair, did a courtesy and said to him, "I didn't know you lived here, Bother."

All smiles, Yu Sheng said, "Please come in, Elder Sister."

She reeled inside. The other ladies knew that Sister Mo was stopping at her relative's place, and so they continued their trip home, leaving Sister Mo's sedan chair bearers waiting outside the gate.

Sister Mo was led into a room where she saw a table covered with wine, food and dry fruit. She said to him, "I don't understand why you bothered to get such a feast prepared."

Yu Sheng replied, "You rarely come this way, Elder Sister. It's just an ordinary meal that I am presenting to you as a token of my hospitality."

Intentionally wishing to have the two of them left alone, Yu Sheng waited on her personally. He poured the wine and treated her attentively. An old saying goes, "Tea enhances the beauty of flowers; wine stirs amorous desires." Sister Mo had been in a drunken stupor before she arrived. Now Yu Sheng kept pushing more drink on her, as if he were quietly rowing a boat to catch a drowsy fish. She turned red but had to consume the drinks repeatedly offered to her. Wholly overwhelmed by intoxication, she felt the surge of her desire. Looking askance at him, she began to pass lustful glances at him and to utter obscene expressions. Yu Sheng took a seat by her side and offered her yet another drink. She took half a sip before he took a sip. Then, holding some wine in his mouth, Yu Sheng craned his neck over toward her, as Sister Mo leaned forward to take the wine from his mouth and gulp it down. After that she stuck out her tongue out while he sucked it. The heat of sexual desire overran them, as they hugged and made their way into bed. There they undressed and made love.

One of them took up the act vigorously in drunken dizziness, while the other performed in merry soberness; dizzily she moved like a butterfly who had lost her way among flowers, and soberly he went at her like a bee gathering honey from a stamen; her passion remained high in drowsy excitement, while his enjoyment came with a tinge of frivolity; though the love continued with different sentiments, they reached a convergence of gratification.

At the peak of their love-making, Sister Mo in extreme passion moaned and said, "Sweetie, Second Brother! You're the only one I love. I'm longing to fly away with you to enjoy ourselves! My wretched husband is not as interesting as you, yet he keeps watch over me. Oh, Second Brother, you are far more tender to me!" As she said this, she wiggled her hips, hugging Yu Sheng, then murmured, "My dear, Second Brother."

Sister Mo was drunk but very excited. In her dizziness she couldn't tell exactly who she was with. It was a matter of "uttering thoughts in drunkenness" or "telling truth upon drinking." She loved Second Brother Yang. But now in her intoxication she mistook Yu Sheng for him and was airing her mind to her present partner. Yu Sheng had heard about her affair with Second Brother Yang and knew she was now confused. He thought to himself, "You bitch, you only keep your lover in your mind! I'll take advantage of that and coax her secrets from her."

He then said to her, "How can we escape and enjoy ourselves?"

Sister Mo replied, "As I told you the other day, we will take his valuables with us and run to another place to live a happy life. It's been difficult to get a chance. On the day of the autumnal equinox that louse of a husband will go to town on his government business. Let's take off that night."

Yu Sheng then asked, "How can we get away?"

Sister Mo said, "You can row a boat down there and then move the things into the boat. We'll leave at night. It will be too late when he returns from town and learns about it."

Yu Sheng said, "Should we have a secret signal on that night?"

Sister Mo said, "Just clap your hands outside and I'll come out to meet you. I'll get ready and wait for you. Don't be late." After that she murmured many more lewd expressions than sensible words. Yu Sheng picked up those important words and bore them in mind.

Soon they finished. Sister Mo adjusted her hairpins and lurched off the bed. Yu Sheng called on the sedan-chair carriers, who earlier had been treated to dinner, to help her into the sedan chair and she went off. Yu Sheng went back into the house, very happy about the good time he had had as well as the secret plan she had told him about.

He smiled. "Marvelous, marvelous. I was surprised to hear about her intention to elope with Second Brother Yang. She took me for Second Brother Yang by mistake. Isn't that interesting? Now I'll take advantage of her confusion and rent a boat. On the designated night I'll take her away to another place and enjoy her for some time. Won't that be wonderful?" A dissipated man, Yu Sheng secretly rejoiced at his gain. He made arrangements for the boat and waited for the hour to arrive.

Meanwhile Sister Mo returned home overpowered by the effect of the wine until the following day. As if she had awoken from a dream, she could not recall accurately what had happened the previous night in Yu Sheng's place, except for some dim memory of her telling Second Brother Yang about the date to leave. Hence she got things ready and waited. Second Brother Yang, however, was not aware of Sister Mo's scheduled date of departure, though she had earlier told him a couple of times about her intention of fleeing with him.

After the second watch on the night of the autumnal equinox, Sister Mo, who had been waiting at home, heard the clapping of hands outside. She clapped her hands in reply. She then opened the door and went out. Seeing a man faintly out there in the dark, she thought it was Second Brother Yang. She ran back into her room and brought everything out of her wardrobe and packed her suitcases, while the man received one piece after another and put them into the boat. Worried about being discovered, she did not use a light outside the room. She put out the light in her room, locked the door and went over to the boat in darkness. The man supported her as she got on board and then the boat immediately started to move. Hastily the two of them whispered to each other. Sister Mo thought she was with Second Brother Yang. She couldn't recognize the man as he did not show his face clearly in the dark. After one day's urgent preparation for the trip, Sister Mo was finally at rest upon getting into the boat. Exhausted, she could not do anything. She tried to talk to the man but received only a taciturn reply. So she lay down and went to sleep with her clothes on.

When morning arrived, they were on the Luhe River, about one hundred *li* away from home. Sister Mo woke up and saw that the man sitting in the boat with her was not Second Brother Yang but Yu Sheng from outside Qihua Gate. Stunned, she asked him, "Why are you here with me?"

With a smile, Yu Sheng replied, "Elder Sister, you came to my home after your visit to the temple the other day, and had a drink with me. I appreciate your kindness in giving me the opportunity to have a good time with you. You personally told me about our departure tonight. Why are you surprised?"

Dumbfounded for awhile, Sister Mo slowly recollected that night she had drunk in his home and made love with him. Probably I mistook him for my lover and told him of my thoughts. She thought she must have scheduled the time to flee with him, because she hadn't known it was with Yu Sheng instead. Now she couldn't undo the matter. She could only go with him. She thought, what can I later say to Second Brother Yang? She then said to Yu Sheng, "But where shall we go, Brother?"

Yu Sheng answered, "Linqing is a big port. I have a friend there so we can settle in that place and start a business. We'll live together. Don't you think we'll have a good life?"

Sister Mo said, "I've got a large sum of money with me. That should start you in business."

Yu Sheng replied, "Excellent." Thus Sister Mo went with Yu Sheng to Linqing.

Let's now pick up another thread of the story. Xu De returned home after finishing his business to find the room stripped of all its contents. He swore, "That bitch must have gone with the adulterer!"

He checked with his neighbors. They said, "The lady disappeared at night. The following day we saw the door was locked and did not know what had happened inside. You might think about the matter. it must be a man who has seen her a lot in the past that has taken her away."

Xu De said, "Isn't it very clear? She must have been taken to the home of Second Brother Yang."

The neighbors said, "Yes, we would guess so too."

Xu De then said, "The disgrace to my family is no news to you. Now she's disappeared. It's unquestionably because of Second Brother Yang. This matter has to be settled in court. I would appreciate it if you would appear in court as witnesses. Now I'm going to find Second Brother Yang and argue with him."

The neighbors said, "Who does not know their affair? When you need us in court, we'll surely put in a good word for you."

Xu De replied, "I will appreciate that."

Then Xu De angrily raced to the home of Second Brother Yang, when Yang was coming out of the house. Xu De grabbed him and said, "Where did you take my wife?"

Second Brother Yang knew nothing about what had happened, but Sister Mo had been constantly on his mind. As the news exploded on him, he was shocked and said, "I absolutely know nothing about it. How can you accuse me?"

Xu De said, "Who in this neighborhood does not know that you have seduced my wife? But you want to deny it. Let's go to court! You must give me back my wife!"

Second Brother Yang said, "I have no idea where your wife has gone. I've stayed at home and done nothing related to her. Why are you asking me about her and taking me to court? I have nothing to do with her." Not listening to him, Xu De seized Second Brother Yang and turned him over to the local authorities. Then he was taken to the department of the garrison.*

Xu De had many connections and got a lot help from the government. The head of the department of the garrison put Second Brother Yang into custody. The next day Xu De had his indictment of Second Brother Yang granted from the prefecture's department of inspection. The department of the garrison was authorized to examine the case. The head of department interrogated Second Brother Yang. At first Second Brother Yang denied any relation to the missing of Sister Mo. Xu De and the neighbors all gave their testimony of his

---

*During the Ming Dynasty, a department of the garrison was set up with the director and deputy director in charge of the town's security.

illicit relationship with her. The head of the garrison ordered that he be tortured. Second Brother Yang could not stand it, so he admitted to the adultery he had committed with Sister Mo over a long time.

The head of the garrison then said, "If the adultery is true, you must have taken her away."

Second Brother Yang said, "Though I participated in adultery, I really have no knowledge of her disappearance."

The head of the garrison then asked Xu De, "Does your wife have another lover?"

Xu De said, "No. Second Brother Yang is the only one she has kept."

The local authorities also said, "He is her lover, which is known to everybody in the neighborhood."

The head of the garrison then shouted at Second Brother Yang, "Do you still want to deny the facts? You must tell the truth. Where have you hidden her?"

Second Brother Yang said, "She is not in my place. How can I know where she is now?"

Flying into a rage, the head of the garrison shouted, "Clamp him up! Make him tell."

Second Brother Yang had to confess, "She talked to me about our fleeing together. This is true. But we did not schedule a time. Now I don't know where she has gone."

The head of the garrison said, "Since you talked together about fleeing, you must have some knowledge about her whereabouts. I think what you've done was to put her away in a secret place, then deny the fact here so as to continue your affair with her later. I'll send you to jail and bring you up for interrogation every three to five days. Let's see how long you can hide her!"

Second Brother Yang was put behind bars, and every few days subjected to inquisition and torture. However, he told nothing. Xu De came periodically to urge the head. Second Brother Yang was punished with the repeated beatings on his buttocks, but the interrogation was fruitless.

Second Brother Yang could not stand it any more. So he also filed an indictment with another government office over the false charge and unjust imprisonment. However, it was well known that Xu De had lost his wife and Second Brother Yang's adultery was undeniable. So no one would free him. Some people who doubted his crime and showed sympathy toward him urged him to have notices posted, offer a reward and hire men to hunt for the missing woman. But nine out of ten people examined said that Second Brother Yang was responsible for putting his lover away. Who would admit that he had been wronged? Thus it was the payment Second Brother Yang received for his seduction of somebody else's wife.

Let's leave Second Brother Yang with his troubles for the moment and turn again to Yu Sheng, who had carried Sister Mo away that day to Linqing. They settled down in a rented house and continued with their affair for awhile. But the thought of her relationship with Second Brother Yang lingered in Sister Mo's mind. She grappled with her reluctance to be with Yu Sheng and was saddened all day long, heaving great sighs. Yu Sheng found both Sister Mo and himself lacking appeal for each other after an initial two months of copulative bliss. Uneasy, he figured, "I'm now spending the money she brought with her. The money will be all gone one day. I'm inexperienced at doing business. What will I do then? Moreover, she's not my wife and that will become gradually known to the outside. I can't stay long with her. I will have to return home. How can I live here for very long? I'd better sell her to someone. She is good-looking and may be worth one hundred *liang* of silver. With that sale plus the rest of her money, I'll be able to live pretty well."

He learned that Mother Wei, the mistress of a brothel in front of the post station by the pier of Linqing, maintained a group of prostitutes. Mother Wei needed many women for her thriving business. He asked someone to take a message to Mother Wei. Mother Wei came one day, on a pretext that she was on a visit to see a relative, and saw Sister Mo. Mother Wei paid eighty *liang* of silver after a bargain was reached and was then ready to take Sister Mo away.

Yu Sheng said to Sister Mo, cajolingly, "Mother Wei is one of my remote kinswomen. She's very good-natured. We're in an alien land and it's good to have her around to dispel boredom. Some days ago she came to see you. Now you should pay a return visit." Sister Mo was interested in social activity because that is the nature of women. Having heard his words, she started dressing herself up. Yu Sheng rented a sedan chair and sent Sister Mo to Mother Wei's home.

Sister Mo noticed that Mother Wei was not particularly warm in meeting her, but only looked her up and down with smile. Then she saw many prostitutes about. She wondered, "What kind of remote relative is she? This is a brothel, I think." After having a cup of tea, she rose and began to take her leave.

With a smile, Mother Wei asked her, "Where are you going?"

Sister Mo replied, "I'm going home."

Mother Wei said, "Why are you still talking about your home? You belong here."

Taken aback, Sister Mo said, "What do you mean by that?"

Smiling, Mother Wei said, "Your man, Master Yu, received my payment of eighty *liang* of silver for the sale of you to me."

Sister Mo said, "Nonsense! My body is mine. Who can sell me?"

Mother Wei said, "I don't care whether the body is yours or not. The silver was paid. You're now mine."

Sister Mo said, "I'm going to reason with him to make it clear!"

Mother Wei replied, "I think he is seven or eight *li* away from here by now, on his way back home. How will you catch him? You can make a good living here in my house. Just be at ease and settle here. Otherwise you are asking for a thrashing with a discipline club!"

Knowing that she had been cheated by Yu Sheng, Sister Mo broke into tears because she had been wronged. Mother Wei yelled for her to stop, threatening her with punishment if she did not. The other women came over to calm her down. Basically Sister Mo deserved no praise for her former conduct in terms of morality. Now she was ensnared and was not in any position to reverse the situation. She simply yielded in obedience and became a prostitute in the house. It was retribution for her ignoble deeds.

After she sank into prostitution, Sister Mo often thought to herself, "I had really intended to run away with Second Brother Yang and lead a happy life. But I made mistake when I was drunk, giving an opportunity for that wretch Yu Sheng to sell me here! I wonder how things are with Second Brother Yang? I've been away from home all this time, and I don't know what has happened to him." She was restless with these thoughts. Occasionally she revealed her mind to some of her clients, but no one really cared what she said. So her days often passed in weeping.

Time shot by like a flying arrow and four or five years elapsed before one realized it. One day a customer arrived for prostitution. He stared at Sister Mo as if he knew her, while Sister Mo also saw a familiar face in him. They both wondered.

Sister Mo broke the silence by asking, "May I know who you are, sir?"

The customer replied, "My name is Xing Feng. I live in Zhangjiawan."

The mention of Zhangjiawan brought tears to Sister Mo's eyes. She said, "Since you're from Zhangjiawan, I wonder whether or not you know a government assistant called Xu De?"

Surprised, Xing Feng said, "Xu De lives in my neighborhood. He lost his wife years ago. I thought you looked familiar. Are you his wife?"

Sister Mo said, "Yes, I am Xu's wife. I was abducted and brought here to suffer. Your face rang a bell with me and I decided I must have seen you before. It is a surprise that you're our neighbor, Master Xing!"

It turned out that Xing Feng was also a philanderer, who used to be attracted to Sister Mo because of her beauty. So he quickly recalled her now. He then said to Sister Mo, "You don't know, madam, that while you are here, one man suffers a great deal."

Sister Mo asked, "Who?"

Xing Feng rejoined, "Second Brother Yang was sued by your husband and has been in jail for years. He must have been beaten innumerable times. He's still imprisoned, but can't clear himself."

Sister Mo's heart sank at this news. She said softly to him, "It's not appropriate to talk here. Stay with me tonight and I'll have something to tell you."

That night Xing Feng slept with her. Sister Mo told him in detail about her relationship with Second Brother Yang, about Yu Sheng's deception through posing as Second Brother Yang, and about her abduction. Then she said to him, "In terms of our relation as neighbors, please do me a favor by going to my home and telling them all about this. First, I'll be able to get out of here. Second, it will clear Second Brother Yang of the charge — that will be a meritorious deed I should perform so as to obtain the gods' blessings. Third, I'll be able to confront Yu Sheng, since he has made me suffer a great deal. I would like to take a few bites out of him in revenge."

Xing Feng said, "Sure, I'll tell it when I get back. Second Brother Yang, Xu De and I were brought up together as friends. Furthermore, there is an offer of a reward posted everywhere in this case, which I'll certainly try to claim. Why wouldn't I go and report the matter to the government? Yu Sheng is well known for his cunning. It would be outrageous to let him remain at large. It's time for his downfall."

Sister Mo said, "You should keep this matter secret. If you let it out, the mistress of this house will put me away."

Xing Feng replied, "I'll keep it between us and won't say a word about it to anyone else. Once I get back home, I will tell the authorities." They agreed on the plan.

Upon arrival at home, Xing Feng found Xu De and said to him, "I know your wife's whereabouts. I saw her personally."

Xu De said, "Where is she?"

Xing Feng said, "Let's go to the government office and I'll tell you what has happened."

Xu De went with Xing Feng to the department of the garrison. Xing Feng then presented a statement which read:

I am Xing Feng from Zhangjiawan, presenting this lawsuit on the abduction and sale of a woman. Xu De from my native place Zhangjiawan lost his wife, Sister Mo, and brought a lawsuit, but the case has remained unsolved. I saw with my eyes the woman working as a prostitute in a brothel run by the family of Wei in Linqing. The woman said she was sold there by Yu Sheng, a knave. The sale and prostitution of a good woman is a criminal offense, and whoever knows the facts should report to the government. I swear my statement is based on truth.

The head of the garrison put the statement on file at once. When he sent a report to the prefecture's department of inspection, he gave a secret order to arrest Yu Sheng for interrogation. Yu Sheng could not deny the facts and confessed all his offenses. He was imprisoned, to be sentenced when Sister Mo arrived and confronted him in court.

The head of the garrison then sent an order, following directions from the department of inspection, that the plaintiff, Xing Feng, and Sister Mo's husband, Xu De, go with the runners to Linqing and help arrest Sister Mo and the mistress of the brothel, Mother Wei. The Linqing government at once sent men to the house of Wei. The arrest was a "job as easy as catching a turtle in a jar." The Linqing government, after making the arrest, sent the group back to the department of the garrison. At that time Second Brother Yang was still in jail. After hearing the news, he filed a petition with the county's department of the garrison, stating that he was innocent and happy to see himself cleared of the charge. His petition was approved and he was told to wait.

With the people concerned brought to court, the head of the garrison first called Sister Mo for questioning. Sister Mo presented a complete narrative of Yu Sheng's taking her away by deception to Linqing and his selling her into prostitution. The head of the garrison then called up Mother Wei, and asked, "Why did you purchase the wife of an honest man?"

Mother Wei replied, "I run a brothel, which provides me with a living. Yu Sheng told me that he wanted to sell his wife. I thought that it was alright for a husband to sell his wife, so I made the purchase. How could I know he had abducted her?"

Xu De came forward and said, "My wife fled with many of my valuables from wardrobes and boxes. Now that they are captured, the stolen property should be returned to me."

Sister Mo said, "Yu Sheng sold me to the house of Wei, so I stayed there empty-handed. He seized all my property. This property has nothing to do with the house of Wei."

Smiting the table, the head of the garrison shouted, "What a vicious man Yu Sheng is! You took away a woman for sex, and then sold her to the brothel. You also seized her property. This is grossly offensive!" He then cried, "Give him a sound beating!"

Yu Sheng protested, "I admit my offense of selling her to the brothel. As for the elopement, she followed of her own accord. I did not abduct her."

The head of garrison asked Sister Mo, "Why did you run away with him? Tell the truth. Otherwise you are asking for punishment!"

Sister Mo had to confess to her offense of committing adultery with Second Brother Yang and to eloping with Yu Sheng, whom she mistook for her lover. The head of the garrison laughed and said, "That's why your husband, Xu De, sued Second Brother Yang! Though Second Brother Yang served a few years of imprisonment, Xu De's charge was not completely false. Sister Mo admits her offense, but how can you, Yu Sheng, deny your crime of taking advantage of her in abducting her?"

He gave the order to beat Yu Sheng with forty severe strokes of a lash and sentenced him to military service and the return of all the valuables he seized from Xu De. In addition, the eighty *liang* of silver Yu Sheng obtained from selling Sister Mo had to be turned in to the government. Mother Wei had bought a good woman in ignorance of the truth, so the nature of her offense was commitment of an unintended crime. She was to give Mo back, but not to deliver the money that Sister Mo had made during her years in prostitution. Second Brother Yang had committed adultery but was not involved in the crime. According to law, he was punished with flogging and then paid bail for himself. Since Xing Feng had made an accurate report, he was granted the reward. The verdict was thus delivered. Sister Mo was returned to Xu De.

But Xu De said, "My wife fled home and deserted me years ago. She later became a prostitute. What shame I will have to bear by taking the bitch back to my home! I'm willing to divorce her in court and to let her marry someone else."

The head of the garrison said, "This business I will leave to you. Take her back for the present. When you find a man to marry her, come to court for the registration."

The other people returned home after the court session. Second Brother Yang thought to himself, "Somebody took Sister Mo away but I was wronged in being imprisoned for years. I must right this wrong!" He told this to his neighbors in order to show his intention of confronting Xu De. Xu De was a little worried, so he begged the neighbors to mediate the dispute.

The neighbors consulted among themselves and said, "Since Xu De wants to terminate the marriage and look for someone to marry his wife. Why not let Second Brother Yang marry her so that the grievance between him and Xu De will be cleared?"

They talked to Xu De, and the latter responded, "I understand that Second Brother Yang was wronged. I don't object to your plan."

Second Brother Yang heard of it. He was overjoyed that the matter had played into his hands. He smiled and said, "If I can have Sister Mo, I will not complain, even if I were to be given a few more years of imprisonment."

The neighbors double-checked that the three parties were in agreement and then reported this to the government. The head of the garrison understood that it was not fair to have had Second Brother Yang imprisoned for those few years, and he therefore approved the neighbors' request, permitting Xu De's divorce and Second Brother Yang's marriage. Sister Mo was very happy in marrying her lover. She had learned the lesson from her years of suffering and renounced her past behavior of flirting with men. She remained faithful to Second Brother Yang. Perhaps Second Brother Yang's marriage to her was predestined by fate. Though he finally married his love, he suffered a lot. So this was by no means an enviable experience. People should take a lesson from this tale.

Tale 19

An Ingenious Thief Conveys His Sentiment with a Plum;
A Gallant Burglar Plays His Game with Adroitness

During the reign of Jiajing [1522-1567] of our [Ming] dynasty there was a thief named Lazy Dragon in Suzhou whose thefts were extraordinary and numerous. Despite being a thief, he maintained a sense of justice and gained a great deal of enjoyment through his deeds. Therefore his story is interesting and this poem describes it:

> *Who say's in stealing there's no art?*
> *A clever thief performs unusual deeds.*
> *You'll be convinced a vulgar robber he's not*
> *If you see how he helps those in need.*

It is said that a man lived in the first alley by the Temple of Mystery, east of the town of Yazi in Suzhou. No one knew his real name. He later styled himself Lazy Dragon and that was what people called him. His mother lived in a village. One day she had wandered out and it began to rain. She entered a deserted temple for shelter. This was the Temple of the Third Brother in Straw Sandals. As she sat there and the rain continued, she fell asleep and had dreamed that a god came to her. When she returned home, she had found herself pregnant. Ten months later, she gave birth to Lazy Dragon. Lazy Dragon was short, sprightly, brave, intelligent and generous. When he engaged in stealing:

> *he came softly as if he were a boneless creature easily blown away in the wind; for a demanding mission, he could leap up to the roof of a house and move along the roof-beams; for an easy task, he could cross a wall and pry open a door; he was quick in making decisions about what effort might be required of him; working with his mouth, he could produce the sound of a cock, dog, fox and mouse; clapping his hands, he made music that could only be played on a bamboo-flute, drum and stringed instruments; like a ghost he left no trace of his coming and going; resembling a storm he attacked with force and unexpectedly; unmatched in power, he was truly the best thief in the world.*

He was not only competent in those skills, but he had also acquired a few other extraordinary abilities. From his childhood he could walk on the wall with his shoes on; he could speak all the dialects in the country. He could stay awake the whole night, running, and sleep days on end without consuming any food or tea, as Chen Tuan* had done. Sometimes he drank a few sips of wine and ate a couple of mouthfuls of food, not much to stave off hunger. Sometimes he observed a fast for days and did not feel hungry. His soles were stuffed with straw ash, so that when he walked he made no sound. In wrestling, he moved his arms and turned himself around as swiftly as a wind.

An old saying goes, "Birds of a feather flock together." Lazy

---

*Chen Tuan was an ancient Taoist. It is said that he could abstain from eating and drinking for over one hundred days.

Dragon tended to show his skills and abilities off and to mess around with young rascals. That is why he developed the stealing habit. Among the well-known thieves he associated with, there were:

Reed Stem, who was as skinny as a green reed and was a good slinger; Thorny Hawk, who, upon spotting someone around, would hide on a roof-beam like a scorpion; and White Girdle, who, with a piece of white silk tied around his waist and a big iron hook fastened to the end of it, would toss the hook up, catch it on something, climb up the silk and then descend again, all in nimble fashion.

These thieves were the stealing masters of the local area. But Lazy Dragon's remarkable powers won their esteem, for they found his skills overshadowing theirs. Single and without family fortune, Lazy Dragon did not depend on anyone for living. He took the world at large as his home. No one could tell where he stopped at night. During the day, he sometimes appeared around town and sometimes sneaked into the home of some family, leaving a trace that instantly vanished before he was detected. At night he often stole into a rich residence and found shelter there. Getting into a huddle like a hedgehog, he might sleep on exquisitely constructed roof-beams with the design of a hawksbill turtle on them, or inside a building of newly-weds, or behind the wooden screen in a young lady's bedroom, or in a colorfully decorated pavilion. He could sleep anywhere and, at the same time never miss a chance to steal. Because he could sleep any time of the day and kept to mysterious behavior like a dragon, people addressed him as Lazy Dragon, just as he referred to himself. Wherever he hit a target, he would draw a plum on the wall of the room and write some characters in white chalk against a black background, or in black coal against a white background. Therefore he was also sometimes called "Plum Bough."

One year at the beginning of the reign of Jiajing a crocodile sprang out from two hills in the Dongting Mountains and cliffs fell down by Taihu Lake, exposing an ancient tomb, with a burgundy-painted coffin and countless treasures. The treasures were later stolen, but word of this spread to the town. Lazy Dragon went there, rowing a boat with some of his friends. He saw that the coffin's binding vines had been cut off. Looking inside, he only saw a dried skeleton. At the side of the tomb was a broken tombstone with undecipherable characters on it. Lazy Dragon believed it was the tomb of an ancient prince and his heart sank. He then shut the coffin, hired a few local men at his expense to give it a burial and made a libation in front of it. As Lazy Dragon was leaving he stepped on something. He bent over to pick it up. It was an antique copper mirror. Quickly he slipped the mirror into his sock so it would not be seen by the others. When he got back to town, he ran to a quiet place and removed dirt from the mirror for a closer look. It was a small mirror, about four or five inches in diameter and shining brightly. Around the handle on the flipside were a few blurred designs of strange beasts, fishes and dragons. It was green and bore traces of cinnabar and mercury. A tap on it gave a clear sound. Knowing this was a treasure, Lazy Dragon hid it on his person. At night he took it out and then the darkness was lighted up like broad daylight. After acquiring this mirror, Lazy Dragon carried it all the time. It proved a great help for him in moving around at night because now he need no longer use fire for light. Where other thieves avoided dark places, Lazy Dragon walked in as if he was sauntering around by daylight. His stealing was thus made easier.

Despite his thievery, Lazy Dragon was meritorious in a few ways. He did not seduce women. He did not enter the house of virtuous and unfortunate families to steal. He was always a man of his word, believing in brotherhood and charity — he gave his stolen goods to people in poverty or desperate situations. He loved to offend parsimonious and evil rich persons, and take advantage of situations to make fun of them. So wherever he went he had an army of followers. His fame of righteousness spread far and wide. He would laugh and say, "I don't have parents or a wife as dependents to feed. Helping the needy by taking from the haves is the heavenly law, and has nothing to do with my benevolent nature."

One day it was said that a rich merchant had given a deposit of one thousand *liang* of silver to the weaver Zhou Jia. Lazy Dragon decided to steal the money. However, he got drunk and ventured into the wrong house, one that belonged to a poor family that had only a big table in the room. Looking about, Lazy Dragon detected nothing else. Since he was already inside the house, he was unable to find a quick way out, so he lay prostrate under the table and listened to the husband and wife talking over a meager dinner.

Sad and gloomy, the husband said to the wife, "We have no way to pay our debts. I'd rather die."

The wife said, "Why are you talking about dying? You'd better sell me in order to survive." Then they sobbed.

All of a sudden Lazy Dragon jumped out, and the couple was terrified. Lazy Dragon said, "Don't be scared of me, you two. I'm Lazy Dragon. I heard people talk about a rich merchant around town, but entered your house by mistake. I see you are suffering from poverty. I'll give you two hundred *liang* of silver to help you start a business. Never take your own life."

The husband and wife had learned of his name before, so they saluted to him and said, "If you are so kind to us, we can survive." Lazy Dragon left, and a watch later a big thud was heard in the room. The husband and wife stepped forward to look. On the floor was a cloth bag holding two hundred *liang* of silver. This was the silver that Lazy Dragon stole that night after the rich merchant left with the weaver. The husband and wife were overjoyed. They set up a memorial tablet to him and worshipped him throughout their lives.

A man, who had been a close friend of Lazy Dragon in childhood and was reduced to poverty later, stumbled across Lazy Dragon one day. The pauper in rags was embarrassed to meet his former comrade, so he raced past him holding a fan to shield his face from view.

Lazy Dragon grabbed him by his clothes and asked, "Aren't you Mr. So-and-so?"

The pauper was flurried and replied, "I'm too embarrassed to see my friend." Lazy Dragon said, "You're in such a deplorable state, let's go together tomorrow to visit a wealthy family and obtain something for you. But you mustn't tell anybody." The pauper knew Lazy Dragon was a masterhand and knew he was not joking. The next evening, he went to see Lazy Dragon. They arrived at a manor house, which belonged to a senior official.

Lazy Dragon let the pauper wait outside, while he climbed a tree and got inside by crossing over the wall. He didn't come back out for quite a while. Holding his breath, the pauper squatted by the wall waiting. A few dogs kept by the family ran over and barked at him. He had to move away along the wall. Then he heard water splashing inside and saw something like a cormorant diving from the wall and dropping to the ground in the dark woods. Going closer, the pauper saw it was Lazy Dragon, completely wet through.

Lazy Dragon said to the pauper, "I almost got killed for you! There's a huge amount of gold in the house and you can measure it by the bushel. I stole some gold from the room, but the dogs barked annoyingly and the host was awakened. For fear of being caught by the host, I dropped it by the path and fled over the wall. I'm sorry it's your bad luck."

The pauper said, "You're experienced and never fail to make it. Today it's indeed my bad luck." He sighed disappointedly.

Lazy Dragon said, "Don't worry. I'll take care of it later." The pauper went home disheartened.

One month later Lazy Dragon ran into the pauper again on the street. The pauper implored him saying, "I'm so poor that I went to the fortune-teller today. I was told that I will have good luck and receive wealth. The fortune-teller said, 'There'll be a windfall coming to you. Someone will bring it to you.' I thought that if it is not you, who else?"

Lazy Dragon laughed and said, "I had almost forgotten the chest of gold and silver that I took the other night. But I thought, if I handed it to you immediately, you might not be able to hide it and the loser might discover it. So I dropped it in the pond of the family that night to see what would happen. Now a month has passed and nothing has happened. That family may have given up searching for it. You can have it without getting into trouble. I'll make another trip for you tonight."

The pauper waited until dusk. He came to see Lazy Dragon and they went there together. Lazy Dragon entered the residence and came out moment later, carrying the chest on his back. They rushed to a quiet place and Lazy Dragon took out his magic mirror for a light. The chest was full of gold and silver. Lazy Dragon did not touch it, nor did he count it.

He simply gave all of it to the pauper and said, "This fortune should last you your whole life. Spend it wisely. Don't be like me, Lazy Dragon, getting by from day to day without being financially established half-way through my life." The pauper was grateful and expressed his thanks. With the money he started a business and later became rich. This is only one of many good deeds that Lazy Dragon performed.

Reader, you may wonder, was Lazy Dragon so remarkable in his stealing, that he never slipped? He did occasionally find himself landing in trouble. But he was capable of quickly finding a way out of his predicament.

One night he stole into the home of a family. Seeing the closet open, he slipped into it to pilfer the clothing. However, the family shut the closet door and locked it before going to bed. Lazy Dragon was thus enclosed in the closet. But he hit upon an idea. He wrapped himself up in the clothes, and made a bundle of them that he set inside by the closet door. Then he produced the sound a mouse chewing on the clothes.

The hostess of the house called an elderly woman servant and said to her, "Why did you let a mouse become shut in the closet? It may damage the clothing. Let it out and drive it out of the room." The elderly servant picked up the light and moved to the closet. No sooner had she opened the door than the bundle of clothes rolled out. Instantaneously Lazy Dragon rolled out with the bundle and snapped off the light in her hand. The servant was astonished, letting out a cry. To prevent the family from being aroused, Lazy Dragon clutched the bundle and shoved the woman at the same time. She stumbled, as Lazy Dragon flashed through the door. Some people of the family came and tripped over the elderly woman servant, mistaking her for a thief. They gave her a good beating. She yelled in pain as servants rushed in with lights from outside. They then realized they were beating their servant and stopped the beating. But Lazy Dragon had vanished a long while before.

A weaver received some silver from a customer for the weaving of a few bolts of silk and gauze. The husband and wife stored the silver in a treasure box and set it on the bed by the wall. They went to sleep on that bed, paying particular attention to the box at night. Lazy Dragon heard of the silver and decided to steal it. He sneaked into the room. With one foot on the side of the bed, he reached into the bed to get the box. The wife awoke and felt there was something on the side of the bed. She touched it with her hand and recognized it to be a man's foot.

So she held it tightly, calling to her husband, "Get up! I've grabbed a thief's foot."

Immediately Lazy Dragon picked up one of the husband's feet and gave a pinch. Feeling the pain, the husband cried, "It's my foot! It's my foot!"

Realizing she was wrong, the wife let go, and Lazy Dragon shot out of the room holding the box. The husband and wife shouted at each other. The wife said, "I held the thief's foot in my hand, but you wanted me to release it."

The husband said, "No, it was my foot. Your pinch is still hurting. How could it be the thief's foot?"

The wife said, "Your feet were on the other side of the bed. I held a foot on this side of the bed. Besides I did not pinch."

The husband said, "If that is so, then the thief must have nipped my foot. But you should not have let go of his foot."

The wife said, "When I heard you yelling, I was shocked. I thought I was mistaken, and so I released it. He fled. Since a thief came, we must have lost things!" They reached for the box, but it was gone. The husband and wife then complained against one another for most of the night.

That same night Lazy Dragon went to a clothing store to rob it. But it was too dark to see clearly. So he took out his magic mirror to light the way. An old saying goes, "Walls have ears and doorposts have eyes." He did not know that a husband and wife were making love on the second floor of the house next door. They saw the flash of light in the neighboring store, and quickly realized something was happening there. They ran over to knock on the window, calling out, "Be watchful, my neighbor! You may have a thief in your house."

The store owner jumped up and shouted, "Stop thief!" When Lazy Dragon heard the shout, he looked for a hiding place and saw a big jar in the yard for storing thick soya bean sauce. It had a bamboo-mat cover. He ran over to the jar, took off the cover, jumped inside and stayed squatting there after he put the cover back on the jar. The family searched with lanterns, but they did not find anybody, so they went to the rear of the house. Lazy Dragon thought to himself, "They did not look inside the jar. If they don't find anything in the rear, they will surely come back to check this jar. I'd better hide where they have already checked." Then he realized, "I'm soaked through with soya bean sauce. If I climb out, I'll surely leave a trace." He took off his clothes and crawled naked out of the jar. Then he ran to the gate of the house and opened it, leaving a line of footprints on the ground. He turned around, ran back into the clothing storage, and hid himself there.

The family found no one at the back of the house and so they went to check the jar. They found a set of clothes inside. Knowing these were not their own, they said, "It's the thief's clothes." They also saw the footprints on the ground leading to the gate, which was left open. They all said, "The thief saw us searching for him so he hid himself in the jar. When we went to the back of the house, he took off his clothes and fled. It's a shame we checked here too late. Otherwise we would have caught him."

The store owner said, "We frightened him out of the house. It's all right. Close the gate and go to sleep." They thought the thief was gone. They stayed awhile and fell into sound sleep, ignorant of the fact that the thief had not yet left.

Lazy Dragon picked up a few of the best dresses and tied them around his body. He then put on an old blue overcoat. He selected some silk clothes and wrapped them up with a quilt, and rolled it into a bundle. It took him quite awhile before he leapt out from under the eavesdrop, carrying the load of clothes, with the family still asleep.

As Lazy Dragon jumped onto the street, it was not dawn yet. He walked forward and bumped into a few of early risers. They saw Lazy Dragon walking alone with a heavy load at that early hour. Suspecting him of a crime, they stopped him and asked him, "Who are you? Where have you been? Tell the truth and we'll let you pass."

Lazy Dragon said nothing. Instead, he slipped out a cloth ball, like a feather-stuffed ball, from under his elbow. He dropped this on the ground and ran away. The men swarmed around the object and saw it tied closely with threads. They thought it certainly must be something valuable, so they scrambled to untie it. They undid one layer after another, as if they were peeling a bamboo shoot. It was tightly bound. After they had untied quite a bit of it, they still saw there was no end to it. When they came down to a roll the size of a fist, they became suspicious, saying, "What is inside?" They were curious and continued to untie it. In the end there were just rags and scraps of cotton strewn all over the place.

As they were in a hubbub, a group of people arrived, running, and shouted, "You stole our clothes and are dividing them among yourselves!"

Before a reply could be given, the new arrivals began to swing their sticks and boards to beat the group of men. Unable to fend off the blows, the men scattered, leaving an elderly man behind. In the darkness his face did not show clearly, so they continued to beat the elderly man all the way back to the store.

The elderly man yelled, "Stop! Stop! You're mistaken!" But the men were so excited they didn't listen to him.

As it became daylight, the store owner recognized the man to be his son's father-in-law, a man who lived in countryside. The store owner stopped the beaters, but the elderly man already had a swollen face. The store owner apologized to him and set a table for forgiveness. He then mentioned the burglary that had taken place that night.

The elderly man told him, "I was with a few friends coming this way before dawn. We saw a man carrying a big load, so we stopped him for questioning. He dropped a cloth ball and we scrambled to look at it. He took the chance and ran away. The cloth ball was nothing but rags. We were cheated and failed to capture him. When these men hit and struck indiscriminatingly, my friends fled. It's a pity that the thief is now well on his way."

When the men heard the story, they were surprised and regretted their rashness. The tale of the mistaken beating of the store owner's son's father-in-law spread among the neighbors and became the butt of ridicule. It happened that Lazy Dragon took his leisurely time to make the cloth ball when he had been hiding inside the clothing closet, and he carried it with him for the sake of misleading his pursuers in case he was discovered. This was one of many instances in which he used his wits to free himself from a crisis.

Lazy Dragon became quickly well known for his remarkable stealing skills. The garrison commander Zhang, who was in charge of security learned about him. He sent patrols to bring Lazy Dragon to his office, where he asked him, "Are you the ringleader?"

Lazy Dragon replied, "I don't steal or rob. How can I be a ringleader? No lawsuit has been brought against me in court. And I don't have any connection with thieves and robbers either. I only have a few skills and play one or two tricks occasionally on friends and relatives. If you find no offense in my action, lord, I'd like to offer to do any kind of demanding work for you in future."

Seeing that Lazy Dragon was small and nimble and had a brisk tongue, the commander thought to himself, "With no stolen goods as evidence, he can't be charged." Furthermore, Lazy Dragon had offered service in the future. The commander found a possible assistant in him, so he rejected any idea of charging him.

As they were talking, a man called Lu Xiaoxian from Changmen arrived with a gift of a red-beaked green parrot for the commander. The commander had the cage containing the parrot hung under the eaves and said to Lazy Dragon with a smile, "I have heard that you are remarkable in your skills. In spite of your claiming playful conduct and a clean record, I doubt that you're completely free of stealing. Today I'll let you go without charge, but I want to test your skills. If you can steal this parrot tonight and return it to me tomorrow, I'll renounce any charges against you."

Lazy Dragon replied, "That's easy. Let me do it and bring the parrot back to you tomorrow morning." Kowtowing, he took his leave.

The commander at once called two soldiers and said to them, "Watch the parrot closely. A slight negligence on your part will incur harsh punishment." With this order, the two soldiers stayed on the watch under the eaves that night, not moving one step away from the spot. But later their eyelids began to droop as they battled sleepiness with difficulty. A spell of dozing seized them. Occasionally they were suddenly roused by slight sounds. It was indeed a rough time for them. Before dawn Lazy Dragon arrived on the roof of the commander's study. He pried open a few rafters and slid down into the room. He saw a soft silk cloak perfumed with a southern wood fragrance, a beautiful turban on a small table, and a hanging lantern with the characters "Suzhou Patrol" painted on it placed against the wall. An idea struck him. He put the cloak over his shoulders and the turban on his head. Then he slipped a lighter from his sleeve, pulled out the lampwick and lighted the hanging lantern. With the lantern in hand, he walked in imitation of the old commander. He came to the door of the main room and opened it. Then he set down the lantern and stepped out walking along under the eaves in the dim moonlight. The two soldiers were struggling to keep awake. Lazy Dragon gently kicked them and said, "It's getting towards daybreak. Don't stay here any more. You may leave." As he said this, he reached out to take hold of the parrot cage and then meandered back with it to the entrance to the inner quarters of the residence. The two soldiers were worn out with drowsiness, scarcely able to open their eyes. After hearing the order, they felt a complete release, as if granted a special amnesty. With no thought about the consequences, they departed.

Soon it was morning. Commander Zhang came and saw the parrot gone. Immediately he called the two soldiers, but they were not around. He sent for them. The two soldiers arrived, still drowsy. The commander shouted, "I wanted you to watch the parrot closely. Where is it now? Why did you come from the other direction?"

The soldiers replied, "About the fifth watch, you, lord, personally came out, took away the parrot and released us. Why are you asking us about it now?"

The commander yelled, "Nonsense! When did I come out? It must have been a ghost you saw!"

The soldiers answered, "There is no mistake about the fact that you personally came to us. We both were here. How could we both be wrong?"

The commander understood that something had gone amiss. He went into his study. When he looked upward, he noticed that a few rafters had been moved. He decided that Lazy Dragon must have entered from up there. As he was pondering the matter, Lazy Dragon arrived with the parrot. Smiling, the commander emerged and asked Lazy Dragon how he had made away with it. Lazy Dragon recounted his posing as the commander by wearing the turban and taking away the parrot. The commander was delighted and praised him immensely. Later Lazy Dragon periodically offered a few gifts to the commander, while the commander never hesitated in entrusting him with personal requests. With this support, Lazy Dragon started to carry out his business easily. Since ancient times, all police officers patronized thieves.

Even though Lazy Dragon was a thief, he liked to play tricks on people. One gambler, who had won a bet and was on his way back home carrying one thousand *liang* of silver on his back, encountered Lazy Dragon. Pointing to him, the gambler said jokingly, "Tonight I'm going to tuck this money under my pillow. If you can take it away, I'll treat you to dinner tomorrow. If you can't, you'll have to treat me."

Laughing, Lazy Dragon said, "Okay, let's do it."

Upon getting back home, the gambler said to his wife, that he had won a bet and tucked the winnings under his pillow. His wife was joyous. She killed a hen and warmed wine. They had dinner together. The chicken was not completely eaten so the leftovers were put away in the kitchen. Before going to bed, the gambler told his wife of his bet with Lazy Dragon about stealing the money. They slept in a state of alertness.

Meanwhile Lazy Dragon had been hiding outside the window, listening. Knowing that the husband and wife were rather vigilant, he realized he would have no chance to get the money while they were in bed. Then he suddenly hit upon an idea. He slid into the kitchen, picked up a chicken bone, stuck it into his mouth and chewed on it vigorously, making the sound of a cat eating the chicken.

The wife heard this and said to her husband, "We've got half the chicken left. Tomorrow it can feed us for another dinner. Don't let that cat get it." At once she got out of bed and ran to the kitchen to check. Lazy Dragon by this time was already in the yard. He tossed a rock into a well, and the sound of a plop was heard.

The gambler was surprised and called, "Be careful. Don't slip and get killed in the well just for that small bite of food." He raced out of the room to look for his wife. Lazy Dragon then sneaked into the bedroom and took the money from under the pillow. In the darkness the husband and wife called and responded to each other. Assured that nothing had happened, they went back to the bedroom, hand in hand. But they saw the pillow had been moved a distance away on the bed. They reached for the money. It was gone.

The husband and wife mumbled complaints against one another and said, "We were not asleep, neither us, and yet we failed to guard our possessions. Truly he made fun of us. It's ridiculous!"

The next morning Lazy Dragon came with the money, claiming his triumph. Laughing, the gambler took a few hundred pieces of cash from the money he had won, bought wine in a wine store and treated Lazy Dragon.

As they drank, they talked about the happening of the previous night, clapping their hands and laughing. The store owner noticed them and stepped over to ask why they were laughing. After being told the story, he said to Lazy Dragon, "I heard of your remarkable skills long ago. Now I'm convinced it's true." Pointing to a tin winepot on the table, he said, "If you can take this pot away tonight, I'll also treat you tomorrow."

Lazy Dragon laughed and said, "That will not be difficult either."

The store owner said, "But you're not permitted to ruin the door or window. Just do whatever you can to get it from the table."

Lazy Dragon said, "All right." Then he took off.

The store owner had the door shut safely. He toured the room with a lantern to make sure that there was no possibility for Lazy Dragon to enter the room. He thought, "I'm going to let the lantern stand on the table and I'll sit by the table, watching the winepot. Let me see how he steals it!" He did sit there well into the night. Nothing happened. Then he became drowsy. Unable to stay alert, he struggled to keep from dozing off. At first he barely could keep his eyes open. But pretty soon he collapsed and reclined on the table in a sound sleep. Lazy Dragon had been watching closely outside. So he now ascended the roof and moved one of the tiles. He quietly lowered a hollow bamboo pole with a hog bladder fastened tightly to its end. He managed to stick this into the opening of the winepot. The winepot, like those from most wine stores, had a bulging body and a narrow neck. Lazy Dragon blew air through the bamboo pole until the hog bladder ballooned, completely filling the pot. He then stopped the air from escaping by holding his hand over the end of the bamboo pole and slowly pulled the pot up. Then he moved the tile carefully back in place. The store owner woke up later. The light was still on but the winepot was gone. He jumped up to check around the room. The door and window were closely shut. He was absolutely mystified.

Another day Lazy Dragon was standing with a few young men in a tavern at Beitongzimen. They noticed a boat moored by the bank of the river on the bow of which a young master from Fujian Province was having his servants dry some beautiful clothing and bedding. The clothing and bedding presented a quite spectacle, which drew watching crowds. One quilt particularly stuck out because it was from fine Indian brocade.

Envying the young master's showing off of the possession, the men said jokingly, "What can we do to take his quilt away and make fun of him?" They turned to Lazy Dragon and said, "It's time to let him know your skills! Don't tarry."

Laughing, Lazy Dragon said, "Okay, I'm going to attack him and get it tonight. Tomorrow you can return the quilt to him and get a reward. We can then go and have a drink together."

He went to a washroom and took a bath. Then he came back to the river bank to watch the boat. After the sounding of the second nightly watch, the young master and servants, satisfied after drinking, put out their light and turned in, all sleeping together on the floor of the boat. But Lazy Dragon had already seized his chance to steal aboard and join them. Speaking their local dialect, Lazy Dragon jostled and shoved, disturbing the men, who mumbled complaints. He pretended to fall asleep and uttered words in a Fujian accent. As he jostled and bumped them, he gripped the quilt and rolled it into a bundle. Then he muttered that he would have to go out for piss. He opened the boat door, walked out and urinated. Then he leaped onto the bank, without being noticed by the men.

When morning came, the quilt was found to be gone and an uproar ensued. The young master sighed sadly. He talked with his men, saying that to go to the law for the loss of the quilt was not worth the bother, but to give up searching for it was something he really hated to do. He offered one thousand pieces of cash to anyone recovering it.

Lazy Dragon came on board with his men and said to the young master, "We have seen the quilt you lost in a place. If you give us the reward, which we can use to buy some drink, we'll bring it back to you." Immediately the young master asked one of his servants to get the money ready and said, "Once I get back the quilt, I'll give the money to you."

Lazy Dragon said, "You may have your house retainer come with us to get it."

So the young master asked a trusted servant to follow them. They went to a pawnshop in Huizhou, where the stolen quilt was stored. The servant said to the owner, "This quilt was on our boat. How did it get here?"

The pawnshop manager said, "This morning a man brought it here. We noticed it was not made in this area, so we were suspicious. We would not lend money to him. He said, 'If you have doubts about it, I will bring a friend here as a guarantor, and then you can give me the silver.' We said, 'That will do.' But that man left and did not return. I figured the quilt had a suspicious origin. Since you say it's yours, you may take it away. If the man comes back, I will catch him and bring him to you."

They returned the quilt to the young master and told him the pawnshop owner's words. The young master said, "We're away from home. It's good to have the quilt back. Why bother to catch that thief?" He gave the one thousand pieces of cash to Lazy Dragon and his men, who took the money and had a good time at a tavern. Lazy Dragon, of course, had talked to the pawnshop owner in advance so that he could leave the quilt there as part of his plan to claim the reward. There were too many such stories to tell.

Although Lazy Dragon loved to play tricks while stealing, he would not let anyone whose behavior annoyed him go without being disturbed, combining his tricks with ways of harming them.

A group of thieves invited Lazy Dragon to tour Tiger Mountain, to treat him to wine. They stopped their boat at the back of a rice store by the side of the Shantang River. The thieves usually went in and out through the store to buy firewood and wine.* The rice store owner hated being bothered by men mooring their boats by the bank and going through his store, so he harshly rejected their request.

---

*Many houses in Suzhou are situated between rivers so people often go through a house or store to do shopping.

The thieves argued with him, but Lazy Dragon winked at them and said, "All right. He will not allow us a way through. Let's go down the river and find another store. Why should you be mad?" Then he told them to release the boat and they were on the way again. The thieves, however, were still angry. Lazy Dragon said, "Don't talk about it any more. I'll take care of him tonight."

They asked him about his plan. He said, "You should go and find me a ferry boat. Please leave me with a vessel of wine, things to warm the wine with, firewood and charcoal. Set them in the boat. I want to enjoy the beauty of the moon throughout the night on my way back home. You'll know my plan tomorrow. I'm not going to tell you anything about it now."

That night after their feast at Tiger Mountain, Lazy Dragon told the thieves to leave and come back the next morning. He only asked that one man who was good at cooking and another who could row the boat stay with him on his trip back. As they neared the rice store, Lazy Dragon could see that it had closed for the day. At that time many boats sailed to and fro on the river, while people on the boats enjoyed the beautiful sight of the moon and sang songs. The family of the rice store owner were all asleep. Lazy Dragon moored his boat by the side of the rice store. During the day he had noticed a grain bin that was located in one corner of the store, close to the deck leading to the river. Lazy Dragon took out a knife and cut away at the bin. A piece of board came off, leaving a big hole. He pulled from around his waist a hollow bamboo pole and stuck one end of it into the bin, which he shook a little. Rice streamed down from the bin through the pole and into his boat like water falling. Lazy Dragon drank wine and enjoyed the beauty of the full moon, his laughter mingled with the gurgle of the rice rushing down. Other boats went past without noticing what was going on. The sleeping family of the rice store could have never found what was happening. As the constellations moved across skies, the rice stopped flowing. Lazy Dragon figured that the grain bin had become empty and his boat was full. He called for the boat to be released gently. As he moved to a quiet place, the thieves ran up. Lazy Dragon told them about the incident, and they broke into laughter.

With a cupped hand expressing his thanks, Lazy Dragon said, "Please share the rice among yourselves as a token of my gratitude for the wonderful dinner you gave me last night." He left without taking any rice with him. When the rice store opened, the family discovered its grain bin was empty, but they didn't know when and how the rice had disappeared.

At one time in Suzhou a cylinder-shaped hat became a fashion and flighty youngsters all adopted the style. A group of Taoists of the White-clouds Temple, on the east side of the south garden, also each had bought one of these hats in case they could go out on a tour posing as ordinary persons. One summer day they scheduled a tour to Tiger Mountain and rented a boat, with wine prepared. There was a man called Gauze Weaver the Third, who was the third son of Weaver Wang. On friendly terms with the Taoists, he often took part in such parties. But his inclination for petty gains and his lack of manners in drunkenness annoyed the Taoists. So they decided not to invite him on the tour this time. Gauze Weaver the Third, however, learned of their planned tour and resented their desertion of him. He found Lazy Dragon and talked to him about disrupting their tour. Lazy Dragon agreed to do so. He stole into the White-clouds Temple and took away all the hats the Taoists regularly wore.

Gauze Weaver the Third asked him, "Why didn't you take their new cylinder-shaped hats? Why did you want the Taoist hats?"

Lazy Dragon rejoined, "If they had lost their new cylinder-shaped hats, they would have given up their plan for tomorrow's tour. What could we do about them then? Don't worry. I'll take care of it." Not understanding his intentions, Gauze Weaver the Third said no more.

The following day the Taoists, all in civilian dress looking like ordinary young men, went out by boat for fun. Donned in black clothing, Lazy Dragon followed them onto the boat and squatted near the rudder area. The Taoists took him for a boat-hand, and the boatman thought he was a servant of the Taoists. So no one was suspicious of him. As the boat left the bank, the Taoists unbuttoned their clothes, threw their cylinder-shaped hats to the side and started to drink merrily. Lazy Dragon seized this chance and slide those hats into his sleeves. Then he took out the Taoist hats he had stolen the day before and placed them where the cylindrically-shaped hats had been. As the boat went under a bridge close to the bank, he leaped out onto the shore.

When the Taoists were ready to disembark, they found their cylinder-shaped hats gone and their regular Taoist hats neatly there in a pile. They shouted, "Strange! Strange! Where are our hats?"

The boatman said, "You took care of them yourselves. Why ask me? My boat is safe. Nothing could have been lost."

The Taoists searched again and there was still no sign of the hats. They asked the boatman again, "You had a short, black-dressed man on the boat earlier today, who just awhile ago went onto the bank. Bring him here and he may know where the hats are."

The boatman said, "I didn't have such a man with me. He came here with you."

The Taoists yelled, "How could we know him? You must have worked together with that burglar to steal our hats. Our hats are each worth a few *liang* of silver. We can't let you do this!" They seized the boatman, who protested by yelling at them. Crowds gathered on the bank to watch.

One young man jumped onto the boat and said, "What's happened?"

Different stories were told by the boatman and the Taoists. The Taoists knew the man and thought he would put in a word for them. But on the contrary, the man rebuked them by saying, "You're all Taoists and supposed to wear Taoist hats on board. Now you've got the Taoist hats there. Why are you asking for cylinder-shaped hats? Clearly, you're making a false charge against the boatman."

The watching crowds realized that these were Taoists, and believed that they were trying to blackmail the boatman into giving them cylinder-shaped hats. An uproar ensued and a few idling rascals stood out brandishing their fists and saying, "These contemptible Taoists are outrageous! Let's beat them up and send them to court!"

The man gestured with his hand to stop them, saying, "Leave them. Leave them. Let them go." Then he leaped onto the bank. The Taoists called for the boat to start, in fear of drawing further trouble. They had lost their cylinder-shaped hats and were exposed as Taoists. Their tour ruined, the Taoists beat a retreat in frustration.

Can you figure out who the man was who leaped onto the boat? He was Gauze Weaver the Third. After the trading of the cylinder-shaped hats for the Taoists hats, Lazy Dragon told him about it and let him reveal the Taoists' identity to disappoint them. Back at their temple, the Taoists were still blaming the boatman when Gauze Weaver the Third came in, returning to them the stolen hats.

He said to them, "When you go out for feast and show yourselves with cylinder-shaped hats next time, be sure to let me know." The Taoists then realized that Gauze Weaver the Third had poked fun at them. They had heard of Lazy Dragon long before and knew that Gauze Weaver the Third was a close friend of his. It was obvious to them that this was Lazy Dragon's work.

At that time there was a county magistrate in nearby Wuxi who was notorious for his greed. A man came to talk to Lazy Dragon and said, "The Wuxi county magistrate has a huge amount of wealth which he came by through dishonesty. Why don't you steal some of it and share it among the poor?" With this plan in mind, Lazy Dragon went to Wuxi. At night he stole into the office of the county magistrate and saw that it was indeed a treasure-house, where:

chests were placed one after another filled with bolts of brocade and silk, and shelves were loaded with a variety of precious items; piles of shoe-shaped ingots of gold and silver, not wrapped in paper, stood in packed lines; containers, half of them not made of pottery, burst with gold and silver; an elephant tusk was there that often found its use in a servant-girl's poking of the fire; a rhino's horn was used as a soup ladle for children; no one knows for how many generations the family had procured its wealth by bullying and breaking up other families; the fortune was also gathered as a result of seizing government property in an administration of disorder; every effort was made to hand down the wealth to future generations; yet the county magistrate was cheeky enough to claim to be the people's parents.

Seeing the tremendous wealth, Lazy Dragon thought to himself, "The doors and gates are shut tightly and the watchmen's clapper and bell keep sounding. I can't take a lot away." Then he saw a small, heavy box and figured it must hold fine gold and silver, so he picked it up and carried it with him. Then he thought, "In a government office, the loss of this will draw a lot of suspicion to the innocent tomorrow." He took out a brush and drew a plum on the wall by a shelf. Then he quietly climbed under the eaves and got out onto the street from the back of the office.

A few days later the county magistrate examined his official savings and did not find the small box containing about two hundred *liang* of gold, which was equal to over one thousand *liang* of silver. He searched everywhere and then saw a plum painted on the wall in fresh ink. Stunned, the county magistrate said, "Evidently, it was not a man from my office who painted it. Who has the guts to come to my bedroom to steal something and then calmly leave this plum drawing as a challenge? I'm sure he must be an extraordinary thief. He must be caught!" He called a group of capable runners in to look at the drawing.

The runners were surprised at the sight of the plum drawing. "My lord," they said. "We know this thief, but we can't catch him. He's the most remarkable thief in Suzhou, a man called Lazy Dragon. Wherever he goes, he leaves a drawing of a plum on the wall as a sign of his identity. He has super skills, and all his life has been untouchable. He is also a strong believer in brotherhood and keeps a large number of sworn followers. If you try to find him, it may give rise to further trouble. In comparison, the loss of gold and silver is nothing. We'd better leave him alone, lest we'll run into trouble."

Flying into a rage, the county magistrate cried, "You idiots! If you know his name, how can you say you're unable to capture him? You must have kept close connections with the thief, and are now saying these words to shield him. You deserve a sound thrashing! Now I want you to catch him. I'll postpone the punishment for you. If you fail to arrest him within ten days, you will all die!"

The runners dared not reply. The county magistrate called in a writing clerk to compose the order of arrest, assigned two runners to the mission, and sent a report to the county governments of Changzhou and Wuxian. He had made up his mind to capture the thief, and the runners could do nothing but set out on the trip to Suzhou.

As they entered the gate at Suzhou, Lazy Dragon was standing there. Patting him on the shoulder, one of the runners said to him, "Old dragon, why did you steal our master's treasure and leave a drawing behind? Now we have an order to arrest you. What should we do?"

Lazy Dragon said, "I'm sorry to have bothered you two. Please come with me to the restaurant. Let's sit down and talk about it."

Lazy Dragon pulled them into the restaurant and started to drink. He then said to them, "Let's talk about this. The county magistrate is pressing you to catch me. Why should I cause trouble for you two? Give me one day. I'll send him a message. Then he'll definitely cancel his order and call you back. How about that?"

The runners said, "It sounds good, but you took too much of his money, most of it gold, according to him. How can you make him renounce his order? If we fail to bring you to him, we'll be in trouble."

Lazy Dragon said, "Even if I wanted to go with you now, the money is not with me."

The runners asked, "Where is it?"

Lazy Dragon said, "I gave it to you two right after I took it." The runners said, "Don't try to fool us, old dragon. Government business is not something you can trifle with."

Lazy Dragon said, "I don't usually talk nonsense. Go back to your homes and you will see." Pulling on their ears, Lazy Dragon whispered, "Go and search in the tile cracks on your roof. You'll find it."

The runners knew of his remarkable skills, so they figured, "If he tells the county magistrate the stolen goods are in our homes, we'll be involved in the case. How can we?" So they said to him, "We're worried. We won't bring you with us now, old dragon. What do you want us to do?"

Lazy Dragon said, "Please go home. I'll be there soon after. I can assure you that the county magistrate will never push you to arrest me and you'll be fine." As he said this, he took a pack of gold from around his waist, about two *liang* in weight, and divided it between them, saying, "Take it for traveling expenses."

An old saying goes, "A runner loves money just as a fly sticks to blood." Seeing the shining gold, how could the two runners hold their avarice in check? They took it joyously, thinking to themselves, "Who can be sure that this is not part of the gold he stole from the government office?" They thus feared even more going with him to see the county magistrate.

They parted. Lazy Dragon set out at night and arrived in Wuxi the next morning. That evening he stole into the government office. The county magistrate had two wives and stayed that night with the elder one. The younger wife went to sleep alone. Lazy Dragon went to the young wife's bedroom. Lifting the bed curtain, he reached inside. He touched the young wife's black hair, in a coil lock on top of her head. Lazy Dragon gently cut it off with a pair of scissors. Then he located the chest that contained the county government seal, managed to open it, and put the skein of hair into it. He closed the chest and drew another plum on the wall. He then left without touching anything else.

The next morning the young wife woke up and found her hair loose. She was curious. When she stroked it, she found her topknot missing. She gave a yell, which immediately summoned a shocked group in the government office. They asked her why she had cried out, and she said, "Someone's played a trick on me and cut off my hair!"

The county magistrate was called. He arrived and saw his young wife look like a mendicant Buddhist monk sitting on the bed. He was confounded. Recalling her lovely dark hair and comparing it with her present state, he felt sorry and baffled, murmuring, "The gold was lost and the thief is still at large. Now I've had another break-in! I can lose anything but the county government seal!"

At once he went to check his seal chest. He found the wrapping and lock intact. He opened the chest and saw the seal on the top shelf untouched. He breathed in relief. Then some of the hair sprang into his sight. He lifted up the top shelf and saw the skein of hair at the bottom of the chest. He examined the other things, which were all there as before. Then he saw a plum painted on the wall, which was exactly the same as the one found days before. Frightened out of his wits, he said, "It's turned out to be the same man! I guess that, since he was closely hunted by my orders, he has used his power to send me a message. The cutting off of the hair shows me that he could cut off my head. And putting the hair in the seal chest shows me that he could also steal my seal. He is indeed an extraordinary thief! The runners advised me to leave him alone. I realize now that what they said is correct. If I continue to hunt for him, I'll be killed. The loss of gold is alright. I can make up for it by fleecing a few more rich families. However, I should stop pursuing this business." He drew out a bamboo slip to cancel the previous command and summon back the two arresting runners.

The two runners who had parted from Lazy Dragon a couple of days before had returned home. As they were told, each started searching on his own roof and found a pack of gold with the seal of the date and month in agreement with those for which the gold was lost in the government office. They wondered when Lazy Dragon had put them there. They were scared. With his fingers between lips, one runner thought to himself, "We did the right thing when we gave up our efforts to carry out the order to bring Lazy Dragon to the government office. Otherwise he would have made a confession about the gold's whereabouts and the stolen gold would have been found in our homes. Then we would never have been able to clear ourselves of the charge of theft. The problem we have now is how to report back to the county magistrate."

While the two runners were worried and talked with each other, a messenger arrived from the county government office. They became frightened, thinking that they would be punished for their failure to capture the thief. But it turned out that the messenger reported the cancellation of the order to arrest Lazy Dragon. The runners asked the reason. The messenger told them of the recent occurrence and said, "The county magistrate is terrified now. How can he press for fulfilling his order of arrest?" It then dawned on the runners that Lazy Dragon had kept his word and struck home his threat by using his powerful skills. Their admiration for him rose higher.

Toward the end of the reign of Jiajing, there was a county magistrate of Wujiang who was greedy, corrupt, cunning and cruel. One day he sent men with gifts to Suzhou to invite Lazy Dragon to meet with him. Lazy Dragon accepted the invitation and arrived.

He said to the county magistrate, "I wonder for what purpose you want to see me."

The county magistrate replied, "I have heard that you're a well-known thief. I've got a top-secret mission for you to complete."

Lazy Dragon said, "I'm merely a local rascal. Since you lower yourself to see me, I will do my best to be of your service."

The county magistrate asked his men to leave them alone and he then said quietly to Lazy Dragon, "The imperial inspector is currently staying in my county and finding fault with me. I can't tolerate it. I'd like you to go to his office and steal his seal so he will lose his position. Then I'll be at ease. I'll give you a reward of one hundred *liang* of silver for your service."

Lazy Dragon said, "Don't worry. I'll surely bring his seal over here to you."

Lazy Dragon went to the office of the imperial inspector that night and brought the seal back. He presented it to the county magistrate, who was overjoyed and said, "A wonderful performance! You're a good match for the legendary figure, Red String, who stole the golden chest."*

Immediately he gave Lazy Dragon one hundred *liang* of silver and asked him to leave the county at once. Lazy Dragon asked, "I appreciate your kindness of giving me the handsome reward, but I wonder what you will do with this seal."

Laughing, the county magistrate replied, "With this seal at my hand, the imperial inspector can harm me no more."

Lazy Dragon said, "You've treated me with kindness. But I have to give you a sincere suggestion." The county magistrate asked, "What suggestion?"

Lazy Dragon said, "When I hid myself on the rafter in the office of the imperial inspector, I saw him sitting by candlelight, perusing documents and writing government files rapidly. He is an intelligent

---

*Red String was the heroine of a legend. She stole a gold chest from at the pillow of a powerful warlord and greatly intimidated him.

man and you can't deceive him. I suggest you return the seal to him tomorrow, telling him that you recovered it during your nightly patrol but failed to catch the thief. The imperial inspector may be suspicious but will be grateful to you and afraid of you. He will have to change the way he has treated you."

The county magistrate said, "Nonsense! If I return it to him, he will definitely do the same as before. Go on your trip and leave me alone!" Lady Dragon dare not say anything more and he sneaked away.

The next morning the imperial inspector needed the seal for his work. He opened the seal chest and found it empty. He called his men to search thoroughly, but they could find no trace of it. The imperial inspector figured, "I know who took it. That county magistrate knew that I was finding fault with him. This is his area and he has many people working for him. He must have asked someone to steal it. I've got an idea of how to deal with him!" He told his followers not to release a word of the matter, and wrapped up the seal chest as usual. He then quit observing his routine court office on an excuse of sickness, leaving all the government files in the hands of the inspection director. His faked illness went on for days. The county magistrate understood the imperial inspector's anxiety, and was pleased. However, the county magistrate had to pay an obligatory call on him to show his respect.

On hearing of the county magistrate's arrival, the imperial inspector told his servants to open a side-gate and let him in. The county magistrate was then shown directly to his bedroom. The imperial inspector chatted with him cheerfully about local customs and conventions, the handling of the government budget and grain levies, and shared his thoughts on each issue in an easy manner. Tea was consumed one cup after another. Finding the imperial inspector to be so honest and frank, the county magistrate was puzzled. During their talk, the kitchen was suddenly reported to be on fire.

The imperial inspector's team of personal servants, the gatekeepers and cooks all rushed in, calling, "The flames are raging. Please leave here, my lord!"

In fright, the imperial inspector leaped up. He held the wrapped seal chest in his hands and gave it to the county magistrate, saying, "I will ask you to take my seal. Please keep it in your county's storeroom and send men immediately over here to fight the fire."

The confused county magistrate could find no excuse to reject his request and so he carried the empty chest out of the room. When the local fire fighters arrived, the fire was extinguished. As a result, two kitchen rooms were destroyed but the offices were intact. The imperial inspector then called for the gate to be shut. It was a ruse that the imperial inspector had arranged after the loss of his seal.

The county magistrate returned home and thought to himself, "He handed me an empty seal-chest. If I bring it back to him, he will find it empty. Then I will not be able to clear myself of stealing the seal." Unable to think of a way out, he opened the chest by moistening the seal strips on the lid and put the stolen seal back into the chest. Then he wrapped it up again as usual. At the court session the next day, he returned the seal chest to the imperial inspector. The imperial inspector asked the county magistrate to stay with him, while he checked the seal. That day he used it on many government papers that he had not had a chance to seal before his sickness. The same day the imperial inspector gave his order for departure and quickly left Wujiang. However, he quietly told the provincial governor about the county magistrate's deed. They together composed an impeachment document against the county magistrate and presented it to the imperial court. The county magistrate was thus sentenced and stripped of his position. When leaving his post, the county magistrate said to his subordinates, "Lazy Dragon was farsighted. I regret that I did not listen to him and so I've come to this ending."

Lazy Dragon's reputation for remarkable skills reached far and wide and, occasionally, drew suspicion on him for various cases of theft, which got him into trouble. The government storeroom in Suzhou once lost ten silver ingots. The thief-hunting runners talked to one another and one said, "It's a mysterious loss. Could it be that Lazy Dragon stole them?"

Actually Lazy Dragon did not steal them but knowing he was suspected, he wanted to uncover the truth. He thought that the storeroom keeper might know something about it so he hid himself in the government compound at night. He hid near the bedroom of the storeroom keeper and heard him talking to his wife.

The man said, "I stole the silver but Lazy Dragon is suspected of doing so. I've thus got a stroke of good fortune. However, how can Lazy Dragon admit the crime? I'll write an indictment tomorrow, listing all his deeds of crime and present it to the prefecture magistrate. I don't think he will not become my scapegoat!"

Lazy Dragon heard there words and thought to himself, "Ouch. I didn't steal the ingots. Now the storeroom keeper wants to escape punishment for his offense. Government officials favor each other. Besides, I don't have a clean record. If he accuses me in court, how can I clear myself of the false charge? I may as well flee from here to avoid the torture of a beating on the false charge." He then set out at night for Nanjing, where he posed as a blind fortune-teller wandering the streets.

A man called Zhang Xiaoshe from Town Yiting at Taicang in Suzhou Prefecture was noted for his incredible ability to identify thieves. He went to Nanjing and ran into Lazy Dragon on the street. He thought, "This blind man looks suspicious!" Taking a closer look at him, he recognized him to be Lazy Dragon.

He grabbed Lazy Dragon and pulled him into a quiet place, saying, "You stole the silver from the prefecture's storeroom. The government is hunting for you. But you ran here and are protecting yourself in this way. How can you fool me?"

Gripping his hand, Lazy Dragon said, "You know me pretty well and should clarify the confusion about me. Why do you also accuse me? The truth is that the storeroom keeper stole the silver. I heard him and his wife talking to each other about it. He's the thief, I'm sure. He wanted to shift the blame onto me by bringing a charge against me in court. I was worried that the government would listen to his false charge, so I fled here. Would you please go to the government office and present the truth in court? You'll receive the reward and clear me of the wrong. I will give you something as a token of my appreciation. But please do not reveal my identity here." Actually Zhang Xiaoshe had received the assignment from the prefecture government to investigate the loss of silver. With the truth of the crime revealed, he let go of Lazy Dragon and returned to Suzhou to report. The silver was then confiscated from the storeroom keeper's home, and Lazy Dragon was cleared.

Zhang Xiaoshe received the reward for his report on the thief. He then went back to Nanjing and saw Lazy Dragon again, who was still roaming the streets. He hit Lazy Dragon on his shoulder with his hand and said, "Now your wrong is righted in Suzhou. Why are you so forgetful about your promise to me?"

Lazy Dragon said, "I'm not. Go home and search in your stove ashes. You'll have my paltry gift."

Zhang Xiaoshe left Lazy Dragon and went home. He searched the stove ashes and, indeed, found a pack of gold and silver. However, buried together with it was a sharp knife. Sticking out his tongue, Zhang Xiaoshe thought, "This tough thief! He was worried that I would keep bothering him, so he gave me something to thank me and sent a knife to me at the same time as a threat. I wonder when he was here. He's really so powerful. I'm afraid. I will never bother him again."

After he met Zhang Xiaoshe a second time in Suzhou and learned from him about his freedom from any charge, Lazy Dragon was still worried that he might be the target of other people's attacks. Therefore he quit stealing and settled down to make a living by fortune-telling. He lived in Changgan Temple and died a natural death there a few years later. A lifelong, hardened and mighty thief, Lazy Dragon did not receive any government punishment, such as torture, beating or character-tattooing on his arms. Today the natives of Suzhou still talk a great deal about his deceptions and tricks in stealing. Among those who engage in petty theft, he can be considered an admirable outlaw. His behavior was quite different from that of government officials who, though imposingly dressed, were greedy double-dealers seeking wealth at the expense of moral values. It is a shame that Lazy Dragon could not have put to use his exceptional skills in launching secret assaults on enemy military camps or in working as a spy in times of war. How many exploits would he have achieved for the country? It is a shame that at a time of peace, when law and order reigned, he could only perform his skills on small matters and become a subject of anecdotes.

Glossary

chi 尺   A length unit equal to 0.33 or 1.09.

cun 寸   A length unit equal to 3.33 cm or 1.3 in.

fen 分 [1]   A weight unit equal to one-tenth of a *liang*, i.e. formerly 0.11 oz (0.3 g), currently 0.18 oz (0.5 g).

fen 分 [2]   A length unit equal to 0.33 cm or 0.13 in.

fen 分 [3]   A unit of area. One *fen* equals 66.67 square meters.

jin 斤   A weight unit equal to 0.5 kg or 1.1 lb.

jinshi 进士   Literally meaning "enter officialdom." A scholarly honor granted to successful candidates of the national civil service examination.

juren 举人   Literally meaning "recommended person." A scholarly honor granted to successful candidates of the provincial civil service examination.

li 里   A length unit equal to 0.5 km or 0.31 mile.

liang 两   A weight unit equal to formerly 1.1 oz (31.2 g), currently 1.76 oz (50 g).

mu 亩   A unit of area. One *mu* equals 666.7 square meters or 0.1647 acres.

sheng 升   A unit of capacity equal to 1.76 pt.

qian 钱   A weight unit equal to formerly 0.11 oz (3.12 g), currently 0.18 oz (5 g).

qin 琴   An ancient stringed musical instrument.

xiucai 秀才   Literally meaning "outstanding talent." In the Ming and Qing dynasties *xiucai* referred to students of the county-level public schools. In the Tang and Song dynasties, it referred to examinees in the national level examination.

图书在版编目 (CIP) 数据

二刻拍案惊奇: 英文 ／ （明）凌濛初著; 马文谦译. − 北京: 中国文学出版社, 1998.12
ISBN 7-5071-0401-X

I.二… II.①凌… ②马… III. 话本小说−中国−明代−英文 IV.I242.3

中国版本图书馆 CIP 数据核字 (98) 第 05596 号

二刻拍案惊奇
凌濛初

翻　　译: 马文谦
中文责编: 高　苗
美　　编: 李　力

熊猫丛书
*

中国文学出版社出版
(中国北京百万庄路 24 号)
中国国际图书贸易总公司发行
(中国北京车公庄西路 35 号)
北京邮政信箱第 399 号　　邮政编码 100044
1998 年 第 1 版
ISBN 7-5071-0401-X/I.412
04000
10-E-3282P